Diary of a Hapless Househusband

Sam Holden is the pen name of an author and journalist. He lives in Wiltshire with his wife and two children. This book is partially based on his experience of (briefly) swapping roles with his wife.

Diary of a Hapless Househusband

SAM HOLDEN

arrow books

Published in the United Kingdom by Arrow Books in 2007

1 3 5 7 9 10 8 6 4 2

Arrow Books
The Random House Group Limited
20 Vauxhall Bridge Road, London SW1V 2SA

Random House Australia (Pty) Limited
20 Alfred Street, Milsons Point, Sydney,
New South Wales 2061, Australia

Random House New Zealand Limited
18 Poland Road, Glenfield,
Auckland 10, New Zealand

Random House (Pty) Limited
Isle of Houghton, Corner of Boundary Road & Carse O'Gowrie,
Houghton 2198, South Africa

Random House Publishers India Private Limited
301 World Trade Tower, Hotel Intercontinental Grand Complex,
Barakhamba Lane, New Delhi 110 001, India

Random House Group Limited Reg. No. 954009

www.rbooks.co.uk

A CIP catalogue record for this book
is available from the British Library

The Random House Group Limited makes every effort to ensure that the
papers used in its books are made from trees that have been legally sourced
from well-managed and credibly certified forests. Our paper procurement
policy can be found at: www.randomhouse.co.uk/paper.htm

Mixed Sources

Product group from well-managed
forests and other controlled sources
www.fsc.org Cert no. TT-COC-2139
© 1996 Forest Stewardship Council

ISBN 9780099509363

Typeset by Palimpsest Book Production Limited,
Grangemouth, Stirlingshire

Printed in the UK by CPI Bookmarque, Croydon, CR0 4TD

This book is for
TOBYN and VANESSA ANDREAE

With thanks to Nikola Scott, Tif Loehnis, Jenny McVeigh, Rebecca Folland, Kirsty Gordon, Annabel Venning, Carla Filmer, Julia Weston, Samantha De Mello, Jo Evans and Tara Douglas-Home

Thursday 24 February

Strange thing happened at work today. I got an email from David, the managing director, which was clearly meant for someone else. Chris, I suspect, as we both have the same surname. This happens a lot. The email mentioned that 'the new Dudley business would shortly be in the bag', and soon it would be 'champagne all round – for ever'. What irks me is that new business is one of my responsibilities, so why had I not been told? And who or where or what the hell was 'Dudley' anyway? Assuming Fiona had made an uncharacteristic mistake, I somewhat tetchily asked her whether she had been giving me all my memos. She swore she had, and, no, 'Dudley' didn't mean anything to her either. I apologised.

Was tempted to email David back, asking him what it was about, but something told me not to. Don't exactly know why, but there was something uncharacteristically shifty about it. Went through the internal phonebook, and found that we don't have a soul in Dudley. I printed the email out and then deleted it. I then deleted it from my 'deleted items' just to make sure, although I expect there'll be a copy on the server somewhere, and certainly in David's sent items. I'm going to leave the printout hidden here at home.

Perhaps I'm being a little suspicious, but I don't like being kept out of the loop. Am I being superseded? If I am, then it's no doubt because of my almighty balls-up with Lockhart Armstrong last month. David still blames me for losing that account, which is – and I will only admit as much in this diary – not entirely unfair. The truth is, we simply didn't do a good job with them and, as it was on my watch, it was my fault. I still wince when I think of their MD telling me, rather loudly, that if anyone needed management consultancy it was us. Given I've been doing this for over a decade, it really hurt.

Chris has always wanted my job, so perhaps he's set something up on the sly in Dudley that will curry favour with David. Whatever it is, it stinks. Dudley of all places! Christ!

Train getting back home was hideously late and packed, and I had to stand for the first forty minutes. It's at times like these I wonder what the hell I am doing with my life. Fifteen years ago I was reading modern history (Nazis mostly) at university, and naively promising myself I would spend my years exploring the world and writing exciting books about my experiences. These days my travels only extend to the 18.35 back home, and the only writing I do is this diary. Or a report for one of the firms we advise. How in God's name did I go from history to life as a management consultant commuting back and forth every day?

Didn't get home until nine, by which time the children were in bed and Sally had already eaten. I told her about the email, but she said I shouldn't worry about it. I said it looked as if I was being sidelined, but she said that was surely unlikely, as David was a fan of mine. I emphasised her 'was', saying that the Lockhart Armstrong thing was still causing bad blood, and besides, David was such a slimeball it was impossible to tell how he felt. Anyway, I was too tired to argue. I hope she's right, but Chris's stock is high these days. Consoled myself with the only bottle of wine left in the house – pinot grigio – whose insipid contents I drank rather too quickly and felt somewhat smashed. Watched some C4 Yank comedy featuring a lot of very thin women. Sally laughed all the way through. I didn't get it at all. Decided to watch some Nazi documentary on UKTV History in the kitchen instead. There's nothing like the war to cheer one up.

Friday 25 February

Today was our seventh wedding anniversary. I got up at the usual time and brought Sally breakfast in bed – nothing more than a few croissants and some coffee and orange juice. Oh yes, and an expression of pure lechery on my face – I always think she looks lovely when she's just waking up. Her features went from quizzical to smiling and finally settled on a frown.

'What about Peter and Daisy?' she asked.

'They're still asleep,' I said.

3

'But they'll be awake in a second, and when they come in here they'll wreak havoc.'

'It'll be fine,' I said, my usual catchphrase that presages a major disaster. 'Peter went to bed late, and Daisy can't exactly get out of her cot.'

Sally arched an eyebrow.

I slipped back into bed, desperate to re-create the first morning we had spent as a married couple some 2,500 days ago in an absurdly large suite that Sally's parents had paid for. Sally had emptied the entire contents of her honeymoon luggage on the floor of our room, and insisted I watch her try on every item of her new wardrobe. I seem to remember it took *hours*, and as she started asking questions about whether this or that suited her, I had to remind her what the ultimate purpose of this little burlesque was meant to be.

This morning, Sally started hurriedly eating her croissant while eyeing the baby alarm. No floor show today. Resigned, I picked up my coffee, thinking how she'd barely changed – her brown hair still long (no sensible 'mum' hair for Sally), her face just as pretty as when we first met. All in all, still highly delectable, no seven-year itch for me. She had a cool job too (a LOT cooler than mine). Until Peter came along, Sally had basically been a spook, working for what she only ever referred to as the 'ministry'. (In fact, it took her ages to tell me what her real job was, and until we started going steady I was under the impression she worked in the Department of Agriculture investigating global grain production.)

But what about all those years learning Russian? I had

asked, when the blue line had come up on the pregnancy test and she'd announced she would be giving up work after her leave. All that time perusing intelligence reports of tank movements in Tajikikazahturkastistan, all that time climbing up the greasy pole at the ministry, now she was just going to jump off? Yup, she had said, it was either one or the other, no point in doing two jobs badly. Someone else could be a Central Asian defence analyst, but nobody else was going to bring up *her* children.

'Why are you eating so quickly?' I asked.

'Because I want to finish before the children get here.'

'It'll be fine.'

I then took a dainty nibble of croissant and a comparatively refined sip of coffee.

'This is nice,' I said. 'Happy Anniversary, darling.'

Sally mouthed something back, sending a shower of croissant crumbs flying over the duvet cover. Of course, this had to be the moment Peter burst in, declaring he had had a dream about giraffes. (It's always giraffes. Every morning.) Told him he could go back to bed if he liked. He said he wanted to get into MummyandDaddysbed, and could he have cake, too?

And then my coffee got spilt. A violent burning sensation on my stomach which spread rapidly southwards. I leaped out of bed – orange juice went EVERYWHERE – and dashed to the basin, frantically splashing cold water all over my pyjama bottoms. It was no good. I had to remove them, and continue the splashing. All I could hear was

Sally's laughter and Peter's cackling. I shouted that it bloody hurt, but this only caused more hysterics. After a few moments, the pain died down, and I inspected myself for signs of damage. There were none.

The bed, though, was trashed – duvet covered in orange juice, coffee and croissant crumbs, and then Daisy started crying.

'I'll get her up while you sort this,' said Sally.

She got up and gave me a kiss.

'A nice idea,' she said. 'Can you pick up a new duvet from Farrell's on your way back from the office?'

Saturday 26 February

Afternoon spent at Sally's godson's third birthday party. Village hall and bouncy castle smelling of rancid feet. Peter kept being knocked over by larger children. Felt guiltily heartened to see he took his revenge by pushing over a boy half his size. Such is the chain of things. If I ever get shafted at work, I'll shaft someone else in turn. I could make the bouncy castle into a metaphor for the office, but I can't be bothered. Best mate Nigel was a good host as usual, and plied us hombres with suitable amounts of surprisingly pleasant supermarket own-brand cava. Plastic cups though. Still, at least it was cold. Robert's breath is getting worse. Why doesn't Rachel do anything about it? Sally tells me Rachel's breath is just as bad – perhaps it's some sort of kink. They're a bit like that those two. Does wife-swapping still go on? If so, I bet they're up to it. But the breath surely holds them back.

Asked Nigel about the market for people like me.

'It's a little, er, *rarefied*,' he said.

'You mean it's non-existent?'

'Not exactly. I'll have a look around if you like. Anyway, I thought things were going well for you there?'

'They're going fine,' I replied, a little too high-pitched. 'But, you know, it's always nice to know what's out there.'

Nigel gave me the kind of look that suggested he'd heard this a thousand times.

'Here's an idea,' he said.

'What?'

'You could stay at home and look after the children.'

I scanned his face for signs of irony. There were none, at least not immediately. Much laughter ensued. Ho-ho. I playfully made to punch him in the stomach, which caused him to flinch, which in turn sent his cup of cava down my jeans. Result – everyone assumed I was incontinent. It hasn't been a good forty-eight hours for my lap.

Got back home in time for the ritual of children's supper – bathtime – storytime – milk – brush teeth. I find the whole process utterly draining (especially after too much afternoon drinking) and it involves rather too much physical exertion. Peter decided he had to have a large cardboard box in the bath – a pirate ship apparently – which Sally said was not allowed. I told her it was harmless, and Peter, sensing I was on his side, egged me on. Box went into bath, closely followed by Peter and Daisy. Predictably, box started to disintegrate and quickly ended up a brown soggy mass.

'I want you to fix it!' Peter moaned.

'I can't,' I explained through gritted teeth. 'It's broken now.'

Naturally this infuriated Peter, whose mind's eye was not so much seeing the demise of five sides of cardboard, but the wreck of a valued toy. Box went dripping downstairs, making carpets wet. Came back up, helped finish off bath and then processed Peter, who insisted on writhing and wriggling while I got him into his pyjamas.

'Just stop it!' I finally yelled, grabbing his ankle firmly to stop him twisting, but like some sort of rubber-limbed fakir, he managed to rotate 180 degrees despite my grip.

'I. Am. Made. Of. Jelly,' he told me, which made me laugh.

I find it impossible to get genuinely angry with him – unless I'm horrifically tired – because whenever he's being naughty I think it funny as well. Sally says this is 'unhelpful'.

Read Peter a *Thomas the Tank Engine* story – utterly boring, but he loves them. Noticed that the one I'm reading features a mildly anti-Semitic passage in which a 'Jeremiah Jobling' refuses to hand over a bootlace required to get some engine back on the rails.

'Can I have it again?' Peter asked. I indulged him and he fell asleep after two pages. I closed the book and just looked at him for a couple of minutes as he gently breathed through his slightly open mouth. So precious. Reflect that I see the children asleep more often than I see them awake. I'm up before they are and back after they're in bed.

Sunday 27 February

Spent much of the day worried about work and the EMAIL and have been rather foul to Sally. Snapped at her a few times, and told her I wasn't going to make Daisy's lunch because I didn't think it was my job. I didn't really mean it and regretted it straight away. Apologised instantly, but she was still infuriated.

'You've got no right to treat me as the default parent at the weekend,' she said.

I never know how to answer this, except to say I'm the breadwinner.

So: 'But, but, I'm the breadwinner,' I said.

'That hardly gives you the right to act like some Victorian!'

She was right – saying things like that does make me sound crusty and old-fashioned.

'Perhaps you're insecure,' she said. 'Trying to flex some sort of male muscle.'

'Fnar fnar,' I went childishly, which helped to break the ice or at least to crack it a little.

Anyway, day not helped by presence of Sally's mother, who Peter adores in equal measure to my loathing. I know it's such a cliché to hate one's mother-in-law, but I really, really do. Jane is always dressed in some rectangular red outfit, and has this huge mouth out of which barbed comments issue every fifteen minutes. She looks like a malevolent postbox.

Barbs today included, 'Sally's looking very tired.' 'Can't you afford to buy some *nice* clothes for Daisy?'

'This wine has a funny taste.' 'Are you thinking of moving soon?' 'How old is your car?' All of these I can stick except for the one about the wine, about which she knows sod all. The car is old, and the house is too small, and Sally probably is tired, and yes, Daisy's clothes are all hand-me-downs from friends, but none of this is her wretched business. If she was so bloody worried about our condition (which is not exactly parlous) then why doesn't she open that socking great bank account of hers and give us a fat pile of cash? A hundred grand would do, and she could afford it easily. I know why she doesn't – she doesn't like me, that's why. If Sally had married someone posher – someone like ex-boyfriend, ex-colleague and all round Mr Perfect, Nick, who Jane just adored – then maybe we'd get our hands on her dosh.

After lunch (beef, which I deliberately cooked rare because I know Jane hates it like that), I had to get out, so I took Peter and Daisy for our weekly walk, or rather a drag. Daisy sat in her pram and gurgled cutely round the circuit, whereas Peter was tired and whinged the whole way.

I tried to explain that the weekends were special days because Daddy wasn't at work, but he told me he wanted to see Mummy. I find this rejection mildly upsetting, but I suppose it's fair enough. Just because the Sunday afternoon walk is one of the highlights of my week, it doesn't mean it has to be for them. After all, I'm just some bloke who turns up twice a week. Sally's here all the time. That's why she's better placed to look after them at the weekends.

Plus, as soon as I try to help, she always tells me I'm doing something wrong. Anything that deviates from her routine is immediately slapped down.

The thing is, if her domestic life were a *business*, it would be obvious what's wrong. When I try to explain to her, in management consultancy terms, that her routine is suffering from systemic atrophy and a lack of fluidity, she tells me I should keep that sort of talk for the office. Children aren't like companies that can be 'repurposed' she says. She's wrong. Much as I complain about my job, the truth is a little management consultancy would work wonders for Sally's routine. I'm just too much of a coward to suggest it. But it would be interesting. I might ask Jim at the office to work up some models, throw what he likes to call 'blue sky' on this.

Monday 28 February

Most of my day was occupied by trying to work out once again what 'Dudley' referred to. It's become an obsession, and I know I should get on with the Everest of stuff I've got waiting, but I can't help it. It's a niggle that's turned into a neurosis. I phoned Clive in Birmingham (I know, it's nowhere near, but it's the nearest we get) to ask him whether we should do something in Dudley. He thought I was barking.

'Dudley? Dudley's the last place we'd do anything. Have you ever been to Dudley?'

'No.'

'Well, if you'd ever been, you'd know it's not for us.'

'Have you ever been?'

'God no.'

'So anywhere you haven't been isn't worth visiting?'

'Precisely,' he replied. 'Why do you think I haven't been abroad in fifteen years?'

Fiona suggested that perhaps Dudley was a person, so I took another look at the internal phonebook – nothing. I don't know why this is annoying me so much, but there was something suspicious about that email. AND, it is my job to look after new business, so I need to be involved. If I'm being left out, then this augurs badly.

Got home in good time. Read Peter another *Thomas the Bloody Tank Engine.* Sweet that he's so into it, but – GOD – I wish he'd ask for something else. Nevertheless, read it as excitingly as I could, which apparently wasn't good enough, as he fell asleep halfway through. Tucked him up and gently removed a giraffe from his hand. Daisy was asleep on her front, her bum in the air. Why do they sleep like that? Mystifying.

Sally looked tired, said her day had been stressful. She'd been clamped – something to do with chasing a dog down the street outside the supermarket – I lost the gist of the story well before she got to the end.

Nothing on the box. Monday night's always bad for Nazis, even on UKTV History. Who gives a toss about what the Stuarts did for us anyway?

Thursday 3 March

The last few days have been infuriating. Along with every-thing else I've got to get on with, I've spent as many spare minutes as possible looking into what Dudley means. Yes, I know, I should just leave it, but I've gone through every wretched file – digital or otherwise – I can get my hands on. What makes things more complicated is that I don't want to attract suspicion. Chris – of all people – found me in the records room on the third floor today, and asked what I was up to. I wanted to tell him it was none of his business, and reprimand him for being so cocky – techni-cally he is subordinate to me – but afraid a bit of guilt stopped me. Told him that I was looking for stuff about Exeter, to which he just went 'ah', and glided away like the snake he is. (Do snakes glide? Sort of.) There is something repellent about Chris. Dark-eyed, and looks like a sweaty Russell Harty. I don't go in for astrology, but when I found out he was a Scorpio it made total sense. Outwardly he's friendly, but there is something glossily dark and sinister about him, sting in his tail, etc., especially since the Lockhart Armstrong fiasco.

Home too late. Sally looked upset and told me I could have warned her. Truth was I completely forgot. Told her as much.

She then half-jokingly said, 'Some wives would think you were having an affair.'

'I'm not having an affair,' I said sternly. 'In fact, I resent the implication.'

'Well what am I supposed to think? You've been getting in late most of the week and with hardly any explanation.'

'I've told you,' I said. 'I've been trying to work out what this Dudley business is.'

'Pah.'

'You're being neurotic,' I said, which didn't help.

Ate an angry supper alone in the kitchen in front of *Secret Weapons of World War Two*. Interested to discover that V2 rockets travelled so fast you would see and hear the explosion before you heard them approach. Awesome. Bed now. No chance of sex I expect. I shall try though. Want to prove that I'm not having an affair, although quite how having sex will achieve this I don't know. Besides, I heard that men who have affairs do it more with their wives – reawakened libido. So if I do want sex tonight, perhaps Sally will suspect something. Oh God, this is hopeless.

Friday 4 March

Today I took the unprecedented step of committing a crime, or at least I think it's a crime. I logged on as Chris and went through his emails. It was childishly simple to guess his password – I got it right on the third try. It was 'Linsey', the name of his plain wife. Despite the faithful cuteness of his password, my snooping confirmed my suspicion that he and Charlotte in accounts were having an affair – and, bizarrely, a hitherto unsuspected mutual interest in bird watching. It looked as though it had been going on for months. What does she see in that worm? Still, judging by their correspondence, it's pretty passionate stuff. Their favourite lunchtime haunt would appear to be the Thistle Hotel – how seedy. Amazing they haven't yet been busted, because everybody goes there for sales conferences, etc.

Anyway, to get to the meat of the matter, I went through a whole medley of messages between him and David that carried the subject 'Dudley'. David's messages are very guarded, and he tells Chris he should proceed with caution. On a few occasions he reminds Chris that he, David, is the MD, and only he will greenlight it. However, most curious is David's repeated assertion that he wants everything to be kept discreet. I printed them all out. It looks as though they are on the fiddle, but then that may be paranoia. Maybe they are cooking up something that's perfectly legit but somewhat risky? Whatever the case, there's little I can do, because I came by the knowledge illegally. It's not worth risking my job for this, not after the Lockhart Armstrong business, and especially with demand being so 'rarefied'. All I can do is to keep an eye out.

Sally thinks it was very very wrong of me to go through the emails. I told her that was a bit rich, coming from someone who worked with information that was presumably gathered by spies. Still, I do feel guilty now, but I just had to find out more. She told me I should go to see Sir Roger, the chairman, but my evidence is not good enough. Besides, I can't just blurt out that I've been hacking into a colleague's emails and I've found something I don't like. No. I shall need more proof. Tomorrow we're off to stay the weekend with our old friends Ant and Melissa in London. Hellish drive. Should be fun though.

Sunday 6 March

7/10 weekend. Subtract one point for conversation utterly dominated by merits and demerits of private education. Subtract another for Ant's largely rubbish wine. Subtract another for abysmal dinner guests last night – some odious couple from I forget where. He (I can't remember his name) was a former financial adviser but has given it up to be a music teacher and kept banging on about how 'brave' he was. She (I think she was called Petruchia or something similarly annoyingly Shakespearean manqué) banged on about how they were going to educate – let me get this right – Xave, Calypso, Clem and Ralf. For heaven's sake! Xave – boy or girl? Clem – boy or girl? Calypso – ice cream. Ralf – ugly and trying too hard. Why do all these people have to give their children such ridiculous names? Sally and I feel inestimably smug with our totally workmanlike and conservative Peter and Daisy. Safe, unoriginal and solid. They've been good names for centuries, and they'll do the pair of them for their next eight or nine decades. Or maybe their generation will live to a hundred? So long as they don't eat too many Pork Gobblers or whatever rubbish they'll get at their school, state or otherwise.

Vomitella maintained that Charnborough was a 'marvellous' school. I told her that I'd never heard of it, and there was no point sending one's children to some incredibly minor public school. She didn't like this one bit, and looked at me as though I was one of her peasants. Mind you, Revoltina is actually all fake posh and I doubt whether her family has ever owned a peasant in centuries. Neither have the illustrious Holdens, but then I don't claim that we have, and neither do I bang on about how 'mahvellous' my children are. (Clem's already on grade 6 viola. Is he/she really?) Despite – or because of – Ant's wine (some Gallo Brothers plonk) I got smashed way too quickly and fear I insulted Excreta and dull – but oh, so very brave – husband. Sally said I got a little loud, which is code for rude and offensive.

Sunday was perfectly pleasant though, and after lunch walked round the common. While Ant and Melissa were ahead of us, Sally and I tried to dispel our hangovers with one of our favourite park games: analysing the other parents. We have isolated at least three types of fathers so far, for example, which we have organised into a classification pompously called the Holden Fatherhood Taxonomy.

First, there is OKD – Overly Keen Dad – who tries to do too much and prove what a Modern Man he is. He can easily be identified by his wearing of cargo trousers, rectangular glasses, cooler-than-cool trainers, and tight trendy T-shirts, even though he is nearing forty. He spends his whole time in the park, showing the rest of the world that He Loves His Children More Than You Love Yours. Thus, he rolls around with them on the grass, and tickles them constantly, laughs too much, plays frisbee in a demonstratively athletic way, gives the children their bottles on the park bench, etc., etc. He wants everybody to know he is not just a Good Dad, he is Terrific Dad. In a few years' time his children will see through him and regard him as the fraudulent twat that he is.

17

Next is OFD – Old-Fashioned Dad. He is the opposite of OKD. He normally wears a V-neck jersey, cords, brogues, a checked shirt – i.e. he dresses like his father. OFDs are often to be found in pairs, walking several steps ahead of their wives, sensibly dressed stay-at-home mums who are minding the children. OFD loves his children in an undemonstrative way, although he has no interest in the tiresome business of actually rearing them. At teatime and bathtime he can be found reading *The Economist* in his study which he leaves at 6.50 to read the children a story before returning to the drawing room where he will have a whisky and watch the *Antiques Road Show*. In short, OFD is a fogey, and regards children as a woman's job. His wife is likely to be in agreement with him, because she is that sort of 'gel'. (A few years ago, she would definitely have worn an Alice band.)

Then there is PDD – Perfectly Decent Dad – who dresses in unshowy but not particularly fashionable clothes – chinos, long-sleeved T-shirts, rollneck jumpers, button-down shirts (often blue), and a pair of desert or Chelsea boots, although Docksiders are the most likely. He does his bit with the children and genuinely enjoys being with him. However, he does regard his wife as the default child rearer. He tries to help more, but finds it a little tiresome.

Personally, I think I am a PDD, although Sally thinks I have a large dollop of OFD in there, partly because I have this shameful interest in the *Antiques Road Show*.

By our reckoning, some 60 per cent of those fathers in the park were PDDs, 15 per cent OFDs and some 25 per cent were OKDs. Pushed Daisy a bit in her clonezone three-wheeler, displaying token New Manism. Gave a few knowing nods to other PDDs in similar position. Looking round the common, hard to imagine any of us used to go clubbing. As for most of the women, they all look so . . . *sensible*. Their hair short, their clothes machine-washable and baby puke-proof, boobs sucked into pitta breads by their children whereas most men I know are *growing* breasts. Is that all marriage is about? A gradual process of mammary transference? It's affected Sally too. Don't get me wrong, she looks fantastic when she gets dressed up – well, how often does that happen? – but her clothes are so damn practical these days. She used to wear sexy knee-length boots the whole time, but now she just wears stuff from that Sloaney catalogue – flat-soled shoes, predictably colourful cardigans, etc. And skirts, when did she last wear a skirt? Whenever I moan about this, she always ripostes that high-heeled boots and miniskirts aren't the most practical things to wear when looking after children. What if the skirts were made of leather? I once asked. Surely they could be easily wiped clean of child gop and would also keep me happy? That nearly earned me a left hook. Perhaps I should try wearing heels and a skirt one day, she said. That, I said, would require a severe amount of waxing. Such high wit.

Got back home around 7.30, the children having slept all the way. We unloaded them gently and carried them up the stairs like UN sacks of grain. Peter woke briefly and asked if Tom – Ant's son – had come back home with us, and I told him a white lie that he had. He smiled and went straight back to sleep. I looked at him for a minute or so.

He looks increasingly like Sally – the same large brown eyes, the same defined eyebrows. If Peter is as handsome as Sally is pretty, he should break a few hearts. As for Daisy, it's too soon to say. Bizarrely, she's blonde – neither of us is blonde – and I fear she will inherit my stocky rugby player's physique. Well, it was a rugby player's physique. God knows what it is now. If I spent two months in a boot camp I might get back to my glory days, but chances of this are zero.

It's now 9 p.m. and I have the most dreadful Sunday feeling. I have an inkling this week is going to be some-what momentous. Sally gave me one of her head massages, which was wonderful. Felt miles better afterwards. Almost better than sex.

Monday 7 March

I'll write a longer entry tomorrow because it's late and I'm pissed and very tired. All that needs to be said at this point is that it has happened. I'm out. Gone. Sacked. Shafted. Those arseholes. I will kill David. Slowly. Pliers and blow-torch, à la *Pulp Fiction*.

Tuesday 8 March

It was all very sudden and humiliating. The phone went at three – it was David's secretary, Debbie, asking me to come up right away. It was clear from her voice that I wasn't being asked up for a pay rise. I put on my jacket – protection? – and walked up slowly in a pathetic attempt to show dignity.

I had to sit for a demeaningly long time in the anteroom to David's office. Further confirmation that things were very bad was the absence of coffee. Debbie ignored me, and just typed away furiously fast. I noticed she is one of those people whose heads rocks from side to side as they type, as though they are on a boat. Flicked through some boring trade mags on the coffeeless coffee table, finding it impossible to take them in – well, no change there.

David was to the point.

'I'm terminating your employment with immediate effect.'

'Why?'

'Because you have contravened paragraph fourteen of your contract.'

I looked back at him blankly. He had obviously prepared for this, as he thrust a copy of said contract towards me. I had to lean forward to grab it. I scanned down to paragraph fourteen. 'Any employee found misusing and/or abusing the electronic systems of the company shall be dismissed.'

I closed my eyes. Fuck.

'I have here a log of you accessing Chris Holden's user account from your own terminal.'

Another sheet of paper, another lean forward. My first thoughts were about what I was going to tell Sally. To get sacked for snooping on others just looked pathetic, childish. To make matters worse, there would be no severance pay, nothing.

I was determined not to go without getting my tuppence worth.

'What about Dudley?' I asked, closely scrutinising David's face.

Colour only drains from people's faces in bad books, but if this had been a bad book then David's face would certainly have gone white.

'What about Dudley?' he replied, slowly.

'Just something I heard,' I said, suddenly realising that my lie was completely pointless. After all, David would know which of his emails I had read.

'For your information,' he replied, 'Dudley – which you've no doubt read about in *personal* email correspondence – refers to a management buyout. I needn't remind you that as your confidentiality agreement will follow you to the grave, you are not entitled to breathe a word about it. If you do, I will sue you.'

Whatever colour *I* had left probably really did drain from my face. Fuck, I kept repeating internally, fuck fuck fuck. Hence all the secrecy, all the 'champagne for ever' emails. But why was I not consulted? I asked as much.

'Two words,' David replied. 'Lockhart and Armstrong.' More internal fucks, the rhythm of which was interrupted by David handing me a large black bin liner.

'I don't believe it,' I said. 'I expect I'll be accompanied by a security guard.'

Wordlessly, David looked over my shoulder, and there indeed was Terry, the guard from downstairs. I stood up, knowing it was time to leave. I held out my hand to David, feeling rather like having to thank the headmaster for caning me. David shook it awkwardly, his grip small and wet. To think I had regarded him almost as a friend. I'll get you, I thought, I'll bloody get you.

The walk across the floor was the worst. It's one thing to be sacked, but quite another to have to suffer the humiliation of being frogmarched across to your desk, there to fill up your bag with several years of mementoes, rubbish and whatnot. In went the photographs of Sally and the children, in went a tracksuit and trainers (barely used), a squash racket (never used), some trade mags (unread), a hippopotamus tooth (don't ask), and a couple of books. Fiona came over and asked me lots of whats and whys, and I just told her I'd give her a call later in the week. I walked out, solemnly, to the scaffold accompanied by Terry, who was just as self-conscious. At least fifty pairs of eyes were on us. I told Terry I'd never known it so quiet, and he laughed a little too loudly. Humouring a dying man. Just as his laugh petered out, the bag split, scattering my stuff all over the floor. 'Not even a decent sack,' I said, and Terry laughed again.

Uncharacteristically drank three cans of beer on the way home. Strange being on the train so early, surrounded by people not wearing suits. Took my tie off. By the time I got in, I was feeling mildly pissed, which I topped up at the Railway Tavern, a really foul place, full of toothless men with toothless dogs, and, occasionally, toothless wives. I couldn't face the idea of going home, but two pints of Guinness gave me courage of sorts. I got back at seven – an hour earlier than usual – to find Sally reading to the children while they drank their milk. Two of the three looked delighted to see me, and somehow I suddenly had to hold back the tears. Sally, though, took one disapproving look at me.

'Has what I think has happened, happened?' she asked.

I nodded, and then came and gave them all a hug, muttering that I was so sorry.

'You smell strange, Daddy,' said Peter.

'You should have a shower,' said Sally, waving my boozy fumes away.

It was at that point that Daisy sicked up her milk. Selfishly, I just walked out of the room. Not my job, I thought, at least not tonight.

Sally was good to me, far too good to me. When I told her why, she allowed herself a rolling back of the eyes and then poured herself a large glass of red wine (something South African from the supermarket – she must have bought it) and knocked back half of it. Could see she was trying not to cry.

'It'll be fine,' I said.

Instant regret.

'Whenever you say that,' she said, 'things normally end up somewhat less than fine. Anyway, I really don't want to talk about it just now.'

This meant supper in a great big stupid silence, punctuated by small talk about the children. Peter had drawn a nice tree at playgroup, and was now able to pee into the lavatory standing up. Daisy has started pulling herself up using a chair . . .

She then asked me what I was going to do tomorrow. Told her I hadn't given it much thought. Would call Nigel. We went to bed early, and had 6/10 sex, which was 6 points more than a fool like me could have wished for. Sympathy I expect.

Today has been strange. I woke at normal time – 5.30 – but did none of that automatically getting ready nonsense. Instead, I just lay in bed, watching the greyness of the light through our curtains. Must get some new ones. They are too thin. By 6.15, the time at which I would normally have left, I heard one of the children cry. Couldn't work out which one it was. They sound increasingly similar. Just as I was about to shake Sally awake, I decided to leave her asleep. The least I could do was to execute the morning routine.

Stumbled into Daisy's room. She was standing up in her sleeping bag, demanding to be set free from her cot. She's nearly one and although she doesn't speak she certainly makes herself clear. I lifted her up and trod gingerly down the stairs, bidding her to shush. She didn't. As we walked past Peter's room, her howling woke up Peter, whom I just ignored. Raced downstairs, and plonked Daisy on the kitchen floor, which intensified her screaming. I could see why – the tiles were freezing.

Picked her up and then looked for a bottle, which I eventually found in the cupboard that contains all the baking products. Huh? Why there? I then realised it was nearly impossible to spoon in the formula unless I put Daisy down, which would only create more noise. So, I tried to spoon it in while holding Daisy, which was a disaster. I knocked the bottle over. This meant having to boil up fresh water, wait for it to cool down, stir in more formula

– a good fifteen minutes at least, a good fifteen minutes of more effing wailing. I decided to use cow's milk instead, and she guzzled that happily.

While she was doing so, Sally came downstairs, my mission to let her have a lie-in clearly a failure.

'What was the swearing about?' she asked.

I told her.

'What are you feeding her then?'

'Cow's milk,' I said sheepishly.

'But she's not supposed to have milk yet!'

'What's wrong with it?'

'She may be lactose intolerant,' said Sally.

'It'll be fine.'

At this point, Daisy revealed that she was indeed lactose intolerant – or at least not used to bovine products – by sicking up her milk all over me and the floor. I looked up at Sally, who had 'told you so' written all over her. At least my motives were noble, I said. Sally said I was very sweet to try, I would know next time, nice idea, etc., etc.

Now sitting in Rose's coffee shop near the station. Rose has a wireless network. Big deal. Rose has sweetly brought me a cup of coffee on the house – do I already look like a charity case? Last week, I was going places. This morning, I'm well on my way to forty, with 'rarefied' skills that can't even feed a one-year-old. And I smell of pukey milk. Must get my act together. Too tempting to wallow in self-pity.

Check for emails containing sympathy and job offers. None. But excitingly I can enlarge my penis, and have a new mortgage. If I answered all my spam, I'd have a cock the length of the street, and a mortgage that would buy every house on it.

Wednesday 9 March

It has not been a great couple of days. First, Nigel tells me there is nothing out there. Second – and this was predictable – Chris has got my job. I spent much of the day making calls, only to have very few of them returned. Andrew Peters at Imprimature (who makes these names up?) says they might have something coming up in the 'mid-future' although he wouldn't say quite how 'mid'. I'm not sure I'd want to work with Andrew anyway. There's something slimy about him. Toadlike. The fact is, word about what I did will get round fast, and nobody will want to employ me. I may well be completely shafted, but I'm not going to admit it yet.

Spend many hours plotting revenge against David and Chris. Imagine increasingly brutal scenarios, which culminate in an image of covering them in petrol, setting them alight, hanging them by their feet from a helicopter, then dropping their, hopefully, still conscious, burning bodies head first into the middle of the M25 at rush hour from 2,000 feet. Decide that this is too warped – and a little impractical – but it's how I feel. What can I do? There must be something. A sensible part of me just tells me to forget it, put it all behind me, but the truth is, I'm still in shock. I always thought I was adaptable, but I fear I'm rather less so than I supposed. What the hell am I going to do now?

*

High – or rather low – point of day was looking after the children from 5ish onwards. Sally announced she was going off for a drink with her sister Victoria, where I expect she will spend the entire time bemoaning my spectacular fall. She doesn't seem to have much sympathy for my reasons for looking through the emails. I tried to dress it up by saying I was attempting to 'gather some intelligence' (i.e. speak her language), but this cut no ice whatsoever. I know I did a Bad Thing by looking through Chris's emails, but it was in a Good Cause, albeit a potentially Good Cause.

Anyway, I didn't have enough time to worry about all that, as I had to process the children until bedtime at 7.30ish (at least it is normally.) Utterly exhausting (although will tell Sally otherwise). Sally told me before she left that Peter had been a little bad-tempered throughout the day, and that Daisy was yet to have a poo. I thought nothing of it and put on one of my old tapes I had found this morning in the attic: *Greatest Hits of the 1980s*. (Stand-out track – 'Michael Caine' by Madness, although bizarrely I also like 'Politics of Dancing' by Reflex, and more disturbingly, 'Bird of Paradise' by Snowy White. My taste can be enormously suspect.)

I decided to mime along to 'Temptation' by Heaven 17, which for no apparent reason made Peter and Daisy cackle with laughter. I think Daisy genuinely believes the sound is coming from my mouth, and she squealed whenever I 'sang' the word *temptation*. Peter then joined in, and soon the two of us were shouting 'temptation' every few seconds. God knows what the rest of the lyrics are. Some woman screaming incomprehensibly in the background about putting her 'die in the hot tub' and it being a 'meal into one shop'. Huh? After the song had finished, Peter said, 'We are cool dudes, Daddy.' His observation was more cute than acute.

After our eighties revival session, Peter asked what he was having for supper. I hadn't even thought about it. I just kind of assumed it happened.

'What does Mummy normally give you?'

'Pasta.'

'Pasta with what?'

'Peas.'

Cordon Bleu stuff. Easy. Just peas – organic of course – it was, then. He looked at it with disdain, the little Fauntleroy.

'Where's the bacon?' he whinged.

'You didn't ask for bacon.'

'But I want bacon!'

'You can't have it!'

He then started yelling about how much he wanted bacon, at which point I started yelling back at him, which resulted in a vicious circle of yelling. This did not impress Daisy, who started bellowing louder – and a lot higher – than Peter or me.

There was only one thing for it. I had to have a drink, so I went to the living room and knocked back a whisky. This is how alcoholism starts. Why aren't all housewives complete dipsos? Returned to kitchen, and found that Peter had thrown his (thankfully plastic) bowl of food on the floor. I yelled at him again, and back we were with Daisy shrieking, Peter yelling and me shrieking. Also struggling to make themselves heard were the Flying Pickets singing 'Only You'. I resisted urge to slug down another glass of whisky and decided I would have to make the peace first. Humility, you see. This was like negotiating with terrorists.

I caved in by presenting Peter with a chocolate digestive biscuit. I always thought I was a good negotiator (how many courses have I been on?) and here I was, giving Peter more than he was asking for. Madness. It was like offering someone £60,000 when they would have settled for £45,000. Just nuts. Perhaps negotiation courses should tell executives to shriek at the people opposite, and pretty soon you'd get what you want simply because the other people would want you to shut up.

All this didn't solve the Daisy problem. She was inconsolable. I lifted her up in an attempt to calm her down, but somehow this made things worse. She struggled – more powerfully than I could have imagined – and nearly landed head first on the floor. What did she want? Food, that was what. Frantically, I scrabbled around in the cupboard and the fridge to find something that would be suitable to give her. All I could find were mysterious Tupperware containers filled with sinister-looking pastes. Could these in fact have been foodstuffs? Surely not. The least inedible thing I could find was mint jelly. Would that do? There was only one way to find out.

She loved it, and ate almost the whole jar. Peter ate another three biscuits, after which I gave him some milk and soon the three of us were the picture of familial contentment. I helped myself to a digestive as well, and eventually found my mind wandering back to 'Dudley'. Just as I was deliberating how I might be able to find out what exactly it might be, an almighty smell emanated from Daisy. The poo had come, and it was bad. Not solid in any way. What the hell had Sally been feeding her? The fact that her poo was presumably organic was little consolation.

It's now 8.30 and I've done my 'bit' for the day. Bathtime was more or less a disaster, and I have no intention of tidying up the bathroom. Sally's still not back. She and Victoria don't normally meet for a drink, it's so unlike them. Instead, they just talk on the phone, or have lunch during the week. Despite being twins, they're complete opposites. Victoria is total Slack Mum to Sally's Ubermum. She probably thinks Gina Ford is a make of car. Victoria lets her two boys (Sholto, seven, and Perry, five – eurgh) stay up as late as they like, and lets them eat ketchup (in- organic, presumably). Victoria's husband, Adrian, ran off a couple of years ago with a beautician, whom he probably fancied because she was tidy. Still, at least I don't have to worry about whether I earn more than my brother-in-law. There's a saying that claims that if you earn one pound a year more than your sister-in-law's husband, then you could consider yourself rich. Well, it wouldn't take much to be richer than me at the moment.

Thursday 10 March
11 a.m.

Great. My suspicions proved correct. It wasn't Victoria. It was Mark Warwick, no less, the head of Sally's old depart- ment at the ministry. He lives a few villages away, and Sally has always kept in touch with him. But that's not all. He's offered Sally her old job back. I don't know what to think. She hasn't accepted it yet, but I can tell she's keen. He'd like her to start in April, just three weeks away. And he's offering her the same salary she was on before, which is only £5,000 less than I was getting. Total maelstrom of emotions, I think the cliché goes.

I'm as surprised now as I was when she announced she was going to give up work. Barring parlous inefficiencies and ill-thought-out time/motion practices in her routine, I thought she was not only looking after the children well, but also enjoying herself. Clearly, by the sound of it, some days were worse than others, but still, I thought she had things on a level. Once in a while she would complain that it would be nice to use her brain again, but I didn't think she was being serious. After all, she still has a stack of esoteric magazines next to the bed, the most obscure of which at the moment is clearly *Tajik Digest*. But over the past few months, the stack has been topped with crap like *A-Listers* magazine. Sally has always hated that sort of dross, so maybe her brain really is starting to turn to goo.

What to think? On the one hand, I'm happy for her, on the other hand, selfishly, I feel utterly dejected. Not only have I been sacked, but my wife has been offered a plum job. There's something else I don't like about it either, if I'm being honest – Nick. Nick is an old flame of hers, and he also works in the ministry. I suspect he still burns a socking great candle for Sally, despite her assuring me that he doesn't. And now he's going to be seeing her every day.

I know I can trust Sally, but it's hardly going to make me feel easy.

But then there is a bigger question, and that's this: who's going to look after the children?

2.30 p.m.

I am, apparently. A long conversation at lunch while Peter was at playgroup and Daisy slept. (A rare event – she doesn't seem to do much sleeping. A sign of intelligence I'm told, but am cynical about such glib reassurances.) Sally has it all worked out. She will go back to work while I stay at home and look after the children on a six-month 'trial basis'.

In short, I will become a househusband – a cultural and social joke, never to be taken seriously again. I can already see the superior smirks of fellow men at dinner parties, the condescending 'oh-good-for-yous' and 'how lucky you are to have so much time with the children' and the frankly dishonest 'I'd love to change shoes with you'. No way. Not for me thanks.

'I don't think I can go from A to Z quite so quickly,' I said. 'I'll need a little time.'

'I went from A to Z pretty damn quickly. Anyway, we haven't reached a decision yet.'

This was said in a tone that left me in no doubt what she wanted the decision to be.

'Chew it over,' she continued. 'There's nothing wrong with being a househusband these days.'

'There's everything wrong with being a househusband.

It goes against my entire grain. I love Peter and Daisy, but I don't think I could spend all day every day with them.'

Sally sighed.

'Us mothers don't like spending all day every day with the children either, you know. This is why they have play-groups to go to. Friends to visit.'

I huffed and I puffed, saying appalling, last-ditch stuff like women are programmed to look after children, whereas men aren't. More paahing. She said Suzie's husband, Digby, had been looking after the children for nearly a year now and was enjoying it. Digby – what sort of name is that anyway? – is a complete wet fish, and couldn't hack it in the real world. Sally said that clearly neither could I, other-wise I'd still have a job. Told her that was unfair, and losing a job didn't constitute not being able to cope. She then piped up that Digby had deliberately left his job at AHG just so he could look after the children, which took a real man. Sniffed Sally's tactic a mile off, and said I wasn't a real man. She said I was a real man the other night, and then proceeded to attempt to seduce me, a ruse so shame-faced, so obvious, so crass, I was immediately forced to give in.

Not much in the way of emails. Nigel says there's nothing around. One from Sally's mother (I haven't told her yet, or my parents) wondering whether I can take the day off for Derek's sixty-fifth. How much I would dearly love to miss that. The day that woman learnt how to use email was one made by Satan himself. I get non-stop drivel from her. Another from Fiona asking how I am. Sweet of her. Only person in that bloody company who's sent me an email. Write her a lengthy reply, and apologise at the end for banging on.

Sunday 13 March

A strained weekend as Sally spent much of the time explaining child-related procedures, which I chose to ignore, or at least pretended to ignore. Peter's clothes are kept here, this drawer for socks and pants, this drawer for trousers (light) . . . felt like that WWII poem we had to learn at school. Henry Reed's 'Naming of Parts' in which the narrator is taught how to use a rifle, and when he's shown how to ease the rifle's spring, his mind drifts . . . Daisy's formula is made thus, and no, she's not ready for milk. We call this milking the Daisy.

By Saturday afternoon, I told Sally it was very sweet of her to tell me all these things, but as I'd be back at work soon, there was really no need. This was deliberately provocative, but she was too intelligent to react. Instead, she just smiled like some Jehovah's Witness who's just been told to eff off. Apparently, there's nothing I can say that will wind her up. It's as though she's approaching paradise. It's the civil service I tell her, she will be commuting and spending her spare hours reading papers on Tregjkdklstani missile silos. She says, yup, can't wait. This is all too strange.

Escaped to the golf course on Sunday morning. Now that *was* paradise. Played with Nigel to whom I told the whole truth about what had happened at work. I could see he was a little shocked. Blot on my copybook, etc., etc., firms take invasion of employee privacy very seriously, etc., etc. Will probably foul things up for a long time. Not good news, to put it mildly. I told him I wanted to find some work urgently because Sally's got this idea about me being a househusband. This made Nigel roar with laughter, and me to fluff an easy chip on to the fourteenth green.

'You'd be brilliant at it!'

'Sod off,' I said, suppressing a glare, my smile false as hell.

'I can just see you in your apron!'

Ha-dee-ha-ha.

This went on rather too long for my liking. He then brought up Digby, and told me that Digby had trousered about £3 million from AHG being taken over, so he had decided to retire. He kept that quiet. Nigel said it was so people like me and him didn't get jealous. Well, I am jealous. If I had three mill in the bank, I'd certainly become a househusband.

Was late back for lunch. Sally normally would have looked daggers, but instead she asked what I had got round in, and how Nigel was, etc. She's being unreasonably reasonable, and I know why. It rained in the afternoon, so we let the children watch *Wallace & Gromit*. Peter sat transfixed (this is worth remembering if the worst happens), but Daisy only occasionally gurgled at the screen and then bellowed because she wasn't being paid enough attention. Helped with the bath to earn some brownie points. Sally told me that this was excellent practice for me. Grrrr.

Monday 14 March

Woke up v early this morning in a shock. Heart palpitating. Enormity of everything that has happened has suddenly hit me. A little late, but then you're not really in charge of your body, are you? Felt weak, strange, breathless, as though I were having a heart attack. I wasn't (clearly) but must have been having some sort of panic attack. Strange and worrying. I told myself I had to accept what had happened, and just forget about David, Chris, 'Dudley', etc. That part of my life was gone, was over.

I rolled over and cuddled Sally who murmured encouragingly. This was a cue to instigate marital relations, to which she seemed amenable enough but just as things were getting interesting, the door burst open and Peter marched in.

'Mummy! Daddy! I've been shot in the neck by aliens but I have been a brave soldier and I am going to shoot the aliens back with my Lancaster bomber and can I have some milk and a cuddle in bed with you?'

No giraffes then. Told Peter to go back to bed and he would have some milk in a minute (which was frankly all I needed for what I had in mind), but this started a gripey whinge, which had to be checked in case it woke Daisy. It did wake Daisy, and so we all found ourselves downstairs – minus Sally – blearily watching a cartoon called *Johnny Neutron* while we gormlessly ate our Grape Nuts and Shreddies combo. I fed Daisy some proper baby cereal, the making of which had seeped in during one of Sally's lectures. Tried changing channel to watch BBC1 news, but

Peter moaned, and frankly I don't much like Violet Freshfield either. Preferred Nicky Stamford, but she's obviously been moved to some daytime news slot, as I don't see her these days. Ominous thought that perhaps I would see her more now. A good thing and a bad thing. Good, because she's nice to look at, bad because presupposes I'm at home during the day.

I've been allowing things to drift. I therefore decided that today would be a Day of Action. Made numerous phone calls, dispatched some twenty to thirty emails, and wrote at least ten letters. Felt better for having done it. Proactive. Real man stuff. I must trump Sally. It's clear that if I don't find a job I won't have anything concrete to set against Sally's not unreasonable demands other than my socio-cultural sensitivities, which mean diddly-squat (I can see why). Also, must get a position that pays more than hers, which will be hard. Doable, though. I hope.

I picked up Peter from his playgroup at 3 p.m. Have only been once, on his first day. It's in a little Portakabin next to the local primary school's playground. Looks horrific from the outside, but inside it's fine. Lots of colourful scribbles stuck to the walls, and a line of hooks with the children's little coats on them. Place is run by a jolly woman called Simone Jolly (amazingly), who didn't recognise me. Other mothers were milling around, one of whom I couldn't help but notice was wearing jodhpurs and black riding boots. She wasn't up to Sally's level, but still. A sudden wave of lust meant that I didn't immediately hear Simone jollily wondering why I was around. Lied and said I was on gardening leave.

'How nice for you,' she said.

'Yes,' I said through gritted teeth. 'It's great to have some time with the children at last.'

(I never use the word 'kids'. Hate it.)

'How long have they got you for?'

'Err . . . a month.'

'So we'll be seeing a lot more of you?'

'I expect so, yes.'

Put on Peter's coat and sloped off, aware of mothers' eyes drilling into my back. Suspicious of man at such a time and place. Or maybe they all fancy me. (V unlikely. Ten years ago, maybe, but not now. The Holden mane is no longer quite so thick and abundant, unlike the rest of my body.)

Wednesday 16 March

First of all – no sodding replies. Not one email, not one phone call, not one letter. (A little soon for the latter, I admit.) Word has clearly gone round as to why I was dismissed. That, and the fact that the market is bad. But still, I'm not exactly unemployable. I did get good results, and that was well known. Just feel an overriding sense of anger that it's boiled down to this.

This afternoon I had intended to play golf, but Sally was having none of it. Instead, she insisted I take the children shopping, and then I could play nine holes. Everything in me militated against it, but I acquiesced and did as she asked, or rather commanded. The trip was a Horlicks. Both children were tired and ratty – Peter having decided that breakfast time should be at around 5.45 a.m. – and I was feeling mildly hungover from having consumed nearly a bottle and a half of Cote Rotie the night before.

Unfortunately, by the time I arrived in town, I realised I had left the large pram – the nice big pram that can hold shopping – at home. I dimly remember Sally muttering something about it as I left the house, but I had pretended not to hear her. I do that a lot these days, I'm afraid. I put Daisy in the clapped-out Maclaren buggy, and then insisted Peter held my hand as we walked. This he refused to do, seeing it as some infringement of his personal liberty. The more I grabbed his arm, the more he struggled, and soon he was yelling at me to let him go. Passers-by gave us strange looks. Nevertheless, we managed to make it to the butcher, the baker, and even the chemist, where we bought enough nappies to last us a nuclear winter. Somehow I managed to struggle to our final destination, the greengrocer, with the immense amount of shopping, the buggy and Peter.

Peter loves the greengrocer's. He sees it as a place in which orange balls (oranges) can be thrown at large green balls (watermelons), and where piles of carefully arranged apples can be made to spill on the floor by his cunning removal of the single item of fruit on which the others are supported. Today was no exception, and I found I had to buy at least a dozen bruised and dirtied Braeburns.

This surplus fruit weighed a ton, and by the time we started back to the car, I was struggling. The shopping bags were hanging off the buggy's handles, and Peter was demanding that the pigeons a few yards away needed to be chased. I relented, and let him run off (we were in an arcade), but after a few steps he tripped and fell flat on his face. I let go of the buggy and rushed forward to save him, only to find that the weight of the shopping caused the buggy to flip back instantly, sending the buggy and its contents – including Daisy – crashing to the ground. I had strapped her in, thank goodness, but she was now screaming almost as loudly as her brother. On a bench, a few single mothers sat watching me, smiling over their Rothmans. Their children looked whey-faced and unhealthy, but at least they weren't being injured on a simple shopping trip. By the time I got back, I didn't have the energy to play golf. Sally smiled contentedly. I swear she's becoming more sinister every day. There's a small element of revenge about all this that I don't care for.

Later that night, I found a packet of cigarettes that Tammy and Paddy had left after a dinner party, and secretly smoked one of them outside. It was my first cigarette in years, and it tasted stale, foul. It did relax me, however, but as I flicked it into the bushes, I vowed it'd be my last.

Thursday 17 March

Came back home after an early drink with Nigel to find the children in bed and Sally wearing nothing but some underwear, high heels and a silk dressing gown. She hadn't done that since one Valentine's Day in our twenties. I know her agenda, but didn't care, and once again fell victim to the tactics of the temptress.

Lots of pillow talk about me being a househusband.

'Why don't we try it for just three months? You know, a probationary period.'

In my post-coital state I murmured some form of assent, which made Sally more excited than she had been when she opened the door. We did it again – well, it was a bit soon – and then went downstairs for supper which we washed down with champagne. Never seen Sally look so happy. Not since our wedding day. If me staying at home puts a smile on her face and earns more evenings like this, then it's got to be worth a try. Sod it, she can deal with the bitchiness of office life, and I'll clear up the poo. What's the difference?

Friday 18 March

It's all happening a bit quickly. After breakfast, Sally announced she was going up to London to see Mark to sort out her new contract, etc., etc.

'But I, um, thought . . .' I stutteringly began.

'What?' asked Sally. 'There's no point in me sitting around for a few weeks is there?'

'I guess not.'

'I'll be back as soon as I can.'

'So I'll be, um, looking after the children?'

'That's the general idea.'

Everything went sort of well until Daisy vomited down

my shirt this afternoon, most of which got glued into my chest hair. What made it worse was that I never found the time to wash it off. When I picked Peter up from playgroup, Jodhpur Mum gave me a funny look. She must have smelt me, even through the jersey and the overcoat. Or maybe I misread the funny look. Perhaps Jodhpur Mum likes me. Enough of this.

We had more champagne early this evening when Sally got back. 'To our new lives,' she toasted. I clinked my glass a little too strongly against hers, and mine smashed. It's just as well I don't believe in omens.

Monday 4 April

It's 10 a.m. on the first day of the rest of my life, and I'm not sure it's going to be a very long life at this rate. I shall have a heart attack by forty, and when that vice grips me round the chest, a small part of me will be willing it to do its best. What a dreadful thing to write, but then again, it's been a dreadful morning. Thank God Daisy is having her nap, otherwise I might have set light to myself.

It started at 6 a.m. (is that really only four hours ago?) when Peter fell out of bed and started howling, which in turn woke Daisy. Instinctively, I turned towards Sally, who looked back at me and said, 'It's your job now. I've got to get ready for work.' I could swear there was a note of cruel joy in her voice. Blearily, I stumbled into Peter's room, and comforted him. As I did so, I realised he was wet right through.

'He's wet!' I shouted to Sally.

'Then you'd better change the sheets!'

Damn. I hadn't thought about the sheets. I debated whether to leave them on. While Daisy carried on bellowing from her bedroom, I took Peter into the bathroom and washed him. He really shouldn't be wetting the bed any more – something needs to be done. Has just occurred to me that I'm now the person who needs to sort it out. But how? How do you stop a three-year-old wetting the bed? Not give him any liquids during the last two hours of the day? That seems a little harsh. There must be a website that will tell me.

Oh, indeed there is. Type in 'stop bed wetting' on Google and up come 20,900 sites. This will take me ages to plough through, but a brief glimpse reveals that many people get their children up in the middle of night to take them to the loo. That's madness! I'm not going to spend the rest of my days – or rather nights – setting the alarm to 3 a.m. and holding a sleeping child over the khazi. I shall have to ask my mother about this. Actually, I'd rather not. That will only open a chink through which she will bombard me with endless 'helpful' tips. And I'm certainly not going to consult Sally's mother. I suspect she won't really approve of me being a househusband. This could be the first time we're in agreement.

Anyway, back to this morning. While I was washing Peter, Daisy continued to bellow. Sally then came into the bathroom.

'Are you going to do anything about Daisy?'

'But I'm dealing with Peter! Can't you do Daisy?'

'I can't,' she said. 'I've got to leave in half an hour.'

'That's plenty of time.'

'No it's not. Besides, you never helped me when you were off to work.'

'But . . .'

'Anyway, can't you at least put some clothes on?'

The image of Sally standing above me wearing a pair of black thigh boots and clutching a whip flickered briefly through my mind, the excitement of which rapidly made me decide that to get some boxer shorts on at least was a very good idea indeed. I did so, and then got the howling Daisy out of bed and removed her from her sleeping bag. Oh Gawd. She was soaking too. Nightmare, and it was only 6.05. I had another 775 minutes to go until they were in bed, which meant I was merely 0.64 per cent of the way through the day. This was hell.

It got worse. Not only was Daisy more than soaking, but she had done another 'nitrogenous spectacular'. While I was dealing with it, Peter was running around half naked, which Sally informed me in passing was playing dangerously. Explained that it was surely impossible the boy had more urine in him, but she told me the supply was seemingly inexhaustible.

Peter confirmed the truth of this by peeing on the carpet on the landing. Sally, who was running down the stairs, turned to complain that the carpet would be stained, but I explained to her, à la *Withnail and I*, that it was unadulterated child's piss, and it would be fine. Apparently it wouldn't, so while Daisy lay naked on the bathroom floor

('She'll get cold!'), I found myself scrubbing Peter's pee ('Don't scrub it! Dab it! Scrubbing will only make it worse!') and all the time feeling ready to storm out the house. However, I bit my lip, convincing myself that I was man enough to do this – all I needed to do was to work out a system. Blue skies, I chanted to myself like a mantra. Imagineer a solution.

After fifteen minutes of much bad-tempered dressing, the children were more or less presentable.

'Is he really going to wear that to playgroup?' said Sally over a mouthful of toast.

Curses. Playgroup. I had quite forgotten. However, I was determined not to let on.

'It's fine,' I said. 'What's wrong?'

'Well, apart from the American-golfer-fashion disaster of mixing that checked shirt with those checked trousers – we'll just let that go shall we? – they're both filthy. Can't you see the egg all down the shirt?'

'No,' I lied.

'There,' said Sally.

'Oh, *that* egg.' Touch of Basil Fawlty.

'He can't go like that.'

'It'll be fine.'

Sally gave me a look, and it was not until she did so that I realised how she was dressed – a nice dark green suit, skirt just above the knee, sheer black tights, and not-quite-slutty-but-deliberately-skirting-dangerously-close-to-being-extremely-tarty heels. She looked great.

'Why can't you dress like that for me?' I asked.

Jealousy made me want to throw egg down her.

'I can't wear a suit here,' she said, 'don't be ridiculous.'

'But you look so nice. Why do a bunch of civil servants get to see you looking like that and I don't?'

Green-eyed monster nearly made me mention Nick, but managed to stop what was turning into an outbreak of jealousy Tourette's.

'You look nice in a suit,' she replied. 'But you wouldn't expect me to want you to wear it all the time at home would you?'

'I would if you really liked it,' I said.

Another lie. Of course I wouldn't. Sally saw through it and gave a 'pah'.

'I must dash,' she said, looking at her watch. 'Wish me luck!'

'Wish you luck? What about me?'

'It'll be fine,' she said with a dazzling smile, and then she gave me a big (to me, slightly condescending) kiss. She then gave the children enormous hugs, begged them to be extraspecially good, and was out the door, a flurry of high-powered defence analyst briefcase, laptop bag, *The Economist* and, for heaven's sake, the distinctive and alluring scent of Green Tea by Bulgari. She hasn't worn that in years either.

Breakfast went more or less well, with Peter knocking his cereal bowl on to the floor when it was thankfully half empty, which required only a few minutes of cleaning and fifty-eight sheets of kitchen roll. Afterwards, I plonked them both in front of the box while I ate a bowl of cereal on my own, reflecting that TV was actually very good for them, and that something called *Fimbles* was, in fact, highly educational. By now it was just gone 7, and I felt absurdly tired, tired as if I had a hangover, which I hadn't. Is this normal?

7.30 a.m.

Decided that Peter wasn't too old for *Teletubbies*.

8 a.m.

Told myself that *Tikkabilla* was also highly educational and would help to teach him about the realities of growing up in twenty-first-century, multicultural Britain and other issues relevant to modern life.

Thankfully, playgroup is only a couple of minutes' walk, so we left at 8.57 to ensure we were in good time. I had hopelessly underestimated how slowly Peter walks, and how fascinating he finds every stone, piece of moss, etc.

We eventually made it to playgroup at 9.30, not least because Daisy insisted on repeatedly removing her left slipper-cum-shoe thing from her right foot and throwing it to the ground. Apologised to Simone, who jollily said it was not a problem, but had I remembered a change of clothes? Change of clothes? No, I had not remembered a change of clothes, as it was hard enough remembering both children. I told her I'd come back with them straight away.

'Sally away today is she?' Simone asked with a knowing wink.

'Yes,' I said. 'She is.'

Pathetic pride stopped me from revealing that she would now be away every day, and Simone would just have to get used to me. As far as she's concerned, I'm still on gardening leave. As I walked away from the Portakabin, I saw Jodhpur Mum drive past. She gave me a little wave and a smile. Sudden rush of excitement. Then felt guilty. Then thought of how nice Sally looked this morning. Then felt jealous. Then felt even more jealous when I thought about Nick. Then felt emasculated. Then felt angry and frustrated and helpless. Then realised I had left Daisy in her buggy outside playgroup.

God knows what the rest of today will hold. I think I shall use these few moments of peace to go and read a magazine on the loo. I can see now why Sally never gets the chance to go. Still, early days. I will show her that the male of the species is perfectly capable of bringing up children, and bringing them up well *and* efficiently. Time and motion studies, timetables, best practice policy documents – the weapons of the management consultant shall be ruthlessly employed to facilitate the task of childrearing. I will not be defeated by two people whose ages do not add up to even ⅛ of mine. Perhaps I shall start a revolution in childcare, and my methods will be adopted by parents the world over . . .

The phone's just rung. Peter's had an 'accident' and could I urgently bring round that change of clothes? This means I have to wake Daisy up. Damn damn damn. I could use a drink. Or perhaps I'll seriously take up smoking again.

Tuesday 5 April

I don't even want to write about today.

Wednesday 6 April

Today was better, but not by much. Eighth circle of hell rather than the ninth. It's just gone 9.30 and I am so tired; structurally exhausted like a condemned building.

I feel twice my age. This is ridiculous. I must get things in order. It's high time I drew up what I have christened the Holden Childcare Programme, but the only problem is, when? There's no time during the day, and in the evenings I'm too knackered. When? I need to develop some kind of programme just to be able to find time to develop my programme.

Have indeed taken up smoking again. Nothing serious, just four or five a day. I won't tell Sally, because she'll hate me for it. Besides, I enjoy a petty sense of rebellion whenever I light up. I may be a househusband, but at least I smoke. *Cool.*

Thursday 7 April

After a few days of rain, it was actually sunny. Not just quite sunny, but 'gosh, isn't it hot for this time of year' sunny. So, after Peter returned from playgroup, I decided the afternoon could be spent outside, the three of us pottering about in the garden. I would read the papers while Daisy gurgled naked under a parasol, and Peter ran around the garden playing imaginary goodies and baddies. That was the idea, anyway.

The only problem was that neither of them wanted to be left alone. As soon as I put Daisy down, she began to scream. Not just a little bellow, but a full primal bellow, one that frightened away the birds. So, instead of being able to read the papers, I had to cuddle her, which was nevertheless quite a cute moment. I stress the word 'moment', because no sooner was she completely relaxed than her bladder decided to follow suit, and I found, for the third time in about ten days, that my lap had become strangely damp. In order to get changed, I had to put her back down, which caused her to bellow louder than I thought possible, which in turn set Peter off, who whined about how much Daisy was screaming. I nearly yelled back at the pair of them, but instead stormed inside to find some new clothes.

Even this simple task was beyond my feeble means. No clean clothes. Nothing. Where had they all gone? I assumed Sally had hidden them somewhere, but no, they were not even in my chest of drawers (where she normally hides them – she also maliciously hides my shoes in the bottom of the bedroom cupboard). After a couple of minutes' frantic searching, the mystery was soon solved: there were no clean clothes. Every pair of pants, trousers, shorts, you name it, was overflowing out of a tightly packed laundry basket in our bedroom. I was tempted to fish out the least offensive item, but I couldn't bring myself to do so. Instead, I opted for a pair of lime-green swimming trunks and a faded black T-shirt we had to wear on Nigel's stag weekend. 'We're here to put the hell in Helsinki!' it read. God how embarrassing, how late twenties. I seem to recall it was Tim's idea, and despite my protestations that there was in fact no 'hell' in 'Helsinki', mob rule won. Still, it was a good weekend, although for some reason it ended up costing around a grand, an absolute fortune back then.

When I came back to the garden, I found Daisy and Peter inconsolable, both no doubt assuming I had abandoned them. How long had I been away? Two minutes? Three? As a means of expressing his temper, Peter had scattered the newspaper over the garden, and was also smeared in black newspaper print.

'Daddy,' he said, 'I'm hungry. Can I have some bread?'

Curses. I had completely forgotten about lunch. It was 1.30 – an hour later than they were used to. I picked them both up, and dashed inside, plonking them in their high chairs before scattering a few hastily torn scraps of bread their way. This seemed to buy me a few seconds to rummage through the food cupboard and fridge. It became quickly apparent that Daisy was not ready to chew great crusts of brown bread, and she started to choke.

Sheer pathetic panic took over. While she gagged and choked, I lifted her out of her chair and patted her on the back. Nothing happened. The sound was horrendous; the poor little thing struggled for air. I dimly tried to recall a parents' first-aid course Sally and I had been on just before Peter was born, and all I could remember was that the worst thing you could do was to put your fingers down the throat, as that could make the blockage even worse. I kept patting, harder and harder, all the time pleading, 'Please don't die, please don't die.'

By now, she was making these alarming wretching noises, and I suddenly realised quite how serious a situation this was. I carried on patting frantically, but it didn't work.

'Just get it out Daisy!' I shouted in frustration. I then remembered that instead of patting, one was supposed to sort of push upwards on their backs, and so I did this instead, with Daisy straddling my left forearm.

After what seemed like hours, a piece of mangled crust fell out on to the kitchen floor. Daisy then started screaming like I had never heard her before, but I didn't care, because screaming meant she could breathe, and if she could breathe then she would live. I hugged her tightly before letting her go again, suddenly realising I might be stopping her from breathing. I kept telling her how sorry I was, and saying, 'There, there' and stroking her little head. The poor thing was so upset, and I found myself having to stifle a few tears.

'You sodding fool,' I kept saying, which caused Peter to pipe up, 'Are you a sodding fool, Daddy?'

To which I replied in the affirmative. There was no denying it.

After lunch (biscuits for Peter, yoghurt and honey for Daisy), I had another sneaky smoke. The drama of today has really made me think about what it is I am doing. It's occurred to me that I'm not meant to be merely 'looking after' the children, but I'm actually raising them – a huge difference. 'Looking after' is what babysitters do for a couple of hours, but a parent has got to do more than that. As a parent, I'm supposed to teach them right from wrong, how to behave, and to encourage them, discipline them, etc., etc. I'm nowhere near that. I'm not even capable of getting through the day without one of them coming close to death. Things must improve.

It's 8.30 p.m. Where's Sally?

Friday 8 April

A change has come over Sally, or at least I think it has. Perhaps it's just my paranoia, but there's a spring in her step, a twinkle in her eye, a certain jauntiness. I thought she'd be knackered with her return to office life, but instead she's fizzing. Last night, she came back home at about 9.30, and couldn't stop talking about what a week she'd had, and how it was JUST GREAT to get her BRAIN working again and how NICE IT WAS to be RESPECTED and not just be treated as a BABY FACTORY. I asked her how the free world had managed to survive without her, and she flicked me a look that went from withering to sympathetic.

'I'm sorry, sweetheart,' she said, 'I forgot to ask you how your day had been. How are the children?'

I began to tell her what had happened from the moment she left the door, unaware that I was going into far too much detail. By the time I had informed her of the fascinating episode of Daisy peeing on me, I noticed her attention was beginning to wander; she was flicking through *Jane's Defence Review* and going 'uh-huh' each time I finished a sentence.

'And then Daisy nearly choked to death,' I said monotonously, ready to see if there was a reaction.

She nearly went 'uh-huh' again, but she didn't, and looked up.

'What do you mean, "choked to death"?'

I told her what had happened, and said I had felt an utter fool, but thank God for that first-aid training. I could see she was riled, and was doing her best not to lay into to me, to say that I was completely incompetent, etc.

'I know you're angry,' I said, 'but it could have happened to anyone.'

'No it couldn't,' she said.

I asked her to explain.

'Because I've yet to feed her food she is incapable of eating, that's why! How many teeth do you think she has?'

I hazarded that she had three, maybe five.

'None, Sam. She doesn't have a single tooth! How do you think she's supposed to chew through a piece of bread?'

I just shrugged, and told her I had fouled up, and it wasn't going to happen again. Apologies were fulsome, but seemed to make little impact.

'Come off it,' I said, 'these things are bound to happen from time to time.'

'So what else has happened? Any other near-death experiences I should know about?'

'None,' I said, genuinely racking my brain. 'Just give me a chance.'

Sally narrowed her eyes. Lee van Cleef in *The Good, the Bad and the Ugly*.

'I hope you're not doing this on purpose,' she said.

'Doing what? Trying to kill our children?'

'You know what I mean.'

'What?'

'I know your tactic. You're trying to make a pig's ear of it so I'll have no choice but to give up work. That's what you're playing at, isn't it?'

'No!' I said, instantly regretting that I hadn't thought of it. 'You're being unfair.'

'Am I?'

Folded arms.

'Yes,' I stressed. 'You are being unfair.'

Sally didn't say anything for a moment. We sat in married silence.

'Nice outfit by the way,' she said.

I looked down at my trunks and Helsinki shirt.

'Off to the beach were you?'

'Ha, ha.'

'Or did you have no clean clothes?'

I sighed. I raised my hands up in the air, and let them drop again. I felt like Woody Allen, or how I imagine Woody Allen to be. I haven't actually watched a Woody Allen film, and have yet to meet someone who has.

'I haven't got round to it yet,' I said. 'Besides, there's nothing to stop you from doing it.'

Sally smiled.

'Has it only taken one week?' she asked.

'Has what only taken one week?'

'This,' she said. 'I've become you and you've become me.'

I chewed it over. She was right. As always.

We both apologised and when Sally got back home this evening I was able to present her with cupboards full of clean laundry. What's more, I had even done the washing-up. One small balls-up is that all Sally's knickers have turned red. At first, I hid them in my drawer, but then I thought she might have thought I was a panty-wearer, so instead I've put them in Daisy's nappy drawer. I shall have to buy her some new undies PDQ.

Sunday 10 April

A mixed weekend. Some improvements with our new domestic arrangements, but one disaster. Improvements first. Sally and I have agreed to let each other lie in on weekend mornings. She gets Saturdays, I get Sundays. This morning was 'utter bliss' as a women's magazine would put it, and I lay in bed until 9.30, doing nothing but drifting in and out of sleep and reading the papers. Sally had even brought me a cup of tea; it was cold, but I had to neck it down so as not to hurt her feelings.

Other improvement. I don't have to do bathtime at weekends. I hate bathtime. It's far too much hassle, and involves a lot of bending over, which I am spectacularly bad at. Instead, I have to do the children's supper, which I don't mind, although am amazed that Sally has let me, considering the choking incident. Maybe I really am forgiven.

However, the disaster, which happened at the supermarket on Saturday morning, overshadowed all. The trip didn't start brilliantly. Before we set off, I found myself reading the paper, assuming Sally was getting the children ready. While I did that, Sally was in fact on the phone to her sister, assuming *I* was getting them ready. When we both found the children were neither shod nor coated, we started to lay into each other. 'I thought it was your job . . .' 'It's not my job . . .' 'Whose job is it?' 'I look after them all week . . .' 'I work hard all week . . .' etc., etc.

Eventually, we got the children ready. I told Sally how much I hated going to the supermarket, but she told me that was no reason for me to wriggle out of going. I told her we shouldn't support it, and we should be doing our eco-enviro-local-organo bit by buying from all the shops in town. Sally riposted that there are hardly any shops in town, and if I fancied tramping round the butcher, baker, candlestick maker with two children and countless bags of shopping, then I was welcome to it. I couldn't argue with that, memories of Daisy keeling over in the buggy are still fresh.

The supermarket was horrific. As soon as we arrived, Peter made straight for the garish Postman Pat van, which he loves sitting in. 'Can I go in that?' he asked.

'Yes,' I said.

'No,' said Sally.

We looked at each other. I never know what to do in these situations. We both like to present a united front, but it's not always possible.

'Come on,' I said, 'there's no harm.'

Sally did Lee van Cleef eyes but gave in.

'All right, but just one go.'

If Peter had been older we would have done a high-five in a display of laddishness. Instead, he had already climbed into the van, and was twisting the steering wheel violently in anticipation. I rummaged in my pocket for a 50p, but could only find pound coins. That meant he would have to have three goes, but I suspected we would get away with it. (Was also mildly interested by the machine's pricing structure and increasing return to scale, but too boring to write.)

For the next five minutes or so, Peter had a great time in Postman Pat's van. It sort of rocked from side to side like a boat in a slight swell, the gentleness of which looked utterly unthrilling. The muffled theme music soon began to annoy the man-tits off me, but I just grinned through it, begging for a paper to read. I looked through the main doors, and there, just on the other side, was the newsagent and fags bit of the supermarket.

Peter looked quite content, and thinking that Postman Pat had a few minutes left in him, I dashed into the supermarket proper and grabbed a paper. Unfortunately, this meant I couldn't see Peter, but I told myself that all that kiddie-snatching was just media hype, and besides, there was no more of it around than there was in the 1950s. In front of me was an old dear buying a carton of Embassy Regals – a whole carton! How could she afford it? I tried to be patient as she counted out a mountain of change on the counter top. Behind her was a fat middle-aged man in shorts who had a fistful of lottery tickets. This was going to take ages, but as I could still hear 'early in the morning, just as day is dawning', I knew it would be fine.

The old woman took AGES to count out her money. I thought she might die before she finished, but eventually she got there. Some £48. All in 2p coins by the looks of it. Her addiction was almost admirable, and if she had survived that long on the weed, then it probably wouldn't kill her.

Now it was the turn of fat lottery man. Naturally, there was some complication, and disturbingly, I could no longer hear 'picks up all the letters in his van . . .' Gently I tapped the man on the shoulder.

'Excuse me,' I asked, in my politest tones, 'do you mind if I quickly pay for this? My son is—'

'Yes, I do mind.'

He had the type of face that was permanently set to 'don't mess with me' mode. Somewhere beneath it was a neck, but I was buggered if I could see it. Old blue tattoos adorned his forearms, and I thought I could detect another partially hidden by a roll of neck fat, but then that may have been some overworked vein. Ashamed by my own cowardice, I slunk back behind him. Peter would be all right.

And then I heard him cry.

'Mummy!' he shouted. 'MUMMY!'

Without thinking I dashed towards the supermarket doors, still holding my newspaper, or rather not *my* newspaper, as the security guard was eager to point out.

'Have you paid for that, sir?'

I struggled to look past him, to see what was happened to Peter, but the guard kept blocking my view.

'Let me past!'

'You're not going anywhere, sir.'

I caught sight of Peter, who was lying on the floor. He had obviously fallen out of Postman Pat's van, and was looking around for Sally. 'Mummy!' he shouted again, his face streaming with tears.

'Goddamn it! That's my son! He's fallen out of that Postman Pat thing! Of course I'm not trying to steal your wretched newspaper!'

I shoved the newspaper in the guard's hand and barged past him, paternal instinct giving me the courage I had singularly lacked when dealing with the fat lottery man. I rushed over to Peter and picked him up, once again telling one of my children how sorry I was, and how I was a silly daddy, and how it would never happen again.

By now, I was vaguely aware of a crowd gathering behind me, which also included a bloke about my age who looked alarmingly like Anthony Perkins in *Psycho*. His name badge revealed that he was in fact no less a figure than 'Neil Colquhoun, assistant manager'. Apparently, he was 'here to help'.

'Is everything all right, sir?'

Sir. How I hate the insincere *sir.*

'Everything's fine, thanks,' I said, smiling weakly.

I heard a few women mumble. 'Fancy leaving a child on his own . . .' 'He's not fit to be a father . . .' 'Anything could have happened . . .' The words got to me, and I just snapped.

'Why don't you just sod off?'

Neil/Anthony smarted at that. He made the most of his five foot six, and addressed me with all the seriousness of a judge sentencing a man to death.

'I'm afraid I'm going to have to ask you to leave the store, sir.'

'Leave?'

'That's right, sir. We do not tolerate abusive customers. Or those who try to shoplift.'

'You've *got* to be joking. I just left him in this Postman Pat thing for a minute and then he fell out and now I'm being . . . being *blackballed*. This is ludicrous.'

'I'm sorry, sir, but would you go?'

The figure of the guard loomed. I couldn't quite believe what was happening. I was being thrown out of a super-market. *Nobody* gets thrown out of supermarkets. I looked at Neil/Anthony, looked at the guard, looked at the tutting biddies, and realised I had better leave. There was no point in arguing. That would have been far too *infra dig*. With my head held high, I walked out of the supermarket, clutching Peter. Unfortunately, I tried to leave through the entrance, so the automatic doors wouldn't open for me. I yanked at the bar, but nothing happened.

'The exit door is to your right, sir,' said Neil/Anthony sarcastically.

'Can I have another go on Postman Pat?' Peter asked.

'No you cannot!'

My sharpness caused Peter to cry, and I found myself apologising.

'I want to see Mummy!'

We stepped out into the daylight. The last time I had been kicked out of somewhere was in Finland, but that was for a cool reason. I had been attempting to dance with the sexiest girl in the nightclub, but evidently she was some sort of gangster's moll, so I got thrown out by a couple of heavies, much to general merriment of fellow stags. I still don't believe there are such things as Finnish gangsters, but at the time I was in no position to argue, otherwise I expect I would have found myself at the bottom of the Gulf of Finland.

I put Peter down and we made our way back to the car. His temper abated somewhat.

'Are you OK?' I asked him, wiping tears off his face with my right thumb.

His bottom lip continued to tremble.

'Daddy,' he said, 'why did we have to leave the shop?'

'Because Daddy was angry with the people in the shop.'

'Why?'

'Because the people thought Daddy had been silly.'

'Why?'

'Because I left you in the Postman Pat van.'

'Why?'

'Because I wanted to get a newspaper.'

'Why?'

'Because I wanted to read the newspaper while you were in the Postman Pat van.'

'Why?'

'Because it's a bit boring for Daddy standing by the Postman Pat van.'

'Why?'

'Because the Postman Pat van is not for daddies but for little boys.'

'Why?'

'Because . . .' I began. 'Look, no more whys, please, Peter.'

'Why?'

Just then, I spotted an anxious Sally leaving the supermarket, clutching Daisy in her arms. She half ran towards the car.

'What's happened?' she asked. 'Why are you back in the car?'

I explained what had happened. Sally looked genuinely agog.

'So you're telling me you've been *banned*. Are you allowed back?'

'I doubt it.'

For the rest of the weekend, Sally accused me of being utterly negligent, and once again suggested that the choking and the supermarket ban were all part of a fiendish plan. She said all this light-heartedly enough, but I could tell there was an underlying sincerity in her humour. I maintained – and this is true – that I can be a little hapless, but things like this were bound to happen from time to time. Sally said she had never had one of the children choke, and neither had she been banned from a supermarket. Well done, I said sarcastically.

Wednesday 13 April

Things have been going a little better, but not by much. I've got into some kind of a routine, but it's not entirely convincing. Everything sort of happens sort of on time, but nothing ever happens particularly well. It seems to take ages to get them dressed, and I have now given up trying to make their clothes co-ordinate. Like my secret smoking, this is partly a small act of rebellion, but may have more to do with the fact that most of the children's clothes always seem to be in the laundry basket.

I have yet to get Peter to his playgroup before 9.10, and even then, he never seems to have the right stuff – I invariably forget to take his lunch on a lunch day, or take lunch when he doesn't have a lunch day. With Daisy, it's just a case of winging it. There's never any structure to my time with her, and we seem to spend most of it doing 'row, row, row your boat' on my lap, which she just adores. I do love watching and hearing her chuckle, but after a while, a man needs a break. However, whenever I put Daisy down, she just bellows. I think she's frustrated that she can't walk. She crawls very well, and she can just about haul herself up to a standing position using a chair or the coffee table, but then she crumples with a thud of nappy on to the floor and bellows again. Because I'm a pushover, I immediately pick her up, and then she's all sweetness and light.

Hoiking her around all day does hamper one somewhat. She sits on my hip even when I'm cooking (I'm sure Sally, or health and safety would have something to say about this), and whenever I try to go to the loo, all hell breaks loose. Today, for example, I didn't even have time to have a crap. There must be something going badly wrong if I can't even do that.

Thursday 14 April

Things between Sally and me are better. Thank goodness. I couldn't stand the supermarket-ban/choking-induced frostiness. As usual, the best way to get rid of the bad odour was to have sex (I put in a middling, somewhat lazy performance, but it was still not bad, I think, especially after a gruelling day) and afterwards we lay in bed chatting good-naturedly. I apologised for being an arse in the supermarket, and she apologised for being overly critical, and told me how it was wrong of her to expect me to get it perfect from day one. With things between us settled, I feel so much more confident in my ability to handle the children.

Please note, 'more confident', not actually 'confident'. The whole business still feels very unnatural. I wouldn't tell Sally this because she would think I was pulling that 'men go out and hunt' line, and I don't want to have a row about that, not when things are going so much better.

Friday 15 April

Things between Sally and me are now worse. This time it's got nothing to do with the children, but the spectre of Nick. Nasty Nick. Nick who, without a penumbra of doubt, is definitely trying to get inside Mrs Holden's pants. Am I being paranoid? No. I know what men are like, and no matter how much Sally protests, I know what's going on. Besides, I've even tried it myself on a few occasions. Historically, pre-Sally, of course.

Sally got back late this evening and, uncharacteristically, her breath smelt of booze. I asked her whether she'd been for a drink, and she said she had.

'Who with?'

She paused.

'Just some people from work.'

'Who? Mark?'

'No, he wasn't there.'

'Was Nick there?'

Another guilty pause.

'Yes.'

'Anyone else?'

'What is this?' Sally asked aggressively. 'I'm allowed to have a drink with whom I please.'

'Was there anyone else there?'

Sally folded her arms.

'And what if I said there wasn't?'

'Then I would be cross.'

'And why would you be cross? Would you be thinking I was having an *affair* with him?'

'No. I would be thinking he was wanting to have one with you, and that having a drink with him, no matter how innocent it seemed to you, would be regarded by Nick as a come-on.'

'Even if that were true, isn't that Nick's problem and not mine? I mean, there may be plenty of men who want to have sex with me, but that doesn't stop me from speaking to them, does it?'

There was something slightly unappealing in the way Sally suggested the potential multiplicity of sexual partners she had at her fingertips, as it were. If I hadn't been feeling particularly insecure before, then I was now.

'You know there's an enormous difference between some bloke in the office fancying you,' I said, 'and having cosy

Friday night drinks with your ex-boyfriend. Come on, Sally! You must see why I'm jealous!'

'Of course I do, but why can't you trust me? Nick wanted to talk about some problems he'd been having, and it was only natural he would want to talk them over with me.'

'*Problems?* What sort of problems? How hard he's finding it working with the love of his life?'

'You're being childish.'

'No, I'm not. What sort of problems?'

'*Work* problems, Sam. At least he talks about his work problems, unlike others, who bottle them up and then go and get themselves sacked.'

'Ouch.'

At this point, I left the kitchen, glass of wine in my hand, and went up to my study. Sally asked up the stairs if there was any supper for her. I almost replied 'fuck you', but thought better of it. Be a grown-up, I told myself, despite the utter childishness of our argument. 'It's in the oven,' I said. 'Keeping warm.' The dutiful bloody househusband.

What fun this is. Do our friends row like this? I sort of hope so. I'd hate to feel that our union was in some way uniquely defective. What annoys me is that this wasn't even an adult argument. It was just plain old jealousy, the sort of row I would have with an ex like Louisa ten, no, shit, *fifteen* years ago. Mind you, my jealousy was fully justified on that occasion. She had been sleeping with Darren (*Darren!*) and her letters from him proved it.

I know I can trust Sally, but for Pete's sake, is it so unfair of me to complain that she's late back on a Friday because she's been having a drink with a significant ex? I have to confess I've always been slightly jealous of Nick, not least because he kept sniffing around Sally when we started going out.

What a fun weekend this is going to turn out to be. I shall insist I have a few hours to myself. I need time to sort out my Childcare Programme. If I can get that cracked, then I'm sure things will start to fall into place. Including our marriage.

Sunday 17 April

Last night we had a dinner party. (Remember them?) I had completely forgotten about it, and was only reminded when Sally asked whether she needed to go to the super-market to buy food for it. Sheepishly, I told her she had to, but I would stay at home and look after the children while she did the shopping. She said I was doing her no favours, because she had a husband who was banned from the supermarket. I told her to lay off.

Anyway, the dinner went fine to some degree. We had Nigel and Clare, Sally's sister Victoria and David (this week's boyfriend), and our neighbours Andy and Linda. In order to prove that things were continuing as normal, I made sure we had champagne as our aperitif (although not Louis Roederer, I'm afraid, just some Albert Etienne stuff which was OK) and some smoked trout on blinis to nibble.

'Glad to see you can still run to the poo,' said Nigel predictably.

I raised my glass back to him.

'No point in dropping one's standards,' I replied. 'Besides Sally's salary is pretty much as mine was.'

Nigel paused for a second.

'How's it going anyway? You know, looking after the kids?'

'Pretty well,' I lied. 'Obviously there are some good days and some bad, but mostly they're good. I still haven't got my routine together yet, but I'm getting there. One of the biggest problems of the day is convincing Peter that he's old enough to put on his shoes, and we always have a night-mare time just before I take him to playgroup. He's adamant that he's incapable of doing it, but . . .'

I noticed Nigel wasn't really listening. A glassily bored expression was smeared over his face, and I saw he was transferring his weight from one foot to another – a sure sign he wanted to walk away.

'Sorry,' I said. 'Boring of me.'

Now it was his turn to lie.

'Not at all,' he said. 'Sounds like you're really getting stuck in. Good for you.'

If it hadn't been Nigel saying it, I would have suspected condescension, but Nigel's too decent and sincere to be like that. We've been friends since we were thirteen, and we know each other well enough not to need to bullshit each other.

'The truth is,' I said, 'I'm finding it tough. I keep making cock-ups.'

'Such as?'

I told him about the choking and the supermarket, the latter anecdote causing vast amounts of merriment, merri-ment which was then shared with the rest of the room.

Sally laughed too, which was a good sign. I'm glad she can see the funny side of being married to quite possibly the only man who has been blackballed by a supermarket. Lots of fair enough jokes about me getting an ASBO next.

At dinner, I placed Victoria and Clare on either side of me. Both of them were keen to hear how I was getting on, and talked to me as though I had just survived a major accident. Lots of wide-eyed sincere questions. 'Are you *all right?*' 'I think you're doing *brilliantly.*' Etc., etc. Clare touched my forearm a lot, which I always take to be flirtatious, but I suspect is just her way.

I told them how I was thinking of applying the methodology of management consultancy to raising the children, which earned rather too much laughter for my liking, especially from Victoria.

'Why is that so funny?' A justified question, I thought.

'Typical man,' said Victoria. 'Always wanting to have a system in place. You're not autistic are you?'

'I think all men are,' said Clare. 'Nigel's obsessed with maps and routes and working out the time it takes to get him from A to B.'

I didn't dare admit I was the same. On a long car journey, I always reset the mile counter, and constantly work out our speed/distance/time ratio, even when Sally is talking. Any journey under an average of 60 mph is slow in my book.

'Well, I don't think I'm *that* autistic,' I replied, 'but it would make life much easier for me if I did, yes, if I did have some sort of system in place. Why not?'

'Because children aren't *employees*, Sam,' said Victoria

in a hippyish way. I like Victoria, but sometimes she will talk as if she is living in San Francisco in 1978. Drawn out words, a lot of 'man' at the end of sentences – dope-smokers' talk. Perry and Sholto are beginning to speak similarly. What a bizarre load of cousins they're going to turn out to be.

'I'm not saying they are,' I said, 'but there are lots of ways in which they can be treated similarly. Goals, incentivisation packages, solutions, deliverables, milestones. You name it, the processes are very similar.'

At this point, Clare and Victoria looked at each other with smirks on their faces.

'I know what you're thinking,' I said. 'Just a typical load of management bullshit. I promise you this is a lot more than "keeping your powder dry" and "running ideas up flagpoles". There's no reason why I can't run a family in the same way as I used to advise people to run their companies.'

A pause.

'I always thought management consulting was a load of bollocks,' said Victoria, lighting up a rollie.

'Well, that's your opinion,' I said. I wasn't going to be drawn into an argument.

'I mean,' said Victoria, before taking a hit on her rollie, 'if you need a management consultant to tell you how to manage your company, doesn't that mean you're a bit fucked?'

'Not necessarily. It might mean you just want to improve things, but you're not sure how.'

Victoria nodded.

'I see. And you think you can make this work with Peter and Daisy?'

'I'm not sure, but I'm going to give it a try.'

'I look forward to seeing the results,' said Clare, her tone suggesting extreme scepticism. I thought this a little unfair, as she's in marketing, and uses words like 'solutions' and 'facilitate' the whole time.

'Just you wait,' I said. 'In a few months, I'll have made my fortune by selling my idea to families everywhere. I'll be the new Gina Ford.'

'Gina who?' asked Victoria, letting her ash fall on to her plate.

The rest of the party passed in a flurry of dashing in and out of the kitchen and countless glasses of red wine. Sally implored me not to have a whisky and a cigar with Nigel, but I felt too bloody-minded. I may be the little househusband, but I am still entitled to smoke and drink what I feel like. As a result, and as Sally predicted, I snored all night, and woke up with a mouth that was desiccated and tasted bitterly poisonous.

Today has been a bit dead. Sally and I are being superpolite to each other, which is a sure sign something is awry. I think she is stressed about work and, let's be honest, about me being at home. I'm stressed about not working and about me being at home. I worry about Nick, she's mad at me for worrying about Nick. It all comes out to the same thing. I hope nobody detected the frostiness between us at dinner. I hate the idea of people yakking about us.

'I wonder if their marriage is in trouble?' I can't stand Schadenfreude, at least not other people's Schadenfreude at my expense.

No brain today to start drawing up the Childcare Programme. Is it just hangover, or is it simply that looking after children causes one's brain to slowly dribble out of one's ear?

Tuesday 19 April

Day from hell. Can't bring myself to write about it, but suffice to say it involved a lot of screaming, whining, vomit and cigarettes. What have I done? I'd do any office job instead of this – anything. I can't believe Sally twisted my arm quite so easily. Well, it wasn't really my arm, was it?

Wednesday 20 April

Today, Daisy actually went to sleep for an hour when Peter was at playgroup. Sally tells me she should have a nap between about 10.30 and 11.30, but under my watch, she has yet to do this. Until today! When she fell asleep, I didn't quite know what to do with myself. A better man would have used it as an opportunity to get on with some cleaning, but not me. Instead, I went to the loo and read the paper for about twenty minutes. For a while, I felt like a real man once more. No one to disturb me, no one to answer to, nothing to do for anybody else – just me, the paper, and my throne. In a word – magic.

Afterwards, I checked my emails. There's still a part of

me that is holding out for an amazing job offer, but I know this is the stuff of fantasy. In fact, any job offer would do. I miss the banter of office life, the availability of intelligent people to talk to. All that was in my inbox was an email from Nigel saying he was still on his mission 'to rescue' me, and a load of spam. In some ways, the spam was more believable.

Thursday 21 April

Sally and I had a rather tense discussion about Easter when she got back. (We don't mention Nick at all. Worryingly, her breath always smells of mints now. Does this mean she is having sly drinks with him?) As had been agreed ages ago, Sally's parents are coming. Nightmare. Sally's parents, of course, means mainly Sally's mother – old Derek is fine, if a little dull – and no doubt she will be full of charming asides concerning my new role. I told Sally I really didn't feel like having them, and couldn't we just bull our way out of it, but Sally was adamant they should come. I wasn't the first man who didn't like his mother-in-law, and I wouldn't be the last, so couldn't I just grin and bear it?

Grinning and bearing it is all I seem to do these days.

Saturday 23 April

Hooray! This morning I started work on the Holden Childcare Programme. At the moment it's not a precise flowchart type of system, but rather a broad strategic document that attempts to evaluate objectives.

My first decision was which type of approach would work best. I opted for what we grandly call 'process consulting' at work. It involves asking the client a series of questions to which you never want a direct yes or no answer, e.g. 'How did you feel about that?' 'What's your opinion?' 'How do you think that could have been done better?' Such questions are intended to get the client to address the core values and goals of their projects. It's a bit like being a psychiatrist, I suppose. You try to lead the client/patient to the root of their problem, and how to tackle it. I think this is easily the best approach to take with Peter and Daisy, as it will get them to learn how to question and evaluate – surely useful skills. (Admittedly, Daisy is a little young, but Peter's recently turned three, and has some grasp of qualitative thinking.) So, I guess the first thing I've established is that I'll be asking them a lot of questions.

Secondly, I've begun to draw up our milestones and our deliverables. Our milestones are, in no particular order:

- To establish a regular and easily implementable routine. This is vital in order to have a firm base to achieve our deliverables (chiefly to get them to bed early).
- To develop 'asset-based thinking'. This is essentially a means of encouraging optimism and a 'can-do' approach for both the children AND me. For example, instead of my thinking that something is getting me nowhere, I shall try to think that something is taking longer than I thought, but can eventually be done. This is the frustrated/feasible axis, and I shall try to imprint this positive thinking particularly on Peter, who is very negative.

- To develop family intradependence. Note: not inter-dependence. There is a big difference. Clearly. There is no room to explain this here.
- Not always to micromanage, but to allow the children to develop their own synergies. This does sound like leaving the children on their own for vast periods of time, but I'd dispute that. Strongly.
- Constant imagineering. It's important for all three of us to think outside the box. That strategy is a goal in itself. In essence, this can mean that if Peter has a good idea, then I'd like to hear from him. Perhaps we can have a suggestion box in which thoughts outside the box can be put in the box?
- Adaptabilisation. I always told companies this was an ugly word for a beautiful thing. We should be in a constant state of flux, always undergoing change. For example, perhaps one day we decide to have lunch not at home, but, say, at the pub.
- Re-engineering processes. Too many of the quotidian tasks are inefficient. We need to streamline them in order to maximise our QoL (Quality of Life) revenue. Basically, this means trying to do things more quickly so I can have time to read the paper on the loo.
- Varietisation. Each day needs to be different. We need to have a lot of emphasis on away-days in which we offsite and re-establish our bonds in a radically different environment. Example: going down to the swings.
- Evaluating risks and issues. Again, this is something that requires regular attention. If we decide to offsite, what are the risks involved? Maybe Daisy could fall off the

roundabout. Issues might include a paternal unwilling-ness to push the swing repeatedly.

It's early days yet, but I'm pretty proud of what I've drawn up so far. I think it might just work. I'll show it to Sally when she's in a better mood with me. I think she'll like it.

Sunday 24 April

What a day. What a great big stinker of a day. Never do I want to see Sally's mother again. Mind you, I expect she never wants to see me again. And, at the time of writing, I doubt whether Sally really wants to see me again either. I don't really know how things got so out of hand, but out of hand they most certainly got.

Things didn't start well when I accidentally spilled red wine down Jane's front – all over a cream cardigan. What made it worse was that she had actually wanted white wine, but I wasn't really listening to her. (Surprise, surprise.) Needless to say, she went ape. 'Look what you've done! Brand new as well! How's that going to come out?' I then offered to pour some white wine on the stain, but she narrowed her eyes in the same way Sally does, so I thought it best to back off. Sally came to the rescue and took Jane upstairs to find her something new to wear. Meanwhile, all this was taken in good cheer by Peter, who said, 'Granny is very funny when she is cross.' I wish I could have agreed with him.

The conversation at lunch was a disaster, not that I had much part in it. I spent most of my time dashing from dining room to kitchen and back again, while simultaneously trying to make sure Peter ate his food and, if I was lucky, managing to eat something myself. All through this, Jane was questioning Sally about our new domestic arrangements, and both of them behaved as though I weren't there. Neither was Derek, who just sat and ate and grinned benignly at the children.

'So dear,' I heard Jane asking as I was making the gravy, 'how much longer is this going to go on for?'

'How much longer is what going to go on for?' Sally replied.

'You know, Sam staying at home. He should really be back at work by now, or at least looking for a job.'

'Mum! We've been through this—'

'It's not right that he's here with the children, it's unnatural. Wouldn't you agree, darling?'

I heard a sort of snort coming from Derek, which seemed to signal non-committal approbation.

'There's nothing *unnatural* about it, Mum. It just makes sense, that's all.'

'Well, I don't think it's right. There's something very left-wing about it.'

I stifled a chuckle as I stirred the gravy, doing my best not to empty half a packet of cornflour into it.

'Left-wing?' asked Sally.

'It's all a bit, you know, *Islingtonian*,' said Jane. 'I expect you two will be eating rolenta next.'

'Polenta,' said Sally. I could hear the exasperation in her voice. 'Anyway, Mum, we've been through this before. I know it wasn't brilliant of him to lose his job, but it's happened. Besides, househusbands aren't that rare these days, and in this way we don't have any financial worries. It just makes sense.'

At this point, I emerged into the room, carefully steering the gravy past Jane's shoulder. Of course, just as I was doing so, she decided to lean back and knocked the gravy boat out of my hands. Result: gravy all down my lap. How many wet laps have I had recently?

'Shi . . . ugar!' I exclaimed – as Sally shot me a warning look. 'Now look what you've bloody done!'

'Who me?' snapped Jane. 'I didn't do anything. You knocked into me. I was perfectly still.'

Peter's laughing didn't help the situation, and even Daisy joined in with some squeals of delight.

'You weren't still,' I said. 'You moved just as I was passing you. You must have seen me.'

'Of course I saw you! I can't help it if you're clumsy.'

'Please,' said Sally. 'Let's not have a row. It's done now. Look, you go upstairs, and I'll clear it up. Mum, would you mind trying to get some more food down Daisy?'

Seething, I disappeared upstairs and gingerly removed my trousers and boxers standing up in the bath, knowing Sally would kill me if I smeared gravy on the carpet. I then showered myself down, hypochondriacally inspecting myself for any signs of third-degree burns. Grudgingly I accepted there were none.

By the time I came back, everybody was eating.

'This lamb is raw, Sam,' Jane announced.

'No it's not,' I said. 'It's *rare.*'

'Why do you insist on eating it raw? We're not wild animals, you know.'

'*Rare*. I cook it *rare* because you keep more flavour. If you overcook it, as you like to do, then you don't really taste anything.'

'It's not safe having it raw like this.'

Be mature, I said to myself. I kept silent and tried to eat. But Jane was determined.

'I hope you don't feed my grandchildren raw meat. They'll get e-boli!'

'E-coli. And no, for your information, your *grandchildren* always have their meat well done, just in case.'

'I'm glad to hear it. At least you've got something right.'

'What?'

'Sally tells me that your new "job" hasn't been going particularly well.'

I put down my knife and fork and shot Sally – such treachery! – an annoyed look.

'What do you mean?' I asked Jane politely.

'Well, it appears that poor Daisy nearly choked to death.'

'What means "choked to death"?' asked Peter.

'It's when food gets stuck in your throat,' I replied. 'And if you can't get it out you can die because you can't breathe.'

'Did Daisy choke to death?'

'No she didn't,' I said. 'She's right next to you, isn't she?'

Peter looked at his sister. They haven't quite bonded yet, but they do exchange some smiles and laughs. I looked back at Jane, catching Sally's eye. She seemed apologetic, but her expression also implored me not to rise to her mother's bait. I took the high road and changed the subject. I raised my glass, and said 'Happy Easter!' Glasses were raised more out of ritual than sincerity. For a while, there was silence, as we tucked into the lamb, which, I must admit, was damn fine. And beautifully rare.

The silence was broken by Peter.

'Daddy.'

'Yes?'

'Is Daisy shit?'

'What?'

A collective gasp from Sally and Jane. A snort type thing from Derek.

'Why is Daisy shit?'

I struggled to keep a straight face. Bad case of church laugh for both me and Sally, who luckily saw the funny side of it. However, Jane was positively shaking with outrage. Derek simply took a slug of claret.

'She isn't,' I said. 'And you must not use that word.'

'But you use it.'

Great. I shut my eyes.

'When?'

'When Daisy choked to death. You said, 'Shit Daisy shit Daisy shit Daisy . . .''

'That's enough, Peter!' said Sally.

'Really,' said Jane. 'I'm appalled, Sam. Language from the gutter!'

Something inside me snapped. I don't know whether it was the clichéd pomposity of her last remark, or the succession of barely veiled criticisms, or the spilling of the gravy, or just everything, but I decided to give her both barrels.

'I do wish you'd just stop this,' I said, as calmly as possible. 'All I've heard since you've got here is non-stop insult and criticism. I'm afraid I've had enough. If you don't like me being a househusband, then fine. But do me a favour and just keep it to yourself, all right?'

Jane stood up and eyed me fiercely. I attempted to do fierce back, but I suspect the effect may have made me look as if I were squinting. Or just plain tired.

'Please you two,' said Sally. 'Why can't we just enjoy the day?'

'It's impossible to enjoy a day here when your husband is so obtuse.'

'I am not being obtuse,' I said, folding my arms defensively. 'Obtuse, Jane, means being slow to understand something. I'm not being obtuse. In fact, I understand what you're getting at all too well.'

'You tell her, boy,' Derek said.

'Derek!' snapped Jane, an exclamation that caused him once more to reach for his glass.

'Sweetheart,' said Sally, 'why don't you just go for a walk, clear your head or something?'

By now, I felt truculent.

'No, I'm having my lunch. I've been cooking all morning, and the last thing I'm going to do now is to go for a walk.'

Meanwhile, Jane shook her head and made a growling sort of 'God' sound.

'It's all right, Jane,' I said. 'Maybe you'd like to go for a walk.'

Her eyes bulged like some sort of toad you see on a wildlife programme.

'We were just about to! Come on Derek, we're off!'

'Really?' asked Derek. 'I thought things were just beginning to get rather fun.'

'Derek!'

Derek obediently stood up.

'Mum! Please don't go. He didn't mean it.'

'I suspect he did.'

'For once I agree with your mother,' I said, a cheap smile on my face.

A few minutes later they were gone. I resolutely sat at the table, eating my lamb and roast potatoes, drinking my claret, and doing my best to pretend that nothing had happened. Pathetic in a way, but at the time I thought it rather admirable. Daisy sat quietly twiddling her hair, and Peter asked why Granny had left.

'Because she was angry with Daddy, that's why.'

'Was she very cross?'

'Yes, she was.'

'Why?'

I felt wretched. I didn't want to tell Peter the truth, although I'm sure he was sensitive to much of the bad blood.

I took a deep breath.

'Sometimes,' I said, 'grown-ups have arguments about things, and sometimes they get cross. But it's OK, it doesn't really matter. I expect you get cross sometimes with William at playgroup, but you're not cross with him all the time. Come on, have some more lamb.'

Peter slowly chewed my words and the lamb.

'But you are cross with Mummy all the time.'

'No I'm not.'

'Yes you are. You and Mummy are always shouting at each other. You are very cross.'

I stroked Peter's head and told him I wasn't cross with

Mummy, or him, or Daisy, and that Daddy would stop shouting. I felt as if I was some sort of vile abusive father, yet all I had done was to have a time-honoured row with my mother-in-law.

Sally returned to the room. She sat down wordlessly and started to feed Daisy. Daisy shook her head whenever the spoon came near her face. Evidently not much of a meat-eater then.

'I'm sorry,' I said to Sally. 'I'd just had enough.'

'Clearly.'

'You've got to agree that she was being dreadful, and basically rude.'

'Yes,' Sally sighed, 'she was. But then you should have just ignored it.'

'Why should I? I don't see why I should be on the receiving end of her barbs every time she comes round.'

Sally took a swig of wine.

'You're quite right,' she said. 'As you always are.'

'I'm not always right. But I am about her.'

Tuesday 26 April

This evening, Sally and I had a council of war. On the train on the way back, she had drawn up a list of where I'd been going wrong and where I'd be going right.

WRONG
Choking incident
Bad language
Leaving Peter unattended

Supermarket ban

Children's diet – no vegetables or fruit appear to have
  been eaten for days

Erratic bedtimes

Lack of cleanliness – children often have dirty faces when
  I kiss them good night

Teeth brushing? I assume this happens sporadically, if it
  all. Peter's breath does tend to smell these days

No clean clothes for anybody

Kitchen filthy

Discipline – Peter doesn't really do as he's told, and he
  answers back

RIGHT

The children seem very happy

I looked at the list in disbelief. I don't take kindly to
being patronised at the best of times, but this was the limit.
I looked from the list to her and back.

'I don't believe this,' I said. 'This is utterly condescending. It's as if I'm your sodding employee. What do
you think I am? Some civil servant?'

'I only made the list so I could crystallise my thoughts,'
she replied. 'I'm sorry if it looks so stark, but I really think
it's important we sort this out.'

Sally's tone was more pleading than bossy. I could see
she was being sincere, but I still couldn't help but feel as
if I were a thirteen-year-old with a bad report.

'You're meant to be my wife,' I said, 'not a headmistress.'
I thrust the list back at her before continuing. 'Besides, if

I'm going to be the one looking after the children, then how I do it is my call. I'm not your proxy, not some au pair or nanny you can boss around. I'm your husband, remember?'

'I know that,' she said, 'and of course you're right. But you must see that some of these things are vital.'

In my heart, I knew she was right. Things have been getting sloppy over the past weeks. I'm just winging it, lurching from one minor drama to another. I'm not looking ahead, and it's high time that the Holden Childcare Programme was fully implemented.

'Things will get better,' I said. 'I promise. But please don't treat me like a child. And besides, after the weekend we've had, I'm not really in the mood for much more criticism.'

Sally nodded.

'OK, OK, crap timing,' she said.

'Have you spoken to your mother?'

'No,' she said. 'Look, could you not just write to her?'

'Write to her? Write what?'

'To apologise, of course.'

'Apologise! For heaven's sake, why? Didn't you hear her? Were you listening at all?'

We hadn't actually spoken about the weekend, and thinking about it now was about as painful as removing shrapnel from one's groin. There was no way I was going to apologise to that woman.

'Of course I was listening,' said Sally. 'I know she was being a bit unfair, but making them leave was going way too far.'

My gob was smacked.

'Whose side are you on?' I eventually asked.

'It's not a question of sides. I just don't want there to be all this bad blood in the air. And we both know that she's not magnanimous enough to make the peace.'

'How can you have blood in the air?'

'What?'

'It's a mixed metaphor. I suppose the blood could be in a very fine mist . . .'

Sally just looked at me.

'Look,' I said, 'I'm not going to apologise. If she doesn't want to see me again, then that's fine by me, because I don't want to see her. If you want her to see the children, then it will have to be when you're around. As far as I'm concerned, I want nothing to do with her.'

'Come on,' said Sally, 'you can't expect never to see her again.'

'Wanna bet?'

Sally held up her hands. 'All right, I see there's no point in talking about this now.'

'Good.'

We stood in silence. I went to the fridge and got out a bottle of white. I took two glasses out the cupboard and offered her one.

'Sure,' said Sally, croakily.

I poured out two large glasses and we both took long slugs.

'Are we all right, do you think?' Sally asked.

'How do you mean?'

'Us. We're not getting on at all. I hate it.'

I took another slug.

'It's just a blip,' I said. 'All couples go through times like this. Come on. We've just got to be strong.'

'I hope you're right.'

Inwardly, I didn't feel so confident. Sally opened the fridge and looked inside. I was conscious of its bare countenance.

'Sorry,' she said, 'but have we got anything for supper?'

'I think there's a pizza somewhere in the freezer.'

For once, we both laughed.

Wednesday 27 April

Today was momentous, as it marked the official start of the Holden Childcare Programme. There were a few teething problems, but otherwise I think it was an enormous success.

The first implementation of the 'process consulting' came during breakfast, which takes place long after Sally has left for work. This morning, Peter was refusing to eat his Rice Krispies, which I know he loves. For some reason he was being bolshy, and under normal circumstances I would have simply told him he wasn't going to get down until he had finished his bowlful. (A threat I somewhat feebly have never carried out, often because there is not enough time in the morning. Also, I suspect, though will not yet admit, that Peter has a stronger will than I have.)

However, this morning I decided to ask Peter a series of questions in order to evaluate the problem.

'How can we improve your breakfast experience?' I asked.

Peter frowned with his expressively thick eyebrows.

'I don't understand, Daddy.'

'How would you like your breakfast to be better?'

'Don't want it,' he said, pushing the bowl away.

I kept my cool and continued to process consult him.

'I know you don't want it, but what I'm trying to establish is a framework in which you do want it. Let's try to zero in on your issues. What is it about the Rice Krispies you don't like?'

Meanwhile, I clumsily pushed apple purée into Daisy's mouth. She clearly was having no issues with her breakfast experience.

'They're boring,' he said.

'Aha! Progress!'

Another frown.

'Perhaps I can make them less boring,' I said. 'Maybe introduce another element. How about I put some sugar on them?'

'I want some bread and jam.'

'Well, you have to eat your cereal first. How about some chopped banana?'

Peter shook his head.

'I don't like banana!'

'Some apple? How about apple? You like apple!'

Peter shook his head.

'No!'

Peter was proving to be a very reluctant consultee, but I was determined. I had to steer him away from yes/no questions.

'Is there any way that you will eat your cereal?'

Peter shook his head.

'In that case, you shall have no breakfast at all.'

I then realised I had deviated from the course of 'process consulting' and back into normal parenting. I corrected myself.

'What is your favourite cereal?' I asked.

'Rice Krispies,' he said.

This was infuriating.

'So why will you not eat them?'

'Because you haven't put any milk in them, Daddy.'

Finally, my process consulting had paid off. At last we had identified his issue. This was rectified immediately, and soon we were in a full breakfast situation once more. I know it's not a brilliant example, but under the previous regime, I would have simply snatched the bowl away and just given him toast with an inordinate amount of raspberry jam. So this can be counted as a triumph of sorts.

Another early (although not quite so successful) implementation came this afternoon, when Peter was insistent that he watched TV. Although he can sometimes be a bit tired after a morning at the playgroup, I thought it best not to cave into his demands. Instead, I sought to address why he wanted to watch TV when it was a perfectly nice day outside, and he has lots of nice toys, etc.

'What do you want to watch?' I asked.

'I want to watch cartoons,' he said.

'What cartoon do you want to see?'

'*Astro Boy*. I want to watch *Astro Boy*.'

Astro Boy? I'd never heard of *Astro Boy*.

'And why do you want to watch *Astro Boy*?'

'Because!' he shouted.

'Because what?'

'Because I want to watch it, that's why!'

He was getting upset and frustrated now, but I was determined to get him thinking about his motives.

'Well, you can't,' I said. 'Besides, I doubt very much *Astro Boy* will be on. All that's on now is probably the news and *Bargain Hunt*.'

'What means *Bargain Hunt*?'

'*Bargain Hunt* is a programme all about selling rubbish.'

'Why?'

'I really don't know why. All I know is that it has a man with an orange face on it.'

Peter giggled a little at that.

'Why does he have an orange face?'

'Because he sits in the sun too much.'

'Can I see?'

I picked up the remote control and turned on BBC1. There, just as I had hoped, was orange man, speaking in his absurdly queeny voice.

'Is that the man?' Peter asked.

'Yes it is. Can you see how orange he is?'

Peter laughed. At this point, Daisy crawled away from the Fisher Price garage (my old one as it happens – it's amazing how many people have still got these and now their children play with them. Interestingly, all the lifts are broken in exactly the same way – a man or a small car stuck in the top bit, thereby not allowing the lift itself to disengage.) She then sort of pulled herself up holding on to the TV screen and stared right close at orange man. A disturbing contrast.

'Baa!' she shouted, jabbing her finger at him.

Peter and I laughed.

'Baa!' we went.

For a few minutes, we watched as orange man talked us through buying tat from car-boot sales. In fact, with my penchant for the *Antiques Roadshow*, I found it quite interesting.

'Can we watch *Astro Boy* now?' Peter asked.

His question snapped me out of my sudden interest in the price of old Bakelite telephones.

'No,' I said. 'It's not TV time.'

'But you are watching this!'

Aware that I was outmanoeuvred, I switched off the TV. Peter began to moan.

'I want it on!'

'You can't have it on!'

'Want it!'

'No.'

Eventually, I unplugged the TV from the mains and put the remote control out of his reach. This caused loads of whining, but I was happy that we had begun to open a dialogue. The Childcare Programme is in its early days, but I'm sure it will work.

Thursday 28 April
10 a.m. (Daisy asleep – hooray!)

Chatted with Jodhpur Mum on the way back from dropping Peter at the playgroup. I was wheeling Daisy back home, and she caught up with me.

'Hello!' she said cheerily.

'Hi,' I said, somewhat taken aback.

True to form, she was wearing shiny black riding boots and the tightest jodhpurs imaginable. I knew right then that I had to buy a similar outfit for Sally. She would regard it as absurd – especially as we don't own a horse, know how to ride a horse, go racing, or even watch the Grand National – but I'm sure she would indulge me. After all, as kinks go, surely it's pretty harmless. It's not as if I want to . . . actually, I won't mention it, and besides, I probably do.

Anyway, here was Jodhpur Mum, all smiley and perhaps a little flirty, but then I've always been crap at establishing the difference between female flirtatiousness and plain friendliness. (No sisters, you see.)

'I thought I'd say hello,' she said. 'My name's Emily. You're Sam, aren't you, Sally's husband?'

'That's right. How do you do?'

I held out my hand, which seemed gauchely formal, but she shook it, albeit with a slight giggle. I felt my heart starting to race, which annoyed me. I don't fancy her – at least not mentally – but my body seems to. Perhaps it's just the jodhpurs, or the fact that Sally and I aren't getting along particularly well at the moment and, being a typical revolting male, I start mentally straying after a row.

'Off riding, I see?'

Dumb question Holden.

'Oh no,' she said. 'I just wear these for fun.'

Even more cretinously, I believed her.

'Fun? Really?' I asked wide-eyed.

'Of course not!' she said, playfully switching the top of

my arm with the back of her hand. 'What do you take me for?'

For a few seconds, I was indeed taking her for a woman who liked to do nothing better than spend her days wearing the type of clothes you got in the opening few frames of a photo shoot in a softcore porn mag. Of course, there was no way I could reply. Instead, I merely mumbled something about not being all there, tough morning etc., etc.

Emily laughed again.

'I quite understand,' she said, and flashed me a slight wink.

Now I was confused. Was she winking because she was showing some empathy for parenthood, or was she winking because she thought I fancied her? The thing is, I don't fancy her. I just happen to fancy all women with above average figures wearing jodhpurs and riding boots. Put her in a pair of dungarees or an everyday pair of jeans, and I wouldn't even tell her the time.

'Anyway, how are you coping?' she asked. 'I gather you're on gardening leave and looking after the children for a while.'

'Well, it, er, has its moments.'

'I'm sure. It does for us all! Anyway, look, I must dash, but would you like to come round for a coffee tomorrow morning? Bring Daisy along.'

Without thinking, I said 'Yes' immediately, followed by a stammering, 'Are you sure?'

'Of course I'm sure. I'll see you at elevenish tomorrow. That all right?'

'Fine, great,' I said. 'See you then.'

She gave me another small, almost imperceptible wink – perhaps it's a twitch – and she ran up the road. Was she doing this deliberately, allowing me to see her from behind? As soon as she was gone, huge amounts of guilt. What do I do? Do I tell Sally or what? If I don't, then it will look suspicious if she finds out. If I do, then she will only suspect something, even though she's got far fewer grounds to, fewer than I have with her and Nick. Logic dictates that Nick and Sally must have fancied each other once, otherwise they would not have gone out together, but I really don't fancy Emily at all. Not one little bit.

Twelve hours later

Well, I've done the decent thing and told Sally. She couldn't have been less interested. She said something like, 'Oh, she's quite fun' and then turned on her electric toothbrush, rendering any further conversation impossible. Sally does seem a bit wiped out by her return to work. It's hardly surprising – the commute alone is exhausting – and by the time she gets back home, she's ready to crash in front of the box. Short temper, too. Much sympathy because I can remember what's it like.

Childcare Programme slightly been on hold today. Daisy has some sort of poo crisis going on. Much time spent changing her. She also seems rather upset. Maybe a bug of some sort. I haven't told Sally. She'll only say I must have given her something bad to eat or fed her with a dirty spoon or something. Partially true. She dropped her spoon and I wiped it clean on the front of my (not terribly clean) T-shirt.

Friday 29 April
7.30 p.m. (Children in bed – although not convincingly. Peter very much awake.)

Something terrible happened today. Really awful. But it's best if I start at the beginning.

Woke up in a fit of nerves about seeing Emily. Sally sensed that something was wrong, and asked if I was OK. Said I was, but in truth, I almost felt sick, as if I were going on a date. What's got into me? Anyway, Sally had no time to worry, as she was out of the door by her usual 6.45. (Our goodbyes get more perfunctory these days. Quick kiss, see you later, have a good day, etc. Going through the motions. Inevitable, as unlikely to give each other a full passionate snog in the middle of a hectic morning, but then again, why the hell not?)

Everything I did until taking Peter to playgroup assumed shades of massive guilt. Even choosing what shirt to wear felt akin to adultery. Should I go for the faded blue one which Sally thinks looks really good on me? I opted to wear a white button-down one instead. Then, more guilt as I even ironed it and put on a clean pair of jeans. Normally I just hack around in whatever I can find, but here I was, making what for me amounts to an effort. I had to stop myself putting on aftershave.

At breakfast, to take my mind off things, I tried some more process consulting with Peter. I asked him what he wanted to do this afternoon. Watch *Astro Boy*. Grr. I didn't have the energy to argue. I announced that we would probably go swimming, which he hates. I have a feeling the 'process consulting' approach might not be working. I think I should just do what PWTD & Partners do and tell them what's what. No consulting, Just 'sulting'. Far easier. Dictator Dad. Anyway, I'm not going to give up, not yet.

On the way to Emily's, I found myself almost shaking with nerves. I nearly cancelled, but thought that was just being ridiculous. Besides, I could do with the company. I hadn't realised how lonely it gets being at home all day with just infantile babble to sustain one. And Radio 4.

In a bid not to give her any idea that I was keen (which I'm not) I arrived at 11.20 – just a little outside what people mean by elevenish. Jodhpur Mum's house was at the other end of the village to ours, and in the few years we'd been here I'd never set eyes on it. Tucked away down a small drive, thatched, and called Fir Tree Cottage, (although I couldn't see a single fir tree), it's cute in a chocolate-box type of way.

When Emily answered the door, the first thing I noticed was that she wasn't wearing jodhpurs. I know it was stupid of me to think she might be, but I've got so used to seeing her in them that it didn't occur to me she might have a more varied wardrobe. God, how sad. She was in a skirt and a pair of knee-length boots. Nothing too tarty – just sensibly tarty. Hardly any heel on the boots, skirt not short but then not long.

I started getting the same feeling I had when I was about to enter a girl's flat for the first time at the end of an evening. Nervous expectation, the giggly offer of 'another drink' (never a 'coffee' because that was just too obvious), the sitting down on the sofa and the rest of it.

The first thing that struck me about the inside of the house was that it was almost as messy as ours. Garish plastic toys lay underfoot, a huge pile of washing-up teetered in the sink, tea-towels hung on the back of kitchen chairs, sofa cushions had not been plumped up in ages, a few too many dead insects along the off-white windowsills. It wasn't scuzzy dirty, just comfortably messy. No having to take your shoes off here, although I did notice the somewhat muddied riding boots in the hall. I plonked Daisy in the middle of a load of toys in the living-room-cum-playroom and followed Emily into the kitchen.

'What can I get you? Coffee? Tea? Wine?'

'If you had asked me that question after twelve, then I'd probably have gone for the wine, but I think I'd better have a coffee.'

'You sure?'

'Yup.'

'Because I'm going to have a glass of wine.'

'Really?'

'Well, why not? It's a nice day.'

She had to be an out-and-out alkie. But then so am I.

'All right then, why not?'

Emily smiled. A slight tingle of excited fear ran down my spine. What the hell was I doing?

'Good!' she announced, clapping her hands together.

A few minutes later, we were sitting in the living room, drinking some pleasantly light Alsace, the French windows open, and the smell and sounds of spring wafting in. Daisy was obligingly playing with some plastic pots and pans, and for the first time in weeks, I felt relaxed. I sat back in a battered armchair and sighed.

'Thanks for this,' I said, holding up the glass. 'Very decadent.'

'Not at all,' she said.

For a few minutes the conversation was stilted, awkward even. Again, it reminded me of those far-off chats with girls on sofas at 1 a.m. This time, however, girl and boy were firmly seated opposite each other, Emily lounging almost disgracefully on a sumptuous sofa. I'd never really noticed her hair before, but it was long (a lot longer than Sally's) and in the light it was kind of glowing. Crash! Another guilt wave swamped over me.

'My favourite time of the day,' she said. 'All the children out of the house, and time to myself.'

'Heaven,' I said. 'What are their names again?'

(In truth, I had no idea how many or what sort of children she had.)

'Well you know about Thomas, he's Peter's friend.'

'Of course.'

'And then we've got twin girls, Flora and Louisa. They're six and at school.'

I was relieved by the lack of wanky names. Flora was sailing a little close, but it was acceptable. It would pass any grandparent test. I looked around the room, and saw the usual smiles in frames. Smiles on the beach, smiles in the snow, smiles next to cakes, smiles next to old people. Same set of photos as ours. Nothing wrong with that.

'So that must be your husband,' I said, pointing to a

picture of a dark-haired bloke wearing a dark blue roll-neck jumper. He looked nice enough, decent sort of face, good husband material.

'That's him,' said Emily. 'That's Jim.'

'I can't believe we haven't met before,' I said.

'Well, he works terribly late.'

Turns out that Jim is in recruitment. No surprises there. Everyone apart from me is in recruitment. Perhaps I should have been in recruitment. But then I would have been just another bloke in recruitment.

I looked at Emily on the sofa. If I hadn't been married, and Daisy wasn't there, and if she hadn't been married (although maybe this one is less important – I don't know Jim), then I would have been tempted. She was *clearly* flirting with me, offering me wine in the morning, allowing her skirt to ride up her thighs. Everything was so provocative, and even as we chatted about who we knew, and people in the village, and how nice it was not to be in London, she was adopting a sequence of nearly provocative poses – whether it was letting her hair fall slightly across her face and leaving it there for just too long, or stretching her legs along the length of the sofa, or bending over in front of me to help Daisy with a toy, all were calculated – I am sure – to seduce me, or lay the groundwork.

I actually began to get a little discombobulated. What was she? Some kind of frustrated housewife who only exists in porn mags? Or maybe there really were lots of women like her, bored with their husbands and wanting a bit on the side. I'd heard our postman services at least six women down the valley (as it were), but I'd never believed it.

Looking at Emily, I wondered whether she might have been one of Phil's regular deliveries.

Still, displaying my usual lack of spine, I accepted another glass of wine. So long as I remained in control and didn't flirt back, I saw no reason why I should feel guilty. If Emily wanted to lay it on, then fine, let her, but I wasn't going to do anything about it, bad patch with Sally or no. Feeling comfortably self-righteous, I leaned back in my chair.

Emily then asked me if I was going back to work. When I told her I was at work, and my job was the same as hers, she looked shocked and then flashed me a brilliant smile. (Emily does have very good teeth, I'll give her that.)

'So that's it? You're a househusband?'

'Why not?'

'I thought you were on gardening leave.'

'That's just what I told Simone a while back. But no, Sally and I have decided she was to go back to work while I did the whole househusband thing.'

'How are you finding it?'

'Pretty good, actually,' I lied.

I then proceeded to bore Emily about my 'process consulting', which earned a similar reaction to that displayed at the dinner party the other night. I said that even though it was early days, it was proving very successful. This was bullshitting of the worst sort, but I couldn't help myself. I didn't want to admit that I was finding it tough. After all, I *should* be able to manage as well as any woman.

'Well, I suspect you need to process consult your daughter's nappy,' she said. 'There's something pretty smelly going on in this room, and I hope it's not you.'

I took Daisy upstairs with her changing-mat-cum-nappy-and-wet-wipes holder. Emily had directed me to Thomas's room, where she said there was an old changing mat on top of a chest of drawers. I gingerly placed Daisy on the mat, before opening up the holder to discover there were no wet wipes. A few weeks ago, I would have instantly blamed Sally, but now it was nobody's fault but mine.

Nevertheless, I removed the nappy carefully as though it were a bomb. A few seconds later, I was wishing it was. This was not a normal nappy, but something that should have been banned by the Geneva Convention – a real dirty bomb. It had exploded everywhere, and there was a real risk that, having taken the nappy off, it was going to spread elsewhere.

Most normal people would have shouted down the stairs for some assistance, but I couldn't bring myself to. After all my bullshitting just now, it would have been too embarrassing to admit I could not cope with something as simple as a dirty nappy. If I'm honest, it was also because I was trying to impress Emily, wanted her to see that I was the type of man who could do a nappy without complaining. Why be the cliché useless man?

Frantically I opened the chest of drawers, looking for something – anything – that I could use to clean Daisy. All I could find were freshly laundered clothes, some of which looked alarmingly of the adult variety, and specifically, of the adult female undergarment variety. I had only been in the house for a few minutes, and already I was rifling through Emily's knicker drawer. Not good. Why did she keep her underwear in here? Wasn't there room in their own bedroom? Probably not. There's not much room in ours.

The rest of the chest contained jerseys and other unsuitable items. Knickers, it would have to be knickers. I was tempted to dash into the bathroom and get some bog roll, leaving Daisy on the chest but a) she might have fallen off and/or b) she might have started playing with her poo, as is her wont. I scrabbled around the knickers, desperately trying to find a pair that weren't too new-looking. I fished out a grey pair of M&S undies. They looked suitably old, although I suspected they were old favourites. Too bad.

The knickers did the job. Not convincingly, but they did it. I wrapped the filthy nappy around them and then looked in the holder thingy for a nappy-sack. Shit. There wasn't one. Thinking it wouldn't be a problem, I breezily returned downstairs, clutching Daisy and the nappy-cum-knicker combo. I put Daisy down.

'Where's your bin?' I asked. 'This is pretty radioactive.'

'Here,' she said. 'I'll take it. I was just going to get our bottle.'

(I briefly noticed the 'our'.)

'No, no,' I said, 'I really wouldn't. It's um, pretty gruesome.'

'I'm a mum, remember!'

She held out her hand. I wasn't in a position to say no. All I could do was to pray that I had sealed the nappy up tightly enough.

'Hold your nose!' I said nervously.

'It's a good one, isn't it?'

'It is rather!'

For what happened next, I blame the glue used by the Comfies factory. As Emily took the nappy, one of the adhesive wings suddenly detached itself, and, like a chrysalis opening, or a time-lapse rose, the nappy blossomed open to reveal its guilty package.

I saw Emily look at it, look at me, and then look back at it.

'Knickers?'

Her voice was unusually high-pitched.

'Er, yes,' I said. 'Old pair of Sally's. Run out of wipes so I'm using up all our old underwear, tea-towels. Green initiative sort of thing.'

This was pathetic.

'These look like *my* knickers.'

I shook my head like Alan Partridge. I tried to keep calm.

'Er, are your knickers M&S?'

'Yes.'

'Well there you go. Doesn't every woman in the UK own several pairs of M&S knickers? What I wouldn't do to have a hand in them.'

Emily looked at me quizzically.

'In the business itself I mean,' I flabbered, 'not the knickers themselves. Ha ha!'

'They *are* mine, aren't they?'

'No, I swear they're not.'

'They are. They've got the same small tear in the waistband. I've had these ones since university.'

Fuck. These pants had some serious history. I was torpedoed now. No way out of it.

'I'm so sorry,' I said. 'I just didn't have any bloody wipes, and I didn't want to leave Daisy on the chest . . .'

At least she was smiling.

'You could have shouted down.'

'I know, I know, but I wanted to . . . Oh, forget it. Look, I'll buy you a new pair.'

Arched eyebrow.

'OK, three pairs.'

Two arched eyebrows.

'And what would Sally say? I don't think she would take kindly to you buying another woman items of lingerie.'

'Yes, you're right. No, she wouldn't. Could you buy them and I'll pay you back?'

Emily was laughing now.

'Don't be silly! They're just an old pair of pants.'

She stepped forward and looked me directly in the eye.

'You don't have to buy me a thing.'

She held my gaze and then I looked down at the nappy and knickers.

'Please don't tell Sally about this,' I pleaded. 'Or anyone else.'

'Don't worry,' she replied, also looking down at the nappy and knickers. 'This shall be our dirty little secret.'

Indeed it is. Sally's just got back in. Should I tell her or what? Answers on a postcard. Usual address.

Saturday 30 April
Noon

Traumatic evening. Last night Sally came home at about 9 o'clock and promptly burst into tears. She was inconsolable until I sat her down with a glass of wine and asked her what was wrong.

'Everything,' she said.

Churning, wrenching, acidic feeling that this was going to be something to do with Nick.

'Oh dear,' I said, smiling carefully.

'I just hate everything at the moment.'

'I know we've been through a bad patch, but—'

'It's more than that, Sam.'

'Oh.'

'We seem to spend a lot of time bickering, yelling, arguing. We never seem to laugh any more.'

I was sitting next to Sally, my arm round her. My grip tightened. She was right. However, I was still expecting the word 'Nick' to pop up at any moment.

'I know,' I said. 'But it's a tough time, and it would be for anybody. I've lost my job, you're back at work for the first time in ages, and I'm finding being a househusband a struggle.'

I looked at her, but she just stared down at her drink, sniffing back some tears.

'But we'll get through it,' I said. 'We've just got to work on it.'

'I feel I've been horrid to you,' she said.

Uh-oh. This was definitely about Nick. The churning was getting worse. This was it. I was about to find that she had cheated on me. That she had enjoyed another man's body, and that he had enjoyed hers. I started imagining the act in lurid detail, and felt almost sick.

'It's Nick, isn't it?'

'Nick?' she went, slightly incredulous.

'Yes, Nick.'

Sally closed her eyes.

'No, it's not Nick,' she exasperatedly retorted. 'Honestly. God, you really don't think I've been cheating on you, do you?'

'Of course not,' I said. 'It's just, you know, it's pretty easy to get jealous when you're sitting at home all day.'

'But this is all part of the problem, don't you see?'

I didn't and looked appropriately blank.

'We've drifted so far apart you don't seem to trust me.'

'It's not that. I don't mistrust you . . .'

'You do. Otherwise you wouldn't keep asking me about Nick.'

Fair point.

'Anyway,' I said, 'let's forget about Nick. Why do you think you're being horrid?'

'That list,' she said. 'I should never have written it. You were right, it was just too schoolmistressly. And insisting you write to my mother. That was wrong of me. She was being perfectly foul to you.'

'Don't worry about it,' I said. 'I needed that list. It focussed my mind brilliantly. Ever since then, I feel that I've been getting on top of things. I know you think it's silly, but I really think my management consultancy programme is beginning to work.'

'Really?'

'Really. Asking Peter lots of questions is starting to make him think about what he is trying to achieve, I'm sure of it.'

Sally looked down at the floor in the living room. It was covered with toys, newspapers, books, magazines, bits of ribbon, scrap paper, logs, at least four remote controls, two old mobile phones, some train track, a handful of teddies, and a couple of photo frames.

'I was about to tidy up before you got in. Sorry.'

'Don't worry about it. How are they anyway?'

'They're both very well. Daisy has been doing some excellent standing, although she's a bit wobbly. And – ta-dah! – Peter even managed to do a poo all by himself.'

'That's great.'

'*I* thought so. How're the Central Asian republics behaving?'

'Badly.'

'Do you reckon they can poo by themselves?'

Sally laughed a little.

'Barely.'

'Just as well they've got you then.'

Another little laugh.

'I'm missing them,' she said, tearful again, looking down at the toys. 'I'm missing them so much. I only seem to see them at weekends, and when I do, the time just passes so quickly. We never have time to sit and just *be*. We're always rushing off somewhere, or shopping, or doing this, doing that.'

'Look,' I said. 'We've got three empty days ahead of us. All we have to do is to get some food. If you look after the children tomorrow morning, I'll get it. The weather's going to be good, so we can just chill in the garden, not go anywhere.'

Sally held my hand.

'Aren't we meant to be seeing your parents?'

'I'll cancel them. I can't face a Bank Holiday drive.'

'What will you say?'

'The normal lie. Peter and Daisy have got foul colds and it's probably best they don't pass them on.'

'You sure?'

'Of course!'

'Thank you, sweetheart,' she said, and kissed me. Properly. We hadn't done that – or what followed – in ages.

Monday 2 May

Typical Bank Holiday. It's rained all sodding weekend. Not just a few showers, but total and utter washout. Instead of sitting in the garden, drinking beer, chasing the children with the hose, lighting up the first of the year's barbecues, looking for the sun cream and all those other delightful springtime activities, we found ourselves marooned inside.

On Saturday morning, we decided to take the plunge and go to the place we hate more than anywhere else in the world – Jungle Jim's Adventure Land. The very name sets me on edge, casts fear into me. What Jungle Jim's Adventure Land is not is its name. There is no jungle, nothing adventurous, no actual land. Neither is there a person called Jim. Instead, it is a sweaty corrugated box in the middle of a trading estate that boasts a few thousand plastic balls, some plastic climbing frames and slides, and a canteen that smells of rancid chip fat, delightfully augmented by the reek of feet. In short, it is a horrific place and a place that, naturally, the children love. Peter loves climbing around the slides and whatnot, and Daisy loves sitting among the plastic balls, throwing them with an admirable sense of purpose. When we got back home, we all had to change our clothes, so imbued were they with the aroma of nastiness. Sally's hair reeked until she washed it. (I decided not to tell her.)

On Sunday, I spent some time redrafting the Childcare Programme. Clearly, I've rolled out the process consulting implementation too early, so instead I drew up a very specific timetable with milestones and deliverables factored in. Yes, it's more dictatorial, but I expect it will produce a highly efficient and streamlined operation.

Example day, which I hope to start on Tuesday.

0600 Wake up (or rather, get woken up by Daisy's cries)
0630 Sam to have had three Ss and be dressed
0645 Sally departs
0646 Start getting children washed and dressed
0700 Children ready for breakfast
0745 Breakfast finished
0747 Upstairs to clean teeth
0751 Teeth cleaned, hair combed

I'm not sure what should happen between now and 0850, when I have to leave the house to take Peter to playgroup. I suspect television (only of the educational variety of course) may play a small part.

0800 SH to visit loo with newspaper while children watch TV

0814 SH to leave loo

0815 SH to tidy kitchen, make Peter's sandwich for playgroup and get some laundry going

0830 Get Peter's stuff ready for playgroup

0840 Get Peter's shoes on

0845 Check have everything, including Daisy

0850 Leave house

0858 Arrive playgroup

Now what? Clean, cook, go shopping, hang up the washing, go shopping again, and all the time look after Daisy and attend to her every whim. She really is pretty whimmish – a very demanding little thing, just like her brother. Are we spoiling them? Or are they just like that?

0910 Return home

0912 Start chore (e.g. one major piece of housework)

1000 Finish chore

1001 Put Daisy to bed

1002 Have coffee, read paper, check emails, make phone calls, write diary

1100 Get Daisy up

1115 Take Daisy for a ride in pram

1145 Return, make Daisy's lunch

1200 Daisy's lunch

1230 End of lunch

1232 Prepare SH lunch (inevitably ham and cheese sandwich)

1240	Eat sandwich
1245	Make coffee
1250	Catch end of *Bargain Hunt* and then watch news
1330	End of news
1340	Go shopping, or at least some expedition that takes seventy minutes (not Jungle Jim's)
1450	Return home
1455	Leave home to pick up Peter
1515	Get back home
1516	Debrief Peter; admire artwork
1517	Stick artwork on fridge
1518	Activity: painting, 'gardening', etc.
1600	End of activity
1601	Children to play quietly until
1630	TV time
1631	SH to prepare children's supper
1649	TV off
1700	Supper
1730	End of supper
1740	Bathtime
1820	Children bathed and dressed (ambitious but doable)
1830	Milk time
1840	SH to read stories until
1900	BEDTIME
1905	SH to pour drink, watch news in kitchen and make supper for adults
2004	Sally home
2005	Kiss Sally

2006   Make Sally drink
2030   Supper

The rest of the day can be left fluid, but largely it's a model timetable. It has enough variance to make it flexible so I shouldn't have a problem sticking to it. I showed it to Sally, who just laughed and all but ruffled my hair.

Today, Monday, the weather has been a little better. For the first time in ages, we sat down for a proper lunch as a family of four. No guests, nowhere to go, just us and a roast chicken. It was heavenly, just being us. We should be us more often.

The mellow weekend has paid off. Sally and I feel like proper husband and wife. Thank God. And I haven't thought about Emily at all. Until now. Bugger. I haven't told Sally about what happened. All I said was that we had a nice coffee, and that we really must get Emily and Jim round for dinner one of these days. Sally agreed, and we spent some time discussing who with. Probably Nigel and Clare – we have them round with everybody. Failsafe friends, who get on with everybody, young or old, rich or poor. Besides, as both Jim and Nigel are in recruitment, they'll have tons to talk about. (Or quite possibly nothing at all.)

Tuesday 3 May

Today was supposed to have seen the successful implementation of the new Childcare Programme Timetable. Unfortunately, things did not go according to plan. In fact, from the word go, they went dangerously awry.

0515   Daisy wakes and bellows, transfer her to cot in spare room so as not to disturb Peter

0520   Tell Peter to go back to bed

0525   Go to Daisy, comfort and try to coo her to sleep

0530   Tell Peter he cannot get into Mummy and Daddy's bed

0532   Attempt to discuss with Peter his motivation for why he wants to get into our bed. What does he want to achieve? How will it benefit him?

0534   Sally announces it is too early in the morning for process consulting, and she is desperate for twenty-six minutes more sleep

0536   Peter goes back to bed, crying

0537   Daisy starts crying

0538   SH and SH bury heads under pillows

0548   Decide lost cause and get up

At this stage, I was so tired, I sort of felt sick and my eyes actually stung. I could tell Sally wasn't much better as she stumbled around with moley eyes. Why do our children need so little sleep compared to others?

0600   Get into shower after Sally unaware this will be last time I have entirely to myself for the rest of the day

0613   Get out of shower

0615   Lacerate my face shaving; realise I am using one of Sally's tiny Bics she uses for her legs

0620   Put on crumpled shirt and jeans only to discover they honk of Jungle Jim's Adventure Land

0621   Look for new trousers; none can be found

0622   Briefly sit down on bed, fatal as nearly fall asleep. How will Sally and I manage today?

0628   Start processing children; Daisy, predictably, has enormous nappy full of gruesomeness, this time do not use a pair of knickers to clean up, decide better if I run a bath

0633   Come back to bathroom to find Peter sitting in bath in his pyjamas, having emptied half a Matey bottle over himself

0640   Finish cleaning Matey off Peter

0641   Get Daisy in bath, cannot see her for bubbles, Daisy shrieks, quickly wash her

0647   Hear Sally say 'Bye' and front door closing

0710   Children more or less dressed

0717   Eat breakfast while watching BBC news

0720   Tell Peter he cannot have cartoons as Daddy is watching the news

0721   Scold Daisy for emptying mushed-up cornflakes on the floor

0723   Clear up cornflakes

0725   Tell Peter he still cannot have cartoons

0730   Return cornflakes to Daisy

0731   Clear up cornflakes

0734   Tell Peter that if he asks for cartoons one more time I shall pour his cornflakes on his head

0736   Peter asks for cartoons. Now in quandary. Must follow through with my threat, but do not wish to set a bad example. Weigh up pros and cons until

0737   Do nothing, can't bear to clear up mess

0802   Eventually finish breakfast

0804   Dump children in living room in front of cartoons

0805   Retreat to our bathroom with newspaper

0806   Hear terrific crash from downstairs. Rush down, pulling up trousers. Peter has pulled a a lamp off a table. Wedding present from someone now smashed

0807   Expel children from room. Much moaning about cartoons. Daisy wants to be held

0815   Finish clearing up lamp; let children back in room

0816   Retreat to bathroom with newspaper

0817   Hear terrific scream coming from downstairs. Rush down pulling up trousers. Peter has cut on bottom of his foot from a shard of bulb. Extract shard. Much screaming, which is mimicked by Daisy

0819   Put plaster on Peter's foot, not before he has trod much blood into carpet

0822   Give Peter consolation biscuit

0824   Eventually give into Daisy's mewings and give her a rusk

0825   Decide to abandon going to loo

0826   Go back into kitchen. A mess. Ignore it. Make Peter's sandwich. Two bits of junk white bread (thought we had some better stuff left) and some Cheddar chucked in the middle. No mayo. Bad for them. Couldn't find any cling-film or tin foil so wrapped it in two sheets of

117

A4. Did the trick. Couldn't find Peter's play-group bag so put sandwich and pair of pants in a carrier bag

0835 Look for Peter's shoes

0842 Still looking for Peter's shoes

0848 Find Peter's shoes

0851 After much fuss, get shoes on

0855 Walk out front door

0857 Return for Daisy

0901 Walk out front door again

0903 Return for Peter's bag

0905 Walk out front door

0916 Arrive at playgroup to find that it is shut for the break

0917 Say 'Shit' loudly

0919 Chastise Peter for saying 'shit'

0926 Arrive back home in foul mood. Now wondering what to do with the rest of the day. Tons of laundry, cleaning, etc., to do, and no way to be able to do it with two children around. Had always thought it would have been possible, but weeks of hell have shown me the light

0934 Turn on TV and mull over what to do for rest of day. Decide shopping is the only thing

0945 Get children in car

0946 Go inside to look for keys

0948 Phone rings. It's Emily, asking if I want to go to Jungle Jim's that afternoon with her lot. Tempted to say no, but common sense dictates that no reason why not, we're all grown-ups, and maybe Jungle Jim's isn't so bad after all.

The shopping, needless to say, was horrific. Having been blackballed from the supermarket, I had to tramp round all the shops in town, and still only ended up with half the things I needed. It wasn't helped by the fact that Peter was walking around with a limp and kept moaning his foot was hurting. Got back at

1145	In time to give children early lunch. Peter rejected his sandwich, so instead gave him a Scotch egg intended for me. Daisy had a jar of something indeterminate but seemed to like it enough to wave her arms around
1214	Turn on TV, find a cartoon channel, plonk them down in front of it
1216	Make my own lunch – ham and chicken sandwich on doughy white bread – comforting junk
1240	Start getting guilty that they're still watching TV
1243	Check emails, surf net, no noise from downstairs
1250	Still no noise from downstairs, worried now
1255	Very quiet indeed
1256	Enter living room. Peter and Daisy not watching cartoons, but drawing. On the walls. With felt-tip. Peter gives me a nervous smile. 'Look Daddy! Look! I've drawn a giraffe!' Peter has in fact not drawn a giraffe but a wallful of blue, red and green spaghetti. Daisy sort of chuckles. Her artwork is over her face

and hands, and around her mouth. Can only assume that there's no such thing as a toxic felt-tip. For once in my life, am grateful to health and safety. Give Peter an immense bollocking. The process consulting can come later. (Although I never encountered the professional equivalent of child-drawing-on-wall.) Peter in tears. I can't get too cross with him because it's my fault for leaving the felt-tips within reach, and hasn't every child tried their hand at decorating?

1305 Pack children into car

1323 Arrive at DIY shop

1330 Buy new paint. Have brought chip of existing paint and get it matched.

1356 Start painting wall. New paint does not match whatsoever, bugger

1410 Phone goes. It's Emily, wondering where I am. Should have been at Jungle Jim's ten minutes ago

1412 Pack children into car

1414 Children asleep

1422 Arrive Jungle Jim's. Leave children in car with windows ajar and doors locked

Emily looked surprised to see me walk in on my own. She gave me a slightly too affectionate kiss on the cheek while I explained about the Great Felt-tip Disaster. She laughed and told me it had happened to her at least three times. I suggested that perhaps a wall in the house could be earmarked for graffiti, but she said they had tried that, and it hadn't worked because only forbidden walls were fun to deface. Reminiscent of overly liberal inner-city councils allowing graffiti artists stretches of wall.

For a while, Emily wasn't quite as flirtatious as she had been the other morning. Perhaps it was the rank smell at Jungle Jim's – it's hardly something you'd splash on as an aphrodisiac. Or the unmentionable knicker incident, which I was so glad she didn't bring up. In fact, we chatted easily about children, locals, etc., although she never once asked about Sally. Mind you, I never once asked about Jim. I was glad she didn't flirt, because I would like Emily and me to be friends, and not to have some dumb *When Harry Met Sally* thing going on. It's just so twenty-something, stuff like that. And most importantly, I love my wife, bad patch or not.

And then Emily mentioned the party. I can't write about it, or indeed about the rest of the day, because it's high time I went to bed. Will tell all tomorrow.

Wednesday 4 May

Oh God. What am I going to do? Go, or not go? Go, and tell Sally? Not go and tell Sally? Not go, and not tell Sally? What does that leave? Go, and not tell Sally, of course, easily the most tempting option.

This is no ordinary party I've been invited to. Not just a coffee with a few housewives but a TrèsRisqué sex-toy party. On Friday. Oh fuck oh fuck oh fuck. This means watching Emily and her friends perusing piles of dildos. (What is the collective noun? An arsenal of dildos perhaps . . .) I'm not prurient, but surely it's no place for a man? When I told Emily this, she said she had asked her friends and they were fine about it. In fact, they thought having a man along might even be useful! In what way?? Do I have to dress up? If so, as what? A gimp? All right, all right, unlikely I know, but I'm beginning to wonder what goes on in this place. Sally never mentioned anything remotely like this.

I said to Emily that surely it was more appropriate she invite Sally, but she was adamant I came, and besides, she said, Sally could come to the next one if she wanted. (Unlikely. Like me, she's no prude, but just not public about what she likes in the boudoir. Unlike Nigel and Clare, who are always banging on about their, er, banging on.)

My one trump card was Daisy. I said there was no way I could bring her. It would just be wrong. Emily shrugged that one off with ease: why not leave her at the playgroup for a couple of hours? Plenty of the other mums were doing the same. Apparently – and this seems somewhat weird – Simone had agreed to it on the grounds that she got a free product. That feels as strange as paying our next babysitter in sex toys rather than cash. 'Sorry, Sophie, we don't have any cash, but how about a nice pair of Chinese love balls? Will they do? A spanking paddle as well? All right – deal.'

I told Emily I'd think about it. And think about it I have. All day. At work, I would have drawn up a list of Hot Buttons and Red Flags. Hot Buttons are the things I like about an idea, and Red Flags are clearly the elements I don't. So, here it goes.

Hot Buttons	Red Flags
Might be fun – should give it a go and not be so prudish	Highly likely to be ghastly – women cackling over vast and garish dildos that can achieve more than any man ever could
Good way to meet new people	What sort of people go to TrèsRisqué parties? Are they people I want to know?
Maybe I could buy something? Sally wouldn't be averse, and besides it would be nice to get hold of something that could give my fingers a rest	The fact that everybody would know what we've got in our bedside drawer. Like to keep these things private. Can't bear the inevitable nudge-nudges.
Good to do things that go against one's grain – a great way to self-reimagineer	Just feels so naff and suburban and wife-swappy

I still don't know. At the moment I'm coming down on the side of not going. I'll just tell Emily it's not my type of thing. Naturally, so far I've not told Sally. There's really no need for her to know.

Peter and Daisy on good form today. At one point, I thought Daisy was going to take a step, but she thudded on to the ground. I think Peter suspected I was pre-occupied, because he once said, 'I am TALKING, Daddy!' I couldn't help but laugh, no matter how bossy it sounded.

Thursday 5 May
Just after lunch

Have been fretting all day. Bumped into Emily after dropping Peter off at playgroup today, and she expressed her rather too ardent hope that I would be coming tomorrow, and not to forget my chequebook. I just mumbled that I would, thinking that over the course of today I would come up with a convincing buller as to why I can't come. However, still can't think of anything. Whatever I say, she'll know I've wimped out. And she'll be right.

Just after tea

I've made up my mind. I'm definitely NOT going. It's just not me, and I don't want to be in a position to have to lie to Sally. I'm going to ring Emily now and tell her that it's just not me; it was really kind of her to think of me, etc., etc.

Just after phone call

I can't believe the phone call I've just had. It went something like this:

Me: Hi there. It's, um, Sam, here.
Her: Hi! How's tricks?
Me: Fine, thanks. Listen, it's about this, um, thing tomorrow. I don't think I'll be able to make it.
Her: Oh no! Why not?

Me: Um, just, well, you know, I don't really think it's, um, my cup of tea.

Her: How do you know?

Me: Well, it's not as if I've been to many TrèsRisqué parties before – actually I haven't been to any – but I'd have thought it's best that they're all-girl affairs. Do you know what I mean?

Her: But the girls are keen to have a man along. It's not like there's a law or anything!

Me: Quite! Anyway, I just think it's best that I don't come along.

Her: Oh well. Seems a shame.

Me: I know. I hope I haven't let you down.

Her: Not at all.

Me: Good. I'll make it up to you. Perhaps you and Jim could come to our next bondage night or something.

Her: What??!

Me: Joke! JOKE! But seriously, we should get you both along to, er, supper soon. It would be nice to meet Jim.

Her: That'd be nice.

Me: OK. I'll get my people to talk to your people.

Her: Fine!

Me: Great. Well, see you soon I hope.

Her: You know, it's a real shame you're not coming tomorrow. You'd have met some fun people.

Me: I know, I'm sorry.

Her: Anyway, I'll do my best not mention our dirty little secret.

Me:	(Speechless)
Her:	You still there?
Me:	Er, yes.
Her:	I mean, I really hope I don't find myself saying that you used a pair of my knickers to wipe—
Me:	Are you blackmailing me?
Her:	Er, *yes.*
Me:	Oh God. You are joking?
Her:	Nope.
Me:	But . . .
Her:	But what?
Me:	That's so unfair.
Her:	Life isn't fair.
Me:	You're a cruel and awful woman.
Her:	Maybe. Anyway, it would be lovely to see you and Sally for supper. Tell her to give me a ring.
Me:	All right, all right, I'll come!
Her:	Whatever brought this on?

I sort of comedically growled at this point and said my goodbyes. I still can't believe it. I've been a househusband for only a few weeks, and I've been blackmailed into comparing dildos with a load of women I've never met.

I had better tell Sally. There's no way she's not going to find out.

Just before bedtime

Have decided not to tell Sally. Have decided I will buy her something as a surprise. My decision may be influenced by the fact that I am feeling very amorous these days now the air has been cleared, and I can tell she is as well. However, she's still somewhat wiped out by work. The day, from start to finish, is some fourteen hours, which only leaves ten hours for supper, chat, bath, some how's-yer-father and then sleep. She's been a little ratty, but a well-timed gin and tonic seems to help. Call it medicinal, or an aphrodisiac.

Friday 6 May
Mid-afternoon (children watching box)

Well, it's been an interesting day so far, to say the least. On the desk next to my mouse is a receipt for enough sex toys to keep a perverts' convention in Amsterdam happy for a fortnight. Oh Gawd. What have I done?

I can't deny that I was pretty nervous when I walked up Emily's drive, having deposited Daisy at Peter's playgroup. She answered the door with a glass of wine in her hand, and she was smoking a cigarette. She wore the tightest pair of skinny jeans, over which she wore a pair of knee-length black boots. (Memo to self: boots for Sally for next birthday.)

'Hello!' she said. 'I'm so glad you've come!'

'Well, blackmail does work wonders.'

Emily winked. This time it was not a tick.

'Our secret is safe,' she said, hammily conspiratorial.

Nervous grin from Holden. She then shouted back into the house.

'Token Man is here!'

More nervous grinning. This was beginning to feel like something out of a porn film. God, if I were a bachelor, I'd be feeling like a pig in clover, but I'm guessing bachelors don't get invited to TrèsRisqué parties. I was invited because I was safe, presumably. How depressingly reassuring.

I followed Emily into the sitting room, which was already a fug of cigarette smoke. Emily thrust a glass of wine into my hand, and offered me a Silk Cut, which I accepted. I looked around the room and the room looked at me. There were a few familiar faces, which I nodded to.

'Hello, Token Man!'

'Hello, Sam,' said a couple of women who I vaguely recognised, but whose names I could not remember.

'I think you're very brave,' said another familiar face.

'What does Sally think?' asked another.

'Um . . .'

'You mean you haven't told her?' asked Emily.

'That's right,' I said. 'I sort of thought, you know, I'd get some things for her as a surprise.'

'Aaah,' went all the girls, as if they had just seen an ickle puppy. How sweet and considerate of me to buy my wife a sex toy as a surprise.

'Better than flowers,' said one, who I later found out was called Stephanie. Vivacious, extremely overweight, and certainly very, VERY open about all matters sexual.

In the centre of the floor were a selection of garishly pink and black boxes, all of which were emblazoned with the ludicrous TrèsRisqué logo, which featured a legged heart clutching a whip. Right.

Emily then introduced everyone again, names I instantly forgot owing to my nervousness. However, I did remember Sue, who was the Party Organiser. She was wearing the shortest skirt imaginable, a sort of tight pink lurex number, and her highlights looked so bad even I noticed them. She looked like a washed-out tart, and as soon as she opened her mouth, her socio-economic incompatibility with the rest of the group became apparent. I tried to wonder whose friend she could possibly be, but my attention was soon distracted by Emily, who was forcing me to sit on the sofa between Stephanie and Sue. There was hardly any room, and I found myself indecently pressed up against both of them. I offered to move, but both Stephanie and Sue pulled me back down, and insisted I was staying right there. Thank God, Sally wasn't seeing all this.

'Right girls,' said Sue, 'let's get cracking, eh!'

Lots of twitters and girly giggles. (I'm sorry, but when girls get together, they really do giggle. It can't be denied.)

'Let's start with a few novelties,' said Sue, 'and work our way up to the more interesting items . . .'

She was interrupted by a buzzing noise coming from the audience, which took me a few dumb seconds to work out. Some of them were pulling rabbit faces as well, which took me even more dumb seconds to work out. I laughed along nervously, stupidly.

Sue opened the first box as though it held pirates' treasure. The women's heads craned forward. Mine stayed still. What the hell were 'novelties'? Sue brought out the first item. I breathed a sigh of relief, while the women sat back, disappointed looks on their faces.

'A board game?' asked Emily.

'This is no ordinary board game,' said Sue, flicking her crap hair away from her face. 'This is the TrèsRisqué Snakes and Ladders game. You play it with your man and it's like normal snakes and ladders. However, every time you go up a ladder, he has to do something to you, and every time you go down a snake, you have to do something to him.'

I nearly said 'go down on his snake', but Stephanie beat me to it, setting the room off into a cackle. I cleared my throat.

'What, um, other things does it suggest?' I asked.

Debbie looked at the back of the box.

'I'm not sure,' she said. 'It doesn't say.'

I took the box from her and studied it. It looked like an ordinary game of snakes and ladders except it featured the TrèsRisqué logo. Not one comedy cartoon penis, nothing.

'I think this is a con,' I said. 'It's just a normal snakes and ladders. I could give this to my children.'

Murmurs of disappointed assent around the room. Token Man had scored a hit. Sue looked daggers at me and took the box back.

'It's one of our top sellers,' she said poisonously.

It was clear that Sue and I were never going to be best of friends. However, she was not to be put off her sales pitch, and after some rummaging, out came that most tedious of 'sexy' novelty gifts – an ice tray with willy-shaped moulds.

'Ho, ho,' I went sarcastically, with newfound confidence.

'Whatever next? An apron with stockings and suspenders on it? An ironing board cover with a naked hunk?'

Sue glanced briefly at the box, confirming that said items were indeed in there. At this point the room went a little quiet, and I became quickly aware that this was neither the time nor place for my sarky wit. Token Man was proving to be a little more of a menace than had been hoped. Emily flashed me a foul look, and I held out my palms submissively.

Sue then proceeded to go through the contents of the novelty box, which were more or less as I predicted. Yes, there were the 'comedy' aprons, there was the edible posing pouch (only 60 calories!) – why? Why would anybody want to eat a pair of pants? – the furry handcuffs, the strip-poker set, the dice with different sexual positions on them, the blow-up male doll (he stays up all night!), toffee body drizzle (Yuk! Yuk! Yuk!) and, finally, the type of present I should imagine is of no use to anybody, a teddy bear in bondage gear. Who would want it? Where would you put it? After just how many seconds of ownership would its appeal – if indeed it ever had any – diminish? Most of the contents of the first box looked tired, as though they had been perused a number of times, and the only purchase was made by Emily, who said she needed a new ironing board cover, and that one would do fine. (I suspect she bought it out of sympathy.)

But things began to get more interesting with the next box – and therefore more embarrassing for me.

'This is where the REAL fun begins,' Sue announced, the lack of excitement in her voice proof that she had perhaps seen one too many sex toys in her life.

The first item to come out was a black whip. Lots of oohs and aahs. Sue demonstrated it against the wall, which she thrashed with a meaty thwack.

'Perfect for keeping your man under control,' she said, the line clearly pat.

'Let's have a go!' asked Stephanie. 'I've always wanted one of these!'

Stephanie then attempted to crack the whip, but failed.

'Here,' said Emily, 'like this.'

Emily then proceeded to demonstrate a brutal and disturbing efficacy with the whip.

'You look like a pro!' said someone.

Emily said nothing, and then, turning to me, cracked the whip just inches from my face, causing me to fall back against the sofa. Net result: I spilled my wine into my lap. (How many times now?) Huge laughs which I had to take in good spirit after my earlier wisecracks. Emily told me I could borrow a pair of Jim's trousers if I wanted. I said I'd be OK, but Emily was insistent and dragged me upstairs.

This was dangerous, I knew it. I was now following Emily into her bedroom, and I felt a twinge of excitement, the kind I hadn't felt since the first time Sally and I had got it together. This was bad, very bad. There was absolutely no doubt she was intending to do something, and there was absolutely no doubt I was going to do nothing about it.

Their bedroom was just as messy as the rest of the house. Not disgracefully so, but just enough to let me know they were real human beings, and not those who like to live in show homes.

Emily looked down at my lap.

'What size are you?'

The *double entendre* was absurd, but she said it with the straightest of faces.

'Thirty-four,' I said. 'What's Jim?'

'Thirty-two.'

'Keeps himself in good shape then?' I asked, as Sally went through the wardrobe.

'Not bad,' she said, before turning around to produce the most garish pair of tartan trousers I had ever seen. They must have been designed by a child with unlimited access to felt-tip pens.

'Here – try these. They've always been slightly too big for Jim.'

What had started as a dangerous flirtation was now turning into a humiliation.

'You're serious? *Those?*'

'Well, there's nothing else.'

There was a hint of a smile on Emily's face.

'You're taking the piss, aren't you?' I asked.

'That's what I said to Jim when he bought them. Look, they're from Ralph Lauren! Designer no less! He wouldn't tell me how much they cost – he never does.'

'They're the most revolting trousers ever created. I'd rather go downstairs just in my boxers than wear them.'

'That'd be a sight! Anyway, I'll leave you here to make up your mind.'

Emily walked out of the room, narrowly brushing past me. Once again, the gesture was ambiguous enough to be interpreted as an accident, but surely she knew that I knew that she was flirting outrageously with me? Still, at least the moment had passed. I could feel my heart thumping away, and I felt angry with myself.

In the end, I went with the tartan spectaculars, which were actually quite comfortable. I could see why Jim had bought them. Whistles and catcalls when I emerged into the living room, which now featured a coffee table covered in various items of S&M lite: cuffs, spanking paddles, chains, gags – you name it, it was there. The throng was pawing over them with a kind of embarrassed hush, each of them no doubt sizing up how exactly this or that could be applied.

Once again, it was Emily who broke the ice, by putting her name down for a pair of cuffs and a blindfold.

'That should put Jim in his place,' said Stephanie, which made the room collapse into giggles of relief and started the ball rolling. Soon Sue was busily filling in her pink order pad. The most popular item appeared to be the spanking paddles, with the room agreeing that most husbands showed a predilection for being spanked, and with Stephanie brazenly stating that she could be a 'naughty girl', and didn't mind putting the slap into slap and tickle. Ooer.

'You haven't got anything yet,' Emily remarked. 'I hope you're not being shy!'

'Um, er, no, just, um nothing that's, um, tickled my fancy yet,' I stammered.

'Go on,' urged Stephanie. 'Surely your wife would like one of these?'

She held up a metal bar with a cuff on either end of it.

'What the hell's that? Looks like something you'd put on a horse.'

Stephanie allowed herself a slight laugh.

'Wrong, Token Man! It's a *spreader bar* of course.'

'Of course.'

'It's to keep your legs open.'

'Right,' I said. What else was there to say?

'Doesn't appeal?'

'I can, um, see the attraction, but I think Sally would think it was like something she'd see at the gynaecologist's rather than in the bedroom.'

'I wouldn't know about that,' said Stephanie. 'Ian likes nothing better than to tie my wrists to the bedstead, spread me with one of these, and then have his way with me!'

The room went a little quiet. The image of Stephanie in such a pose filled our heads (or at least it did mine). Such is Stephanie's girth, I expect it would be impossible to tell when her legs were actually open. No wonder her husband needed this bar thing. The way she spoke about spreading – it made it sound as though her body were made out of cold dripping.

'How nice for you,' I said, the platitude as insincere as a politician working the room.

'Moving on!' said Sue, who now opened another one of her garish boxes. 'PVC and rubber!' she shouted, and once more there was a collective crane of heads.

I was on safer ground here. I reckon there's not one man who doesn't like seeing women dressed in tight, shiny clothes – the tighter and shinier the better. Put a black PVC miniskirt on an average woman with an average figure, and she will turn every head in the room. Sure, all the other women will think she's a complete tart, but men don't care about things like that. In fact, most of my male friends are desperate to get their wives to dress more tartily, but often the wives won't have it. (Those who want their women to dress down so as not to attract attention are mad and insecure, and I don't care about them.)

The first item that emerged was a black PVC catsuit. Involuntarily, I made a kind of 'meow' sound accompanied by a 'well, hellooo'. This had the instant effect of making all the women laugh. I went bright red, but decided, well, what the heck, there was no way out now. I had revealed my fetish, and I might as well capitalise on it. Ever since watching Catwoman on the Adam West *Batman* shows, women in black catsuits have always done it for me. More than jodhpurs even.

'Can I tempt you with something, Token Man?' asked Sue.

I paused. Options sprinted through my mind. Sod it, I thought, I'll buy it.

'Go on then,' I said. 'Put me down for one of those in a size ten.'

'Sally is a lucky lady,' said Emily, looking at me provocatively.

I hope Sally feels the same way. She's never shown much interest in dressing up, so maybe this will convince her. It's just a question of timing. Catch her in the right mood – slightly drunk in a hotel room is normally the best time – and I suspect she'll be game. I also hope she'll be game for all the other things I bought.

Emboldened by my confidence in buying the catsuit, I found myself adding various other items to Sue's list. One black PVC skirt. A pair of thigh-high black boots. Some cuffs. Two sets of Chinese love balls. (What was I thinking? *Two* sets? Why man, why?) Nipple tassels. (I suspect these are ridiculous.) A ball gag. (Sally will never agree to this. What the hell was I thinking?) One vibrator, silver. (This has got to be fair enough. All women have one, apart from Sally. Or maybe she has a secret one. Could this be possible?)

Somehow, I also ended up with a dildo which went under the name of a 'Lusty Girl Pleasurer', although looking down the list I've discovered the Sue has put a 'Y' next to a box which states 'plus Lusty Girl's Anal Love Bulb'. I didn't ask for that! Or at least I don't think I did. I wasn't that smashed – only three or four glasses. What should I do? Phone her up later? 'Hi there Sue, yes it's, er, Sam Holden here. Listen, it's about this Anal Love Bulb you've got me down for . . .' I just can't see myself saying that. Besides, am mildly paranoid that Sally's line of work means our phone may be tapped. I know this is mad, but there it is.

At the end of the party, Sue told me our 'gear' would arrive in a week's time, sent under plain wrappers. I just pray the parcel doesn't arrive at the weekend and Sally intercepts it. The idea of her opening a whole box of pervery at 9.30 on a Saturday morning would be just too embarrassing. Besides, I've had enough embarrassment for one day.

Now all I've got to do is to plan a weekend away. That will be hard, but we both deserve it. In fact, next weekend may well be doable. I'll ask Mum and Dad if they can look after the children. But I only want to go if the 'gear' arrives.

Saturday 7 May

Bad news. Sally told me as soon as she got in last night that she was going off to Kdasfskhaslhdfahistan on Monday morning. Something had just blown up (literally I expect) and a team of them were going out. She couldn't tell me much more about it because it was classified. So strange. I asked her if it was going to be dangerous, but she said it wouldn't be, and besides they would have loads of guards with them. Blimey.

Weird that we both have these secrets now, but they are of such different magnitudes. Hers are about global politics and intelligence matters, and mine is worrying about whether the dildo I've bought her really will have a Lusty Girl's Anal Love Bulb. The weighty matter of whether I've bought the right size PVC catsuit also occupies a lot of my waking hours.

Anyway, we had a lovely evening à deux. I cooked her favourite dish – risotto (I can't stand it – what's so good about cheese and rice?) and after we'd worked our way through the best part of two bottles of Sancerre we retired upstairs. Five-star performances all round. So nice that things are back to normal. It's too easy to underestimate quite how important sex is. Read somewhere that it also releases some chemical that helps build trust. Don't like the idea of being a victim of hormones and neurons, but if it works, it works. Nearly told her about the TrèsRisqué party afterwards, but held back. Spoke mainly about Peter and Daisy instead, who have been remarkably well behaved over the past few days.

Sunday 8 May

So much for the magic of hormones released during sex. It occurred to me while I was cooking lunch that Nick would be going on this trip to Slkstlkdsjfistan. Tried to be big about and just let it go, but instead I asked Sally. I broached it as gingerly as possible.

'Um, sweetheart,' I said, coochily, 'sorry to ask this, but is Nick going on this trip?'

Sally paused. She was attempting to get Daisy to eat some of her mashed-up carrot and parsnip combo I had made on Friday, but was having no luck. She put the spoon down.

'You know I can't really say who's going and who's not.'

'Please don't hide behind all that UK Eyes Alpha bullshit,' I said.

'All right,' she replied. 'He is coming. In fact, he's got to go as this is his patch at the moment.'

'So why do you have to go?'

'Because . . . look, I just can't tell you. Please, Sam, I really don't want to go through all this again.'

I went back to peeling the potatoes. What was meant to have been a nice Sunday lunch was ruined. We didn't mention it again for the rest of the day, but there was no doubt, even as we went for a lovely spring walk, what was on the both our minds. Sally spent a lot of time with the children, telling them to be good while Mummy was away. Peter asked whether Mummy was going away to 'kill some baddies', which offered the only light relief of the day.

God, I'm a fool. It's now 10 o'clock, and I'm about to join Sally in bed. I know what will happen. We'll give each other a duty kiss and then turn our backs on each other. Well, that's not going to happen. I'm going to apologise, tell her I'm a jealous twat, and then make love to her.

Monday 9 May
Lunchtime

Sally left at 5 a.m. this morning. We did make love, but there was something between us that we could both feel, and we broke off halfway through. Utterly depressing. I wish I hadn't tried. No amount of TrèsRisqué toys would have kept me going. Even though I had apologised to her, and even though Sally had accepted the apology, we both knew I wasn't convinced.

She left when I was still asleep, and when the three of us came down to breakfast, she had left a little note telling us she loved us all, and she couldn't wait to see us at the end of the week. She said she would try to ring, but she couldn't guarantee it, as no guarantee that their communications wouldn't be earwigged by the Uitkhdsaldkistanis. Not that a conversation about Daisy's bowel movements would threaten the state of the nation. Still, it all felt very grown-up – she was even getting a military flight out of Northolt. I could just see her getting on the plane with

Nick sitting beside her, and maybe that old frisson of sexual electricity recharging as they flew further and further away from Britain. Fuck. I wish I could stop thinking like this, but I can't. There's a monstrously paranoid part of me that suspects the whole trip is completely made up, and she and Nick are off on some love jaunt somewhere. Did the two of them ever stop loving each other? Why was Nick sniffing around in the early days? Did he think he had a chance? And if so, why?

Stop this. Of course I can trust Sally. If I can't trust her, then what's left? Go to marriage counselling? They'd no doubt say that I was the one who had issues, but honestly, I really don't think I do. I'm just an ordinary bloke who's somewhat jealous that his wife spends a lot of time at work – and sometimes after it – with her ex-boyfriend. Who wouldn't feel jealous? And let's not forget that I'm a house-husband, and as a result, although my day is busy, my brain is not, and it's free to wonder into the realms of the ridiculous. So much for our romantic weekend away with a suitcase full of *items*.

A whole week of this. Damn. I must keep myself – and the children – occupied. They've been somewhat in the background recently, which is unfair. To work!

Tuesday 10 May

I'm getting better at this househusband thing, but I can't say that I'm brilliant. My attempts to adopt the Childcare Programme are reaping very few rewards, if any. Peter seems wilfully unmalleable, and Daisy is clearly still too much at the burbling stage for me to make any headway. Perhaps Victoria was right – children aren't employees. But I'm still determined.

Wednesday 11 May

Woke up last night in a cold sweat about Sally. Dreamed she and Nick were having sex in a tent in the middle of some Mongolian steppes. God knows why Mongolia. Sally's mother was hovering around somewhere as well, wearing a PVC catsuit. I think that was the bit that woke me up. My subconscious is a mess.

Still no phone call from Sally. Half expecting an email, but none.

Thursday 12 May

This morning Phil the postman delivered the parcel from TrèsRisqué. He gave me a wink as he handed it over, despite the fact it had a plain wrapper. He's clearly been delivering a few of them recently.

'Have you got a toy, Daddy?' Peter asked.

'Er, yes,' I said, hoping that these were toys that he would never see.

I couldn't bear to open the parcel. With Sally away, and the bad blood about Nick, the stuff inside would just look tawdry, irrelevant, seedy. Had half a mind to chuck it in the bin, but then held back. Things will change, and besides, the whole lot cost some £200, so I want at least two or three sessions with it! Instead, I put the box in the back of the wardrobe in my study, there to remain unopened for God knows how long.

In order to keep busy, I decided to take Peter and Daisy to Drewfort Castle, a fabulous old place that was sacked during the Civil War. Most of it still stands, and it's a great place for Peter to run around in. Knights in armour are his new thing, and he was delighted when I bought him a knight's outfit from the National Trust shop. I bought Daisy a small plastic sword, which she loved, and brandished aggressively at the other visitors.

For a while, I sat watching the children, and uncharacteristically felt a massive wave of depression. A few years ago, I was a young man about town, cutting if not a huge swathe through the ladies, then at least a few well-aimed slices. Now I am a househusband in the middle of the countryside, hamfistedly looking after two children, with a spouse who is growing ever more distant. Is this how lots of women feel? Do they have these bleak moments in which they think, 'What have I done?'

I know it sounds like bollocks, but all that stuff about needing time to adapt to a new situation really is true. A lot has changed over the past few years, and my life is not turning out the way I thought it would. That doesn't mean it's turning out for the worst, but it's certainly not what I would have chosen ten years ago. If you'd presented the Sam then with the Sam now, he would have laughed and told you to go away.

Perhaps I'm just lonely. I'm missing office life and, frankly, male company. I'm surrounded by women and children most of the time, and I only see men my age when they come round for dinner with their wives. What I wouldn't give for a night in a decent pub up in London with some of the old posse.

Time to be proactive. I shall ring up Nigel and get him to sort something out. Of course the normal problem raises its head – who's going to look after the children? Sally's just going to have to take a day off, although the chances of her taking a day off just so I can get smashed in London are pretty minimal.

Friday 13 May
6 a.m.

Amazingly the children are still asleep, but sod's law I've woken early for no particular reason. Must be the absence of Sally in the bed. Still plagued by thoughts of Nick, but have calmed myself down about it. Must realise it's Nick I mistrust and not Sally. Even so, I can't wait for her to get back home.

Decided to check emails and fart around on the computer. Found myself going to a recruitment agency site and seeing what was around – not a lot, as it happens. I added my details to their database, more out of hope than expectation. Slightly pathetic feeling of having achieved something, even though I know it will come to nought.

However, I have just found something very interesting – a website dedicated to househusbands. It's run by somebody called Danny Wolf-Light, surely the most absurd name in the world. There's even a picture of him, complete with goatee beard and ponytail. (Why do men have goatees and pones? Do they really not want to have sex ever again? Are there any women who find such hair attractive?) On his shoulders is his poor unsmiling son, who is called Sky. For Pete's sake. Sky Wolf-Light. Just as well the 'Wolf' is in there.

The site is full of articles about how to cope with the 'kids' – none of which offer any staggeringly practical advice. Perhaps I should submit my Childcare Programme to them, and see what they think. However, what's tickled my interest is the fact that Wolf-Light and his chums organise househusband day trips. Judging by the photos of the last one, the men all look like complete drips, and their children look faintly embarrassed. Of course, many of the househusbands are firmly in the OKD camp, and are sporting papooses and all that other New Dad nonsense. They look so dreadful that I really must go, just for comedy purposes. If I could convince Nigel to pose as a house-husband and come along, then we could have a hoot.

Chances of Nigel being interested? About 5 per cent I reckon.

Saturday 14 May

Sally got back first thing this morning. She was absolutely exhausted and went straight to bed. I did my best to stop the children pestering her, and eventually took them out for a walk. Peter insisted on taking a stick along, which he used to 'shoot baddies'. I know it's my fault, but perhaps his militarism is getting a little out of hand, especially when he shoots at random old women walking their dogs. Incidentally, Daisy seems to love dogs; every time she sees one, she makes these huge squeals of delight. Peter seems happy just to shoot them. Some of the passers-by find their being shot funny, but some of the more politically correct show their disdain by looking away and refusing to acknowledge him. I just find this absurdly sour.

When we got back, Sally was up.

'How did it go?' I asked.

'Not brilliantly,' she said. 'The people we needed to speak to weren't there, and the people we didn't want to speak to insisted on speaking to us. Still, we made a few contacts.'

'Any dodgy moments?'

'Not really although the whole country is a dodgy moment.'

The unspoken word 'Nick' hung in the air. I left it there, and so did she. I was determined to make Sally's return as cheery as possible, and I cooked us a huge three-course lunch, which Sally wolfed down.

'Do you know what Mummy ate when she was away?' she asked Peter.

'What?'

'Camel.'

'Camel!' Peter and I went unison.

'What the hell does that taste like?'

'Sort of a cross between pork and beef. Actually it wasn't too bad.'

'Where did you have that?'

'In our hotel.'

Slight pause. I found myself imagining her and Nick having dinner together in their hotel. Thankfully, Peter interrupted the conversation by asking whether Mummy had eaten giraffe.

Monday 16 May
7 p.m.

This morning, when doing the laundry, I came across a note in Sally's jeans pocket. It was from Nick. As soon as I read it, I could feel the blood drain from my face. Peter was watching me.

'Daddy, you look funny!'

'What?' I said distractedly, studying the note.

'You've gone all white!'

I walked back into the kitchen and sat down.

'Daddy, can I have a biscuit?'

'Yes, of course.'

I gave him a stale digestive from the jar before re-reading the note.

Sal

It's been quite a week, but I'm glad everything's out in the open now, and I'm so glad you didn't mind when I told you. (Far from it!) Let's keep it secret for a while longer. God knows what I'm going to tell Lucy. It will be so hard for her. But I know this is how it has to be, and it feels so right now. You alone have proved that to me.

N x

It could be nothing, of course, it was vague enough, but I didn't like it all, right from the word 'Sal'. The idea that he had his little nickname for her, for my bloody wife, was a bit much. And the single 'x' too – so much more demonstrative than three of them, which is what friends do on emails. As calmly as possible, I folded the piece of paper and put it in my pocket.

For the rest of the day, I've just felt numb. Angry too. I want to go up to London and kick the crap out of Nick. Tell him to leave my wife and family alone. Thought about divorce too. Would I get custody? I would want it as well.

Read the note repeatedly, and now find it impossible to convince myself that this is anything less than proof that my wife and the mother of my children is cheating on me.

I don't know what to do. For the first time in my life, I feel completely helpless. All because of another man. Fucking jackal.

Sally will be back in half an hour. This is going to be fun. Whatever happens, I don't want the children to hear.

Tuesday 17 May.
5.30 a.m.

I didn't do anything. I chickened out. Perhaps it really is about something else. And if it is what I fear, then what can I do? Now I know what so many cuckolded wives go through. How do they find the emotional strength to stay with their men, even when they know they're cheating? It's the lack of options I hate. If Sally and I split up, what would happen? If I got the children, would she have to pay me maintenance? Feels unlikely. And if she got custody, I'd have to find a job and support them. I'd have lost everything. All I know is that I don't want to lose my family. I'll do anything to keep it together, even if it means grinning and bearing what looks like an affair.

Did it start after eating the camel?

Wednesday 18 May

Bumped into Emily today, who made some noises about my purchases at the TrèsRisqué party – had I used any yet? Was rather sullen with her. Couldn't help but think about a revenge shag. Would I feel better about Sally and Nick if I slept with Emily? Of course not, but I couldn't help thinking it, largely because I'm a man. Mind you, women have revenge shags too. Emily asked what was wrong. Told her the whole process of househusbandry was getting me down.

This is partly owing to the fact that the Holden Childcare Programme is not being implemented as smoothly as I had hoped. This afternoon I decided to adopt some 'varietisation' by taking Peter and Daisy to the church. I know, it's not the most fascinating of places for small children, but I thought it good to expose them to new surroundings, a technique we often used back at work. Granted, we didn't often take our clients to churches – usually it was paintballing – but it's amazing how it becomes much easier to think outside the box if you're in a different, er, box.

Peter wasn't impressed.

'This is boring, Daddy.'

'No it's not,' I replied. 'Look, there's Jesus up there, and there's the organ.'

'Can we go home now?'

'No. Come on, let's explore. There may be some ghosts or something.'

'I don't want to.'

For the next few minutes, Peter and I had a row in the middle of the nave. Jesus looked down at us with contempt. The Good Lord clearly wasn't impressed with this latest strategy in the Holden Childcare Programme.

Peter then started laughing.

'What are you laughing about?'

'Look at Daisy, Daddy. She is eating that book.'

Peter was right. She was indeed eating a book, but not any old book, but The Book. Where the hell had she got that from? I snatched the Bible from her, which resulted in much shrieking. I flicked through the pages and saw she had chewed the best part of the Book of Job. No loss there then. I placed the Bible at the bottom of a pile of prayer books and we scarpered, aware of Jesus' eyes burning a hole in my back.

Thursday 19 May

Sally and I had sex last night. Was the first time in some time. I expected it to feel different, strange, but it felt normal, so normal I began to have my doubts that she was having an affair. (N.B. no TrèsRisqué stuff used as yet.)

'I really missed you,' she said afterwards.

'So did I.'

'Not too pissed off that Nick was there?'

What was this? Genuine innocence, or a brazen tactic? I had to assume the former.

'Well, a bit,' I said. 'I'm sure you imagine what it'd be like if you were in my shoes.'

'Of course,' she said.

All I could think about was the note. I wanted to leap out of bed, grab it from my desk, and chuck it at her, but I knew it would be counter-productive. Instead, I just kissed her.

'Did he try it on then?' I asked as light-heartedly as possible.

'Sam!'

'OK, OK, silly question.'

'For your information, no he did not. And if he had, I would have sent him packing.'

Her words were comforting, not least because I wanted comforting, comforting in the same way as her kisses on my chest. I desperately wanted them to be true. They had to be true.

'We should go away for a weekend,' I said. 'Have some more fun like this evening.'

'I quite agree!'

I thought about telling her about the sexual paraphernalia, but somehow their crudeness would have spoiled what was still a warm post-coital glow. Now didn't feel the right time to tell her about the TrèsRisqué party.

Secrets. Stupid little secrets.

Friday 20 May

During breakfast, I decided to give the Childcare Programme one more push. The idea of a suggestion box occurred to me when I poured out the last of the cereal. I threw out the plastic lining, sealed up the box with some parcel tape and attached a sticker that read 'Suggestion Box – For Thinking Outside The Box'. I then hacked a hole in the front through which the children could post their suggestions. The one flaw is that neither Peter nor Daisy can write, but that didn't mean they couldn't dictate their suggestions. I asked them – or rather Peter – what he and Daisy wanted to do today. I told him that after he had come up with six ideas, Daisy could grab one of the pieces of paper from the box, and we would do that.

I sat excitedly with my biro poised over the first scrap of paper.

'We can watch TV!' said Peter.

I slumped.

'We're not going to watch TV,' I said.

'Why?' Peter whined.

'Because you don't watch TV all day.'

'How about a little bit of TV?'

'No!'

'A tiny bit of TV?'

I gave up. I just had to hope that Daisy would not pull out this particular bit of paper from the 'tombola of activity'.

'All right,' I said, 'I'll put down "Tiny Bit of TV".'

'Hooray!' went Peter, and proceeded to get down.

'Where are you off to?'

'I'm going to watch a tiny bit of TV.'

'That's not how it works,' I said.

'But you said I could watch TV!'

'I didn't. I said it was one of the six things that we *might* do today.'

Peter made a sort of whine and folded his arms.

'Come on,' I said, 'think of some other things we might do.'

Peter looked at the ceiling while Daisy gurgled.

'Um . . .' he said.

'A walk?' I suggested.

'How about killing aliens?'

'Killing aliens?'

'Killing baddy aliens!'

This was clearly not the time to discuss the likelihood of our discovering malevolent extraterrestrial activity on a Friday morning in the middle of the English countryside, so I put the idea into the box anyway, thinking we could make some alien costumes or something. Besides, Peter was showing some imagination, which was great.

'Anything else?'

'Killing sharks?'

'Sharks? Where are we going to find some sharks?'

'In the river.'

'There won't be any sharks in our river. Why don't I put down fishing?'

'Killing fish?'

'No! Why does everything have to be killed?'

Peter shrugged. I wrote down fishing. We could dangle some string into the water.

'OK, we've got three ideas. Now we just need three more.'

More brain racking by Peter, until, with a grin: 'Buy toys!'

'No,' I said, "you have to wait until it's your birthday. But we could put down "make aeroplanes".'

Peter then stuck his arms out and made machine-gun noises. This obsession with war and violence is getting disturbing.

'Two to go,' I said.

'Eat cakes!'

Clearly, Peter's perfect day would consist of a spot of shark hunting, a little alien-clubbing, buying some toys, and then coming home to watch TV and eat cake. Actually, it doesn't sound like a bad day at all.

'I'll put down "cooking",' I said. 'Perhaps we can make a cake.'

I have no idea how to make a cake. Real men don't bake, but I thought I might be able to make some fudge or something.

'Last one,' I said.

'Going in an aeroplane!'

I paused before replying. This was not a bad idea, as there's an old aircraft museum fifteen miles away, in which one can climb around old Buccaneers, etc. I wrote down 'visiting museum' and then added it to the box.

'OK, Daisy,' I said, handing her the box. 'Here goes!'

I jiggled the papers inside like a great showman. The

tension was unbearable. Daisy looked at me and smiled sweetly, totally oblivious as to what she was meant to do. I held her hand, and guided it into the box. Peter couldn't have looked more bored. I wonder where he gets his cynicism? Me?

I made Daisy grab the largest sheet of paper (the one that said 'visiting museum') and went 'ta-dah!' as she brought it out. I opened it up with a theatrical flourish.

'And now, laydeez and gentleman . . .'

Peter looked at me as though I were quite mad.

'. . . today, we are going . . .'

I unfolded the scrap of paper.

I paused.

Shit, I thought.

'To watch a tiny bit of TV.'

'Hooray!' went Peter and got down from his chair. 'TV, TV, TV,' he chanted as he ran down the hall to the sitting room.

I should have just lied. Why didn't I? Anyway, the Holden Childcare Programme needs some serious attention. Scrap one Suggestion Box – For Thinking Outside The Box.

Emily popped round later. She was wearing jodhpurs, damn her.

'I think I have the solution to your problems,' she said, a smirk on her face.

'Which problems?'

'You mean you have lots?'

I laughed.

'No, I just can't think what needs solving.'

155

'Your househusband problems. You said it was all going to pot the other day.'

'Oh yes.'

'Well, why don't you get an au pair?'

'An *au pair*?'

'That's right. My friend Pippa is moving to New Zealand, and they've got this nice Polish girl called Lydia who won't be going with them. So I thought, why don't you take her on? It would be perfect for you. You've got a spare room, haven't you?'

'Er, yes, but . . .'

'And it would only cost you fifty quid a week, which is nothing. Just think, no more chores!'

'Are you on commission?'

'No! I just have your best interests at heart!'

'Look, Emily, it's really kind of you, but I don't think Sally would want an au pair in the house. We've discussed it before, and we've agreed we don't want our privacy invaded.'

'OK . . . but you should think about it. I'm sure Sally could be persuaded.'

'I'm not sure that she could! But thank you, anyway, it's very thoughtful of you.'

'Not at all!'

'Would you, um, like to have a coffee?'

'Sorry – I must dash. Got a horse to catch.'

Dash Emily most certainly did, a blur of black leather and cream jodhpurs down the street.

It was as soon as I shut the door that I had the best idea I've had in my life. It's brilliant, in fact. If Sally has her secrets, then I can have mine. And my secret is going to be Lydia.

Sunday 22 May

A bizarrely nice weekend, helped largely by the fact that Sally did about 75 per cent of the childcare. I suspect this is a result of her sense of guilt concerning Nick, or, if I'm wrong (and I hope I am) by the fact that she has hardly seen the children. This even left me with time to play, of all things, a computer game. Total regression as I relived the Second World War in the comfort of my laptop.

Sally can tell that something's bothering me. Last night she asked me what the matter was, and I said nothing.

'But you seem distracted,' she said.

'Do I?'

'Yes. Please tell me this has nothing to do with Nick.'

'No,' I insisted, hopefully in a convincing manner. 'This has nothing to do with Nick or anything, as there is no "this".'

She eyed me suspiciously.

'You sure?'

'Yes,' I said rattily. 'Perhaps I just need a break, or a holiday or something. It can be pretty relentless.'

'Perhaps we should try to get away for a couple of days.'

'I'd love that.'

'We could leave the children with my mother,' said Sally. 'You know she's always offered.'

As Sally's mother hadn't contacted us since Easter, I

thought it unlikely that she would help. She and Sally talk occasionally, but I and our house have clearly been black-listed, which suits me just dandily.

'We can always ask your parents,' said Sally.

'I'll try them,' I said.

'Where do you think we should go?'

'I don't care,' I said. 'Just so long as it's us and a hotel room, it could be Bognor.'

Sally grinned.

'Well, why not Bognor?'

'You *are* joking,' I said.

'Not all. Sarah at work said it was nice. Up and coming, not spoilt yet. Couple of good places to eat.'

I chewed it over. Apart from the intrinsic comedy value, I could see no reason not to go. Pulse-racing visions of a seedy hotel room and Sally dressed in a PVC catsuit flickered through my mind.

'All right,' I said. 'I'll find us a hotel.'

Tuesday 24 May

Oh God. What have I gone and done? This morning, I woke up thinking that hiring a secret au pair was a stupid idea, but as of next week, one Lydia Komorowski, twenty-three, from Poznan, will be working for the Holden family. Or rather for 75 per cent of the Holden family, as Sally will never know. She must never know. Lydia will not be living with us, but instead she will be staying in Felicity's B&B down the road, at the knockdown rate of £15 per night that I have negotiated.

This means that Lydia will be costing us £155 per week, which I shall have to discreetly loot from one of our savings accounts. That's just over £8,000 per year, a figure I wish I had calculated before I had taken her on. Mind you, the chances of me getting away with this for a year are somewhat slim. Peter is bound to blab something out, or one of the neighbours will let on, but I'm going to give it a try. I feel I deserve it.

I met Lydia this morning at Emily's while Peter was at playgroup. I had been reluctant at first, but Emily was her usual insistent self, and I agreed it could do no harm to meet her. And no harm it most certainly did.

My first reaction was one of disappointment. Lydia was no oil painting. In fact, she wasn't even one of Peter's watercolours. Sounds awful to say, but Lydia is very very ugly indeed. And somewhat overweight. The Gruffalo sprang to mind. But then I swiftly realised that ugly is what I need. If I had a pretty au pair, temptation would lie (or rather, stand) in my way, and even though I'd do nothing about it, I'd really rather not deal with it. Besides, if Sally ever finds out or meets Lydia, then at least she won't have her suspicions.

Despite her enormous unattractiveness, Lydia does have a very friendly face. It's the type of face you look at and can't help smiling. She is charm itself, and even though her English is only marginally better than my Polish, she made all the right noises about how much she loves children, etc. She's also intelligent, and has an economics degree from Poznan University, which I assume is probably more august than 80 per cent of any of the British universities.

'So why aren't you working as an economist in Poznan?' I asked her.

'Because more money here as au pair than being economist.'

'Gosh,' I said, genuinely amazed. 'Even in Warsaw? There must be financial institutions in Warsaw which use economists.'

'The same,' she said. 'More money here! But when my English is good, I would like to work as economist in London.'

'Have you ever considered management consultancy?'

Lydia looked at me quizzically.

'Management consoltanty?'

'*Consultancy.*'

'What is this please?' she mumbled all as one word – 'wotizthispliz'. No doubt it is a question she asks often.

'It's when you advise people on how to run their business.'

Another quizzical look.

'Why? If people do not know how to run business, then they should not run that business? Yes?'

'No,' I replied, resigned. But this was not the time to argue about the role of my profession, or rather my former profession.

'We talk about it another time?' she asked. 'Perhaps we should talk about your children, no?'

I was momentarily taken aback by her bossiness, which I noticed earned badly suppressed grins from Emily and Pippa who were pretending not to earwig our conversation.

'Yes, the children,' I replied, 'good point! Well, there's Peter – he's three and a bit, and there's Daisy, who's a year and a bit.'

'Bit?'

'Bit?'

'Wotizthispliz?'

'Bit?'

'Yes, bit.'

'Bit means, well, you know, a bit more. Extra. On top. You understand. Three and a bit means three and a few months.'

Lydia smiled. Her teeth were predictably grey, like the side of an old whaler, or the exterior of a 1970s hospital.

'I understand. And you have a wife?'

'Um, yes, yes I do. She's called Sally.'

'I like that name.'

'However, I should tell you that Sally will not know about you.'

A very quizzical look. And, from the other end of the living room, a high-pitched 'What?' from Emily.

I explained the situation, as slowly and as Basil Fawltily as possible. Lydia nodded, although it was clear she had not fully understood.

'Excuse me,' she said. 'B&B. Wotizthispliz?'

I told her.

'So I do not live in your cottage.'

I briefly winced at the use of 'cottage'. I like to think we live in a house, but again, such niceties could come later.

'No. You will be a secret au pair. Rather like a secret agent.'

'Like a spy?'

'Yes, that's right! Complete with a Walther PPK!'

'Wotizthispliz?'

'It's a gun.'

'You want me to have a gun?'

'No!'

'I know how to use a gun.'

'All right,' I said, swallowing, 'I hope you won't need to use it.'

'My brother and I, in Poland, like to shoot guns.'

'What at?'

Lydia shrugged.

'You know. Animals. Stuff like that.'

'How nice for them. What sort of animals?'

'Cats. Rabbits. Sometimes old dog.'

There was not much I could say to this. The last time I had shot something was about twenty-five years ago, when I nailed a blue tit with Johnny Graham's air rifle. It had been an exceptionally fine shot, just missing Johnny's right eye and knocking the bird off a clothes line.

'Do you have a gun?' Lydia asked.

If I had, there was no way I was going to let Lydia get her hands on it. Every neighbour's cat would be dead within minutes.

'Er, no, no we don't. We're very strict on guns in England, you know.'

Lydia's crest fell.

'Anyway,' I said, 'back to the children.'

I had brought along some pictures of Peter and Daisy, and Lydia made all the right cooing noises when she

looked at them. I told her the children behaved beautifully, and she would really find it very easy looking after
them. I knew that Emily's eyes were drilling somewhere
in between my shoulder blades, but I resisted the temptation to turn round.

After half an hour, we had worked everything out. She
would start on Monday, and turn up at 7.30. She would
help with breakfast, get Peter ready for playgroup, and
then spend until 9.30 doing some housework. She would
come on duty again at 4 o'clock, and supervise the children's supper and bathtime. Then, in top Victorian dad
style, she would present them to me before I read them a
bedtime story. At 7 p.m. she would get the hell out back
to Felicity's, and hopefully would leave no trace of her existence.

It all sounds easy but I know it's going to be hard, especially making sure Peter doesn't let on. How do you swear
a three-year-old to secrecy? The only solution is surely to
bribe him, and to bribe him well.

My one regret is that Lydia heralds the end of the Holden
Childcare Programme, at least for as long as she is with
us. However, now I will have more time, I will be able to
develop the theory a bit more. I am determined to prove
that the programme is a good one – it just needs some
tinkering, that's all.

Wednesday 25 May

All this Lydia business is at least keeping my mind off the
Nick situation. I've studied the note repeatedly, and no

matter how good a spin I put on it, I can only assume it means something's going on between them. It may not be a full-blown affair, but let's put it this way – it hardly looks compatible with our marriage vows. But, for the time being, I shall keep my mouth shut. I need more evidence. I can't directly accuse Sally of having an affair. It's such a serious thing, and if I'm wrong, well, I'll have severely dented our marriage. I can't wait for our weekend away.

Just looked up some hotels in Bognor on the web. Lordy lord. They're more dreadful than I thought. The most promising looks to be the Imperial, which barely lives up to its name. The pictures on the website look as though they are scanned in from a leaflet printed in 1977. In fact, they must be. You don't have to be a student of fashion to work it out. In the 'check-in scene', the man is sporting a pair of bugger grips and some checked, flared trousers. Total giveaway. And the sofas in the lounge are burgundy. Plus, and this is the clincher, in the photos of 'Nelson's Restaurant' (huh? Did Nelson go to Bognor?) a melon boat can clearly be seen on the nearest table, impaled by a red plastic sword, on top of which is a glacé cherry. Yum. I think I'll book straight away.

Friday 27 May

Lydia came round this afternoon, and her meeting with the children was not a huge success. Peter's first words to her were, 'Why are you so big?'

Unfortunately, Lydia appeared to understand. She

attempted to laugh it off. I could have throttled him. However, laughter did not help Lydia's cause.

'What has happened to your teeth?' Peter asked.

I nearly did throttle him then. Instead, I told him to say sorry, or he'd spend the rest of the day incarcerated in his bedroom. Lydia said nothing, but instead turned her attention to Daisy, who she picked up and started making coochy-coo noises.

Daisy was having none of it. She stared at Lydia, her eyes scanning this vast Polish face, cratered with acne, bulging here and there with medieval protuberances that should have been excised and lanced long ago. It took Daisy no more than five seconds to establish that she was in fact being abducted by some sort of troll, and she yelled. Not a normal yell, but the type of yell you get with babies on long-haul flights.

I swiftly disengaged Daisy from the arms of the troll, whereupon she instantly mellowed.

'I'm sorry,' I said, 'she's always like this with strangers.' And especially with Gruffaloes.

Lydia was nevertheless game.

'Don't worry! She will grow accustomed to my features in the fullness of time.'

I paused to consider Lydia's sudden command of formal English. Had she learned this phrase from some sort of book? Or had she had many occasions on which to practise it?

'Perhaps I should show you around the house?'

'Good idea,' she said.

I left Peter and Daisy in front of the box, while I showed

Lydia where everything was. I'm sure she could have worked it out for herself but, of late, I've become a little queeny about where everything lives. I never used to be like this, but it's only upon Lydia's imminent arrival that I'm starting to feel proprietorial about *my* kitchen. Bizarre.

I then asked her what she would be cooking for the children.

'Lots of fruit and vegebatels!'

Excellent. They bloody need them. I'm sure our children are paler than most. I'm worried that Peter may have scurvy.

'Anything else?'

'Do they like meat?'

'Yes – they're good on meat.'

'Lots of meat!'

'Great.'

'And if they eat all their meat and vegebatels, then they can have puddings, OK?'

'Of course,' I said. 'How about fish?'

Lydia shook her head forcefully.

'I'm sorry,' she said. 'I not like the fish. I think it is disgusting.'

Better and better. I was beginning to like Lydia. I just hope the children will too.

Sunday 29 May

Tuesday is Lydia's first day, and I'm nervous about it. I've been doing a crap job at hiding my nerves because Sally keeps asking me what the problem is. Just say that I'm tired, etc., and looking forward to our break – next weekend, hooray! Sally not convinced, but then she is kind of a spy after all, and it's her job to be suspicious.

Good weekend all in all, except for a semi-disastrous visit to the pub in Lymping Magna yesterday lunchtime. Thought we'd get out, have a change of scene and regretted it within five minutes of sitting down. Numerous problems that can be easily presented in list form.

1. Lack of high chairs

   This was a real pain, and almost caused Sally to leave immediately. I restrained her with my 'it'll be fine' catchphrase, and said I'd have Daisy on my lap. Peter, I maintained, would be OK in a normal chair with plenty of cushions. Needless to say, these arrangements were failures. Peter kept sliding off the chair, and Daisy wriggled so much I'd rather have had a bucketload of tarantulas on my lap.

2. Service was SLOW

   This meant both Peter and Daisy started going berserk. This was not the type of place in which you could leave them to run/crawl around. Instead, we had to bribe them with copious amounts of crisps and Coke, all of which no doubt increased their madness. Foul looks from the ancients sitting near us.

3. No suitable food for children

Normally, I eschew 'Kids' Menus'. Those two words are as depressing as 'house wine' and 'all the trimmings', Jeffrey Bernard regarded the latter as encapsulating everything that is wrong with Britain. But boy did we need a Kids' (or even a Kidz') Menu. The menu consisted of everything that children (or Sally) can't stand. Black pudding, liver, pigeon, etc. As far as I was concerned it was all marvellous – real boy food – but Sally said it looked like the scraps from an abattoir. In the end, we chose rabbit for Peter, which we informed him was chicken. He wasn't fooled, and spat it out in his usual demonstrative fashion. The pub did have some chips though, which Daisy enjoyed munching with her new teeth. Chips was pretty much all Peter and Sally had as well. Meanwhile, I tucked into my black pudding and pigeon combo, followed by calves' liver, all of which was washed down with some IPA. Told Sally I was amazed she had eaten camel in Woahsrhfoiuhjfsfistan, but she said she didn't have that much of it.

4. Nappy changing facilities non-existent

Typically, Daisy decided to release her bowels halfway through my main course, and even more typically, this was not the type of nappy that could just be left to fester for twenty minutes. Sally insisted it was my turn, as she had done all the nappies over the weekend.

'But I've done them all week.'

'But that's your job,' she said.

'But . . .'

'But that's the argument you used on me several months back.'

'Did I?' I asked, genuinely surprised.

'Yes,' said Sally, dipping a chip into the bowl of mayonnaise.

The smell wafting towards me indicated there was no more time to argue. I grabbed the nappy-changing kit from my little backpack thing (I all but have a handbag these days) and took Daisy past a group of nonagenarian diners to the lavatory.

Horrendous sight. The floor was covered in water (or at least I hope it was water) and the urinal was, well, it was unmentionable. The one cubicle had a lavatory all right, but it was not an all right lavatory. It had no seat, making it impossible to use as a ledge. I left, briefly considered using the ladies, and then went to the car instead. Unfortunately some of the nappy's contents made it on to the floor of the boot, but I managed to remove it before any lasting damage was done.

5. Our fellow diners

Throughout the meal, our neighbours – who, as I have mentioned, were pretty old – grew increasingly irritated with the Holdens. I couldn't really blame them, as both Peter and Daisy spent most of their time whinging or crying. Even when there was food, this was often eaten in a somewhat ungraceful manner. Sally complained about this.

'Do you always let Peter eat with his fingers?'

'No,' I lied. 'But I thought for an easy life he could eat the chips like that.'

'Standards are slipping,' she said, albeit with a smile. Meanwhile, all sorts of harrumphs and similar noises were coming from the oldies. I couldn't quite make out all their mumbles, but there were a lot of phrases like '. . . fancy allowing . . .' and '. . . never seen such . . .' and '. . . seen and not heard . . .' and '. . . didn't think they were allowed . . .' and '. . . it's not the same . . .'.

Before the children were born, I would have been the same. Tut-tutting at screaming brats ruining my civilised meal. But now I'm a parent, my militancy has changed and perhaps gone hypocritical. Whereas I could never tolerate children, I now can't tolerate those who can't tolerate children. Places such as the pub annoy me – if it doesn't want families to come, why doesn't it just say so? I'd rather go to a place where we were welcomed rather than somewhere we were endured just so the management could take our dosh.

6. Talking of which, our bill somehow came to £74.67 – God knows how

We're never going to go to the pub again. Not en masse, anyway.

Tuesday 31 May

Today was Lydia's first day, and what an enormous stonking huge great big bloody difference it has made. Revolutionary. She turned up on the dot of 7.30 and went straight to work. No request for a tea or a coffee, no fannying around, nothing. She even turned up with a box of some Polish foodstuff called 'Gruboziarnisty Owies' which she swore the children would love. As far as I could tell from the packet, it was either cement mix or high explosive.

'This testy,' she said. 'My mother gave it to me and my brother every day for many years.'

That was hardly a recommendation, but I was willing to allow it. Peter and Daisy sat patiently at the table, mesmerised by the appearance of the Gruffalo in our kitchen.

'Is Lydia our new Mummy?' asked Peter.

'No,' I said. 'She's here to help Daddy look after you.'

'Why?'

'Because Daddy needs some help, that's why. It's nicer for Daddy to have someone to help.'

'Why doesn't Mummy help?'

'Because Mummy's at work, that's why.'

'Why?'

'To earn money, that's why.'

'Why?'

Etc., etc.

All during this conversation, I kept an eye on Lydia as she prepared her Polish gruel. It was obviously a cereal of

some sort, but it was so grey I could only assume it had
been grown next to a toxic hellhole. She heated it in the
pan with a little water, and the most horrific smell filled
the kitchen. It was like putrefying horseflesh, I'd guess. She
added some salt, butter, and then about quarter of a jar
of clear honey, which no doubt was there to mask the taste.
After a couple of minutes, it was ready.

'There we go!' she announced.

'Er . . . what is it exactly?' I asked, as I fetched the
strongest bowls I could find.

'It's a family secret,' Lydia replied, touching the side of
her misshapen nose. Some secret.

She dolloped it out, and I placed the bowls in front of
the children with loads of yum yum sounds. Peter looked
unimpressed. Daisy looked away.

'Go on, Peter,' I said. 'You must try it.'

'Don't like it.'

I tried to force a spoon into his mouth, but to no avail.
I then tried doing the same to Daisy, but she too whipped
her head away.

'You try some in front of them,' said Lydia.

I flashed Lydia a look. I'm not sure how my look looked,
but I hope it looked like a real look. Unlikely.

'Go on,' she said. 'It is delicious. Pippa's children they
really liked!'

I'd never met Pippa's children, so I could only assume
the poor things now looked like swamp donkeys. I held a
spoon of the matter up to my mouth, thinking that I'd
rather be giving Matthew Pinsent a toe-job. I took a small

bite, taking into my mouth less than the amount of tooth-paste I put on Daisy's pink toothbrush.

It actually tasted pretty nice. Amazing. My 'mmmm-mmms' and 'yummy yummy in my tummys' were therefore genuine. It was basically porridge of a sort, albeit immensely sweet owing to the vast quantity of honey. It was also quite salty as well, owing to the vast quantity of salt. And a unique greasiness, owing to the butter mountain that had gone in.

'This would make a marvellous hangover cure,' I said.

'Aha!' went Lydia, for once knowing what I was talking about. 'Sometimes we put Polish vodka in this to make it for adults.' (Why do Poles always say 'Polish vodka'? I assume it must be something to do with rejecting their former Russian masters and their Russian vodka.)

My example had caused Peter to pick up his spoon, and soon he was trowelling the stuff in.

'This is very nice,' he said.

'What do you say to Lydia for making your breakfast?'

'Thank you, Lydia!' he shouted with a big smile and evident sincerity.

I then tried feeding it to Daisy, who after much cajoling, eventually gave in, and she too was soon tucking in. Even I had a few more spoonfuls, until my mouth stuck.

After breakfast, Lydia whisked the children upstairs to brush their teeth and wash their faces (she would have needed a chisel rather than a flannel) and for the first morning in ages, I had nothing to do. In fact, I didn't know what to do at first. I was minded to clear up the stuff in the kitchen, but I took one look at the pan Lydia has used and decided that was her job.

So, I made myself a pot of coffee, and retreated to my study, where I had a pleasant twenty minutes reading the news online. Heaven. This was like having a wife again.

Actually, I didn't write that.

Wednesday 1 June

It just gets better and better. Lydia is a marvel. If I were Pippa and her family, I would have bribed Lydia to go to New Zealand with us. She's as good at being an au pair as her compatriots are at building. The house looks spotless, and the children are eating proper food for a change. Plus, just two days in, they seem a lot better behaved. I wonder how she does it? Could there be something in the Gruboziarnisty Owies?

Even Sally has noticed a difference. This evening, over supper, she said that the house was looking immaculate.

'Have you had someone in?' she asked.

'Someone in?' I responded.

I cursed inwardly. Whenever I lie, I always ask my interrogator the same question. It's there to buy me a few seconds, but Sally knows me too well.

'You heard me,' she said, with a trace of knowing smile.

'No,' I replied. 'I just think the Holden Childcare Programme is beginning to reap its benefits that's all.'

Sally nodded in an unconvinced way.

'It really must be,' she said. 'Even their clothes are neatly folded and put away in the right drawers.'

Were they? Wow. Lydia was even better than I thought. Sensational.

'Yup,' I said, trying to look smug at my newfound adroitness. 'All in a day's work.'

'I'm very impressed,' said Sally, the smile still there. I got the nasty feeling she was playing with me. At least Peter's kept quiet – mostly because Sally hasn't been around much the last couple of evenings. As to the absurd neatness of the house, I shall have to mess up some of Lydia's work after she leaves in order to make things more realistic. Most people tidy up before their help arrives – I shall be the only person who deliberately messes things up after she leaves.

I went over and gave Sally a kiss.

'I'm looking forward to the weekend,' she said.

'So am I.'

'Are your parents still on for looking after the children?'

Fuckityfuckpoo. I had totally forgotten to ask them. Holden, you toerag, you great big toerag.

'Of course,' I said. 'They're coming to stay here.'

'They're quite happy about it, are they?'

'Yup.'

'Because they've always seemed so reluctant in the past.'

'No, they seemed, um, positively keen.'

'Perfect,' purred Sally.

Thursday 2 June

Bugger. Toss. Balls. My parents can't make it.

'I wish you'd asked us earlier,' said Mum.

'Sort of a last-minute thing,' I told her.

'How about Sally's parents? Could they help?'

'We're not really talking to them at the moment.'

'Oh. Why not?'

'Because . . . well, it's a long story and I'd rather not go into it.'

'Anyway, it would be lovely to see you again soon. We haven't see you in yonks.'

'I know. You're right. We've just been so busy, sorry.'

'How's work going?'

'Fine. Yup, absolutely fine. You know, ticking along.'

I know, it's pathetic, it really is, but I still haven't had the courage to tell my parents I was sacked. I'm like one of those men who doesn't tell his wife he's lost his job, and still goes out to work each day with his Tupperware box of lovingly prepared sandwiches in his otherwise empty brief-case. The thing is, I'm too cowardly to accept the inevitable bollocking I'll get from Dad. I really should tell them, I know, but there's never been a decent opportunity, not least because we never see them.

Anyway, larger problem is that we're going away tomorrow night, and we still don't have anybody to look after Peter and Daisy. Using Lydia has crossed my mind, but I'll never get away with it. And there's no way I can bring myself to speak to Jane – we have been incommunicado since the great lunch fiasco. But we HAVE to go on this weekend. We need time to ourselves, and also, I want to have filthy, degraded, haven't-done-that-before sex.

Friday 3 June

Hooray! Or not rather not hooray, but sort of hooray. Sally has got to work tomorrow, so our weekend is cancelled. Sheer relief that my incompetence was not exposed, but also much frustration not to be going on our filthy weekend. The Imperial will not refund my deposit, but that's fair enough. Sally is very apologetic, and I am being magnanimous about it, which is somewhat underhand as the weekend looked like a non-runner anyway. Sally said she wouldn't be working too late, so I told her I would cook her something fab and then we would have a dirty weekend – or rather night – at home. Sally told me she liked the sound of that. Poor woman, she doesn't know what she's letting herself in for.

This week has been a revelation. I feel like a new man. Lydia, in a funny sort of way, has given me back my pride and also my libido. I feel awake, normal, bright-eyed, bushy-tailed and all the rest of it. I still do quite a lot of childcare, but I'm not doing all the cleaning and laundry and all that stuff I'm just so bad at.

Peter likes Lydia a lot.

'Lydia,' he announced at teatime today, 'you are my friend.'

Lydia's great big Gruffalo face melted into something approaching cuteness.

'Thank you, Peter,' she said. 'You are my friend too.'

And then she came over and gave Peter a big hug. He hugged her back. Tidal wave of guilt. He hasn't been this affectionate towards Sally in, well, actually I don't think he's ever been this affectionate towards her. Lydia then went to hug Daisy, but she screamed. You can't have it all. Still, at least Lydia was trying. If Daisy understood words, then I'd have had words with her.

After bathtime, I spoke to Peter about keeping quiet about his new friend.

'You must remember not to tell Mummy about Lydia,' I said.

'Why?'

'Because it is a surprise.'

'Why?'

'You know when you get a Christmas or birthday present and it is wrapped up so you can't see it?'

'Yes?'

'Well, it's like that. Lydia is a secret surprise.'

'Are we going to wrap Lydia up and give her to Mummy?'

Jesus. What a present that would make. Here, darling, a Polish warthog. You shouldn't have. No, really, you shouldn't have.

'No!'

'So when will Mummy see Lydia?'

'One day,' I said. 'But not now, OK?'

'OK.'

'Good.'

I watched while the ratchets and gears in Peter's brain chugged and whirred. He then looked up at me.

'Daddy.'

'Yes?'

'Shall we tell Mummy about Lydia tomorrow?'

'No! Not tomorrow, or the day after that or the day after that or the day after that. Not until I say, OK?'

'OK.'

The chances of Lydia staying undercover are minimal. Today I paid her first instalment. It didn't hurt, but I know it soon will. Sally's pretty good at monitoring household expenditure. I wish she were like Clare, who has no idea. Nigel's always pulling fast ones over her. He tells me that he never asks permission to buy things, as a) he's old fashioned b) it's his money and c) Clare never agrees with him anyway, so what's the point of discussing it? Unfettered non-new-man joy.

Sunday 5 June

This weekend did not go quite as planned. Not by a long chalk.

It started well, though. Perhaps rejuvenated by the presence of Lydia, the Saturday-morning shop went swimmingly. Because I suspect it's too early to attempt a return to the supermarket, I had to drag the children from the green-grocer to the butcher via the open-air market and the baker's, and bought all sorts of delicacies for what was intended to be Saturday night's big Session of Passion. My plan was to start with something simple – smoked trout from the Old Smokehouse, and then follow it with a small rack of lamb with a herb crust. Pudding was to be lavender crème brûlée. (I'm so keen, I even have one of those blow-torches.) Wine was to be champagne, followed by some burgundy, and then some more champagne to go with the pudding. All in all, nothing too fatboy. Both Sally and I find that full stomachs are not conducive to convincing sack action. Besides, it's impossible to perform the full sexual repertoire if there is a severe danger of flatulence.

When we returned, I had a full New Dad moment when I got Peter and Daisy to help me make the crème brûlée. They had great fun whisking up the cream, and naturally I allowed them to lick the ingredients off the whisk and out of the bowl. Surely only the most hard-hearted of parents would disallow this?

Afterwards, we did our normal circuit, and Peter once again massacred the majority of the passers-by with his stick machine-gun. 'This is a Schmeisser,' he kept telling people, who mainly looked utterly confused. I sometimes think I'm teaching him a little bit too much about the Second World War. He already has an overly developed love of my old *Commando* comics, and he can't even read. Hopefully, he'll soon get bored and move on to liking things that are normal for his age, such as, well, to be frank, I have no idea. Robots? Cars? Action Men? I have no idea, partly because I don't think I was entirely normal at his age either. With me, it was dinosaurs to the exclusion of all other toys. I could say the word 'palaeontologist' frighteningly early, even though I wasn't sure what it meant. The war came later, much later, but now I've infected Peter with it, I don't know whether there's any cure. Girls, I expect, will see it off.

Without women, all men would be nerds, I'm sure of it. Unless one is totally committed to one's own special geekiness – collecting football programmes, recording episodes of *Countdown*, learning capital cities – we drop our embarrassing habits as soon as we reach adolescence. There's just no way a decent sort of woman is going to go for a bloke who likes to go metal detecting. It doesn't matter that said bloke may be perfectly well adjusted, have a huge willy, etc. – all the woman will see will be the hours the bloke spends scouring cold beaches for Coke-can ring-pulls from 1978 and 2p coins.

The only nerdiness that men can get away with is an interest in sport, because this is considered an essential part of masculinity. Even though 99 per cent of women don't like the fact that their man spends Saturday afternoon on the terraces/golf course/at the track/in front of the box, they know this is such an accepted element of male behaviour there is nothing they can do about it. At the risk of being New Mannish about it, what women don't realise about the male interest in sport is that it's got bugger-all to do with athleticism and a lot to do with statistics. That's what all those funny tables are about in the back of newspapers. They're packed with stats, acre upon acre of bloody stats. Average lap times, run rates, world rankings, number of caps, minutes before first goal, previous form, split times, number of corners taken, possession percent-ages, maximum speeds – sport doesn't bring out the dormant hunter-gatherer, it brings out the inner accountant.

One of the reasons Sally was attracted to me was that I have very little interest in sport. In fact, I can clearly remember the moment I told her this on one of our first dates. Her eyes widened, and I'm convinced she squirmed excitedly in her seat. I must ask her exactly what she thought. Hopefully something like, 'What a real man to admit that he doesn't like sport' or 'Mmmm – plenty of intimate Saturday afternoons à deux'.

Anyway, back to yesterday. When we got back from the circuit, I left Peter and Daisy in the living room watching *Maisy* mouse. I then prepared their lunch, while listening to the radio, marvelling at what a top day I was having. For once, I was really enjoying looking after the children, and I was certainly relishing the thought of quality nookie later with Sally, complete with Lusty Girl Pleasurer (plus Lusty Girl's Anal Love Bulb). I was even pretty relaxed about the whole Nick situation, 85 per cent believing that I was being paranoid, and that there was a perfectly reasonable and innocent explanation for the note.

At first, I just thought it was the normal Daisy scream, one engendered by Peter having pushed her around, or stolen a toy off her. But this was different – it was urgent, high-pitched, a scream of pain rather than of frustration. It was different enough for me to stop cutting the cheese and rush through to the living room, where I found Daisy crouching next to the TV. We've got – or rather had – one of those DVD-cum-video machines, and while the *Maisy* DVD was playing away merrily, the video slot was playing host to Daisy's right hand. She was desperately trying to wrench it out, and the more she wrenched, the more she screamed.

In retrospect, I am pretty impressed with my first re-action, which was to turn all the hi-fi and video equipment off at the mains. Of course, this instantly caused the volume of noise in the room to double, as Peter started bellyaching that the TV had been turned off and why couldn't he watch

Maisy like Daddy had said he could, and Daddy and Daisy were in the way of the TV, and why couldn't he turn it back on? I ignored him, bent down and tried to wriggle Daisy's hand out of the video slot.

However, every time I tried to pull it free, no matter how gently, Daisy's screaming just got worse. The poor little thing. I must admit I found it pretty hard to be all ice man while she and Peter bellowed, and I implored them both to calm down.

'There, there,' I kept saying, 'Daddy will get you out in a second.'

But Daddy could not get Daisy out. In fact, Daddy feared he might have got Daisy's hand even more wedged in. Daisy was screaming so loudly now, that I really thought she might have broken a finger. For the next few minutes I kept trying to release her, but nothing worked.

I only had one option – I would have to take the machine apart. That would probably see the end of its life, but given the choice between my daughter's hand and a three-year-old Sony DVD/video player, it was a no-brainer. Besides, by now, images of that American bloke who chopped off his own forearm in order to free himself from a rock were starting to parade through my somewhat panicky mind.

I ran back into hall and found my tool kit in the downstairs cupboard. I scrabbled through it, cursing at how haphazardly I had stored its contents. Eventually, I dug out a couple of screwdrivers, both of which looked far too big. Back in the living room, I found Peter about to turn on the switch, which caused me to run over and yank him away. I fear I may have pulled him a little hard, because he shrieked in pain. I spent a few vital seconds trying to calm him down, but he kept telling me how I had hurt him. Enormous guilt, felt like a childbeater, but knew it was in a good cause.

Accessing the screws on the video player was no easy task. As they were located on the bottom and the rear of the machine, I had to move Daisy and the machine as one unit away from under the television. This was made harder by the fact that – geek that I am – there was a heavy amplifier on top of the DVD/video (I like to have my war films LOUD) – which also had to be moved. Every slight movement of the electronics and Daisy caused her to cry even more. This was getting bad. I was tempted to phone for an ambulance, but I didn't think I had got to that stage yet. Besides, what could a paramedic do that I couldn't?

Soon, I had the DVD/video away from the TV and disconnected from the mains and from the myriad other pieces of equipment. Like a bomb-disposal expert, I carefully unscrewed the back of the player in an attempt to remove the metal casing. Unfortunately, and most unlike a bomb-disposal expert, I had completely the wrong tools for the job. The screwdriver was far too big, but I could just about gain enough purchase to slowly remove the screws. All this time, Daisy was bawling. I kept trying to calm her down, but perhaps my panicky tones were most unsoothing. At least Peter had quietened down, and was now watching what I was up to with a timeless male fascination for the insides of machines.

'What are you doing, Daddy?'

'I'm trying to get Daisy's hand out of the video player.'

'Why?'

Just as I was about to answer him, I thought this was not the time for an extended 'Why' conversation. Instead, I told him sit on the sofa and read one of the many *Maisy/Thomas the Tank Engine/Mr Men* books scattered around the house.

'But I want to watch TV!'

'Peter!' I snapped at him, in a way that I had never snapped before. I must have looked scary, because he instantly retreated.

After another minute, I lifted the lid off. Or rather, I half lifted the lid off. The only way to get it completely off was to remove Daisy's hand, which was of course impossible and clearly the whole target of the exercise.

'Fuck,' I said quietly.

'What did you say, Daddy?'

I ignored him, hoping that would be the end of it.

'Did you say "fuck", Daddy?'

'No, I said 'fulge'.'

'You said "fuck". What does "fuck" mean, Daddy?'

I nearly said 'fuck' in response, but found a small portion of self-control.

'*Fulge.*'

'*Fuck.*'

My attention reverted to the video player. Although Daisy's crying had subsided somewhat, she was still not enjoying herself. I examined the machine, to see if there were any other ways of taking it apart, but there was no joy. There was only one thing for it – take her to hospital.

This now posed the tricky problem of how I was going

to get Daisy into her car seat with a video player attached to her hand. It was clearly going to be impossible, and could well end up breaking her arm or wrist. So, I decided there was another thing for it – I would have to call an ambulance. I racked my brain for other solutions, but there weren't any.

For the first time in my life, I dialled '999'. I waited for ages, and eventually a voice answered that sounded as though it was 3,500 miles away, and coming from the bottom of the ocean.

'Emerg . . . serv . . . require?'

'Ambulance, please!'

'Where . . . call . . . om?'

'What?'

'Where . . . from?'

I gave her the address.

'What's . . . emerg . . . ?'

'My daughter's hand is stuck in a video recorder.'

'What?'

'What?'

This was getting confusing.

'Please,' I shouted, 'just send the bloody ambulance.'

'Calm . . . sir.'

'I'm perfectly calm!'

I wasn't. Daisy's crying was getting worse. This really was becoming an emergency.

The ambulance arrived within ten minutes. There's nothing like hearing the sound of a siren and knowing that the vehicle making that noise is coming to help you, and is not chasing you in order to put three points on your licence. The paramedics, who were called Ian and Tracey, walked briskly into the living room, a blaze of bright green, yellow, fluorescent strips, big red bags full of kit. They and their stuff seemed to fill the room, turning what had been an everyday living room in something you rubberneck on the side of the motorway.

'How long has her hand been trapped?' asked Ian, who just looked like the most reliable man in the world.

'About half an hour. I tried taking the machine to bits, but no luck. Hence calling you.'

As Ian fiddled with the machine, Tracey comforted Daisy. I was depressed to see that Daisy calmed down immediately.

'There, there, Daisy,' she was saying.

'Do you have many of these?' I asked her, pointing at Daisy.

'None,' she said. 'At least not yet!'

That somehow made it worse. If she had been a mum, then OK, I could have coped with Daisy's sudden mellowing, because Tracey would have given off secret mum smells and vibes.

'Can I have a look at this?'

It was Peter, who had somehow managed to extract part of a defibrillator from one of the big red bags.

'Put that down!' I barked.

Peter looked cheekily back at me, and continued fiddling with it.

'You'd better do as your dad says,' said Ian, holding out his hand.

Peter complied instantly. What was the secret here? Go around dressed as a paramedic?

Ian turned to face me.

'Well, the good news is that I don't think she's badly hurt. The bad news is that we can't do much here. We'll have to take her in.'

I momentarily closed my eyes. Mine and Sally's night of filth was retreating rapidly.

'You sure you can't do anything here?'

'Positive. We don't have something to cut the machine away, but they do down at the hospital.'

'She'll be OK, Mr Holden,' said Tracey, and I was genuinely reassured. 'We won't go back under blue, so you can follow us.'

'Under blue?' I asked gormlessly.

'The blue light.'

'Of course. Sorry.'

'Not at all.'

'Does this happen often?' I asked.

'More often than you might think,' said Ian. 'I'll tell you one thing though.'

'What?'

'In my experience, household contents insurance doesn't cover the hospital breaking your video player.'

'I think I can live with that.'

We reached the hospital in fifteen minutes, and as a sedated Daisy was wheeled through A&E, we earned a few stifled laughs. Understandable. I would have seen the funny side of it had it not been my child.

Peter and I then had to wait for an hour and a half.

That was just awful, and utterly draining. Every time I asked the nurse behind the counter if everything was OK, she just said it was fine and that I had nothing to worry about. I began to think the most dreadful, horrific thoughts. What if Daisy was allergic to the sedative, and even now was undergoing a huge operation to save her life? Maybe, while they were cutting away the machine, they had accidentally sliced her hand off? Every time I saw a doctor or nurse rush through the doors at the end of the waiting room, I assumed the worst, believing he or she to be on call to help my critically ill daughter.

Eventually, a doctor of about my age came out. He had a big smile on his face, a smile that almost made me wet myself with relief.

'You can go and see her now. She's absolutely fine, although I can't say the same for your DVD player!'

I laughed rather too much as Peter and I followed the doctor, who I noticed was wearing the standard junior doc uniform of chinos and blue button-down Oxford shirt. When I saw Daisy, I almost burst into tears. She was lying in a cot, fast asleep, a bandage around her hand. I stroked her hair. She looked as fragile as she had looked when she was just born. A drip thing was attached to her left hand.

'She's got a slightly nasty cut on her right index finger,' the doctor said, 'but it's nothing too serious. We'll give you some plasters and just make sure you keep it clean.'

'Thank you.'

'Oh yes, and here's your *Maisy* DVD – we managed to save that!'

'Thank you – you've been brilliant.'

'Not at all. In fact, we're getting quite good at doing this now.'

'Really? How do you do it?'

'We use one of those blowtorches you use to make crème brûlée,' he said. 'Works a treat.'

By the time we were discharged and back home, it was six o'clock. There was an answerphone message from Sally saying she would be getting in at about eight, and hoped I was ready in 'every way'. Erk. I felt emotionally drained and physically exhausted. My libido was somewhere in the cellar, and not even a Sally/Elizabeth Hurley sandwich would have seen it climb a single step. Nevertheless, I was determined to press ahead with the evening; I was not going to let her down.

As I had been warned Daisy would be pretty groggy, I put her straight to bed after a cursory bath. The poor little thing. It must have been terrifying for her. Peter was tired as well and, although he had slept in the car on the way back, he was still pretty shattered. He was tetchy and demanding – a sure sign of being knackered – so I bribed him with a few biscuits to keep him sweet.

As soon as they were asleep, I went into our bedroom to get everything ready. I laid out all the items on the bed – the catsuit, the PVC skirt, the thighboots, the ball gag, the nipple tassels, the handcuffs, both sets of Chinese love balls, the vibrator, and finally of course, the Lusty Girl Pleasurer (with Lusty Girl's Anal Love Bulb). The room looked like an S&M dungeon. If I had had time, I would perhaps have opted for a less in-your-face approach to getting Sally to perform my sordid little fantasies.

The one problem was that the Lusty Girl Pleasurer was stuck inside some fiendish packaging (which, bizarrely, featured a picture of a naked man in a cowboy hat), packaging that my tired and clumsy fingers were incapable of opening. I took the Lusty Girl Pleasurer down to the kitchen, where I managed to hack it out. In the cold light of the kitchen, laid on the work surface next to the raw rack of lamb, the Lusty Girl Pleasurer looked like a very ugly thing indeed. In fact, it was about as erotic as an egg whisk or a turkey baster. Purple and pink, about a yard long, a protuberance growing from near its base like some sort of garish tumour, there was nothing sexy about it at all. Still, it was TrèsRisqué' bestselling item, and tens of thousands of women can't be wrong.

Finally, I prepared supper, getting the crust ready on the lamb and peeling some potatoes which I was going to sautée. I also thought it was high time for a glass of wine, so I cracked open the first bottle of rosé of the year. It had nearly been summery today, and I needed something light and refreshing to pep me up.

By 7.30, everything was in place. The lamb was ready to go in the oven as soon as Sally arrived, and the smoked trout was already artistically laid out, complete with a dollop of crème fraiche, some perfectly cut wedges of lemon and a few leaves of coriander. Quite gay, I know. The crème brûlées were in the fridge, ready for their crusts to be immolated later. The dining-room table was laid, complete with wedding-present silver candlesticks (never used), wedding-present Limoges plates (never used), wedding-present linen napkins (used once, too much of a hassle to launder and iron), and some cutlery I had never seen before in my life.

By eight o'clock there was still no Sally. I tried her mobile, but it went straight through to answerphone. Not much surprise there – the reception round here is pretty patchy. So, I sat down in the kitchen and turned on the TV and helped myself to another glass of rosé. I was feeling tired, very tired, but I was determined to see the evening through. It would have been too easy to have quiched out. The last thing I remember was looking at the Lusty Girl Pleasurer (with Lusty Girl's Anal Love Bulb) on the table in front of me, wondering whether it – or indeed I – was going to see any action that night.

The next thing I knew was someone shaking me awake. I opened my eyes, and all I could see was the Lusty Girl Pleasurer (with Lusty Girl's Anal Love Bulb) right in front of my eyes. In fact, things were worse than that. My mouth was actually TOUCHING the Lusty Girl Pleasurer (with Lusty Girl's Anal Love Bulb). Yuk yuk yuk yuk. My head darted back rapidly in disgust, too rapidly for Sally, whose face I butted with the back of my head. She let out a screech of pain and held her hand up to her nose. I, in my groggy state, just looked at her gormlessly while blood started to trickle down the back of her hand.

'Quig,' she said, 'geb me a hunky!'

'What?'

'A hunkerchif.'

I grabbed innumerable sheets of kitchen roll and handed them to her. Gingerly, she dabbed her nose, and held her head back.

'Don't do that!' I said.

'Why nob?'

'Because you might give yourself a haemorrhage.'

'Whad do you kno aboub thad?'

'I just heard it somewhere.'

I got Sally to sit down at the kitchen table and, as she ministered to her nose, I could see her eyes looking downwards at the Lusty Girl Pleasurer (with Lusty Girl's Anal Love Bulb).

'Wob the hell is thad?'

'What the hell is what?' I asked, pathetically buying time.

'*That*,' said Sally, taking the kitchen roll away from her nose.

I had to be blunt.

'It's . . . ah . . . well, it's a Lusty Girl Pleasurer.'

Sally was speechless. I filled the silence in a moronic way.

'With a Lusty Girl's Anal Love Bulb. I think you can see how it works. If you put this bit like this . . .'

Sally held up her free hand.

'Not right now, thanks.'

I put Lusty Girl Pleasurer down.

'Where did you get it from?' she asked.

'From that sex shop in town.'

I couldn't face telling her about the TrèsRisqué party.

'You went *there*? When? What did you do with the children?'

Bugger, I hadn't thought of that.

'Well, it was when Peter was in playgroup . . .'

'So you took Daisy in there?'

'Um . . . um . . . not exactly.'

'What do you mean?'

'I left her outside.'

Oh God, this was sounding so bad.

'You left Daisy in her pram outside a sex shop so you could go in and buy that?'

'Well, not exactly outside, but in a sort of hall area. You know, a sort of vestibule-type thing.'

'So they have a pram-parking area do they?'

'Well, you know, it is sort of like that.'

'I can't believe it.'

I said nothing and looked at my watch. It was ten o'clock!

'How come you're so late?' I asked.

'Something came up,' she said. 'There've been lots of bombs going off in the region. I'm so sorry. I must say, if I'd known you were going to skewer me with a rectal probe I might have stayed up in town.'

Nick. All I could think of was Nick. She had been seeing Nick. I blurted it out.

'You've been seeing Nick, haven't you?'

'Not this again.'

'Admit it, you have, haven't you?'

'Of course I've *seen* him,' said Sally, 'just like I've seen everybody else in the office today. If you don't trust me, why don't you bloody well ring him!'

Sally fiddled around in her handbag for her mobile and scrolled through its numbers. She was clearly finding it hard to do so and simultaneously hold the kitchen towel to her nose. She removed it which was a bad idea as the blood was still trickling fast, fast enough to splash on to the table, and, gross upon gross, on to the Anal Love Bulb bit of the Lusty Girl Pleasurer. Not nice. I debated whether to move it away, but just left it there.

'Here!' she said, holding the phone out to me. 'Call him! Ask him if he's sleeping with me! Go on!'

Sally was a little hysterical, and I did what all men try to do in these situations and appear as calm as the iciest of icemen. It's complete bollocks, as inside I was raging. I looked at the phone.

'Darling, please. There's no need to be like this. Besides, there's no reception.'

Sally snatched the phone back.

'There's at least one bar – go on, call him!'

'No. Please. Just put the phone down.'

'It's not a gun, Sam!'

'Just put it away.'

'Sam!'

'All right,' I said, 'I apologise, I've still got the green devil about Nick.'

'It's got to stop, Sam!'

'I know.'

'We can't carry on like this.'

'I know.'

'So what are you going to do?' Sally asked.

I held my hands up helplessly in the air.

'I don't know!' I blurted.

Without thinking, I then picked up the Lusty Girl Pleasurer (with Lusty Girl's Anal Love Bulb) and thwacked it hard on the table out of frustration. It kind of wobbled in my hand, as though it were quivering with its last few dregs of life. Sally burst out in snotty nosebleed laughter. I started laughing as well.

'That really is the most ridiculous thing,' she said.

'I know. I'm sorry. I shouldn't have bought it.'

'It just so . . . so big,' she said.

'Unlike me then,' I winked.

'Come on,' she said, 'let's at least eat something. How long has that trout been out?'

After we ate, we went to bed, but didn't have sex. Instead, we just cuddled. My mind was occupied by the vast quantity of perv-gear I had hidden under the bed, wondering how I was going to get away with Lydia, and cursing myself for being so bloody jealous. I never used to be like this.

Today has been quiet. I told Sally what had happened to Daisy yesterday, and she was surprisingly chilled about it. She was more bothered as to why I hadn't told her about it last night, but I said it didn't feel like the right time. It never feels like the right time for anything these days.

How ghastly. Self-pity. I do so hate it.

Tuesday 7 June

After countless emails, a boys' night has been arranged up in London on Friday night. It will be me, Nigel, Robert (and his smelly breath), Paddy, Ed and Rich. A good quorum of old buddies. It'll be so nice to see them again, and have a night of not bothering about anything domestic and just getting on with the serious business of getting utterly wazzocked.

Lydia continues to be a star. I've had to continue to bribe Peter with treats and the occasional toy to stop him from mentioning our 'secret friend' to Sally, but it's totally worth it. Everything runs so smoothly these days, and I see my role more as a delegator or an administrator. Balls to the Holden Childcare Programme. All I needed to do was to hire more staff. How many management consultants tell you that I wonder? Answer: none.

Thursday 9 June

Thank God. Sally and I had sex last night. Was at that stage in which we hadn't had it for so long I was worried we'd slip into the habit and never have it again. No perv-gear though, didn't seem right. It will come out one day, I swear.

Saturday 11 June

It's 9.30 p.m. and I still feel hungover. There is no doubt that last night I got the drunkest I had been since the Helsinki Stag Experience. A great evening, but I ended up melancholy and with a feeling of being left behind. Sideshow exhibit. An also-ran.

We started in what had been our usual haunt, The Venning Arms on Walters Street. As soon as I walked in, I suddenly felt naked as I was the only bloke not wearing a suit. Leather jacket had me marked out as someone different, someone perhaps a bit arty. Plus, I hadn't realised quite how long my hair had got.

'Who's the fucking hippy?' shouted Ed across the bar.

I held up two ironic peace signs and then gave Ed a non-gay hug. Hadn't seen him in ages, and he gave me a non-gay hug back. Difficult one to get right, the non-gay hug. It's not really a hug, but merely a mutual slap on the back as you're shaking hands. If you do anything like hold or squeeze, you run the massive danger of being assumed to be gay. Some men refuse non-gay hugs, believing them to be gay no matter what. I suspect blokes who don't do non-gay hugs are in fact gay, and are attacking in others what they fear in themselves.

It's a bit like urinal etiquette in which, upon entering the bogs, you are obliged to choose the Urinal of Conspicuous Heterosexuality. For example, if you're faced with a bank of three urinals and there's a bloke peeing at one of the end ones, then the LAST THING YOU DO is to use the middle urinal. Definitely gay. Other options: if faced with three empty urinals, which one do you choose? Answer: NOT the middle one, as this obliges subsequent pissoiristes to use a urinal next to you. Definitely gay. OK, one more. Here's a tricky one. In a bank of six urinals, three men are using urinals 2, 5 and 6. You have the choice of 1, 3 and 4. Obviously you have to stand next to somebody, so which urinal do you go for?

|1 |2x |3 |4 |5x |6x |

(x indicates being used)

Answer: NOT 1 or 3, as this pairs you off with the bloke at number 2. You might as well tell him that you love him.

The correct answer here is 4 as it's the position with the least suggestion of homosexuality.

Anyway, hugs were exchanged with everyone else, and soon the six of us were breaking each other's balls just like old times. No actual *conversation* was taking place – it never does – instead it was just an exchange of one-liners, bon mots, mal mots, quotes from films, insults, recent jokes, anecdotes about women, more quotes from films, anecdotes about work, car specifications, air miles, and reminiscences from university days.

Naturally, most of the joshing aimed at me was predictable and fair game.

'How're the nappies?'

'Wearing an apron yet?'

'Has Sally given you a monthly allowance?'

'How're all those housewives?'

And then, 'Been to a TrèsRisqué party yet?'

I chewed this over, but couldn't resist telling the truth for the sake of group jollity.

'In fact, do you know what? I have.'

Lots of wooohoos, etc., etc. Then, what I had stupidly not anticipated was the intense grilling regarding what I had bought. By that stage, I was still not hammered enough to reveal anything barring the purchase of a few 'sordid items'.

'Don't tell me,' said Nigel. 'A Lusty Girl Pleasurer!'

'Complete with Lusty Girl's Anal Love Bulb!' shouted everyone else.

I could feel myself going bright red, something that hadn't happened since school.

'How did you know?' I asked Nigel.

'Know what?'

'That I had bought one of those?'

Nigel looked at me, and then I looked back at him, both of us realising what had happened.

'I didn't know!' he said. 'The old Lusty Girl is a legend.'

And then he and everyone else (apart from me) burst into hysterics. I felt immensely square – clearly I had not mugged up enough on my sex toys. I sheepishly sipped my pint of bitter. Nigel then explained why the Lusty Girl was a legend. Apparently, a few months back, Rich had bought one for his wife, Lucy, who was so revolted by it that she threw it in the bin. The next morning, to her horror, she saw a dustman fish it out of the rubbish and show it to the rest of the crew, who all pointed excitedly at the house and made the expected noises. Since then, Lucy has hidden from the dustmen, although every time they come (when they are not on strike), she can hear their jeers and whistles. It's got so bad that Lucy wants to move house.

After a couple more pints, I soon found myself unable to keep up conversationally. Alcoholically, at least for the time being, I was fine, but I was beginning to feel out of my depth. Everyone was talking about work, who was up and who was down, bonuses, how well Pacific (non-Japan) funds were doing, how Quigley Fletcher were going to post record profits, the copper market in the US, how RTY were in trouble and had just sacked their CEO Brian Leavis, and why the Chancellor's latest tax was just mad.

A few months ago, I could have kept up with all this. In fact, I might well have been the one leading the conversation, but it's all gone, and gone so quickly. *The Economist* still arrives at home, but I never read it. Most of the time it stays in its shrinkwrap, which is only removed in order to get it recycled. Sally has been pestering me for ages to cancel our subscription, but it's part of my old life I just can't let go of. I think she understands this, and she's not moaned about it of late. Mind you, something quite different has happened with *A-Listers*. Sally now barely looks at it, but I've begun to read it as avidly as some girl reading a crap piece of chick lit. I find myself endlessly interested in so-and-so's love life, and paparazzi shots of footballers' wives shopping in Bond Street. It's almost a dirty little secret, and I'd never admit it to any of the lads.

At some point we found ourselves at the inevitable Chinese restaurant – Lee Hoo Fook – where we ordered just about everything on the menu. The meal passed in a daze of crispy duck, gelatinous unidentified meat, Tsingtao beer, prawn crackers – you name it. In fact, a lot of Tsingtao was drunk, and by the end of the evening I felt woozily terrible. I had reached that state of drunkenness in which I was desperately trying to prove my sobriety. My efforts only made everybody else laugh, and the word 'lightweight' was bandied about, as it often is.

We left at about 10.30, just in time for Nigel, Ed and me to catch the last train home. All I could think about was how expensive the meal had been – some £55 each. In the taxi on the way to the station, we swigged a small bottle of whisky Ed 'just happened' to have on him. (Is he turning into an alkie? I thought those quarter bottles of whisky were for dossers.)

Whatever sort of whisky it was didn't agree with me. As the cab rocked and rolled its way to the station, I could feel that sort of light-headedness I know presages a major chunder. Nevertheless, I managed to keep it together until we got on the train. For a bit, I was fine, but then the train started to move – as is its wont.

'You've gone as white as a sheet,' said Ed.

I dimly remember getting up, rushing to the lavatory, only to find it locked. I had no choice but to be sick in whatever I could. In this instance it was the bin in the vestibule. I was sick in it at least five times, to such an extent that £55 worth of Lee Hoo Fook's finest MSG-enriched chunks of gop spilled down the sides. Not good. Before I fell asleep, I remember hoots of derision from Ed and Nigel. Fair enough.

This morning I woke up at Nigel's house, having slept very badly for about five hours before his children woke me up. Not good. Clare offered me some breakfast, but the very thought of food made my stomach turn. I kept saying it must have been the Chinese, but she said I should consider the possibility that it just might have been the booze. She had a point.

I drove back home late morning, probably still hideously over the limit.

'My God, you stink of booze,' said Sally when I gave her a kiss. 'You should have a bath.'

'I already have.'

'In that case you should brush your teeth, wash your mouth, anything.'

'I already have.'

I must have looked shit. I didn't dare look in a mirror for fear of committing suicide after I had done so.

'Sweetheart,' I asked plaintively, 'do you mind if I go to bed? I think it's best that I do, so I'm on good form for the rest of the day.'

Sally looked at her watch.

'Don't forget we've got Rachel and Brian coming over for lunch, and we haven't been shopping yet.'

I nearly cried.

'Can't we just cancel them?'

'Hardly! They're probably already on the road. It's at least a two-hour drive.'

It should be a ninety-minute drive, but Brian drives like a pensioner.

'OK,' I said. 'Just one hour, I beg you.'

My begging worked, but when I woke up, I felt even worse. Typical. Perhaps I am a lightweight.

Monday 13 June

It's still bothering me, this being a lightweight. Not an alcohol lightweight, but a lightweight generally. It has been one of my fears since becoming a househusband that nobody would take me seriously. (Maybe they never took me seriously in the first place, but that's another matter.) I can't join in the conversations about Big Boy stuff any more, and not one of my friends has any real interest in what my days consist of. It's not surprising. They're barely interested in what their wives do all day, so why should they be interested in my tales of Peter and Daisy and getting the laundry ready and cooking and cleaning, etc? I didn't dare tell them about Lydia. (How can we trust others to keep our secrets if we cannot keep them ourselves? – La Rochefoucauld.)

To think I used to believe I might be an important type of person one day. More than a childish ambition – a proper grown-up one. To be respected, to make a difference to the world, and above all, to be raking in money as fast as I could manage. It's all gone. I'm just a bloke who stays at home and clears up after his children. I try to convince myself that nurturing two young lives is as important as being a CEO, but it's just not. Maybe women can convince themselves it is, but it's not in my competitive male psyche to see being a househusband as on a par, let alone on the same golf course.

Golf. Now there's something I'd like to do again. Now that Lydia has settled in nicely, I might try to nip off tomorrow morning for nine holes. Got to be worth a try. I'd feel rich then.

Near Lydia miss this evening when Sally came back. Female hairbrush in downstairs loo.

'Whose is this?' Sally asked.

I knew full well whose it was, so I struggled to keep cool. Iceman.

'Dunno,' I said, and walked into the kitchen as if I had no interest in it whatsoever. Inside I was quaking.

'Strange,' said Sally.

'Hmm?'

'I said it's strange.'

'Perhaps it's Rachel's,' I said.

'Oh yes. It may well be.'

Genius Holden, I thought, you bloody genius.

'But there's dark hair in it,' said Sally.

You moron Holden, I thought, you bloody moron. Rachel is blonde. More blonde than Marilyn Monroe sitting on the beach.

'Perhaps she used it to brush Holly's hair,' I said.

Once again, genius Holden. Rachel's daughter Holly has jet-black hair.

'Oh yes,' said Sally again. 'That'll be it.'

She came over and ruffled my hair playfully.

'You'd make quite the secret agent,' she said.

I laughed hollowly and we kissed.

'Here,' I said, 'give me the hairbrush. I'll post it back to Rachel tomorrow.'

Sally handed it over. I don't know why, but I've got a bad feeling about that hairbrush. It's on the desk in front of me as I type. If Sally had looked at it more closely, then she would have noticed a distinctly Polish-looking word on the back of the handle. Phew. If she had seen that, then I would have been buggered – with the hairbrush probably.

Or the Lusty Girl Pleasurer (with Lusty Girl's Anal Love Bulb). I suspect that would hurt.

Tuesday 14 June
2.30 p.m.

Looked at that househusband website this morning, the one run by that weirdy-beardy Danny Wolf-Light. Turns out they've got an outing this Friday. Am sorely tempted. Will email Nigel to see if he wants to take the day off and come with me. It'd be nice to have someone with whom I can take the piss.

9.50 p.m.

Turns out Nigel doesn't want to come. Says he is too busy. Hardly surprising. I told Sally about it, who agreed it sounded awful, but that I really should go, just for comedy value. That's one of the things I like about Mrs Holden – she's as cynical as her husband. I'll send Danny Wolf-Light an email tomorrow. I hope it's not too late.

Spent much of the day reading a book. Sheer joy. Guilty joy though, while Sally sweats away in London.

Wednesday 15 June

Hooray! Or quite why I should be cheering, I don't know. I've just had an email back from dannywolf-light@house-husband.com (possibly the worst email address any self-respecting man could have) saying they'd love to have me on board on Friday. He and twelve other househusbands are going to Longwhip Zoo, and 'It promises to be a day full of fun and bonding!!' Sounds a bit dubious to me. Cost is £5 per child (sorry, 'kid') and £10 per househusband. Plan is to meet at the zoo at 10.30, have 'lunch/nappy change' at 1.00, and then a walk (optional) in the nearby countryside. No mention of going for a pint, I see. How can men bond if they don't have a drink in their hand? It's impossible.

Thursday 16 June

Another near Lydia miss this evening. This afternoon I had my first game of golf in months (what joy, although I played atrociously) and like a moron, I simply dumped my clubs and golf shoes by the back door and left them there. Sally noticed them after half a minute of being back home.

'Been playing golf, have we?'

'Playing golf?' I asked, back with my old lying tick. I must learn to stop this.

'Yes – your shoes and clubs are by the back door.'

A nervous pause while I feebly constructed some buller in my head.

'That's right. I have been playing.'

'With the children?'

'Not exactly. I took them for a walk in the field by the river, and thought it might be fun if I hit a few balls around.'

'This needed your golf shoes, did it?'

'Yes. There's no point in practising in any old shoes. If you do, your swing and stance can all go to pot. It's one of the first things my dad taught me.'

Sally nodded, evidently bamboozled by this utterly feasible piece of golfing arcana. Of course, it's complete crap, but I thought it not bad for spur of the moment.

'Daisy loved watching the balls fly away,' I said, adding a touch of verisimilitude. 'And I even let Peter try a few swings with the putter, although he just wanted to use it as a gun.'

'Typical,' said Sally. 'I wish he would grow out of this gun business. I'm sick of being shot.'

'We've got another, what, eight, nine years of it, I'm afraid.'

'Is that how long it is?'

'Pretty much. I seem to remember shooting my parents until I was about twelve.'

'Are all little boys as violent as you were?'

'No, but most are reasonably violent.'

'Thank God for Daisy,' said Sally. 'Adds some civilisation to the family.'

'I wouldn't bank on it. She seems to like playing with sticks these days, and makes a kind of banging noise.'

'Oh God, she's been infected by Peter.'

I opened a bottle of 2001 St Joseph. I was secretly celebrating my clandestine game of golf, and how Lydia had changed my life.

'And me, I'm afraid,' I said. 'I think I probably encourage the guns 'n' ammo behaviour a little. Inner boy, etc. Regression.'

'Give me a glass,' said Sally, a comedy resigned expression on her face.

'How was work by the way?' I asked.

'Fine thanks. And . . .'

Sally took a swig of wine.

'And what?' I asked.

She looked pointedly at me.

'*And* you'll be glad to hear Nick has moved departments. To the Latin America desk. So there's *really* no more need for you to be jealous about him.'

This was great news. Fanbloodytastic news. First, a sly game of golf, and now no more weaselly Nick sniffing around my wife. I took a mouthful of wine and reflected that life was just dandy. Who cares if I can't hold my own with man talk any more? So long as I've got Lydia around, I might as well be retired. Nowt wrong with that.

Friday 17 June

Today was the Househusband Outing. A day never to be repeated. A day of comedy, tragedy, and strange facial hair. The drive over to Longwhip, some hour and a half, was pretty painless as the children slept most of the way, which meant that I could listen to an unfeasibly nerdy podcast about pinot noir. It's the type of thing Sally finds doubly disturbing because a) I'm nerdy enough to know how to podcast and b) I'm nerdy enough to listen to a podcast about wine. I've tried to explain to her how podcasting works, but like programming the video, she can't – or refuses to – understand it.

As soon as I pulled into the car park at the zoo, I almost turned round. There, gathered underneath a green banner with white writing that read 'The Band of HouseBands' was a group of the most uninspiring men I had ever set eyes on. They were all dressed in OKD clothes such as combat trousers, pale green Che Guevara T-shirts, absurd trainers, and all, as far as I could tell, were wearing trademark 'I'm different, me' black rectangular glasses. Also, and this is what made me nearly turn round, they all sported some form of comedy beard. Some had the standard goatee.

Others had the goatee-light, aka the Soul Chip, aka the Ziff, aka the Annoying Bit Just Underneath Your Bottom Lip Which Makes It Look As If You Haven't Shaved. Others had sculpted sideburns. One even had an Errol Flynn moustache, which might have been forgivable had he not been a ginger.

But I got out of the car anyway. Determined to put my prejudices to one side for one day, I resolved to muck in with this bunch of New Men/Keen Dads. I woke the children up gently, knowing by now that if I swiped their sleeping forms out of the car, they'd be crotchety for the best part of an hour.

'Are we at the zoo?' asked Peter, staring vacantly at the gravel.

'We are indeed.'

'Can we see a giraffe?'

'I hope so,' I said. 'I'm sure they must have lots of giraffes.'

I put Daisy into her pram, which I unfolded with a lot of difficulty. I bet the 'HouseBands' are oh-so-whiz at doing prams. Slowly, the Holden family made their way to the banner, taking in more details of the varieties of facial hair, as well as the assortment of papooses and Himalayan-ethnic-type stuff used for transporting children. I made myself a private wager that there was not one carnivore among them. Yoghurt-knitters. Even the children were dressed dreadfully, the poor things. They all seemed to be wearing garish clothes made out of hemp and other no doubt 'green' materials.

'Hi,' said a bloke walking towards me. He had the full sculpted sideburns and a goatee, plus some sort of

Guatemalan satchel, the type of thing a girl buys on her gap year to prove her identification with oppressed peoples and then leaves in the back of her new Golf. This had to be Danny Wolf-Light.

'Hello,' I said, holding out my hand.

Danny didn't take it. Oh no. Danny didn't do handshakes. Not Danny. Far too Western, man. Instead, he held his hands together in prayer, and then, bowing his head slightly, went 'Namaste'. For fuck's sake! This isn't some sort of leper colony in Bhutan, I felt like saying. This is Longwhip bloody Zoo. There are people here arriving in Ford Mondeos. Just over my shoulder down the road was a new Barratt Home development. This was England. The United Kingdom.

'You must be Danny,' I said. 'I'm Sam, and this is Peter and Daisy.'

'Nice names,' he said.

He chewed them over.

'Peter – radical. Don't know many Peters. Daisy – nice. Like the flower. Cool. Like it.'

'And yours is called Sky?' I said, trying to keep a straight face.

I noticed Danny looking me and up and down, clearly unimpressed by my baggy chino shorts, checked short-sleeved shirt and standard-bloke Docksiders. I was not going to fit in sartorially, at the very least.

'Yeah,' he said, a little distracted. 'Sky. And I've got another little one called Freedom.'

He gestured towards the satchel thingy, and I peered into it as though I were looking down a well of indeterminate depth. Sure enough, tucked inside was a not very large human being. The child was most certainly not living up to its cretinous name.

'Hello, Freedom,' I said. 'Boy or girl?'

'Girl of course,' said Danny.

'Of course. And how old is Freedom?'

'She's four months.'

'Sweet little thing,' I said.

'Whatever,' said Danny. 'C'mon Sal, let's join the others.'

'It's *Sam*,' I said pointedly. Already, particles of frost were beginning to develop in the air.

'Yeah, Sam. Names is names.'

Whatever. I walked over to the banner with the children, ruing my lack of balls that would have told him to eff off and have got back into the car and driven straight home.

I was introduced to at least twelve HouseBands, all of whom had names like Tet, Crip, Finton, Plaz and Womble. Their children's names were even worse. I wish I'd written them all down, but some of the best were Moby, Twelve (huh? never found out why), Tree, Kind (pronounced as in 'kindergarten'), Poplar, Bramble, Cent, Apollo, Affrika, and here was the worst – Xayla-rae. (I've had to confirm spelling of that on the web.) Jesus. (Which would have been better than any of those.) And, because of the gender unspecific hair and clothes, it was near impossible to tell what sex any of these children were. I suppose it shouldn't have bothered me, but it did for their sakes. How the hell are these children going to get on in life with these absurd names? It's so arrogant of parents to label their children alternative before they've got the chance to be so. Maybe Xayla-rae might like to be an accountant, but he (she?) will have no chance with a name like that. At least with neutral names like Peter and Daisy, our children can choose whether they want to be suits or hippies. These children have no chance. Ironically, poor Freedom will be straitjacketed by her very name.

I handed over a £20 note to Danny, who put it in his satchel thing on top of Freedom.

'Er,' I said, 'I think you've put it on top of your daughter.'

'That's right,' said Danny. 'I want her to get to hate money from an early age.'

'Ah,' I went, my revelatory expression dangerously sarcastic.

Danny eyed me suspiciously. He clearly hated me as much as I hated him. Men like me, in his ordered alternative world, weren't supposed to be HouseBands.

As we walked through the turnstile, Peter said, 'Daddy, who are all these people?'

'They're other little boys whose daddies stay at home and look after them.'

This clearly meant nothing to Peter.

'Are these rubbish people?'

I looked around, praying nobody had heard. Plaz and Finton were right behind us – they must have done.

'Er no,' I went. 'Anyway, are you looking forward to seeing the animals? Which one do you want to see most of all?'

'But they are *rubbish* people,' Peter insisted. 'Their clothes are made out of rubbish.'

I closed my eyes. Privately, I agreed with him. Their clothes did indeed look like they had been made from rubbish – bits of old yak, etc., but there was no way I could agree in public.

'They are not rubbish people, Peter,' I said quietly. 'And don't say it again.'

'Why?'

'And don't ask why either.'

'Why?'

'Peter!'

The menace in my voice was sufficient to shut him up. I turned round to see Plimsoll and Nob (or whatever they were called) giving me foul looks. They clearly thought Peter was merely rehashing what I had told him, but the truth is this was all Peter's work. In fact, I was almost proud of the lad.

The zoo was pretty much as I expected. The animals looked bored out of their weirdly shaped skulls, although the children were delighted. Daisy gurgled extremely noisily, which was very satisfying to hear, although I felt I had wasted her £5 when she even gurgled at a pigeon walking across our path. Peter saw his giraffes, and very happy he was with them too.

The people who were the least happy were Danny and his HouseBand cohorts.

'I'd forgotten how inhuman zoos were,' said Danny.

I nearly corrected him, but thought that discretion was the better part of pedantry. In fact, I had been surprised Danny had chosen somewhere as potentially politically incorrect as a zoo to hold the outing.

'I agree,' said Glib as we looked at a particularly docile python. 'These animals are like political prisoners.'

I couldn't hold it in any longer.

'Political prisoners?' I said. 'How on earth are they like political prisoners?'

'Well,' said Glib (or whatever, names is names), 'they are held here against their will and they have committed no crime.'

'So are household pets,' I said.

'I don't have a household pet,' said Splib.

'But zoos do a lot of vital work in helping to preserve endangered species,' I said. 'Besides, they're also educational. Otherwise we wouldn't be bringing our children here, would we?'

Splurb didn't reply. Somewhere behind me, I heard someone mutter 'fascist' – the normal response of the weirdy-beardy to any opposing point of view. I turned round.

'*Fascist?*' I said. 'How does defending zoos make me a fascist?'

'Whatever man,' said Danny, sensing that trouble was brewing. 'Just chill, all right?'

I despise being told to 'chill'. Nothing makes me more angry. Just as I was about to fly off the handle, Peter asked a most apposite question.

'Daddy,' said Peter, 'what's a fascist?'

'Someone who doesn't tolerate the views of others,' I said loudly.

Clearly my response wasn't for Peter's benefit, as there was no way he understood what 'tolerate' meant.

'What means tolerate?' he asked.

'Er, sort of not listening,' I replied. 'Fascists are people who don't listen to what other people have to say.'

'Are you a fascist, Daddy?'

I heard bearded laughter from behind me.

'No, I'm not,' I said.

'Mummy says that you never listen to her.'

Cue enormous laughter, which I had to join in with. Inwardly, I wanted to feed Peter to the boa constrictor. I decided to keep quiet although by now I was inches away from getting into a fight, something I hadn't done since school. There was something about this group that set me on edge, really riled me.

Danny tried taking on the role of UN mediator to defuse the situation.

'I'm getting the vibe that there's a lot of progesterone about—'

'Testosterone,' I said, unable to control my impulse to correct him.

'Whatever you want,' said Danny.

'Well, it's not a case of whatever,' I said. 'Progesterone is the sex hormone found in women, testosterone is the one in men.'

I nearly added that in any case Danny was probably right. This lot were full of progesterone.

'All right, Simon,' said Danny, 'have it your own way. Tostesterone. Cool. Anyway, there's too much of it around. I think we should go for our picnic a little earlier and chill.'

'Good idea,' I said. 'Where do we get the food from?'

'You mean you haven't brought your own?'

'No,' I said, 'you didn't say.'

'I didn't, but the website did.'

'No it didn't,' I said through gritted teeth. I was right, and I've just checked again to make sure. No mention of bring your own lunch.

'Shway,' said Danny (whatever that meant). 'There'll be plenty to go around. I'm sure the rest of the group will be able to share their food with you and Patrick and Buttercup.'

By now, I was getting immune to Danny's misnomers. I looked round the group, all of whom avoided my gaze. Talk about being a total pariah. Anyway, it didn't matter, because there was bound to be some sort of café.

'Don't worry,' I said. 'I'll pick something up from the restaurant or whatever.'

Danny held up his hands.

'You'll be taking your life in your hands there,' he said.

'I'll chance it,' I said.

Gratifyingly, the caff (for it was no café) served the kind of crap that one wants on such an outing. Burgers, hot dogs, crisps, Coke – all the rubbish that one's body craves after a morning of looking at orang-utan poo and being insulted by a bunch of goatees.

I ordered myself a burger and hot dogs for Peter and Daisy. I laced them all with extravagant amounts of ketchup (apart from mine – I hate ketchup) dispensed from those horrible plastic tomatoes, the ones where you have to unpick dried coagulated ketchup from the nozzles. I added copious mustard and onions to my burger and then we joined the hippies on the picnic mound. For good measure,

I bought Cokes, and the most artifical-looking ice creams I could find.

Danny and his friends went silent when we approached; they had clearly been talking about me. This wasn't paranoia, just the type of intuition one gets after spending time with people who are the complete opposite to you. We sat down with them on the picnic mound, from where we could see animals all around us. I broke off some hot dog for Daisy, who ate it with relish. Peter tucked into his as well, and licked the ketchup off it as though it were nectar. I took a huge bite of my burger, and did my best not to gag – it tasted of old monkey. I thanked God it was smothered in onions.

Our rampant carnivorousness certainly shut up Splib, Belby and who have you. I looked at what they were feeding their children – a predictable New Age mush of mung beans, fungus, dried fruit, ethnic breads, etc., etc. The HouseBands watched with amazement as the children and I feasted on our e-numbers, GM additives and prions. Their children looked positively jealous, so much so that one of them – I think his name was Pewt or something similar – came up and asked if he could swap some of his lentil surprise for some of my burger. I had no desire to eat any of his veggie crap, but I was delighted that one of the little hippie kids was breaking from the alternative mould.

'Of course,' I said triumphantly, and ripped him off a hunk of monkey.

'Stop it!' shouted one of the dads. 'Pewt! No! I said "No!"'

The next bit was like the scene from a film, in which

the hero rushes forward to stop his friend doing something awful. Slow motion, complete with the slowed-down voice of the hero, which sounds like some roar coming from the bottom of the ocean. The father – Tet, I think – ran towards us, his hand held out. Meanwhile, little Pewt was ignoring him, and blithely chewed the meat. I watched his face light up – once more a film moment, the little Dutch boy getting chocolate for the first time from a GI. All Pewt needed to say was 'This good' to complete the scene.

As Pewt chewed, his father grabbed him.

'Spit it out!' he shouted. 'Spit it out!'

Pewt looked up at Tet gormlessly.

'Why?' he asked through his food.

'Because that's poison,' Tet flabbered. 'Come on! Spit it out!'

'No!'

Tet then shoved his hand brutally into Newt's mouth and tried to extract pieces of flesh. Too late! Newt had already swallowed it, anticipating his father's move. Tet was almost in tears, which would have made me laugh had I not been so shocked by the violence of his reaction.

'How dare you feed my son meat!' he shouted at me.

I kept chewing, trying to avoid gagging on it. It was pretty gruesome stuff, but I had to hold my ground (and my stomach).

'He asked me,' I replied. 'I thought today was all about sharing.'

'But not about sharing meat!'

'What's wrong with meat?'

'What's wrong with meat?' shouted Tet, his voice high-pitched and hysterical. 'My son has spent the last five years of his life avoiding any form of contaminant, and now you've gone and ruined it all!'

I couldn't bring myself to apologise. This was ridiculous.

'What do you think we should do, Danny?' Tet asked. 'Stick some fingers down his throat?'

At first I thought he was referring to me, but then I realised it was to his poor, frightened, bewildered and pale son, his pallor no doubt a product of his unhealthy diet.

'You can't do that!' I said, standing up. 'Just leave him alone.'

'Don't you tell me what to do with my son!'

'I will if you abuse him! Trying to make him sick is cruel.'

Mischief got hold of me I'm afraid, and I offered little Pewt the rest of my monkey burger.

'Here,' I said, 'why not finish it?'

Before I could blink, Tet made to strike the poisonous parcel out of my hand. Blinded perhaps by fury and too much facial hair, he missed, and struck my forearm instead. It hurt, not least because he was wearing all manner of absurd Celtic rings and all the usual wanky fingerwear.

I reacted badly to this, very badly, and motivated by anger and a highly juvenile streak, I then attempted to shove the monkey burger into Tet's mouth.

'Why not try some yourself,' I shouted. 'C'mon, get it down!'

Tet tried to stop me, but he couldn't. Some of the burger went in, and he spat it out, all over me. We then engaged in what could only be called a very gay fight, which involved lots of slapping. We must have looked as if we were practising our doggy paddling.

'Hey, guys!' shouted Danny. 'Break it up! Today is about harmony and peace!'

I felt some not particularly strong hands pull me away.

'Chill,' I kept hearing. 'Chill, shway, man, shway.'

'I would chill,' I snapped, 'if you stopped telling me to.'

'I think it's perhaps best if you left us,' said Danny.

'You're damn right,' I said, looking down at my shirt which was missing three buttons.

'I just don't think you're appropriate material for our group,' Danny continued. 'We're looking for a more cohesive dynamic.'

Cohesive dynamic?

I eyed Danny suspiciously. There was a pause until realisation finally dawned.

'Did you use to be a management consultant?' I asked him incredulously.

Danny looked flustered. Gone was the hippy swagger.

'Um, not really, no,' he mumbled unconvincingly. Of course he had been, the hypocrite.

'Who did you work for?' I asked, beyond pleased to have found someone who seemed to share my life – even someone as annoying as Danny.

By now, the group, who were pretty agog to begin with, were even more agog. Very very agog. Danny didn't reply.

'Come on,' I said, 'spit it out. Debentine? Massey Lowe? GTR?'

'Well,' said Danny, 'if you must know, it was GTR. But only for a couple of years!'

'Well I never,' I said, attempting to do up my shirt. 'I was at MWS.'

'MWS? Did you know, um, Clive up in the Birmingham office?'

I could tell Danny was having a tough time saying words like 'Clive' and 'office'. The fact that he knew Clive of all people was a real surprise.

'Sure,' I said. 'I know Clive. Haven't seen him in ages. How do you know him?'

'We were at school together.'

'Freshams? Ha! You – at Freshams? I don't believe it!'

'Yeah, well, I didn't have much choice back then.'

'When did you last see Clive anyway?'

'Last week,' said Danny. 'In fact, it's rather bad news. He's just been given the push.'

That brought me up short. 'Really, why?' I asked. Danny just shook his head and shrugged, then turned back to his group of househusbands.

Later, in the car on the way back home, I had to stop to be violently sick. I don't know whether it was the monkey burger or reawakened thoughts about work. I felt a bit better afterwards, but not much.

Sunday 19 June

I spoke to Clive this evening. Poor bloke. He's absolutely gutted and still in a state of shock about being booted out.

'They just summoned me to London,' he told me, 'and I was marched in to see David, who said I was being made redundant on the grounds of "cultural incompatibility", whatever that means.'

'Nothing else?' I asked.

'Nothing. They've given me two years though, which I assume to be nothing less than hush money.'

Two years. Wow. That was a lot. Well over £120,000 by my reckoning.

'Hush about what?'

'About everything that's been going on.'

'What's been going on?'

'Lots of rumours mostly,' he replied, 'but obviously it's hard to keep tabs on the London office from Birmingham.'

'What sort of rumours?'

'Rumours about a management buyout. The one I'd heard was that Chris and David are deliberately running the company down to make it cheaper for them to buy. There's no proof to it, but it wouldn't surprise me.'

Wow. This was huge. Part of me wanted to tell Clive what I knew, but I thought it best to err (uncharacteristically) on the side of caution, especially as I only knew one thing. Well, one word, really. Dudley. Was Dudley Chris and David's codeword for running the company down? I badly wanted to say something to Clive, but if he blurted out that I had told him something, and if Chris and Simon found out, they'd sue me. I've absolutely no doubt about that. And being sued, just when life is finally settling down, is the last thing I want.

Before we hung up, Clive told me that Danny's real name

is Daniel Alexander Pettigrew-Wolfson, and that his father is in fact a baronet! Said that Danny was a complete berk, and didn't have what it took to be a management consultant. I replied that on the face of it, neither Clive nor I seemed to have what it took which went down like a bag of cold sick.

We ended the phone call by agreeing to keep in touch, and if there was any news regarding the company that we'd share it. One thing we already share is a desire for revenge although mine has waned over the past few months, but this management buyout has made me furious all over again. I'm so out of the loop now, there's sod all I can do about it. I'll just have to wait and see. So sodding frustrating.

Nice weekend, though. Everybody v happy. It's so nice that all feels normal and settled again. I feel wretched that the equilibrium has only been reached thanks to a) the presence of Lydia and b) the absence of Nick. Still, there it is. Daisy has been doing some excellent standing, and can even walk about two steps if you hold her hands. Huge smiles and giggles as she does so – lovely to watch.

Monday 20 June

More golf today. I could get used to this life. One thing has occurred to me, and this is a worry, is that Sally is taking some holiday in the middle two weeks of July. I shall just have to pay Lydia to stay at the B&B. I don't suppose she'll mind.

Sally and I discussed options for where to go. We haven't

booked anything, because we didn't know how we were going to be doing financially. I've looked on the net, and flights are all ruinously expensive. I've said we could just go down to Cornwall or Devon, but Sally says that is just so dull. She was thinking South of France, but I can't be bothered. Flight + car hire + hotel/cottage = real hassle and far too many £s. Or s rather.

Wednesday 22 June

Yet another near Lydia miss this afternoon. God it was close. Too close. Yet again, the day had gone swimmingly. Lydia had arrived bang on time, as usual, and had cooked a huge bowl of Gruboziarnisty Owies which the children now adore. What's more, Peter, the little linguistic genius, is able to say Gruboziarnisty Owies perfectly. Lydia has also taught him a little bit of Polish as well, and he can now say 'Hello' and 'thank you' as fluently as any native. Lydia says his accent is still very British, but she will work on it.

The miss came when Sally was kissing the children good night. She had come back a little early, which was great, and had read them their bedtime stories – *Postman Pat* for Peter, *That's Not My Fairy* for Daisy. It was sweet watching her read to the children, as she only usually manages to do so at the weekends, and I even took a quick picture of them both sitting on her lap.

She then tucked Daisy into bed, or rather cot, and did the same to Peter. She kissed him on the cheek, and then said 'night night'. Now, Peter normally replies with a 'night

night' as well, and sometimes embellishes it with a 'mind the bed bugs don't bite', but this evening, '*Dobry wieczór późny, Matka.*'

Sally startled backwards.

'What was that, Peter?' she asked, smiling.

Peter let out a little laugh.

'*Dobry wieczór późny, Matka,*' he repeated.

It took me a few more nanoseconds to realise what was happening. Peter was saying good night in Polish. Fuck, all I could think was, fuck. This was the end of Lydia teaching him Polish, or even worse, the end of Lydia. By the end of the week, Sally would have her deported back to Poznan for being a spy or something.

Sally turned to me.

'What did he say?'

I thought it best to be as nearly honest as possible. My life seems to revolve around near-truths these days.

'It's Polish!' I said, a little too high-pitched.

'Polish?' said Sally. 'Why's he speaking Polish?'

'I thought you'd be impressed!' I said, stalling pathetically, and not wishing to use my normal lying tic by repeating Sally's question.

'I am,' she said, 'but where did he learn it from?'

I saw Peter opening his mouth, about to say 'Lydia', despite the countless bribes that have found their way into his outstretched hand over the past weeks.

'The television,' I almost shouted out. 'You know, CBeebies.'

'*CBeebies?*'

'CBeebies? No maybe not, CBBC I think it was, you know the one for older children.'

'CBBC is teaching children to speak Polish?'

I nodded unconvincingly. Peter tried opening his mouth again, but I rushed over and kissed him good night.

'You've been a very good boy today,' I said. 'And well done with that Polish. You're a very clever boy. Tomorrow I shall get you a new aeroplane.'

'Oh,' he went excitedly, 'a Lancaster bomber?'

'Yes,' I said, saying anything to get the subject off Slavic languages.

I ushered a slightly bewildered Sally out of the room.

'Polish?' she kept asking, 'Polish?'

'That's right,' I said, almost pushing her downstairs. 'They teach lots of languages on CBBC. And a very good thing too.'

'I thought you'd be the last to think that,' she said, 'with your Little Englander ways.'

'I resent that,' I said. 'I'm keen to embrace diversity, and if Peter can learn a few words of Polish and Bengali or whatever it is, then so much the better in my view.'

'You sound like an MP.'

I laughed and opened the fridge, willing it to swallow me up. I would have happily spent the rest of the night curled up with the selection of stale cheeses we never seem to throw away. Instead, I pulled out a half-open bottle of rosé and poured us a couple of glasses.

'In fact,' I said, 'I've even learned a bit of Polish myself.'

'Oh yes?'

I looked at Sally straight in the eyes.

'*Ja miłość ty*,' I said.

'What does that mean?'

'I love you.'

Sally's face creased into her loveliest smile. We had a long hug and a protracted kiss, from which she suddenly broke off.

'They did the Polish for "I love you" on CBBC?'

Darn. I cursed myself for gilding my lily of lies.

'Er, yes, they did. It was a little scene in which people were saying "I love you" in lots of languages.'

'And "good night" in lots of languages?'

'No,' I said firmly. 'Today was a kind of special Polish day. Hence Peter knowing his good night, Mummy.'

'I'm just so surprised.'

'Well, there are a lot of Poles around these days.'

'I know. What time was this on anyway?'

'About 5.30. Just after they'd finished their supper.'

Sally took a swig of wine and sat down at the breakfast bar and flicked through the paper. We spent the next few minutes in companionable silence while I started chopping the ingredients for the stir fry.

'*Bob the Builder*,' said Sally out of nowhere.

'Who?'

'*Bob the Builder*,' she said, holding up the TV-listings page.

'And?'

'Well, it says that *Bob the Builder* was on at 5.30. Nothing about Polish for Kids or whatever.'

My heart thumped.

'It was part of *Bob the Builder*. The plot was all about Bob being undercut by a team of dastardly Polish builders, but in the end they became friends and they taught Bob some Polish.'

Sally looked at me, and I looked back. Her look was

suspicious, but not bad-tempered. A comedy narrowing of eyes.

'I look forward to seeing the next one,' she said. She was clearly as unconvinced as anyone would be, but she was struggling to establish in her head what the truth might be.

'Yes, you should. Bob is very educational these days. Or should I say Bob the Bildski.'

'Builder?'

'God knows,' I said. 'I didn't watch all of it. What do you think I do? Watch TV all day?'

Sally gave me another hug and a kiss.

'No,' she said. 'Of course not. In fact, I'm very proud of you. Everything is looking immaculate. You seem to have settled into the swing nicely, and I can't deny that I'm a little jealous. You're starting to make it look far too easy!'

'Ah well, the good old Holden Childcare Programme. Reaping its rewards.'

I felt like a skunk, but at least I was a skunk that had had a narrow (and undeserved) escape. This business with Lydia is going to end badly, I know it. A sensible man would get rid of her now, while the going was still almost good. But I'm not a sensible man. I'm a lazy man who likes to try to wing it.

Pretty much a normal man then.

Friday 24 June

Emily came round today, the dangerous little lust bucket. She asked whether we were free for supper next Friday. I said 'yes' immediately, keenly, because I'm desperate for a social life, frankly. She then asked whether we'd had the chance to use the TrèsRisqué items I'd bought. I sort of spluttered a reply.

'Er, well, you know, perhaps, maybe, not all of them, you know . . .' etc., etc. My normal meaningless bluster.

'Because it would be awful if they just sat in a bag at the bottom of a cupboard,' she said, appallingly knowingly.

'Quite,' I replied. 'Anyway. This supper. Anything you'd like us to bring? Sally makes a great apple crumble.'

'Surely it's the househusband's job to whip something up?'

'Women can cook as well, you know.'

Emily laughed. 'I certainly can't. Jim hates my cooking. He's a real kitchen Nazi.'

'Same here!' I said. 'Although it's not Sally's cooking I can't stand, it's Sally cooking.'

Emily frowned in incomprehension.

'I don't mind eating what she cooks,' I said, 'it's just that I can't stand watching her do it. She's a little absent-minded, and often leaves things on or in for too long. More often than not, garlic and onions get burned rather than sweated, once-tender pork turns stringy—'

'Get you,' said Emily. 'Sweating, indeed! You sound even more of a Nazi than Jim. I didn't think that was possible.'

'Well, I don't deny it. I'm the Gruppenführer of the kitchen.'

'Well, Guddenfurger—' said Emily.

'*Gruppenführer*,' I said.

'Sorry, I'm not good on my Nazis,' she said. 'Anyway, Gruddenführer, why not bring round a starter?'

'All right,' I said. 'Have you anything in mind?'

'No, you choose. Something light as we'll be having lamb for the main course probably.'

'No problem.'

Emily left a few minutes later after asking me how things were going with Lydia. Said they were going brilliantly. Just as she left, I pleaded with her not to mention my attendance at the TrèsRisqué party, or indeed rifling through her pants, and, whatever she did, NOT to mention Lydia. She chuckled, winked, and said that my secrets would always be close to her chest. Crassly flirtatious, but helps the day go by.

Saturday 25 June

'Sam!'

I knew I was in trouble just from the tone of Sally's voice.

'*Sam!*' she shouted again, from the study.

It wasn't a bossy shout, but rather a 'you'd better sort this out quickly' shout. I assumed some sort of computer balls-up, which, in a sense, it turned out to be.

I went into the study to see a shocked Sally looking up at me from the computer.

'Sam,' she said, pointing at the screen, 'what's all this?'

'What's all what?' I asked, craning forward.

'This!'

She had the web browser open, and was running her finger down the items in the history window. It was not a pretty sight. Among the sites visited were 'XXX Hot Lesbian Love', 'Fisting Times', 'Rubber Nuns', 'Anal Monsters',

'Rug Munchers', 'Finger Lickin' Lesbians', 'Fudge Factory' and 'Lindi Lovetruck's Lezzie Lust'. All in all, heaps of fun, but certainly not heaps of fun looked at by me. Lydia, it had to be Lydia. I was fucked, frankly, or perhaps even fisted. Did I claim the porn was mine in order to cover Lydia, or did I deny the porn and admit Lydia? Talk about a rock and a hard place. Or something like that. How many other men have to make these decisions? Not many, I'll warrant. The other thing that occurred to me as I worked out what to say was the fact that Lydia seemed to go for predominantly lesbian websites, something I would have found somewhat exciting had Lydia not looked like the Gruffalo.

I decided the best tactic was to be brazen about it. Nothing wrong with porn, etc. I needed Lydia more than my reputation. Plenty of my friends look at porn, and some of their wives as well (maybe all of their wives), so perhaps it was best to just 'confess'.

'Yup,' I said. 'You've got me bang to rights.'

Sally was speechless.

'I'm sorry,' I continued. 'I wouldn't worry about it, it's just porn.'

'But it's so seedy. I thought porn was the type of thing you looked at when you were a teenager.'

Sally clicked on Fisting Times. Not good. Up popped a lurid pink and yellow website of gynaecological excess. XXX Hot Lesbian Love would have been fine (I'm guessing) but not Fisting Times.

'But, Sam,' said Sally, visibly upset, 'this is just *foul*. These women are in pain. Look.'

'They're not in pain,' I said. 'They're just acting.'

'But she's got a whole arm . . .'

'Computer trickery, that's all.'

Sally closed the window and opened up Rubber Nuns which actually looked quite good. Lydia clearly has some sort of taste. I'm with Sally on the fisting, but this was OK – sexy and kinky rather than just plain sordid.

'Nuns, Sam?'

I sort of tossed my head from side to side, working out what to say, and ended up just shrugging my shoulders.

'So is this what you want to do? Dress me as a rubber nun and then fist me?'

It had to be admitted that the first part of this little scenario wasn't entirely unappealing, but I thought it best not to push my luck. (What luck?)

'Um . . . not exactly.'

Sally looked back at the computer and clicked on a few links, bringing up page after page of filth. Lydia's filth. Not my filth.

'And do you . . . you know . . .'

'What?' I asked gormlessly.

'You know!'

Still gormless.

'What?'

'Wank, Sam!'

'Oh! Wank! I see what you mean. No, no, I don't wank in front of them.'

'So you just look at them?'

'That's right.'

I knew how unlikely this sounded. So did Sally.

'That's even stranger,' she said. 'I'd have thought the whole point of these sites was so tragic men could have a wank.'

'Well, aha, you see,' I began, a tone of pathetic triumphalism in my voice, 'I'm not one of those tragic men who wanks in front of these sites. Not me. Too sad. I just enjoy looking at them. Come on, what red-blooded male wouldn't enjoy looking at some porn once in a while?'

'What, even Anal Monsters?'

I peered at the screen. Images of enormously fat women appeared, all of whom were apparently treating the sewer of the body as a playground.

'I sort of went there by mistake.'

Sally looked at the history window.

'I see you had to look through at least forty pages of Anal Monsters before you realised your mistake.'

'I was sort of curious.'

I began to feel angry. Angry with Lydia. Angry with myself for getting into this situation. And a bit angry with Sally for being ever so slightly censorious. Shit, Ed just tells his wife he looks at porn, and that's that. Started off day one of their relationship by saying he loved porn, and she'd just have to accept it, which she has apparently.

'Look, sweetheart,' I said, 'there's nothing that bizarre about looking at porn. I mean I was thinking that perhaps we should look at it together . . .'

'What? Settle down for a nice evening in front of Fudge Factory?'

'Well, not Fudge Factory, but something a little more tasteful.'

'Lindi Lovetruck's Lezzie Lust?'

I hummed and hahed.

'Mmm, maybe not that either, but I'm sure there's plenty of porn that's couples friendly.'

'But you just haven't found it yet?'

'We can always have a look if you want.'

I studied Sally's face, hoping for a sign of assent. Perhaps a porn-hungry libidinous devil lurked inside her, ready to spend hours surfing the web for filthy images of beautiful people doing ugly things.

'No thanks,' she said. 'I think I'll keep porn as your department, along with the whatever it's called.'

'What's what called?'

'The dildo you had in the kitchen. The Lusty Woman Arouser.'

'Oh, the Lusty Girl Pleasurer (Plus Lusty Girl's Anal Love Bulb).'

'How could I forget?'

I began to get a bit more annoyed.

'If you don't mind me saying, I think you're being a bit of a prude.'

'Prude?' said Sally, affronted.

'Yes.'

'Because I don't want to sit and look at Fudge Factory with a piece of industrial-sized rubber tubing up my bottom?'

'You could have put it more elegantly than that.'

'Well, it's not a very elegant thing, is it, Sam?'

'I suppose not. But then sex isn't exactly elegant, is it?'

'Yes, but there's no reason to introduce garish bits of equipment.'

I thought of the TrèsRisqué collection lying unloved at the bottom of the cupboard. The chances of it being dipped into were looking remote.

Sally continued, 'Besides, I thought we were doing just fine with the equipment we were born with.'

'We are,' I said, which was the truth. After all, I don't look at porn. At least not very much. And whenever I do, I erase the history in the browser. I'm not a porn junkie (unlike Ed), and although like most married people I wish we could have more sex, I'm always happy with it when we have it. The worst thing about all this was that I was being forced to defend a position that wasn't even mine. And such a dirty position as well. Like Sally, I have no interest in seeing fat German men shove their limbs up fat German women. If only Lydia had been looking at somewhat tamer stuff.

Sunday 26 June

Today has been a little strained. Sally has kept asking me questions about my supposed pornography habit. How often do I look at it? Do I think I should see a psychiatrist about it? What else did I like looking at besides Fudge Factory and Fisting Times? Did I not think there was something wrong with me? Do your friends look at porn? And on it went, sometimes within earshot of the children. I tried in vain to explain that it was OK to look at porn, so long as you didn't do it too much, but Sally said that I clearly did do it too much, and that what I was looking at went way beyond the bounds of normal healthy sexual activity. I just gave up in the end, and went to my study. Sally came into the room repeatedly, no doubt checking that the only thing I had in my hand was my mouse.

Grrr. I'm going to murder Lydia tomorrow.

Monday 27 June

I confronted Lydia after she had scraped the pan free of Gruboziarnisty Owies, a task that normally takes her some ten to fifteen minutes. God knows what that stuff is doing to the children's stomachs, but they seem to be thriving on it. I just hope it doesn't make their skin as greasy and blotchy as Lydia's.

'Ah, Lydia,' I said, 'there's something delicate I need to talk to you about.'

'Delicate?'

'You know, awkward.'

'Auk word?'

'No, awkward. Um, difficult. Something difficult to discuss.'

Lydia's face fell.

'You know what I'm going to say, don't you?'

'You not want me no longer?'

'No!' I said. 'Nothing like that.'

'What is it please?'

'It's about the computer.'

'The computer?'

'Yes, something that was on it.'

'But I cleared it up.'

'Um, I don't think you really did.'

Christ, I thought, was there more?

'But I was very careful and used a damp cloth and wiped everything off.'

I frowned. Revolting images flooded through my mind. Lydia and Fudge Factory and a damp cloth. This was seriously detumescent stuff.

'I'm sorry,' I said. 'I don't understand.'

'The coffee,' she said. 'I spilled the Nescafé on to the keyboard, but perhaps I did not do good job cleaning.'

'What coffee?' I asked. 'I didn't see any coffee.'

'It is all right then?'

'No, I mean, yes. There's no coffee, but it's what's on the computer that I need to talk about.'

She said nothing.

'Some of the websites,' I said.

Again, nothing.

'I don't think they are, um, very suitable to be looked at in a family environment.'

Lydia started looking sheepish. Although she probably couldn't understand my every word, I'm sure that something was getting through.

'I mean, you can look at what you like somewhere else,' I continued. 'It's a free country. It's just that I don't want you to look at such material on my computer. I'm afraid Sally thinks that it is me who has been looking at it.'

Lydia was staring down at the floor. Her big Polish face was ready to burst into tears.

'Look,' I said, 'there's nothing to be upset about. Looking at this stuff is perfectly normal . . .' (Except perhaps for Fudge Factory.) '. . . but just not here, all right? It doesn't alter my opinion of you, and I want you to stay. The children love having you and you are very good with them.'

'I am very apologies, Sam,' she said, her bottom lip blubbering.

'That's all right,' I said. 'Just no more, OK?'

'I promise.'

'Good.'

'I am ashamed. The things I look at, they are not good.'

'Well . . .'

'No! They are wrong. It's just that it is not possible to help me.'

I began to feel sorry for her.

'Honestly, Lydia, don't worry. It's just porn. Everybody looks at it.'

'Do you look at porn?'

'I have done in the past.'

'What porn do you like? Pretty girls?'

I felt somewhat uncomfortable discussing my porndilections with Lydia.

'Of course,' I said. 'Anyway, that's not the point. Fact is, Peter is getting old enough to work the TV, and it'll be the computer before you can say "mouse".'

Lydia looked frantically around the floor.

'Say 'mouse'? Where is mouse? Sure not a rat? We have rats in Poland!'

'There is no mouse. It's just an expression. Anyway, no more porn, right?'

'I understand. No more porn. It will be good for me, I think.'

And for me too.

This afternoon, I took Daisy and Peter for a walk, and we looked at the fish in the river, the bees feeding on the flowers, and the butterflies lazily wafting around. Idyllic. Why we're not in London. Felt wholesome, innocent, decent, a far cry from all the nonsense of the past few days. We got back to find that Lydia had baked an enormous cake by way of an apology. We stuffed our faces, although I suspect she had used cement mix instead of flour as it weighed a ton. Still, as with all Lydia's cooking, the children enjoyed it, and by the end of the afternoon I felt very happy families. A shame that Sally wasn't around to share it. Cunningly, I threw the cake into the wheelie bin before she got back. There's NO WAY she'd believe I'd make a cake. Real men don't bake. All the blokes I know who cook (and these days that's most of them) can just about do anything in the kitchen apart from make things like apple crumble and cakes. There's something a little girly about being into patisserie, darling.

Wednesday 29 June

We still haven't worked out where we're going on holiday. Sally suggested I might like to take in some strip shows in Thailand while she took the children somewhere more salubrious. She was joking, I think.

Saturday 2 July

All my fears about Emily have come to fruition. Our evening with her and Jim was like nothing else. In fact, Sally and

I are still in shock. We don't know whether we dare set eyes on either of them again. The only small mercy is that, thank God, it's someone else in the doghouse for a change.

The evening had started off conventionally enough, and my starter (a kind of designer, revamped, reworked, prawn cocktail I had thought up for the new millennium – yes, quite wanky) had gone down well. Jim was just as I had expected – solid, oozed good-bloke, not too bright, but then not too thick either. Nice to have around. Maybe even good for a pint at some stage, I thought initially.

The Emily/Sally axis was less promising; I could tell Sally found Emily perhaps a little too ditsy and arm-touchy. However, as it was only I who could tell, it didn't really matter. Besides, both Sally and I have found ourselves having to become far less socially fussy since we moved out of London, and we are more forgiving than we were. In London, you can just write off people who rank at 80 per cent likeability, whereas out here you have to be content with about 40 per cent. Harsh but true.

Emily was also dressed more tartily than Sally. In fact, she was dressed how I would like Sally to dress. Short black skirt, sheer black tights, classy-looking suede high heels, a cream rollneck top and some understated jewellery. Sally didn't look dowdy, but her clothes looked a bit worky by comparison. Black trousers which had been in the wash fifteen too many times, an equally tired light blue top, which was at least tight. Heels fine as well, but all in all, and this feels treacherous, I thought Emily was better turned out. Jim and I wore Docksiders and jeans. Natch.

As the evening wore on, we put away a fair amount of

booze. It was good to see that Jim just poured away merrily, and there was no need to ask for one's glass to be topped up. We gossiped about locals, how nice it was not to be in London (the more time we chat about that subject, the more I feel we may be in denial), what it was like me being a househusband. Everybody really enjoyed the story of my day out at the zoo, even Sally, who had heard it eight times.

It was only after dinner that things took a turn for the bizarre/worse/positively outrageous. We sat down in the living room, a room I still associated with sex toys, and Emily put some music on the hi-fi. True to generational form, it was a greatest hits album from the 1980s. On came 'Temptation' by Heaven 17, and Emily started dancing while Sally, Jim and I sat with glazed, slightly pissed looks on our faces.

At first, Emily's dancing was just the normal girl-at-wedding-type stuff, bit of a wiggle but nothing too co-ordinated or flash. Then, to some song by A-ha, Emily's dancing became positively hooker-like. She swayed. She looked us each in the eye provocatively. She ran her hands slowly up and down her thighs. I think she may have even caressed her breasts. I looked at Jim, but he was just sitting there with a faintly dirty leer on his face. Sally and I stole a glance at each other, and smiled nervously.

Emily then held her hand out to me.

'C'mon, Sam, why don't you have a dance?'

'Who me?'

'Yes, up you get. Come on!'

I briefly caught Sally's eye. I could tell that she was not

happy with this – what wife would be, frankly? – but I knew that she knew that it would have been plain rude of me to just refuse. So, I did the gentlemanly thing and got up.

Like many Englishmen, I am an absurdly bad dancer. I lack the necessary bone or muscle that Frenchmen and Italians are born with enabling them to bend somewhere in the middle. I can move my hips backwards and forwards, but I can barely move them from side to side, and neither can I rotate them. They perform what is biologically required of them, but nothing more. My hips, then, are the basic unmodified version, bottom of the range hips. Hips 1.0.

I stood nearish to Emily and started sort of transferring my weight from one foot to the other, an activity that could barely be described as dancing. Unfortunately, Emily was having none of it.

'C'mon you fuddy-duddy,' she said. 'You can do better than that! That's worse than my father and he's seventy-two!'

Emily then grabbed me around the waist and pulled me towards her. She proceeded to jiggle, wiggle, bump, grind, gyrate and generally dance in the most provocative way possible. Anybody would have thought there was no one else in the room, and that neither Emily nor I were married. I did my best to accompany her, but not in a way that would have made her feel I was reciprocating her advances. Once in a while, I caught Sally's disbelieving wide eyes over Emily's shoulder, and all I could do was to raise my own skyward. Jim, meanwhile, was just looking on with that same slightly sordid leer.

It was not until Emily's next words that we realised in what deep trouble we found ourselves.

'Your husband's very good-looking, Sally,' she said, looking straight at me.

I don't think I've ever been in a situation in which I couldn't believe my ears, so this was a first for me. There was no doubt what we had stumbled into: a wife-swapping evening, and it was an evening I wanted to get the hell out of. I did my best Hugh Grant 'Osh-gosh-you-can't-really-mean-me' splutter, letting my head sink to my chest in order to create what I hoped to be an enormously un-attractive double chin.

It didn't work. Emily kept dancing with me as though she were a Brazilian hooker. At one point, I swear she waggled her bum towards me in the way that lapdancers do. Apparently. She must have been absolutely smashed, but she seemed pretty compos mentis.

'He's a very handsome man,' said Emily, this time addressing Sally.

'Thank you,' said Sally weakly, nervously. 'Well, Jim is very handsome too.'

AAAAAAGH! Wrong thing to say, Mrs Holden! Very, very wrong! So unspeakably wrong. Within a nanosecond of the words leaving her mouth, Sally knew she had fouled up royally. I knew she was saying it out of politeness, but for Emily it was just what she wanted to hear.

'I'm glad you think so,' said Emily, winking.

Sally's smile could not have been more frozen. I could almost hear her cursing herself.

'Why don't you dance with Jim?' said Emily. (In fact, it was more of a command than a question.)

'C'mon, Jim, get up!' said Emily.

Soon, much to Sally's evident discomfort, she and Jim were sashaying around the living room to 'Careless Whisper'. This was getting REALLY bad. It was one thing to have Emily dancing with me, but quite another watching my wife being serenaded by a drunk neighbour. It crossed my mind that I should break off the dancing, but I was still feeling English and polite.

I began to curse George Michael as the song went on and on. I've just looked up how long it is – 5.03 minutes – but it seemed eighteen times as long. The words suddenly seemed to be appallingly appropriate, especially all that stuff about losing crowds and being stuck in this dance for all time. Or something like that. Boy did it feel like that.

Towards the end of the song, Emily left no doubt that she wanted some hot suburban wife-swapping action. She laid her head on my shoulder, and pressed her body tightly against mine – ALL her body tightly against mine. The worst thing about it was the unstoppable feeling of desire my wretched sodding hormones were engendering. While my body braced itself for action, my head and heart were violently screaming to run out of the door with Sally. Knowing what was stirring down there, I tried to move my groin away from Emily, but she continued to press against me which made the situation even worse. Much worse. She looked up at me with a proud little smirk and raised her eyebrows coquettishly, as if to say 'I like that'. If I'd had a knife in my hands, I swear that I would have chopped the wretched thing off. All I could hope was that Sally wasn't having a similar effect on Jim.

The music ended and Emily released me from her

clutches. At first I thought we were finally free, that perhaps my paranoia had made me imagine the whole thing, and that I was being unduly square about what had merely been a slightly drunken dance. I glanced at Sally, who was being released by Jim. Things were looking better.

'Let's do something really outrageous,' said Emily.

'What?' I asked.

'Let's do something bad,' she continued. 'Why don't we take our tops off and then carry on dancing?'

Oh fuck, I thought. Now what? Now what? The worst thing was that to refuse would make us look like prudes. No one wants to be thought of as a prude, but neither did I want to watch Sally having sex with Jim, and nor did I want to cheat on Sally with Emily, no matter how revoltingly dirty she would be. (I bet *she* looks at porn.) Another reason of course is that my torso is utterly unshowoffable. These days, I'd rather drop my pants than take off my shirt.

Up till that moment, wife-swapping was one of those things that Sally and I had often joked about with friends, especially with Nigel and Clare. (That now takes on a massive retrospective significance.) Car-key games, *The Ice Storm*, 1970s pool parties – all these were surely the stuff of myth. I suppose we joked about it because it was a kind of acceptable way of suggesting infidelity and not acting upon it. After all, if you've been married for quite a few years – and we and most of our friends have been – then of course the dark, nasty, immoral part of your psyche considers what it would be like to shag someone else. And that someone else is usually one of your wife's friends. And then the darker, nastier, amoral part of you fantasises about – better still! – your wife getting it on with one of her female friends. (Are there any men in the world who actually find lesbianism repellent?) And of course, the next stage is to imagine yourself having a threesome with them. Worse still, not one day goes by without you thinking of this and, although your rational side knows it will never happen, your purely sexual side regards it as a tragedy that you will die in a nursing home of some hideous cancer at the age of eighty-three having never had the pleasure. Neither do you regard the idea of your wife having sex with a woman as infidelity, which seems to suggest that male sexual jealousy emanates not from the act itself but from the fact that another man is trampling on your territory. Other girls aren't a threat. Other men most certainly are.

Naturally, you don't say all this stuff in front of your wife, because she would think you were the nasty, amoral, revolting little pervert you, in fact, really are. Besides, Sally has about as much interest in lesbian sex as I do in Man Love, so I know it's never going to happen. So, even if Jim hadn't been there, I knew there was 100 per cent no way that I would be enjoying a Sally-Emily sarnie.

Back to Emily's kind invitation that we take our tops off. Even as she was saying it, she was hitching up her top, exposing a respectably flattish stomach. I had to take the lead, because Sally was now approaching catatonia. Jim was unbuttoning his shirt, revealing a black coir mat of chest hair.

'I really think we ought to be off,' I said. 'Babysitter and all that.'

I knew how feeble this sounded, and predictably Emily was having none of it.

'C'mon you guys! It's just a bit of fun.'

It probably would have been fun if Jim weren't around and Sally was into lesbianism, but we were rapidly heading for a situation that was more uncomfortable than being tortured with a Lusty Girl Pleasurer (complete with Anal Love Bulb).

'No, Emily,' I said firmly. 'It's just not us. I'm sorry. Call us terribly square, but we're very happy with each other.'

By now, Emily had her top off, and hairy Jim was standing in only his trousers, a convict gorilla on the run. Sally held my arm tightly. It was as if we were being mugged, which in a way we were. My fear was that Emily might play the blackmail card. She would bring up my cleaning Daisy's bottom with her knickers, and reveal my presence at the TrèsRisqué party. If she did that, then I would . . . well, I didn't know what I would do.

As it was, Emily knew the game was over.

'All right,' she said, looking somewhat hypocritically put out, 'have it your own way. Enjoy the next forty years with just each other.'

'We will,' said Sally. 'Look, we're not offended or anything, it's just not our thing. I know it happens a lot, but sorry, not us!'

Sally and Jim replaced their tops. There was bad temper in the air, a temper which I tried to dispel. God knows why I felt beholden to do so.

'I have to say, Emily, that we're very flattered that you asked us,' I said.

I felt Sally's grip on me tighten, fearful I was going to say something craven and dumb.

'Let's go,' she said.

'OK,' I replied. 'Look, um, it's been a really lovely evening. The lamb was delicious by the way.'

Emily ignored me as she started to tidy up the glasses and ashtrays. She was obviously embarrassed she had chosen the wrong targets for her ménage à quatre.

'Thanks,' she said sarcastically. 'The prawn cocktail was very . . . tasty.'

'Good,' I said. 'I'll pick up the plates in the morning.'

'Fine.'

'Good night, then.'

We gave each other pecks on the cheeks because we are English. It was hard to imagine that just a few minutes before Emily had been frotting me. Jim saw us to the door, enquiring in host mode whether we had everything, coats, etc., lovely evening and all that.

Sally and I didn't talk about it until we heard the babysitter's car drive off. I poured myself a large Calvados, and an Amaretto for Sally. Together, we collapsed on to the sofa bed and said, simultaneously, 'Fuck me.'

So we did.

Best we'd had in weeks. Months perhaps.

Sunday 3 July

Have spent the day in shock. We kept asking each other whether what we thought had happened had actually happened, and we agreed that it had. I don't know how we're going to look Emily and Jim in the eye again. Perhaps we'll have to move house. So distracted were we, that even Peter asked us whether we were all right.

'Why do you ask?'

'Because you are very quiet.'

'Am I?'

'And if you are very quiet, then you are ill.'

'Don't worry, Peter, I'm not ill.'

I had to hug him. Sally and I went 'aah'. It's impossible not to be too sentimental with children.

We've decided on a holiday plan. We're going to Brittany (not Bangkok, unsurprisingly). Sally's godmother is lending us her house there for a knockdown rate. Thank God it's so cheap, as the ferry is sodding expensive. Nearly £600! Still, it's cheaper than flying and hiring a car, and this way I'll be able to bring back all sorts of goodies such as wine, mustard and jam. I always buy lots and lots of these last two, as the pots are designed to be used as glasses when they're empty. I can't think of one English jam or mustard manufacturer who does this. Why the hell not, frankly? I'm not Mr Green, but it does seem a waste. Anyway, I'm old enough to remember when one got money back on bottles. Why did that go away? It's nuts.

Monday 4 July

Neither of us knows why, but the close encounter with Emily and Nick seems to have caused an enormous boost in our sex life. One of the TrèsRisqué items made it out last night, but not even this diary is going to find out which one. Delighted that Sally enjoyed it as much as me. (And no, it was not the Lusty Girl Pleasurer. I can't see that ever making an appearance. I might as well throw it away. Or hawk it at a car-boot sale.) My suspicion is that neither of us wants to feel a prude, so having vast amounts of reasonably energetic sex seems to have dispelled that fear. In a way, many thanks to Emily and Jim.

Tuesday 5 July

Saw a jodhpur-clad Emily walking ahead of me on the way back from dropping Peter off at playgroup. I held back, hoping not to engage her in conversation, but some sixth sense made her turn round. I almost hid behind a bin, but thought better of it as she would have certainly seen me. She waited for me to approach which was maddening, as I expected her to turn on her heel in a huff.

'Hello, Mr Holden,' she said in her normal flirtatious manner. She was clutching a riding crop, which added the flavour of dominatrix (whatever that tastes like). It wouldn't have surprised me if she had said, 'On your knees, worm.'

'Hi there,' I said breezily. 'Thanks for the very, um, enjoyable evening the other, um, night.'

'Not at all,' she said. 'I know *you* enjoyed yourself.'

'How do you mean?' I asked gormlessly.

Emily stole a quick glance at my groin. Oh God, I thought. The woman was insufferable.

'Quite,' I said. 'Anyway, we must have you round at some point.'

'Would love to,' she said.

'Perhaps when we're back from holiday.'

'Great.'

A brief and extremely pornographic image of Sally and Emily crossed one of the darker corners of my brain. I dispelled it. Sometimes it is a real curse to be a man. I know our sex drive is useful, but does it have to be quite so unruly? I felt that I should mention something about what had happened, but I was just too English. Instead, I said, 'I must do you my Moroccan chicken dish.'

I felt like such a bloody prude. In fact, I felt like a dull little hausfrau who bangs on about recipes and housework.

'Sounds lovely,' said Emily, forcing a smile.

'Good,' I said. 'Well, we're back from holiday at the end of this month, so perhaps then.'

Emily nodded.

'Great,' she said.

Although she was being taciturn, she was still smiling. She knew that I knew that I was making small talk.

'I'd just like to say one small thing,' she said.

'Yes?'

'In fact, two small things.'

'Go ahead.'

'One, I'd really appreciate it if you kept what happened quiet.'

'Not at all,' I said. 'You've been very discreet about the nappy-changing disaster.'

Emily laughed.

'And the other thing?' I asked.

'We don't have to swap.'

I swallowed. I think I understood her.

'You get my meaning?' she asked.

I did. She was basically saying she and I could have an affair. Heart raced, mind went no, no, no. Normal and typical internal masculine conflict. Jesus. I hadn't been hit on so obviously since I was a teenager, and even then, I don't remember it being this easy.

'I do,' I said. 'But I don't . . .'

'Just think about it,' she said. 'No rush. Talking of which, I must get on my horse. Byee!'

I waved goodbye pathetically as she paced off. All I could think was that Emily was the type of woman I would have loved to have met as a bachelor, but she was the last woman in the world I would have wanted to have married. Poor Jim. Although Jim probably does the dirty anyway.

I haven't told Sally yet, and I don't think I'm going to. It would annoy her beyond belief. I can keep Emily under control, and hopefully maintain a friendship. It's not as though we can afford to lose friends.

Thursday 7 July

Increasing feelings of guilt about Lydia today. We've started to bond, if that's the right word. Not romantically, but in a pleasantly domestic way. This afternoon was a classic example. We were both standing near the hob – she was frying up something Polish that had just seen me preemptively removing the battery from the smoke alarm, while I was making a cup of tea. The children were watching the box in the living room, and for a while, Lydia and I stood next to each other in a brief and easy silence. I had the radio on, and was vaguely listening to the cricket score. I wasn't particularly interested in it, but the series had taken on a national importance, so I thought it best to keep informed for pub-talk purposes. (What pub talk? I never go to the pub.)

'Wotizthispliz?'

'What's what?'

'Thiz. On the radio.'

'Cricket.'

'Cricket? What is thiz?'

'It's a game. Bat and ball type thing.'

'How do you play?'

I sighed inwardly. The chances of successfully explaining the rules of cricket to a Polish au pair were less than zero. What were the chances of explaining what a Silly mid-off was, or the exact LBW rule? I had tried explaining the rules to Sally on a drive up to Scotland four years ago, and it took until Nottingham for her to realise that the wicket keeper was not on the batsman's side. It was exasperating, especially when she asked, just after we had crossed the border, 'What's an over again?' I've always thought that if we have another war, and Englishmen find themselves locked up in foreign POW camps, then the best way to screen for stool pigeons would be to get anyone suspect to explain the rules of cricket.

So I decided not to explain the rules of cricket to Lydia. Instead, I just said that to do so was as hard as getting me to learn Polish by bedtime. She looked a trifle disappointed.

'Nothing personal, Lydia,' I said as the kettle came to the boil. 'It would just take too long.'

Lydia nodded reflectively.

'I understand.'

I took the kettle off the hob.

'You are a very kind man, Sam.'

'Thank you, Lydia,' I said, genuinely touched.

'You are very good to me,' she said. 'I want to be staying to do good job with you and Peter and Dizzy.'

'Well, I want you to stay as well,' I said, holding the kettle between us. 'The children like you very much, and so do I.'

Guilt, lots and lots of guilt. The better she gets with the children, the more sheepish I feel. It would be so much easier if she were awful, then I could just get rid of her. But I need Lydia as much as she needs me.

Saturday 9 July

Close one with Peter today about Lydia. It came up during lunch, when Peter asked whether he could have some 'gruboes' (his word for Gruboziarnisty Owies) instead of the ham and cheese we were eating.

'What?' asked Sally.

'Gruboes,' said Peter. 'I want some gruboes, not this.'

'Don't say "I want"!' I reprimanded.

'*Please* may I have some gruboes?' he asked.

'No,' I replied. 'You eat what's on your plate.'

'What are "*gruboes*"?' Sally asked, not unreasonably.

'Cereal,' I said. 'You know, cornflakes. We call all breakfast cereals gruboes.'

'How did that come about?'

I looked at Peter, who was about to open his mouth.

'Come on,' I said, 'eat some ham.'

'But, Daddy . . .'

'I said eat it, Peter!'

I picked up a large piece of cold pig and shoved it in Peter's mouth.

'All right, sweetheart,' said Sally, touching my forearm, 'you don't have to force feed him.'

'Sorry, yes, you're right. Sometimes he does need a little encouragement.'

By now, I was hopeful that the conversation would move on.

'So, gruboes?' asked Sally.

'What?'

'Gruboes. You were going to tell me why cereal was called gruboes. Come on, I don't see them that much, I miss out on all these little things.'

I popped a large piece of ham into my mouth to buy myself some time. I pointed to my lips to indicate that I had no wish to speak with my mouth full of food. (It's never stopped me before, as Sally is always at pains to point out.) I eventually swallowed when to have continued chewing would have looked like excessive mastication.

'They're called gruboes,' I began slowly, 'because I kept saying "have some grubbo" at breakfast time. You know, grub. It sort of mutated from there.'

'Daddy,' Peter started, 'I thought they were called gruboes because they were from Poland.'

Daggers emanated from my pupils.

'No,' I said, 'they've got nothing to do with Poland.'

Now it was Sally's turn to chew on a piece of ham.

'There seems,' she said, just as she was finishing her mouthful, 'there seems to be a bit of a Polish theme developing.'

'Peter's a little obsessed with Poland after that *Bob the Builder* episode, aren't you?'

Peter just looked confused. Poor lad. I owed him a toy.

'The Polish are getting everywhere these days!' I joked. Weakly.

Sally smiled out of politeness. Remarking on the ubiquity of Poles was utterly dreary in its unoriginality.

'Anyway,' I said, 'what shall we do this afternoon?'

'A walk?' said Sally.

'Good idea.'

'It's a shame,' said Sally. 'Gruboes and all. I'm going to miss Daisy's first steps, I just know it. I'm missing out on so much.'

Sally looked slightly tearful. Not floodgates, but just sort of wistful. I held her hand.

'You're working so hard,' I said. 'Don't think for a second I'm not grateful.'

'You all seem to be enjoying yourselves so much with your secret language and everything, and I just feel like a bystander.'

'You're not.'

'Yes. No. Well, I know I'm not, but I do feel it. I can see what men feel like now.'

'Yes, but the difference between you and a lot of men is that they don't mind being semi-detached.'

'That's awful. My father wasn't like that. Neither are you.'

'I know, but believe me, most blokes I know can't really stick being at home.'

'That's so sad.'

'Well, maybe. But maybe they're programmed that way.'

'I just don't believe it. You seem to have adapted remarkably well. Who would have thought it?'

Guilt. Once again, massive waves of guilt. I haven't adapted, but now I have the Gruffalo, I'm giving the impression of a more than competent househusband. The house is clean and tidy. The children's clothes are ironed and in the right drawers. They are well fed. Despite Peter's little 'I want' outburst at lunch, they are getting better at their pleases and thank yous (even if they are sometimes in Polish). In short, everything, as far as Sally is concerned, is 100 per cent smooth. And I am making it look smooth. And, to add to the guilt, it is Sally's money I am spending on Lydia. So far, Lydia has cost us nearly £1,000, and it's going to be hard to hide that hole in our finances.

I know what I must do. I must get rid of Lydia, and for so many reasons – the porn, the secrecy and most of all, because it's just not right that Sally works her arse off unknowingly paying for an au pair while I play golf. At the end of next week, we shall go on holiday. I shall sack her on Monday and give her four weeks pay and accommodation. That seems fair. I know she won't see it that way.

I must step up to the plate and do my duty. England expects. As does my wife.

Sunday 10 July

Torn between whether to get rid of Lydia or not. Feels a bit wretched abandoning the poor girl but a) she is an adult and b) I am giving her four weeks' notice, which is more than generous. However, I must do it. Even if it means that things go back to Disaster World. I owe it to Sally, and to Peter and Daisy. They can't eat Gruboziarnisty Owies for the rest of their lives, otherwise they'll look as unhealthy as if they were dragged up in an Estonian nuclear wasteland.

Had lunch with Nigel and Clare today, who both remarked how well I was looking. Normally these comments are reserved for Sally, and she mentioned it on the way back as she studied her reflection in the passenger-seat vanity mirror. (Yes, amazingly, I drove back. Such is the power of guilt.)

'Eurgh,' she sighed. 'I look dreadful.'

'No you don't,' I said, not looking at her.

'I do. I look *old*.'

'Not true. You look lovely. Just the same as the day I met you.'

'Very sweet of you to say so, but you know it's not true.'

'C'mon,' I said, 'you look a hell of a lot younger than most of our friends.'

'I don't. Clare looked great today. And it was you who got all the compliments.'

'Hardly.'

'Clare said she's never seen you look so well since she's known you.'

'She's very kind.'

'Anyway, she is right – you do look well.'

I looked away from the road briefly and gave Sally a kiss.

'And you look well too,' I said. 'Very well. Ravishing.'

Sally made another groan into the mirror.

'I wish. I've got lines everywhere. It's like that desert in Chile. And I think I need some sort of bagectomy under my eyes. Look!'

Sally turned to face me and pulled down below one of her eyelids. OK, so she had slight bags, but nothing notice-able. Of course, I said something along the lines that anybody can make it look as if they've got big bags if they pull their skin down.

'And I've got zits.'

'Where?'

'Don't pretend you hadn't noticed them.'

I stole a glance away from the road. We were now on a dual carriageway, so I had to be quick.

'Where?'

'Here. Here. There. Here. They're everywhere.'

'I can't see a thing.'

(This was the truth.)

Sally made another groan. She then opened her mouth and bit her teeth together. More groaning.

'My teeth are so yellow.'

'No they're not. Besides, white teeth are less healthy than yellow teeth.'

'Who cares? I want white teeth.'

'Get them whitened.'

'Costs a fortune.'

'How much?'

'I don't know. Hundreds. But that's not all I need. A chemical peel. Some Botox. I could spend £20,000, easily.'

'Sweetheart, you really do look lovely. I know wives never believe their husbands when they say this, but you must. Come on, you're easily the best-looking of all our friends.'

'Even Lucy?'

Erk. Lucy is married to Tom, and is a complete babe. Mind you, she is about ten years younger than the rest of us. She was born in the 1980s! Fancy that! She had never actually heard of Talking Heads, which is just terrifying. The royal wedding, the Falklands War – these are things of which she has no memories. Bizarre. And Tom has married her. I wonder what they talk about? I don't suppose they do a lot of talking.

'Even Lucy.'

'Now I know you're lying!'

I was lying, of course I was lying. We all know that our spouses are not as good-looking as the latest Hollywood pin-ups, but we don't like to say that to each other.

'I'm not lying,' I maintained. 'Lucy's looks are very shallow.'

(She looks like a classy page-three girl, if there can be such a thing. A sort of Sloaney Suzanne Mizzi. Wow. Where did that name come from? What the hell happened to her?)

'I thought men liked shallow.'

'Not me.'

'So what am I? Deep-looking?'

'I'd say that you look very attractive, sexy, gorgeous and characterful.'

Another groan.

'Now what?' I asked.

'Characterful,' she repeated. 'That's another word for old.'

And on it went. All the way back home. I didn't mind. It's part of the deal, isn't it, to allow each other to wallow occasionally in a bit of self-pity? Sometimes it's hard to reconcile the fact that tomorrow morning Sally will be attending a conference about the future of the Central Asian republics.

While she does that, I'll be sacking someone from Poland. That's globalisation for you.

Monday 11 July

Today was the day of the Great Lydia Sacking. It went as well as might have been expected, which was not well at all. In fact, these bruises are going to be pretty hard to explain to Sally. I shall just have to keep my left arm and shoulder hidden from her, which is not easy, as she lies to my left in bed and, as I don't normally wear pyjamas, it's going to be very tricky.

It didn't help that the children were around (no more playgroup until September – yikes!) which made it impossible to have the guaranteed uninterrupted one-on-one time I needed with Lydia. However, I waited until Daisy was having her afternoon sleep, and plonked Peter in front of a *Scooby Doo* DVD. I then went into the kitchen, where I found Lydia ironing my shirts. I wished she was doing

ANYTHING but that – in fact, I would rather she had been looking at Fudge Fist or whatever. But too bad. There was no other time.

'Lydia,' I said, smiling slightly.

'Yes?' she asked, looking up from the ironing. (Lydia is a brilliant ironer. I think her fantastic strength in her right arm manages to exert more newtons than an elephant made of lead.)

At first, I didn't know what to say. I felt so sorry for this poor, decent girl, who'd had the guts to leave Poland, try to learn English, and create a new life for herself away from some dingily grey, freezing housing complex on the outskirts of Poznan.

'I'm afraid I have some bad news for you,' I said, doing my best not to be a coward and look her in the eye.

'Yes?'

'I'm afraid I'm going to have to let you go.'

'I don't understand.'

'I'm going to have to let you go,' I repeated.

'But you are not holding me.'

Fool, Holden, I thought. She's not a management consultant. I might as well have told her I was restructuring, and needed to reallocate some personnel, with a view to some permanent downsizing in the au pair department.

'I'm afraid that I can no longer employ you.'

'Oh,' said Lydia, the little colour she had bleaching from her face.

'I am very sorry, but it—'

'Is it Internet?'

'No! It's got nothing to do with that. It's just that I think it is wrong I do not tell Sally that you are here. I think I should look after the children by myself.'

'This is very sad.'

'I know, and the children will miss you very much.'

'I will miss them as well. And I will miss you, Sam.'

I became aware that Lydia had left the iron in the middle of one of my shirts. One of my Zegna shirts, the type of shirt I was able to afford when I had a job.

'Ah, Lydia, the iron, it's um . . .'

'Sorry!'

She moved the iron, but it was too late. There was now an iron-shaped burn mark on its back.

'Sam! I am so sorry. I pay you for this shirt.'

'Please, don't worry. It's not important.'

'But it is nice shirt.'

Was, I thought. It *was* a nice £125 shirt. It was now something that would be used to polish shoes or apply dubbin to Peter's football boots in years to come. The world's most expensive rag.

'Honestly,' I said, teeth gritted, 'it doesn't matter.'

Lydia placed the iron on its rest.

'Look, Lydia, I've decided you can stay at the B&B for another four weeks, and I shall pay you for another four weeks. I hope that gives you enough time to find something else.'

Lydia had gone very quiet. She just nodded while looking at the burned shirt. It was awful doing this, but I knew it was right.

'You should try to get a job in London,' I said. 'There are many more opportunities for you there. Lots of English schools. Plenty of families who want good au pairs like you. I shall write you a brilliant reference.'

Lydia still did not speak. I walked over to her and stood on the other side of the ironing board, my ruined shirt a kind of crap metaphor.

'I work for free,' she said.

It was a tempting offer, but one I had to refuse.

'I'm sorry Lydia, that's a very kind offer, but I really must try to look after Peter and Daisy all by myself. It's not fair to my wife that I pretend I am being the brilliant house-husband, when all the time it is you feeding the children, washing up, cleaning the house, doing the laundry, doing the ironing, washing them, getting them into their pyjamas . . .'

As I was saying all this, part of me thought I was bonkers. I was going to go back to all those chores, all those things I hated and did so badly. Perhaps a compromise, one day a week? But I knew that would never work, because it wouldn't suit Lydia, and Sally never had any help. No, I had to be firm.

Lydia started sobbing a little. I felt gauche and English. What do you do when a twenty-three-year-old Polish woman breaks down in tears because you've just sacked her? The only thing I thought I could do was gently place a comforting hand on her shoulder.

Bad mistake.

'Do not touch me!'

Paf! Smack! Oof!

The next thing I knew was an intense pain in my left shoulder and upper arm. Lydia had clobbered me with the amount of might the Poles should have had at their disposal in September 1939.

'Fuck!' I shouted.

My initial reaction, upon receiving such a level of pain, was to lash back, but I stopped myself quickly. Not only would it have been wrong, but getting arrested for beating up my secret Polish au pair would have quite possibly seen the end of my marriage.

'You not touch me!' she said. 'It is unfair just after "letting me go".'

It almost sounded like a passable pop lyric. *You always touch me/Just after letting me go.* Perhaps it already is.

'I'm sorry, Lydia, I just wanted to comfort you.'

'Do not!'

My arm throbbed unbearably, and for a brief moment I wondered whether she had broken it. (Yes, male hypochondria.) However, I was more concerned that perhaps she was going to go psycho. The knife block looked worryingly close to her. What a way to go. Slashed to death in one's own kitchen by a lunatic Polish economics graduate. The iron was another possible weapon. Ouch. I held my hands out plaintively. In truth, if it came to a fight, I doubted whether I would win. Besides, I'm not as cunning as the mouse in the *Gruffalo*.

'Perhaps you should go back to the B&B and we can talk tomorrow?' I suggested.

The slightest hint of off-pink returned to Lydia's face. (She was back to her normal colour.) She nodded. She had seen sense. The threat of violence, which had hung so menacingly, had lifted. Slowly, she turned to the switch in the wall and turned off the iron. She then looked back at my shirt.

'I am sorry with thiz.'

'Please don't worry.'

A few minutes later, she left, constantly apologising about the shirt. She didn't apologise about my arm/shoulder, although to be fair, she probably didn't know her own strength. As soon as she had gone, I took my shirt off to examine the damage. It was pretty bad, and as I type this, I can feel pains shooting up and down my left arm. Or maybe I'm having a heart attack?

I'll have to wear a T-shirt in bed tonight, no matter how hot it is. I just can't think of a buller.

Tuesday 12 July

Sod's law that Sally was feeling frisky last night (as was I). However, I had to feign great weariness in order to wriggle out of any activity that revealed the massiveness of Lydia bruises, which presently look like someone has squashed a handful of plums on me. What's more, they bloody hurt, and it took a lot of effort to stop wincing every time I picked something up – even a plate proved to be a painful proposition. I felt guilty to deprive Sally of a perfectly reasonable request for oats, but at least I had sustained my wounds in a good cause. The annoying thing is, the bruise has got worse. I might just be able to get away with it for another day or two, but on holiday, no chance. I'd better have a good buller by then.

Lydia came round at teatime. Even though we haven't

known her for a long, it was a very moving occasion. She had bought Peter and Daisy a couple of little presents – a toy car for him, and a finger puppet for Daisy. It was very sweet of her, and I told her so.

'I wish I could have bought some more toys for them, Sam. They are very lovely, your children. I hope one day I have children so lovely as Peter and Daisy.'

Her words almost brought tears to my eyes. Not only was it a kind thing to say, but I also felt awful for her. Will she ever have children of her own? I do hope so. There's always someone for somebody, but Lydia needs to do some serious gearing up of her presentation. Perhaps leaving us is the best thing she can do. She's in a bubble here. Going to a big city may be the making of her.

'Do you have any idea what you are going to do?' I asked.

'I think London is a good idea,' she said. 'I have a friend who can let me stay a few weeks.'

'Well, you can stay here for four weeks. I promised that.'

'Thiz iz kind, Sam, but there is no need. Pliz. It is too generous.'

I fetched my chequebook and wrote her a cheque for £600. When Lydia looked at it, I almost had to catch her eyes.

'No, Sam, thiz iz too much.'

'Please take it,' I said. 'I feel rotten for letting you down.'

She kept trying to thrust the cheque towards me, and I kept thrusting it back at her – a sort of reverse tug-of-war. Eventually, I won, as I knew I would. It would have been like me refusing a cheque for £6,000. No matter how much

I might pretend I didn't want it, even as I was doing so I would be thinking of ways to spend it.

A few minutes later, Lydia said goodbye to the children and gave them massive hugs. Daisy looked a little confused, but Peter had a good idea what was happening.

'Why are you going, Lydia?' he asked.

'Because I have to find different job.'

'Why?'

'Because I cannot stay here for ever.'

Peter thought about it.

'You are my other Mummy.'

That earned him another huge hug. Lydia fought hard to restrain her tears. When she left, Lydia gave me a huge hug as well.

'Ouch,' I went. Genuinely.

'What's matter?'

'My, um, arm, it's a little sore.'

Lydia frowned.

'From, um, yesterday,' I said.

'Oh yes! I am sorry about thiz.'

She then gave it a playful tap, which caused me to go 'Ow!' again.

'Oh, Sam! I am so sorry.'

'Don't worry.'

We then muttered a few more goodbyes and thank yous before we promised we would stay in touch and see each other again. At twenty-three, I assume Lydia knows such promises are empty ones. They shouldn't be, but they always are. When she left, I almost felt a tear or two, but maybe that was my shoulder.

Wednesday 13 July

First day without Lydia. Utter nightmare. I had forgotten how much there is to do, and in a funny way, how little. Once I had got Peter and Daisy dressed, breakfasted, teeth cleaned, the whole day stretched in front of me, a temporal chasm that had to be crossed. The thing was, how? What was I going to do with them? What did Lydia do with them? For the past few weeks, I've been having it too easy, far too easy.

So I did what I used to do, back in the early days, and wasted our day. We went to the shop to buy the newspaper. We went to the swings for twenty minutes. We came back and I read the paper while Peter and Daisy played more or less together. Then I checked my emails (none, apart from a lot of invitations to meet Polish teens, as well as a whole ream of foulest porn – I know how this happened). By this time, the morning had more or less disappeared, and I cooked them lunch (pasta with a can of tomatoes and some Parmesan – actually not bad). Daisy had a sleep after lunch, and Peter and I watched forty-five minutes of the *Battle of Britain*, which he absolutely adored. Felt enormously proud of him for liking one of the greatest war films ever. Then felt enormously guilty that I had allowed him to watch the scene in which Christopher Plummer gets burned in his cockpit.

'Is he all right?' asked Peter, who looked deeply concerned.

'He's OK,' I replied, putting my arm around Peter, 'it's only his hands on fire.'

'Does it hurt having your hands on fire?'

'Not really. Just a little bit.'

'He looked hurt, Daddy!'

The next scene showed Plummer bailing out, which enabled me to tell Peter that he really was all right.

'Is he still on fire?' Peter asked.

'No! The wind will put him out.'

Peter sucked his thumb agitatedly. Normally, I would have got him to stop it, but in this instance I thought he needed the comfort of his primus digitus.

'Don't worry,' I said. 'He's all right.'

'I hope so, Daddy.'

It's easy to forget how all too real films must be for Peter. A few minutes later I turned the TV off, which heralded much moaning.

'Turn it back on! I want to watch *Battle of Britain*!'

'We can't watch TV all day,' I said.

I wish we could have done. Instead, annoyingly, the sun was shining, so I felt obliged to take them into the garden. We then sort of played with a football, and Peter made a reasonable fist of getting down the slide unaided. (I hate the slide. It's a garish plastic castle which makes the garden look like one of those naff pub gardens, with one of those hideous troll things with arms.) Daisy crawled around picking daisies as it happened, and made a great show of presenting them to me, which was very cute. This went on for half an hour, by which time my lap was covered in daisies, and if I did so much as remove one of them, Daisy would moan. When I did eventually get up, she screamed for about five minutes.

A walk then followed, or rather a sort of amble. Daisy hates being in her pram, so she keeps jerking her body forward to try to get out. I was tempted to take the straps off, but I knew that would see her catapulting herself head first on to the pavement. Peter wandered along swishing a stick at some random plants.

'Where is Lydia?' he asked halfway.

'Lydia has gone to London.'

'When will she be back?'

'She won't be coming back, Peter, she's gone to get a different job.'

'Why?'

'Because she can't look after you and Daisy for ever and ever.'

Peter then entered into one of his half-minute inner ruminations, which involved a little bit of thumb-sucking, and a lot of anxious frowning.

'Will you and Mummy go away soon?'

'Of course not!' I said, paused and gave him a hug. 'Mummy and Daddy are never going away. We are going to be with you always.'

I gave him a big kiss on the cheek, and did the same to Daisy.

'I am glad, Daddy,' Peter said.

I could have cried. I smiled instead. As we continued on our 0.5 mph walk, it occurred to me how much I had missed them. It's not that I'd been away, it's just that I'd not been entirely all there.

We got back home in time for some tea and biscuits, which they ate remorselessly. I knew this meant they wouldn't eat much of their supper, but I didn't care. I was determined we should do some sort of activity, so we decided to draw moustaches on everybody in the newspaper. Peter wanted everybody to be a pirate, which was a great idea. The prime minister looked particularly good with a great big pirate's hat, stubble and lots of missing teeth. In the photograph he was holding his hand up, so I put a cutlass in it. Peter thought this hysterical. Daisy couldn't have cared less, and just scrunched up as much newspaper as she could, covering her face and her top in newsprint.

Supper, then bath, then bed. All went smoothly. I'm now waiting for Sally to get in and then I will cook a pork chop. (Exciting stuff.) It's been a funny day. I can't work out if I'm feeling tired because of looking after them, or because we haven't done enough. I suspect it's the latter. All in all, it's been a kind-of, sort-of, nearly type day. Nothing's happened, but it's been very nice looking after them.

One problem. The house is an absolute mess. Sally will wonder why. I shall have to do a quick tidy in order to live up to my own (undeserved and unearned) reputation. If only there were au pairs who came in between 5.30 and 7.15 – I'd be made.

Either that, or dust down the Holden Childcare Programme. Despite my promises to myself, I hadn't got round to repurposing it while Lydia was around. What exactly did I do when Lydia was around anyway? It's amazing how easy it is just to piss away the days on reading the papers, surfing the web and having lunch.

Friday 15 July
11.30 p.m. somewhere in the English Channel

I'd never realised that getting ready for a holiday could be so exhausting that one needs a holiday just to get over its preparations. The last two days have seen me a) cursing my sacking of Lydia – what pathetic attack of conscience was that? and b) running around like a blue-arsed fly. I thought Sally was going to get today off, but she couldn't, and I had to pick her up from the train station near the harbour. Compared to the rest of the passengers in the queue for the boat, she looked absurdly smart. Mind you, so did the children and I. So long as one is not wearing a wife-beater shirt and doesn't have one's stomach bulging like a muffin top over one's waistband, you might as well be in black tie. Why do English people always look so crap when they go on holiday? Or, for that matter, most of the time? It'll be nice to be in France where even in the smallest villages, people make some sort of effort. I'm determined not to look like a typical Brit on holiday, and am wearing a short-sleeved checked shirt (tucked in), chinos, Docksiders and no socks. I rather proudly told Sally about my sartorial motives, and she agreed that I indeed didn't look like a typical Brit on holiday. I looked like a typical Yank on holiday.

The children have loved being on the boat, partly because I've convinced Peter that there may be some pirates on board. He ran around for the first twenty minutes going 'Arhar, me hearties' to everybody, even an old woman in a wheelchair, who would have made the least convincing pirate possible. ('Wheel the plank!')

We gave them a very late and sluttily beige-coloured supper (fish fingers, chips, bread, biscuits) which they loved. Obviously. They also wolfed down the ketchup, which we never have at home for the simple reason that neither Sally nor I like it. No sinister left-wing reason to it. I always think ketchup adds a false bloody authenticity to dishes whose flesh is so processed, so homogenised, that its relation to its host animal is so distant it may as well have been made in a lab. The satisfying red of ketchup makes the brain think you are eating real flesh, with real blood. Of course, my theory could be complete crap, but no more crap than the children's dinner. Anyway, they're sleeping soundly on the bottom bunks, while Sally is hopefully also asleep. She looked knackered when we picked her up. I'm in the bar, enjoying a nightcap bottle of beer and writing this. Two weeks away – should be great. It will be nice just to hang out as a family again. No stresses, nothing.

Sunday 17 July

The stress started as soon as we got off the ferry.

Sally's godmother had emailed us directions to the cottage, which were the most useless, illiterate, stupid, nonsensical, meaningless, crap, unnecessary and wrong directions I've ever been given. Like all men, I hate directions, and feel that armed with a postcode and a printout from the web, I can get to a bedsit in Omsk without too much difficulty. In fact, I've driven abroad countless times, and have never once got lost. I've negotiated Warsaw on a wet, dark, Friday-night rush hour, negotiated Madrid on a dry, bright, Saturday evening, and found a shortcut to avoid the Washington beltway on a Monday morning. All this on my own, with a map glued to the steering wheel with my thumb tips, and with an occasional glance at a plethora of printouts from the web on the passenger seat. These things I have done. I know how good I am at map reading because I have a penis.

But this was bad, very bad. Not only were the directions written by a woman, but they were being interpreted by a woman – Sally. This might seem horrifically sexist and repellent, but no more so than women complaining that men fart all the time (which they probably do).

The directions started with the words, 'As soon as you leave the port area you will come to a roundabout and some lights.' Well, as soon as we left the port, we came to three roundabouts and no lights. Taking the plunge, I decided to go straight over all three roundabouts, as the other exits all looked as though they were going to parts of town that would not have made a car with British licence plates feel particularly welcome.

'At the fourth roundabout, take right exit to Beauville.' The fourth roundabout had no exits to Beauville, but merely one to the *gare, centre ville* and *autres directions. Autres directions* it was. By now, I could feel my blood pressure rising.

'Your godmother is a complete idiot,' I said.

Sally looked mournfully down at the A4 sheet of directions. You could tell just from the way they were laid out that she was a halfwit.

'I never want to see her again!' I said, as we headed

over another roundabout, heading this time for *toutes directions*.

'You've only met her once,' said Sally, 'and that was just for a couple of minutes at our wedding.'

'Long enough,' I said.

'So she'll join my mother in your little social sin bin, shall she?'

'You bet.'

We still hadn't seen Jane and Derek since the great lunch, and I was not missing them one bit. What we didn't need now was a row about *them*.

But then, the cliché from the backseat.

'Are we there yet?'

'Nearly,' said Mummy.

'Just a few minutes more,' said Daddy.

I glanced at Peter in the mirror. He didn't look convinced. It's the lying they can't stand. Not the journey and its carsick-inducing twists and turns, but the parental BS that states that the destination is nearly upon us.

'Soon you will go under the railway line.' A minute later, we found ourselves driving over a bridge. Sally and I looked out of our respective windows to see the railway line. Beneath us. Not us beneath it.

'Let's turn round and start again,' said Sally.

'No,' I said, unwilling to admit failure. 'I'm sure this is right. It feels right.'

'You have some sort of sixth sense, do you?'

'Something like that.'

'We could always try to find a petrol station and buy a map.'

'A map? Why do you want a map?'

'Aren't they useful?' asked Sally.

'Maps are for amateurs,' I said. 'We'll do this by the power of logic alone.'

'You are taking the piss, aren't you?' Sally asked.

'Half and half,' I said.

So far, my sixth sense was leading us into the industrial heartland of northern France. More railway lines, both above and below. At one stage, vast silos containing some sort of nasty French chemicals. Lorry parks.

'This feels really good,' said Sally.

'I'm sure this will take us back on to the main road.'

Why can't the French label their road signs correctly? Is it merely Anglo-Saxon politeness and practicality that results in our signs in the UK being almost faultless? I rarely hear people saying the signs back home are crap, but over here, everybody moans. Why have them? Why don't they all just say *toutes directions* and be done with it?

After another five minutes, I decided, much against my sense of pride, that we needed to turn round.

'I thought we were going the right way,' said Sally with a note of wifely triumph.

'We were,' I said, 'but the road went wrong.'

Sally giggled.

'You mean the road got lost? It was the road that went the wrong way, not you?'

'Precisely. Bloody French town planners. Useless.'

I put my foot down as we retraced our route. Sally moaned that I was driving too fast, but by now, tired and irritated, I ignored her. I kept wondering why we had spent a small fortune just to be able to drive around countryside not wildly dissimilar to that at home. Wouldn't two weeks at home have been equally relaxing? Or Cornwall? Anywhere but northern French industrial desolation.

'Mummy,' mewed Peter, 'I'm not feeling very well.'

'What's the matter, sweetheart?' she asked.

I looked at Peter in the mirror. He looked whiter than Lydia ever did.

'He's going to be sick,' said Sally. 'Please could you slow down!'

I lifted my foot a nanometre off the accelerator.

'He'll be fine,' I said.

I was still too angry to be told what to do, and even though I knew Sally was probably right, some short circuit in my absurdly aggressive masculine thinking decided the best thing to do at the next roundabout (around our fifty-seventh that morning) was to swing round it like a bad Michael Schumacher.

'Sam!'

'It's fine!'

'Mummy!' cried Peter, 'I'm not feeling very well.'

'Sam! Please stop! Would you please stop!'

It was too late. I looked in the mirror just as Peter brought up his breakfast and last night's supper. All very beige, all very smelly, all very everywhere. I stopped the car in small layby and got out, fuming. Although not fuming as much as Sally.

'What a lovely holiday this is turning out to be,' she said.

Armed with wet wipes and a crushed bog roll from the glove compartment, we did our best to clean Peter and the car. Daisy looked on at the proceedings from her child seat with an air of bemused detachment. Poor Peter was upset, and I felt guilty and apologised to him profusely. I apologised to Sally as well, but got the dagger treatment.

The clean-up took some fifteen minutes, and barring the stench, we did a pretty good job. Peter looked better too, his rosy cheeks restored. We got back in the front and drove off. Just as we did so, the noise of more vomiting came from the back. Our necks swivelled round like owls'.

'Poor little man,' I said.

But it wasn't him, it was Daisy.

'You can do it,' said Sally. 'This is all your fault for driving like a fucking idiot.'

'Don't swear!' I said, the moral triumph of the thief over the murderer.

Sally just leaned her head back against the seat and shut her eyes. She was close to tears. I got out of the car and did the best I could, which was not much.

It took us another hour to find the house – in all a ninety-minute journey to travel some fifteen miles. Still, this place is just what we needed. A large, comfortable, stone cottage, nice garden overlooking the estuary, a little beach for the children and a small restaurant. Perfect.

Since we arrived, we've spent the day stocking up, and working out how to change the gas cylinder for the boiler. I'm terrified I haven't connected it properly, and if either of us lights a match we'll be incinerated. So far so good, and we've all had hot baths. Now sitting in the garden, admiring the view, and drinking a small bottle of the local cider. Some stresses are lifting, but my behaviour this morning still rankles with Mrs Holden. More apologies are in order, I think.

Monday 18 July

Sally told me it's bad form using my laptop on holiday. She's right. I can't type masses while I'm here. The whole point of being away is that we're not just away from people, but also away from our day-to-day activities. So holiday entries will be brief.

Beach today. Fun for an hour, then felt bored. Can't believe we've got two weeks of this. Still, at least Sally is doing lots of childcare. Lazy and selfish of me to think that, but there it is. Would feel a lot worse if I hadn't sacked Lydia.

Wednesday 20 July

Two days of rain. Two days of misery. Two days of claustrophobia, bad tempers and whining. A lot of whining. Sally and I have done our best to entertain the children, but there's not a lot you can do in a house that doesn't have any of your stuff in it. There's no TV either, which rules out an essential piece of child-pacification equipment. We brought one *Maisy* DVD which we played on my laptop almost on a loop yesterday.

Today we've tried to be better parents and more creative. I went into a nearby town and bought some crayons, paints, etc., and the children had a lovely few minutes playing with those before they got bored. What made it worse is that I seem to have bought the only child's paint that leaves a stain. It looks like we're going to have to buy a new table-cloth. And God knows what we're going to do to the floor. It's like Jackson Pollock at the mo.

Despite all this, Sally and I have been getting along very well. It's nice just to be able to 'be' with each other and not run around doing things the whole time.

Wednesday 27 July

Now at that stage of holiday in which one is truly relaxed. The weather has been good. Have established a slower, more mellow routine, and feel one could live like this for ever. Holidays are cruel things in a way. Just as one has successfully reprogrammed one's body, the end of the break draws near. I'm starting to get a little tetchy thinking how I'm going to cope with becoming a proper househusband once again.

Sally asked me how much I was enjoying my new 'job'. I told her that it was going great, and that I had fully come to terms with the fact that this was what I am going to be doing for the next twenty-odd years. She didn't look convinced, and, in truth, neither was I. I asked her how it was going at the ministry, not day-to-day how's it going, but overall. Well, she said, very well. Part of me died when she said that. The better she does, the more likely I am to stay at home.

Increasingly, I find myself thinking about that phone call with Clive, and about what's really going on at work. Perhaps I should just leave it, but it still niggles. Do I want to find out because I want my job back, or is it just curiosity? A bit of both, I suspect. I'll give Clive and Fiona a call when we're back.

Friday 29 July

Last day of holiday, and feel a bit miserable. We've had such a lovely time. We haven't had to go anywhere, do anything, take phone calls, organise things, cook for anyone. All we've done is buy food and drink, consume food and drink, play with the children on the beach, play with each other in the evenings, and generally flop about. I must have put on about half a stone. Deeply satisfying tan. Sally looks a million dollars better than when she came out. Told her so. She was genuinely delighted, as observation had come out of the blue, and was therefore not me just saying it to refute self-pitying statements à la drive back from Nigel and Clare's the other week. Peter and Daisy look better as well. (They couldn't have looked much worse than on the drive from the port.) They've eaten loads, slept loads, and run around loads. I MUST ensure we continue with these energetic days when we get back. The whole of August stretches in front of the three of us, and I've got to do my best in the post-Lydia world. Still, life is sweet. It could certainly be a lot more bitter.

Sunday 31 July

Back home for twenty-four hours and things are atrociously bad. It all started within one hour of our return, and for the most annoying and avoidable of reasons: the post. The problem lay in the post. Normally, when we get back from holiday, I seize on the mountain that has accumulated behind the door, and sort out the dross from the useful and informative. (The worst are the advertisements from the local supermarket – the one from which I'm banned – offering me sixteen anaemic chicken breasts for the price of eight, and eighty-gallon drums of some cola for £2. How can I opt out of this crap?)

This time, however, I let Sally do it while I put the children to bed, the househusband routine already kicking in. By the time I had come downstairs, I could tell Sally was especially livid, more so than with the porn or all that nonsense about Nick.

'What's this?' she asked, holding up a letter.

'What's what?'

I took the letter. It was from the bank. As soon as I glanced at it, I found my right leg starting to shake. I felt slightly faint, as if I had got out of the bath too quickly. I swallowed a couple of times. The letter was from a Mr Martin Nellist, who claimed to be our personal account relationship manager – I had never heard of him. He informed us that he was not honouring a £620 cheque to Lydia Komorowski because there were 'insufficient funds' – only £534.89 – in our joint account. He was going to charge us £34.50 for this letter, and speculated that the payee's bank might pass on their charges in the future. He then invited us to deposit sufficient 'monies' – for fuck's sake – in order to avoid cheques not being honoured. And, by means of a delightful little sign-off, he said that it was the bank's policy to inform credit reference agencies whenever customers issued cheques that could not be honoured. Attached to the letter with a black paperclip was the cheque itself, with all sorts of squiggles and stamps over it. Of course, I did not have time to get livid with the nastiness of the letter because of the heinous crime of going £65.11 overdrawn, because an answer for Sally was more urgent at this stage.

'So who is she?'

I didn't know what to say. I was tempted to lie my way out of it, but that would have been hopeless. If I were a real shit (rather than someone who is just a bit of a turd), I would have said that Lydia Komorowski was a jewellery designer, and I had commissioned her to make a pair of earrings for Sally's Christmas present. I also would have had to have been quicker, because this idea has only occurred to me as I write, and damn it, it would have been a good buller.

But no. Instead, I just looked gormlessly blank.

'Who is she Sam? A *girlfriend*? Is this why Peter is so miraculously good at Polish these days? Do you get her in during the day when I'm not here? Is that what you do?'

I sighed.

'You're partly right,' I said.

Sally looked inestimably pained. She was obviously fearing the worst.

'How?'

'She's NOT a girlfriend,' I began.

I tried to stay calm, to keep the temperature down.

'Then what is she?'

'She is – or rather was – an au pair.'

Sally's mouth fell open. She looked more agog than Danny Wolf-Light had done at the zoo.

'An *au pair*?'

'Yes.'

'I don't understand. An au pair? Here? You've had a secret au pair living here?'

'Not living here.'

'Where?'

'At the B&B.'

Sally held her hands up and let them drop again. She looked defeated, deflated, distraught.

'I . . . I don't know where to begin,' she said.

'I'm sorry. But, look, I've got rid of her. Just before we went on holiday. This money was meant to be her pay-off.'

'Six *hundred* pounds?'

'Yes.'

'How much have you paid her in total?'

'Fifty pounds a week times about seven weeks.'

'Seven weeks?'

'Yes. So about three hundred and fifty pounds.'

'And the B&B? I assume you had to pay for that?'

'I did, yes.'

'So how much was that?'

'I negotiated a special rate of fifteen pounds per night.'

'Oh, hurrah.'

Sally did the maths.

'So all in all, you've – sorry, *we've* paid her almost two thousand pounds?'

'About that, if you count this cheque.'

'You arsehole,' she said coldly. 'You complete shit. You've lied to me all this time. This is almost worse than an affair.'

'Oh, come on,' I said, 'it's nothing like an affair. I don't deny it was deceitful of me, but I wasn't cheating on you.'

'You were *lying* to me, Sam, that *is* cheating.'

'Semantics,' I said pompously.

'Fuck you,' she said without raising her voice.

'Look, all I did was get her in to help. Lots of people have au pairs.'

'You didn't tell me, Sam! It's not the point whether we needed one or not, but the fact that you went and hired one anyway, paid her, kept it quiet, and lied to me about it. For all I know, you've even got Peter to lie to me, which is just despicable. All this time, I've been working hard, being the breadwinner, and thinking what a brilliant job you were doing, and how proud I was of you . . .'

'I never got to see much of that,' I said.

Sally ignored me and continued.

'. . . and how I thought our life had finally found some balance, when all along, all through this, you had just been what? Wanking on your fucking computer while you got some unknown Pole to look after my children . . .'

'*Our* children.'

'. . . spending hours at the golf course, no doubt, going to the pub, doing whatever it is selfish men like you do. Two thousand pounds, Sam! Think what we could have bought with that! Half a term's prep school fees! But it's gone, all because you're a selfish lazy shit who has no sense of responsibility whatsoever. Well done, Sam, well done! Because you've really fucked up this time!'

With that, Sally walked out of the kitchen. I tried calling her back, to say we could have a reasonable conversation about it, that I was sorry. I knew it was hopeless but she would have hated me even more if I had not tried. The only thing I could do was to open one of the thirty-six bottles of rosé I had secreted around the car.

I sat down at the kitchen table and for the first time since I was sacked, I felt myself close to tears. This was just shit, I kept thinking, just awful. Sally was right, I really had fucked up. Had this terrible fear that I was going to lose her, a terrible fear that was confirmed when she came down the stairs five minutes later carrying her overnight bag.

'Where are you going?'

'I don't see why I should tell you.'

Nick's slightly pudgy face wobbled into my mind. Surely not him? It couldn't be possible. Paranoia.

'I think you should, in case there's a problem with the children.'

'Oh, so responsible. You can always call *Lydia* if you need someone to help turn the oven on.'

'That's not what I meant. Come on, just in case there was an emergency.'

Sally sighed, reluctantly seeing the sense in my thinking.

'I'll be at my sister's.'

With that, she turned and left, slamming the door behind her. When most people slam doors, they don't shut, but bounce back instead. Not with Sally. When she slams a door, it always shuts. Emphatically.

I drank the whole bottle of rosé while watching *The Wild*

Geese. Roger Moore and Richard Burton did their best to take my mind off things, but not even they, giants of the screen that they are, could compete with the shock of Sally walking out. We had never had it this bad before, never. I could see why she was hacked off, but I thought she was overreacting.

I slept badly, as did Peter and Daisy, who kept waking throughout the night wanting Mummy, especially Peter who kept demanding to know where she was. He's obviously got used to having her around the whole time, and now she's suddenly gone, it's a bit of a shock to his system. Poor thing. I'm doing my best not to blame Sally for this, but I wish she had stayed here so we could have thrashed it out. Any amount of broken crockery would have been better than this.

Spent much of the day unpacking, washing clothes, sorting stuff out. The children have been playing OKish in the garden, but every few minutes Peter has asked where Sally is, what she's up to, when is she coming back. I've told him soon; she's just gone to see Auntie Victoria. He looks unconvinced.

All the benefits of the holiday have worn off. I feel stressed, guilty, tired, anxious. Funny butterfly feeling around my solar plexus, that before-exams sensation. Perhaps I should take up yoga or meditation to calm me down, but I know I'm too cynical for any of that jazz.

I've tried Sally's mobile a couple of times, but it's gone straight through to answerphone. No reply from Victoria's either. This has set me off worrying that Sally may have gone to see Nick, but I must stop this way of thinking. It's soured our relationship before, and I don't want to add more bitterness, especially now.

Am now in my study, finishing off this evening's bottle of rosé. It's gone warm, and it doesn't taste so good now. Bedtime. Then what?

Monday 1 August

Sally phoned mid-morning from her mobile.

'Hi,' I said, my voice slightly high-pitched with relief that she'd made contact.

'How are Peter and Daisy?'

'Missing you,' I said. 'As am I. Where are you?'

'Where do you think, Sam?'

'I have no idea.'

'I'm at work. That's what I do, I work. Remember?'

'All right, all right, there's no need to be so sarcastic.'

'Has Lydia been round yet?'

'I've told you,' I said. 'I got rid of her before the holiday.'

'I'm afraid I don't believe you.'

'Well, you must.'

'I don't, and, frankly, I don't see why I should. Your track record is hardly exemplary.'

I was tempted to put the phone down. This was going nowhere. It also reminded me of the rows I used to have with significant ex Sarah a lifetime ago. Constant long silences, cat-and-mouse conversations, sarcasm, seeking the moral high ground, all the crappy hallmarks of a shitty relationship. And now it was happening to my – *our* – marriage.

'OK,' I said, seeing no point in arguing. 'Are you still saying at Victoria's?'

'No,' she replied firmly. 'I'm staying up in London. If you need me, I'm on my mobile.'

'So where are you staying?'

'None of your business.'

And with that, the phone went down, and I realised she was back with Nick. Paranoia? Surely not, not this time. This time it HAS to be intuition. It's almost as though she's been looking for an excuse. Although I cannot believe she would leave the children. That would just be biologically bizarre.

Tuesday 2 August

Today has dragged with a capital D. Dragged, then. I'm in too much of a funk to get up and go and do all the exciting things parents are supposed to with their children during the holidays. And even if I could, then those things would be goppingly packed with other people's horrid 'kids'.

In desperation, I looked again at the Holden Childcare Programme in a bid to inspire myself. No joy. The whole thing is a farce. What was I thinking? Everyone else seems to manage without a programme. It is a testament to a kind of arrogant naivety, a complete misunderstanding of human nature. I pulled it off the fridge door and shoved it in the bin. I really did have to shove as well – the bin was packed, and I can never be bothered to empty it.

Unfortunately, Peter and Daisy can sense my mood no matter how hard I try to be cheery.

'Are you all right, Daddy?' Peter asked during lunch.

'I'm fine thanks,' I replied. 'Why?'

'I think you are ill.'

'Why do you think that?'

'Because you look very old.'

Although I couldn't help laughing, this was irksome.

'How do I look old?'

'You look like Granny!'

Great.

'Well, I'm not quite as old as Granny.'

'Yes, you are,' said Peter, his mouth full of cheese on toast.

I didn't reply. This was just grim. For all I knew, Sally was vengefully serenading Nick in some hotel, while I sat in the middle of nowhere being compared to a septuagenarian by our son. All I could think, in a revolting bout of self-pity, was where did it all go wrong?

Sally called at the children's bedtime. We could hardly hear her because she was clearly calling from a bar.

'I miss you, Mummy!' Peter shouted into the handset.

I could just about make out a 'miss you very much' as I leaned near Peter.

'OK, give Daddy the phone now,' I said.

I took the phone from his hand and held it to my ear.

'Hi there,' I said.

But the line was already dead.

Wednesday 3 August
2 p.m.

This is getting out of hand. No matter how sneaky employing Lydia was, no matter how selfish, no matter how lazy, no matter how naughty, it was not an evil or immoral thing to have done. Sally is perfectly entitled to be angry with me, fair enough, but not this angry. She's now been away for three nights, of which at least two may well have been with her ex-boyfriend. What sort of behaviour is that? Immoral if you ask me.

9 p.m.

The phone rang at 7 p.m., just as the children were getting ready for bed. I answered it but didn't speak and handed it straight to Peter, whose little face lit up when he heard Sally's voice.

'It's Mummy!' he said. 'Mummy!'

The corners of my mouth turned upwards in the type of smile I imagine divorced fathers flash when they have to say goodbye to their children after their access day is over. They want to look happy, but inside they're not.

I listened to Sally talking to Peter.

'Have you been a good boy?'

'Yes. I have been very good!'

(This was a lie, but I let it go. Peter had barely eaten all day, and had thumped Daisy harder than I had thought him capable of.)

'Good boy. What have you been doing today?'

'*Postman Pat*!' Peter shouted.

(This was true.)

'Anything else?'

'*Bob the Builder*!'

(Again, true.)

'Just TV?' asked Sally. 'Have you been doing anything else?'

Peter said nothing, the wretch. We had been for a walk, but clearly the goings-on in Greendale were more memorable than a saunter down the river.

'Can I speak to Daddy now, please?'

Peter handed the phone to me. Sod you, I thought, and hung up. Two can play at that game. The phone rang straight away, and I left it.

'Daddy!' shouted Peter. 'The phone is ringing.'

'So it is,' I said.

I opened the back of it and removed the batteries. Silence. It felt neither big nor clever, but at least Sally would know I was angry as well. It might just make her question what she's up to.

I live in hope.

Right, time for a pizza and a bottle of rosé in front of *Force 10 from Navarone*. At least I'm catching up on my war films.

Thursday 4 August

Utterly bizarre day which makes me question whether I am in fact slightly ill in the head. I don't think I am, but if you took today as an example, you might well think I was and with good reason too.

It started when the children and I were in the main car park in town. (Two hours free parking, but you need a ticket. Moronic. Nobody wants to spend ALL day in this place.) I had successfully got Daisy out of her seat and into her buggy, where she waited with her normal degree of frustration and impatience. She hates being plonked into her buggy, and regards it as somewhat insulting. No doubt she is under the misapprehension that she can walk as well as the rest of us. Poor thing.

I then took Peter out of his seat, and he happily climbed out of the car. While he waited next to it, as instructed, I noticed that one of the straps on his child seat was twisted, and I started to unravel it with my left hand before shutting the door.

However, Peter's impatience knew no bounds, an impatience that sought expression in slamming the door shut on my left wrist. Intense pain. Nasty brutal pain.

'Ah fuck!' I shouted.

I pulled the door away as the agony started to increase.

'You little sod!'

I looked down at my wrist and inspected the damage. This time, I was not being a hypochondriac. It really bloody hurt.

'Why the hell did you do that?' I shouted at my son and heir.

Peter autistically refused to look at me.

'Look at me!'

He didn't. I tried moving my wrist. Every time I did so it hurt like hell.

'Look at me!'

I bent down and turned his head so it faced mine. Still, his eyes looked everywhere but towards me.

'Look at me!'

I clutched the sides of his face and held it so he had to look.

'Why did you do that? Why did you hurt Daddy?'

No reply. He knew he had done wrong.

'Peter! I'm talking to you! Why did you slam the door on my hand?'

'Because I slammed it,' came a sotto voce guilty reply.

'I didn't ask what you did, I asked why you did it. Why did you do it, Peter?'

'Because I slammed it.'

I don't know why we adults think that children will tell us why they do bad things. They don't know why they do bad things, but we, in fact, do. They do it because human nature is nasty, sadistic and vicious, and bringing up children is a constant process of eradicating – or at least masking – this. (The expert speaks.) I knew there was no way Peter was going to tell me anything but jack but, as a rational human being, I wanted to know why.

'I'm very angry with you, Peter,' I said. 'You will go to bed early tonight and there will be no TV after supper.'

Peter started to cry, which set Daisy off. Just what I needed. Two screaming children, one estranged wife, a badly bruised and sodding painful wrist, and a mountain of shopping that needed to be done. What fun. All this, because I looked at an email I wasn't supposed to have looked at. What else could go wrong?

My mobile rang. I hurriedly retrieved it from my pocket

and looked at the caller display, hoping it was Sally, hoping it was Sally phoning to say she would be coming home and all was forgiven. But it wasn't Sally, it was Lydia. I knew what she wanted. Six hundred pounds, that's what she wanted.

'Hello?'

'Hello, Sam! This is Lydia!'

'Hi, Lydia! How are you?'

'I am OK, thank you. There is problem with that money you gave me.'

'Oh?'

(Coward, Holden, to feign ignorance.)

'My bank, they sent me a letter saying the cheque was no good.'

'Really?'

'Yes!'

'How strange! I wonder why that happened?'

'I do not know, Sam.'

'I'll send you some more money straight away.'

'Can you send cash?'

'Er, I don't think cash is a very good idea. Postmen can steal cash.'

'You can send special post. I need the money urgent, Sam.'

'OK, OK, I'll send it registered post.'

'Thank you, Sam. Can you send today?'

'Yes, of course. OK, Lydia, I must go. Bye!'

'Bye bye. Thank you, Sam, for this money.'

'No problem!'

I hung up. This was sodding annoying, as we don't have

£600 in our account. We needed an overdraft. I therefore had to add the bank to the list of places we had to visit.

As was predictable, our trip was haphazard. With my left wrist in agony, I had to somehow arrange the shopping in and around Daisy, while I pushed her buggy with only my right hand, which is harder than it sounds. It kept swerving all over the pavement, knocking into pedestrians, and almost sending one of those old women in an electric chair (wrong term?) into the path of an ambulance, of all vehicles.

By the time we got to the bank, the three of us looked like particularly useless refugees. I walked up to the counter and spoke to a predictably hatchet-faced woman called Janet Sykes.

'Hello,' I said, as cheerily as possible, 'I was wondering whether I could speak to Mr Nellist?'

'Mr Nellist doesn't work here,' said Janet Sykes.

'Oh. He's my personal account relationship manager, and this is my branch, so I thought . . .'

'Personal account relationship managers do not work in the branches. They work in regional offices.'

'And where is Mr Nellist's regional office?'

'I'm afraid I cannot tell you that.'

'Why not?'

'Data protection.'

Data protection my arse. Data protection is becoming one of those catch-all reasons functionaries like Janet Sykes use so they do not have to do anything, tell you anything, or be helpful in any way. In fact, I'd say it was worse than health and safety in its effect on chucking treacle in the finely engineered synchromesh of the fourth largest economy in the world.

'So what's the point in Mr Nellist being my personal account relationship manager if I cannot see him?'

'I do not make company policy, sir,' said Janet Sykes, using the word 'sir' in that derogatory manner that people like Janet Sykes are so good at. If it weren't for the bullet-proof glass, I would have grabbed Janet Sykes by her bank-branded neck-scarf thingy and strangled her until Mr Nellist came from his regional office. As it was, shouting was my only weapon.

'Is there anyone here I can see?' I asked.

'Do you have an appointment?'

'No,' I said, my legs giving way slightly out of frustration.

'You need an appointment. Who would you like to see?'

'I don't know who I would like to see!'

'In that case, sir, I'm afraid I don't know how to help you.'

'The manager,' I posited, 'how about the manager?'

'Mr Nellist?'

'Is Mr Nellist the manager?'

'Yes.'

'But I thought he was my personal account relationship manager.'

'This is a different Mr Nellist.'

'Small world,' I said sarcastically. 'Is there any chance of seeing this other Mr Nellist?'

'No, sir,' said Janet Sykes, the 'sir' even more withering.

'Why not?'

'Because Mr Nellist is on holiday.'

Yet more images of a violent death for Janet Sykes flooded into my head. Janet Sykes hanging upside down an inch above a pool full of starving Great Whites. Janet Sykes forced to eat spoonfuls of highly radioactive matter.

'Does he have a deputy I can see?'

'I am Mr Nellist's deputy.'

Fuck.

'In that case, can I see you?'

'Do you have an appointment?'

'No!'

'You will need to book an appointment.'

'Can I have an appointment in thirty seconds?'

'No,' said Janet Sykes. 'It will be my lunch break then.'

'Look,' I said. 'All I need is a five-hundred pound over-draft for one week. Is there any way you can arrange that? How hard can it be?'

'I'm afraid you need an appointment to negotiate an overdraft.'

'Is there *any* way I can arrange an overdraft in the next few minutes?'

'Have you considered our Premier Platinum Plus Express Phone Banking service?'

'No, I have not considered your Premier Platinum Plus Express Phone Banking service.'

'Would you like to see a leaflet?'

'Probably not.'

Janet Sykes thrust a leaflet under the counter.

'This explains everything. The Premier Platinum Plus

Express Phone Banking service can arrange an overdraft for you over the phone in seconds.'

'And how long does it take to register for this Premier Platinum Plus Express Phone Banking service?'

'Ten working days.'

Janet Sykes having her limbs individually hacked off with old knives.

I flicked the leaflet back through the counter.

'That's no good is it? I need an overdraft now, not in two weeks.'

'Ten working days.'

'Same thing. Jesus Christ. Why do I bank with you people?'

Janet Sykes didn't say anything but instead looked at the queue of people who had formed behind me.

'Have you finished, sir?'

'Yes,' I said, my shoulders slumped.

As I walked away, Janet Sykes brought down her 'position closed' blind. Unbelievable. We struggled through the revolting 1970s shopping centre back to the car, my whole being fuming at Janet Sykes and banks in general. How the hell was I going to pay Lydia? I didn't want to let her down, and being in London without any money is no joke. She might have to go on the game. (Unlikely though.)

And then further disaster when we got back to the car. One of the carrier bags split, sending fruit and veg rolling around the car park, smashing a jar of mayonnaise. Peter and Daisy thought it funny, but I found it anything but. I picked up as many foodstuffs as I could, and wearily bunged them into the boot. What a life, what a sodding crap life. Me a househusband with no money. Sally gone. The Holden Childcare Programme in ashes. The inevitable parking ticket on the windscreen didn't make me feel any lower, just more angry. All of a sudden, I was beyond caring. I just wanted all this to end. Not to kill myself, but just to be taken away from the pettiness of it.

What I needed was something to take me out of all this for a bit, preferably something that would bring Sally back and give us a chance to make up. Another sharp pain in my wrist gave me an idea. A self-inflicted wound. A single pistol shot to the foot and I would be out of the trenches, away from the mud and the horror, every morning going over the top to be faced by an enemy who was always there and would always mow you down. All this would be taken away by a deliberate act of self-maiming. I needed to hurt myself in order to feel better. A paradox I would not be able to explain to Peter, or anybody else. A broken wrist, and I would be off games, unable to look after the children. We would HAVE to have some help, and I would be able to get away from the drudgery for a little while at least.

As I type this one-handed, I really do question my sanity when I said to Peter, 'Do you want to shut Daddy's hand in the car door again?'

Peter squinted up at me. Confusion.

'But it would hurt you, Daddy!'

'I know. But I want to see how strong I am.'

Even Peter knew this was a completely crap reason.

'But you didn't like it when I slammed the door.'

'Yes, yes, but Daddy now thinks he is like Mr Strong because he eats lots of eggs.'

I placed my hand in the door frame.

'Go on, Peter, slam it as hard as you can. I'll tell you what. If you do it, I'll give you an ice lolly.'

'Oooh!'

Bribery. So simple. Why didn't I think of it before? While this conversation was going on, I noticed a few passers-by giving me quizzical looks. I just smiled idiotically back at them. Sensing I was mad, they quickly moved on.

'OK, Peter! One, two, three – slam!'

Laughing as he did so, the sadistic brute, Peter slammed the door with all his little might. Crunch. The door whacked into my already bruised wrist with a sickening grind of what I hoped was smashed bones and ruptured ligaments, or whatever it is you have in your wrist. I tried hard not to say 'fuck' out loud, but failed.

'Fuck!' I went.

'Fuck!' went Peter.

'Don't say fuck!' I said, in agony.

'But you said "fuck"!'

I looked at down at my wrist. It hurt, but did not hurt as much as I thought it should to indicate broken bones. Was my brain shutting off the signals of pain coming from my wrist? Was my wrist in fact now broken? No. I knew it could not be, because when things break, they really bloody hurt and swell up and do all sorts of weird things. Nevertheless, it rapidly grew more painful, and every time I moved it, bolts of violent pain shot up my arm. The pain felt great, perfect, ideal – now I would be off games for a while, and able to get Sally to come home.

I loaded the children into the car (with great difficulty) and drove to the hospital. Each gear change brought on fresh torment, and I tried to stay in fourth nearly all the way. Thankfully, the A&E department was more or less empty, as it was not a Friday or Saturday night and therefore there were no drunks to stitch up.

The nurse at the reception desk looked at me wearily as I stumbled in with the children.

'My son accidentally slammed my wrist in the car,' I explained, holding up the bruised body part.

'Can you move it?' she asked.

'A little.'

I tried rotating it, and made a pathetically small yelp of pain. The nurse struggled to keep a straight face.

'It looks like you've just bruised it,' she said.

'Is that all?'

I was severely disappointed. All that pain and effort and just a sodding bruise at the end of it, my great plan shot to pieces.

'I suspect so, but I expect you'll need an X-ray.'

She then took down a few details before ushering me to one of the many plastic orange chairs. The last time I had come here was for the great Daisy hand-in-video incident. The memories probably came flooding back for Daisy as well, because she started to scream. The elderly couple who were sitting opposite looked disapproving. Peter then started whining as well.

'Can you two just shut up?'

'I'm hungry,' said Peter.

As I twisted my wrist to look at my watch, more pain. It was 12.30, at least half an hour after their lunchtime. All the food was in the car, which was miles away. If I were a proper, competent househusband, I would always have some emergency biscuits on me. Except that I am neither proper nor competent, and the only thing I had on me was an old packet of chewing-gum in the back of my jeans that had been through the wash. I couldn't give them chewing-gum – they'd just choke on it. (Still, we were in A&E. If they were going to choke anywhere, it may as well be there.)

I caught the nurse's eye.

'I'm sorry about the racket,' I said. 'Do you know how much longer it will be?'

She looked at the clock behind her.

'Another fifteen minutes.'

'Is there any way I can get these two something to eat?'

'There's a crisp machine in the corridor.'

Crisps it was, and Peter and Daisy were delighted. I bought three bags, and we munched down contentedly, although Daisy was most insistent that she should have all three bags, the greedy little thing.

Eventually, we were led in to see the doctor. It was the same one who had looked after Daisy, and there he was, still in his chinos and button-down blue Oxford shirt.

'Hello, again,' I said.

'Hello,' he said quizzically. 'Have we met?'

'Yes, about a couple of months ago when I brought my daughter in with a video player attached to her arm.'

'I remember now! How is she?'

He looked at Daisy with a slight sense of disdain as she licked the insides of the now empty crisp packet.

'I don't normally give them crisps,' I said. 'It's just that with this I couldn't . . .'

'No, no, no problem at all. Come on, let's take a look at what you've got.'

He studied my wrist, bending it gently in a series of directions, all of which caused me to mew like a lost kitten. I decided I should really make my mews more manly and so the next time he twisted it, I sort of growled. He looked up at me, concerned.

'Did that particularly hurt?'

'Um, er, a little bit,' I said.

He looked down at the wrist.

'It's a very nasty bruise,' he said. 'But I don't think there's any real damage. How did you say it happened? A car door?'

'Yes, that's right. Peter here, *accidentally* slammed the door on to my wrist as I was adjusting the car seat. A nasty *accident* it was.'

'Very. And it just happened the once did it?'

'Yes.'

'Because you've got bruising all over the shop. Normally with something like this, you get bruises on either side, from where the door hits and from the door frame on to which the wrist is hit. But you've kind of got bruising all the way round and as far as up here, and even some on the back of your hand.'

I struggled to explain how this might have happened.

'Well, it sort of happened more than once.'

'How?'

'It was an accident, but you know, real sod's law. Peter did it first when we were leaving, and then again when we got back! Very unlucky.'

'Very,' said the doctor, unconvinced.

'Do you think it'll need to be in plaster?'

'Oh no. You just need to rest it a bit, but there's no damage here. You only need to plaster it if it's been broken.'

'How, um, hard do you think you need to slam a door on to a wrist before it would break?'

The doctor knitted his eyebrows together.

'Why? Were you thinking of asking your son to do it for a third time?'

I started trying to laugh convincingly at the preposterousness of such an idea.

'Good God no! A third time? No! Have you any idea how much this hurts?'

'Don't worry, I'm only joking. I don't think you're quite the candidate for Munchausen's.'

'That's when people hurt themselves to get attention, isn't it?'

'Something like that. And Munchausen's Syndrome by Proxy is when they hurt other people in order to get attention for themselves.'

'And what's it called when you hurt yourself in order not to get attention, just to lie low, you know, have a break.'

I was getting some really suspicious looks by now.

'That's called depression.'

I inwardly baulked at this. The last thing I suspected myself of being was a depressive. I get down, like everybody else, but I have never been bitten on the ankle by the 'black dog'. Not as far as I know. There must have been another explanation.

'But those people in the trenches who shot themselves. What about them? Were they depressives?'

'Well, they were either suffering from stress or something else,' the doctor replied.

'What would that have been?'

'Cowardice, I suspect.'

'Ah.'

Great. So I was either depressed or a coward. My money was on the latter. Or perhaps it's both. I must sort myself out. Getting your child to wound you is not the product of a healthy mind. The doctor told me that if I was feeling depressed, then I should go to my GP. I told him everything was tip-top, and I'd be fine.

The phone rang at 7 p.m. again. I was tempted to pick it up, but I ignored it. Peter wondered why I left it, but I just mumbled something about being too tired to bother with it, which was true. He and Daisy are missing Sally, and so am I.

Saturday 6 August

Sally came back last night. It was a complete surprise, partly due to the fact that I had accidentally left the phone off all day. The children and I had another one of our nothingy days, which was partly justified by my near-cripple status. Even changing Daisy's nappy is painful, so the idea of us all going out is a step too far.

The key in the door turned just as I was settling down to watch the news with my nightly bottle of rosé. At first I thought it was burglars, and I got half-heartedly to my feet, clutching my wine glass – hardly the most effective of weapons.

'Hi,' said Sally, walking into the living room.

'Hi,' I said, and went over and hugged her.

The hug was sort of reciprocated, if you'd call resting your hands on someone's back their fair share of a hug, which you probably wouldn't.

'How're the children?'

'Fine,' I said. 'They went to bed about fifteen minutes ago, so they're probably asleep.'

'I'll go and have a look.'

While she did that, I grabbed another glass from the kitchen, and emptied some almonds into a bowl. We reconvened in the living room a few minutes later, Sally having changed into her jeans.

'Thanks,' she said icily, taking the glass of wine. 'What have you done to your arm?'

'It's my wrist. Peter slammed it in the car door.'

'Ouch.'

'It was. I had to go to A&E, but they said it's just bruised. Nothing much. It's fine. Looks worse than it is.'

I was being terribly brave. In truth, it still hurt like fuck. Sally sat down.

'How've you been anyway?' I asked.

'Fine,' she said.

'Are you planning on being with us permanently now?'

'Yes. Although if it weren't for the children, I'd probably still be up in London.'

The implication was clear: she wasn't here to see me.

'How is Nick then? All well? Glad to have you back?'

'Don't be ridiculous, Sam.'

'You stayed with him, didn't you?'

'Yes. But we're adults. Just because you're under the same roof as a woman doesn't mean you have to shag them.'

'That's not how men think.'

'Men like you perhaps,' said Sally, 'not Nick.'

'He's so special.'

Sally ignored that.

'Well,' I continued, 'what else am I meant to think? My wife and I have a row, and my wife disappears up to London to stay with her ex-boyfriend. It doesn't look great, does it?'

Sally looked me straight in the eye.

'I'm not cheating on you, Sam, nor would I. All I expect from you is the same honesty I show you.'

She looked scary. I can see why Sally is so good at her job, telling Aashfjdgkstanis what to do. Hard negotiator. Merciless.

'Look,' I said, 'I've apologised for that, and I'll say it again – I'm sorry. I didn't really think the implications through. It was thoughtless of me.'

'You're always thoughtless, Sam.'

Here comes the character assassination.

'Please let's not spend the evening slagging each other

off,' I said. 'It's clear there's nothing either of us can say that's going to make everything peachy, so why don't we just watch a film or something? I'll sort some supper out. What would you like?'

'Curry.'

'Excellent! I'll order some delivery.'

'Do they deliver out here?'

'They use minicabs.'

'Sounds expensive.'

My shoulders slumped.

'All right,' I sighed, 'I'll make us some eggs and bacon.'

'No, let's have a curry.'

'You sure?'

'Yes.'

Sally's return made me realise quite how financially impotent I have become. And it's going to get worse because she won't trust me one jot after the Lydia business. I'll probably have to ask permission for everything I buy – humiliating. Who knows? She may even try to put me on some sort of allowance. Housekeeping money, darling. Which reminds me, I must sort out Lydia's money.

We spent the evening mostly in silence, watching endless episodes of *Friends*. (I'm aware that men aren't supposed to like *Friends*, but the truth is, I do. It's probably part of the same gene that governs disliking sport.) Even though we hardly spoke, it felt companionable, warm almost. I don't know what to think about Nick. Sally sounds so convincing about him, but that dreadful note still rankles. It's clear he's made a move, and she hasn't (I hope) responded to it. But it's obvious there's still a Nick-shaped hole in her heart. Yeeurgh. How cheesy does that sound?

When we went to bed, it all felt very awkward, and Sally got undressed in our bathroom. We lay like strangers next to each other, and gave each other an almost formal kiss good night. Still, she's back, and I'm delighted, not just for me, but for Peter and Daisy who were thrilled to see their mother first thing this morning.

When she was giving them both a hug, our eyes met, both of us thinking that we have a lot of hard work to do. Me more than her, probably.

Sunday 7 August

It's been scorching today, and we've spent all hours outside. The children have been splashing around in the paddling pool, and Sally and I have been sunbathing and reading the papers. I cooked my signature boned leg of lamb on the barbecue (Sally had to buy the meat from the super-market), which was delicious. It was great playing happy families again, and what made it better is that it didn't feel like acting. Sally and I even made each other laugh, but at one point I could tell she stopped herself, keen not to get sucked back in quite so readily.

We even did bathtime together – haven't done that in ages – and the children loved having us both there. They showed off by splashing as hard as they could, and totally ignored Sally's attempts to censure such disgraceful behaviour. Soon, we were even wetter than the children. After we put them to bed, we changed out of our wet clothes, something I normally see as a prelude to a bit of how's-yer-father.

Sally was having none of it. She froze as soon as I kissed her, and moved my hands away from her as though I were a sexually incontinent teenager at a disco.

'I don't think I'm quite ready,' she said.

'Am I still in the doghouse?'

She allowed herself a smile.

'Mostly,' she said.

'Is my nose at least sticking out?'

'No,' she said, looking down, 'but something else clearly is.'

We laughed, and left it at that. This time, Sally didn't hold back. Laughter-wise, that is.

Now feel deeply frustrated, out of which feelings of para-noia regarding Nick are beginning to grow. I must stop them, strangle them at the root, but what else am I supposed to think?

Wednesday 10 August

Right. I've had enough of this. Sally has been back INCRED-IBLY late three nights in a row now. She claims it's about work, but I know it's not. It's bound to be to do with Nick, fucking sodding twatting Nick. I've restrained myself from getting angry with her, because I know she'll only throw Lydia back in my face (an unpleasant image). So instead I've decided I'm going to stalk my own wife. It's all arranged. Tomorrow, I am leaving with the children with Emily, to whom I have promised a case of wine, an offer I knew she would readily accept. I'm then going up to London mid-morning to hide near Sally's office – all day, if required. It seems mad, yes, but it's the only way that's going to make me feel sane. Another paradox in my life.

Friday 12 August
6.30 a.m.

I'd thought I'd get up early and write this, as a) I haven't slept well, and b) there'll be no time later, and I want to get it all down while it's still fresh in my head, because yesterday was something else. I've never had a day like it. Lots of resolution, closure, cleared air, etc., and now all parties can move on. I'm glad I did what I did, no matter how low it must have seemed.

Everything started smoothly. I left Peter and Daisy with Emily just after 10. She asked if I had time for a coffee, which I didn't. Even if I had, I doubt I would have accepted. I most certainly would not have wanted that kind of temptation, a temptation I might have been powerless to resist with my neurosis about Sally and Nick.

Instead, I caught the 10.30 and was up in London just before noon. At every station I thought about getting off and going back home, telling myself all this was surely completely nuts, and I was clearly in need of psychiatric treatment. What sort of man got his son to slam his arm in a car door? What sort of man stalked his wife around London? Things were getting a bit out of hand.

I took the tube to the station near Sally's office, which is in the middle of Whitehall. Lots of large government buildings, anonymous, faceless, like giant filing cabinets. The last time I had gone there was when I picked Sally up on one of our first dates, when she was very junior and I was the up-and-coming thrusting and reasonably moolahed consultant. A long time ago. I remember spending £84 on dinner (a LOT of money then), and doing my best to pretend to hide how much it was. I sort of wanted her to know, but then I didn't want to look like the type of berk who showed off. (A sort of half-baked berk, then.) Afterwards, we went into Soho and drank cocktails in some crappy dive, but lots of fun all the same. I can dimly remember we both got howling, and ended up at her flat, where we had our second (or was it third?) snog. She didn't invite me in for coffee, and neither did I ask. I didn't want to push things in that direction too quickly, because I knew this one was special. Besides, I was quite glad I wasn't getting involved with the sort of woman who readily issued 'Access All Areas' badges. Anyway, all this was a long time ago, ages in fact.

The first thing that occurred to me when I arrived outside the office was the lack of cover. There were no trees, no benches on which I could sit and read a paper, nothing, except for a small sandwich bar diagonally across from the main entrance. I had come armed with a paper, my laptop and several magazines, and decided it would be my home for the rest of the day. I ordered a coffee and a sandwich filled with gunk, and sat at a table near the window and waited.

And waited. By 1.10, there was still no sign of Sally. Perhaps she wasn't going out for lunch today, I thought, perhaps she had already bought her sandwich at this very shop. I was then filled with horror that if she did come out she would make straight for here, in which case I would be busted.

''Ere, are you 'avin' anyfing else?'

It was the bloke who ran the sandwich bar. I looked up at him and smiled. He was cleaning tables, and clearly wanted to clean me away as well.

'Cos we're gonna get busy in a few minutes.'

It was vital I kept my chair.

'Could I have another sandwich, please?'

He looked mildly surprised.

'All right. What do you want?'

'What was the one I just had?'

'A chicken, turkey, ham, bacon, egg, lettuce and mayo super club.'

So that's what it was. Essentially, just mayonnaise with unidentified bits in it, but not bad.

'OK,' I said. 'I'll have another one of those.'

'You sure?'

'Sure – no breakfast.'

I resumed my watch from the window. Plenty of people were leaving Sally's office, some of whom were coming into the sandwich bar, but still no Sally. Then, just as my sandwich arrived, a large black Rover drew up outside the main entrance. I could tell that the driver had a hat on, so he was in fact a pukka chauffeur, not just some recently redundant middle-aged bloke in the company car he'd been allowed to keep.

Out of the building walked Sally, looking very crisp, very

professional, very impressive. Totally un-mum, utterly unlike herself at the weekends. This was the side of Sally I never saw, the high-powered defence analyst, the woman who flies to dodgy parts of the world in a Western attempt to make them slightly less dodgy, or if not less dodgy, then at least our type of dodgy.

The chauffeur sprang out and opened the car door; Sally acknowledged him with the graciousness of someone who is accustomed to such things happening. I could just about hear the car door clunk expensively shut. Where was she going? I wondered. I took a mouthful of sandwich and gloop, absent-mindedly noting that a dollop of mayo had splodged on to the middle of my keyboard.

Then, suddenly a male figure appeared at the building entrance, wearing a smart two-button grey suit, a pink shirt, and a dark blue tie. Very elegant, very dapper, very much my wife's ex-boyfriend. Nick. I almost stood up in shock, but restrained myself. This time, the car door opened from within, and the smarmy git glided in, no doubt to cosy up next to my wife, the bastard.

Red mist descended like Scottish drizzle. I got up and slammed my laptop shut, dimly realising that the dollop of mayo would now be all over the screen. Fuck, I thought, but there was no time to waste. I chucked a fiver on to the table to more than cover the cost of the heart-stopping gristle, fat, entrail, prion, salmonella, E. coli and choles-terol super club, and stepped out on to the street just as the Rover sped away.

Feeling I was in some cruddy spy film, I hailed a taxi, all the time keeping a panicky eye on the Rover. I then said to the cabbie what I had always wanted to say to a cabbie, albeit certainly not under such circumstances.

'Follow that car!'

'Which one?'

'The black Rover, just down there, see it?'

'Nope.'

'You must! Just next to the bus!'

The cabbie squinted. Fuck, I thought, just my luck, a blind cab driver.

'There!' I almost yelled.

'Oh, I got yer,' he said, finally. 'All right, hop in.'

I jumped into the back and sat bolt forward, all the time keeping my eyes fixed on the Rover. The car was too far away to establish whether there was something illicit going on on the back seat, but at this point I just assumed there was. I felt sick and excited at the same time, a strange sensation that did not satisfactorily complement the one and a half gunk sandwiches. I could have sworn the mayo had been a little rancid, but tried to expel all thoughts of food poisoning.

'I bet this doesn't happen very often!' I remarked to the cabbie.

' 'Bout once a week,' he said.

I felt deflated.

'Mostly people chasing their husbands or wives,' he said. 'Happens all the time. I wonder if there's anybody faithful left in this life.'

As opposed to all those other lives, I thought, feeling even more deflated.

'Who's in the Rover, then?' the cabbie asked.

'Not my wife!' I unconvincingly lied.

'Makes a change!'

'It's, um, well, I can't really say who it is, but let's just say he owes my client rather a lot of money.'

'You a bailiff then?'

'God no! Can't you tell? I thought bailiffs were all fat bald bastards with those giant sovereign rings.'

A silence, during which I realised that my cabbie was in fact a fat bald bastard with a giant sovereign ring. I could do nothing but apologise.

'Listen mate,' I started with false wannabe-Cockney bonhomie, 'I'm really sorry about that.'

He looked viciously at me in his mirror. Shit, I thought, while my wife and Nick are billing and cooing in some hotel, I'm going to be driven out to the East End and shot in the middle of an old warehouse by someone who looks like Bob Hoskins.

'You calling me a bastard, then?'

His eyes were smiling, thank God.

'So sorry,' I pleaded.

'Don't worry about it! But you've given me an idea about what I might do.'

'Might do when?'

'I'm gonna give up cabbying,' he said. 'It's not the same as it was. Back in the old days . . .'

Five minutes of waffle followed about congestion, other people's driving, the lawlessness of minicab firms, and all the other guff that fat bald cab drivers assail you with. At least, to his credit, he was keeping tabs on my quarry.

We headed into Mayfair, and after a couple of minutes they drew up in front of the Clarendon Hotel. We pulled up about twenty yards behind them. This was getting worse, I thought, worse and worse. Lydia looked like a misdemeanour compared to the crime that was about to take place, and at vast expense. Bastards. I felt so angry, that had I had a gun I would have emptied its magazine into Nick's podgy little face.

'Nice piece of skirt your man's with,' said the cabbie.

'Um, yes,' I said. 'Yeah, cor, get a load of her.'

'You gonna go in, then, or are we gonna wait out here?'

'I'll go in,' I said, 'and I'll pay you now.'

'No problem. That'll be seventeen pounds fifty.'

Extortion. Cabs are so expensive these days they are an elite form of transport and therefore should be ineligible to use bus lanes. I always thought the point of bus lanes was to enable poorer people to get around town quickly . . . but enough of this. I gave the cabbie a twenty, and was too craven to ask for any change. Anyway, he had done a good job.

'Here,' I said, 'that should keep you in gold sovereign rings.'

'Ta very much,' he said. 'It should buy at least three more.'

We laughed, and I turned on my heel and looked up at the facade of the mighty Clarendon. Red brick, slightly Gothic, a hotel group flag fluttering slightly, and a doorman wearing elegant livery. It felt like the right place for something dramatic, and my feelings would not be proved wrong.

'Afternoon, sir,' said the doorman as I walked past him with what I hoped to be the appropriate air of relaxed briskness.

'Afternoon,' I replied, vaguely self-conscious that I was completely underdressed.

I walked into the lobby, a luxurious expanse of marble floor, oak panelling, hushed armchairs, rich people. No sign of Sally and Nick – had they gone straight upstairs? I hoped they might have gone to the restaurant instead, so I went to the reception desk and asked whether it was possible to eat.

The receptionist, a man in his late fifties with a very mincing moustache, looked me up and down.

'Of course it is possible to eat here, sir,' he said as though I had asked an idiotic question, which, on reflection, I had.

'There is the brasserie,' he continued, pointing over my left shoulder, 'or there is the Angus Crookall restaurant on the first floor.'

The name Angus Crookall meant nothing to me. Had I lived in London, I'm sure it would have done, but as it was, I just assumed he was the latest voguish twat in a chef's uniform.

'I think I'll try that,' I said.

The receptionist cleared his throat slightly.

'Ahem. We do ask gentlemen to wear a tie in the Angus Crookall restaurant.'

'Do you have a tie I could borrow?'

'Of course, sir.'

He reached down and brought out a vile pink shiny tie, a pinkness I had hitherto assumed could only be found on Barbie outfits.

'Is that the only one you have?'

'I'm afraid so, sir. A couple of gentlemen have just borrowed the rather more sober ones.'

Reluctantly, I put it on, and climbed the stairs to the first floor. At the top, two vast glass doors awaited me behind which stood a flunkey. I didn't want to barge straight in and risk being seen, so I beckoned the flunkey out.

'Can I help you, sir?'

'Um, I'm sorry, this may seem, rather, er, odd,' I began, aware that I would make the worst spy in the world. 'But, I just want to know if there's someone in there.'

'Who would that be, sir?'

'A brunette woman wearing a bottle-green trouser suit.'

The flunkey looked concerned now.

'May I ask why, sir?'

Desperately trying to look cool, I pulled a twenty-pound note out of my pocket. Unfortunately, suave secret agent that I am, the extrication of said note sent a shower of change on to the floor, which I pretended to ignore.

'Take this,' I said, offering him the rather crumpled note.

'Thank you, sir,' said the flunkey.

I stole a glance down at the ground. There was at least three or four quid there, which I couldn't just leave. I didn't look like the type of person rich enough to chuck money away. The flunkey knew I was pretending not to care, so who was I trying to kid? I bent down and picked up the change, noticing how shiny the flunkey's shoes were. I stood up and looked the flunkey in the eye. He was in his late twenties, and his hair was revoltingly slick with gel.

'So then,' I said, 'is she there?'

'Yes, sir.'

My heart fluttered.

'Would it be possible,' I said, 'to sit at a table from where I could see her and she couldn't see me?'

The flunkey thought for a moment.

'Behind her?'

'Yes, of course.'

'I can arrange that.'

'Thank you.'

The flunkey led a very nervous Sam Holden into the dining room, which, thankfully, was packed. Because of the classy sumptuousness of the room – carpets, wall-hangings, massive padded chairs, tablecloths, etc. – it didn't seem noisy. It was the type of place where money comes to mellow, not to shout.

The flunkey showed me to a table near the entrance to the kitchen – always the worst place to sit, even in a place as grand as this. As I sat down, I looked around the room, and two-thirds of the way across it, I could see Sally's back. She was certainly with Nick, but both relief and delight surged through me when I saw she was also with a couple of other men, both of whom looked like Mongols. Ktyteklhdfistanis, that's what they were, Ktyteklhdfistanis. They were both fat and middle-aged and looked incredibly shifty. No doubt Sally and Nick were discussing matters of high Ktyteklhdfistani importance. What a world away from Peter and Daisy, I thought. And what a world away from me.

I was brought a menu and shuddered at the prices. Two courses: £42.50. Three courses: £55. Those were the cheap options. Had I gone à la carte, it would have cost me at least twice that. Anyway, I was not there for the food, but to keep an eye on my wife.

'Sir, would you like anything to drink?'

Different flunkey, same sort of hair.

'Just a bottle of still water.'

I then ordered from the set menu, determined to keep costs down.

For the next ten minutes, I kept a close eye on my quarry. She was clearly leading the conversation, and the two mysterious Ktyteklhdfistanis did a lot of nodding. Nick butted in occasionally, but there was no doubt Sally was the dominant one. There was a nasty moment when she got up to go to the loo, and I angled my head down deep into my starter, which would have tasted delicious had I not been so nervous.

I watched as Sally returned, and saw Nick give her a smarmy little smile. It annoyed the crap out of me, as did the way he ever so slightly lifted his hand up as if to touch her on the back. He was obviously used to doing so, the little snake, and he had only resisted making contact because he was in company.

As the minutes wore me down, I began to grow even more outraged. The group was piling away the red wine, although I saw Sally drank very little. Cool customer. I could only assume the British taxpayer was paying, as the Ktyteklhdfistanis were clearly not drinking on their own tab. If they were, they'd have bankrupted their country.

By the time I ate my main course – cod, I think it was – the Ktyteklhdfistanis were getting pretty howling. Nick was obviously drinking a bit as well, and, although I couldn't be sure, I thought I saw him touch Sally's leg under the table. Whatever the truth of it, I saw red, and nearly got up and went round.

I decided to be more devious. I took a piece of scrap A4 from my laptop bag, ripped it in half, and wrote: 'I know you're fucking her.' I folded it up and waited for my waiter to come over.

'I was wondering whether I could ask you a small favour?' I asked.

'Of course, sir, what can I do?'

'I was wondering whether you could deliver this note to the gentleman on that table by the far window.'

The waiter looked.

'I see,' he said. 'On the table with the lady in the green suit?'

'That's the one. I'd be ever so grateful. However, please don't tell him where you got the note from. Is that OK?'

'Of course, sir.'

'I know this is all highly irregular, but I'll make it up to you on the bill, I promise.'

'No problem at all.'

As the waiter walked off with the little time bomb in his hand, I felt unbelievably nervous. My nerves grew even greater when I saw Nick get up, and worsened when he walked off in the direction of the lavatory.

Oh fuck, I thought.

Instead of turning round, the waiter kept walking towards the table. Surely he wasn't going to leave the note with one of the Ktyteklhdfistanis?

Fuck, fuck, I thought.

I could have screamed as I watched the waiter discreetly hand the note to the Ktyteklhdfistani who was sitting next to Sally.

Fuck, fuck, fuck.

The Ktyteklhdfistani looked puzzled, and unwrapped the note under the table, no doubt thinking it was some sort of secret message from the embassy.

Fuck, fuck, fuck, fuck.

I wanted to run out of the room, run all the way back home to have tea and biscuits with Peter and Daisy while watching *Balamory* and pretend I had never done this.

The Ktyteklhdfistani's face went browny-red. Sally turned to him, and I could see her asking whether everything was OK. He held his right hand up to indicate that he was fine, which he clearly wasn't. If I could tell from that distance, I can only imagine how bad he must have looked from just across a table.

The Ktyteklhdfistani looked around the room, no doubt searching for the author of the note. He looked down at it again, and folded it up and put it in his jacket pocket.

Phew, I thought, I was safe. No doubt the man had a guilty conscience, and he really was fucking someone else's wife, the dirty little Ktyteklhdfistani.

And then disaster.

Horrendous disaster.

Catastrophe.

Sally said something to the man, who put his hand in his pocket and brought out the sheet of paper. He appeared reluctant to hand it over, but Sally was insistent. I could see her head angling down to the table, as if she was trying to look at something on the back of the note.

And then the full horror occurred to me as I looked down at the table at the other half of the scrap piece of paper. On the back of it was one of Peter's drawings – or rather scribbles – which Sally had captioned: 'A spacemen being chased by a giraffe in a Lancaster Bomber', although my bit just read '. . . raffe in a Lancaster Bomber.'

There was nowhere for me to go. Nowhere to hide. If I made a dash for the gents, I would bump into Nick. If I tried to do a runner, one of the waiters would be bound to stop me. My legs felt gelatinous as I watched the Ktyteklhdfistani hand the paper over to Sally, who studied it closely while Nick returned to the table. He too looked at the note, and then together, they scanned the room.

I was caught. A rat in a very expensive trap. I wriggled and squirmed, but I knew the hunter would find me, and sure enough she did. Our eyes met, and I knew I was dead, or something a little worse than dead. The question remained, was she going to come over and berate me now?

My phone rang. Loudly. Half the dining room looked at me as I fumbled in my jacket pocket for it, no doubt thinking, who's the twat in the pink tie? It was Lydia. Of course it was Lydia. Who else would it be? I had to turn it off – there was no way I was going to talk to her now. I could see Sally shaking her head.

'I'm sorry, sir,' said my waiter. 'I'm afraid we do not allow mobile phone usage in the restaurant.'

'Sorry,' I said.

By now, I felt nauseous. Literally nauseous.

'Is everything all right, sir?'

'Er, yes, I mean, no, I mean yes – fine, thanks.'

'You look a little pale, sir.'

'Do I?'

I loosened my pink tie. I started to feel terribly hot. My heart was pounding, palpitating, reacting to the absurd levels of whatever stress chemical it was that my brain was causing to flood my body. I felt ready to faint, and that was exactly what I did.

The next thing I saw was Sally's face hovering above me.

'Sam! Sam! Are you OK?'

Her features sort of swam in front of my eyes like a special effect. Her voice sounded a long way away down a tunnel.

'Sam!'

'Hello,' I said.

At first, I had no idea where I was. I looked around me, and saw I was in an office. A senior-looking middle-aged man was on the phone, and one of the waiters was standing next to him.

'Sam,' said Sally, 'are you OK?'

I had never seen such an anxious expression on her face.

'I think so,' I said. 'Can I have a glass of water?'

The waiter left the room.

I looked up at Sally.

'I'm so sorry,' I said. 'I am so so sorry.'

Sally cupped my face with her hand.

'What are you doing here?'

'I followed you.'

'I can see that, but why?'

'Nick,' I said. 'Because you're with Nick.'

The middle-aged man spoke softly to Sally.

'Do you think he requires an ambulance?'

Sally looked back at me.

'Do you?' she asked.

'No,' I said. 'I'll be fine.'

'You quite sure?' she asked.

'Yes,' I replied.

The waiter brought in a glass of water, which I necked eagerly. It felt so good, so vivifying.

Sally turned to the two men.

'Do you mind leaving us for a few minutes?'

'Of course, madam. If there's anything you require, I shall be in the restaurant.'

A few seconds later, Sally and I were alone.

'I'm so sorry,' I said again. 'But I had to make sure about you and Nick.'

Sally shook her head.

'I wish I'd told you ages ago,' she said.

'Told me what?'

She sighed.

'I'm not supposed to tell you, he swore me to secrecy.'

'What is it?'

I could see that it was a real struggle for Sally to say the next sentence.

'He's gay, Sam. Nick is *gay*.'

My head fell back against the carpet.

'Oh God,' I muttered. 'I'm such a fucking fool.'

'That's why I've been seeing him so much. He wants to sort his life out, and I'm the only person he knows who can help. You see, I know his parents, who are incredibly stuffy and uptight, and we've been discussing how he should tell them. This is hardly something he can talk about with his girlfriend. I was the most natural person for him to turn to.'

'Gay? You . . . you're sure?'

'Absolutely, Sam, one hundred per cent.' She sighed before continuing, 'Perhaps I should have told you ages ago.'

'Oh God,' I went, and then carried on apologising.

I didn't know whether to laugh or cry, so I sort of did both. What a fucking fuck-up.

'It's all right,' said Sally, which it clearly wasn't.

'No it isn't,' I said. 'I've humiliated you in front of those people; probably buggered up the whole of Central Asia.'

Sally laughed slightly.

'Don't worry about them,' she said. 'They're more bewildered than anything.'

I sat up, and waited for a head spin. None came.

'Take it gently,' said Sally.

All I wanted to do was to run away, and ostrich myself.

'Listen,' I said, 'you should go back to your lunch with the Whoojumaflippis. I'll be all right getting home.'

'No, you won't,' said Sally. 'I'll come home with you.'

'Honestly, there's no need.'

'Would you let me go home in similar circumstances?'

I thought about it briefly.

'No, no I probably wouldn't.'

'Well, then.'

I slowly got my feet.

'We need to pay my bill,' I said.

'That's all taken care of.'

'How?'

'Let's just say the department are good customers here.'

'If I'd known that I would have ordered a bottle of wine.'

Sally smiled.

'You sure you're ready to go?'

I nodded.

'OK,' she said. 'You wait here, and I'll go and have a word with Nick and then we'll go.'

Nick. Until yesterday, that name sent ice into my heart because I was convinced he and my wife were having an affair. Now it sends ice into my heart because it reminds me of my utter foolishness.

Needless to say, the journey back was somewhat awkward. I felt as if I were a naughty twelve-year-old boy being escorted back to school after having been caught playing truant by his mother. I felt about as tall as that twelve-year-old, my dignity completely stripped. And it was all my pathetic fault, my pathetic paranoid fault.

Saturday 13 August

Sally and I had a huge chat last night. We both agreed we're going through a rough patch, but neither of us wants to give up. Sally suggested half jokingly that I should see a psychiatrist, but I said there was really no need, and that 90 per cent of my problems stemmed from my belief that she was having an affair.

'But how about being a househusband?' she asked.

I pondered the question. Normally, unless I'm trying to concoct some sort of buller, I never ponder. (In fact, I don't know anybody who ponders.) Finally, after about three years, I said, 'I'm not sure.'

Emphatic stuff. I could tell Sally wasn't exactly ecstatic. If I didn't want to do this any more, we'd have to sort out childcare. Finances. Guilt.

'I'm sorry,' I said. 'That's the truth.'

We were sitting in the kitchen after supper, both of us looking down at our dirty plates.

'I feel we haven't really given it a proper go,' Sally said. 'I nag constantly and you just try to get by. And having Lydia can't really count, can it?'

'All right,' I sighed. 'That's true. The time I've had with the children has been really nice, but it's not exactly . . .' I shrugged lamely.

'But they're long-term projects,' said Sally. 'You don't see the fruits of your labours day-by-day. It's not like working in the City or something where your profit and loss is on a screen in pounds and pence every few seconds.'

'I know, I know. But maybe that's a difference between men and women. We want our achievements to be easily measured, whereas you seem to exist in this far more nebulous world where you can't quite quantify anything.'

Sally laughed a little.

'That's what makes us so sophisticated,' she said, smiling. 'We see the world for what it is. A big grey area, whereas you men are always trying to make sense of it, to categorise, to put this in a box, to put that in another box. You can't do that with Peter and Daisy, at least not until they're at school when you can test them on their times tables and things like that.'

She came round the table and hugged me. It was the first time she had done that in a long time.

'What are we going to do?' she asked.

It sounded as if she really wanted to know. I held on to her hands and let out a long breath.

'I don't know,' I said. 'But then I don't have much choice, do I? You're obviously enjoying work, and I don't want you to leave. The chances of me getting a reasonable job are next to nothing at the moment. It's just . . .'

'What?' Sally asked, releasing her grip slightly.

'Well, I know you said you had to adapt when you became a mum, but you must admit that for a man to make that transition is a lot harder.'

'Go on.'

'And I've found it hard. Hence Lydia, I suppose. When I went to see the lads a while back, I found it incredibly difficult to connect with them. It's as though they'd all gone marching forwards, and I was just left behind with a note from matron.'

'Shouldn't you see yourself as marching in a different direction?' she asked tentatively.

'Fair point,' I replied. 'But what's in that direction?'

Sally went over to the fridge and pulled out a half-full bottle of white wine. She offered it towards me and I nodded.

'You know I've seen these other househusbands,' I said, 'and they're just, well, losers, frankly. They're all trying to be something they're not. I can't believe *any* man really wants to spend his day looking after children, and so, in order to compensate for the fact they've found themselves in a situation they don't like, they overegg how much they adore it. I used to do that at school when I bought an album that was complete crap, and I knew it, and all my friends knew it, yet I could never bear to admit it, so I defended the pile of crap in order to save face.'

'But looking after children is not crap, Sam. It's not like buying some S'Express album . . .'

'How did you know it was S'Express?'

'I didn't! Was it really?'

I then started going 'diddle-duh, diddle-duh, ess express', while playing an imaginary keyboard.

'But it was good that song.'

'It was fine, but did you hear the rest of the album?'

'No.'

'Exactly.'

'Anyway,' said Sally, 'children aren't S'Express albums.'

'I know, but men's attitude towards childcare is similar to mine towards buying a crap album. If they've got to look after children the whole time, then men will try to say it's the best thing that ever happened to them, blah blah. I wish you'd been at Longwhip to see what an absurd bunch they were.'

'You're being too cynical.'

'They all had comedy facial hair, Sally,' I said, 'all of them.'

'You can't judge a man by his facial hair.'

'Oh yes, you bloody can. Come on, you must agree with me. It's even more of a giveaway than shoes.'

'But you don't have to be like one of those men to be a househusband. Nobody's expecting you to grow a goatee just because you're looking after Peter and Daisy.'

'But it's the only way I'd fit in,' I said. 'Otherwise I'm talking to housewives all day, and ultimately they think I'm a little suspicious.'

'Do they?'

'Yes. Nobody's unfriendly, but they all think I must be some sort of threat.'

Sally snorted into her wine glass.

'Not that sort of threat,' I said. 'But, you know, something that upsets the balance. Just the same as a woman appearing in an office that has only had men in it. And, before you start, I'm not saying it's a bad thing, but it does alter the dynamic. Men have had to adapt to women in the workplace, and a good thing too, and women must now adapt to men in the homeplace, if there is such a word.'

'There's not.'

'You know what I mean.'

'I do. And it's a fair point. So why can't you see yourself as one of these great trailblazers? Househusbands should be considered as radical as suffragettes.'

It was a good point, and I pondered into my glass. Whatever it was Sally had given me was a little old, but still, it was cold, so it went down.

'The thing is,' I said, 'I never saw myself as being radical. I just wanted to make a fat pile of cash and be as New Dad as possible without being a Keen Dad. You know, do my fair share of nappies at the weekend, and yet still bring home the bacon.'

'But those days are gone, Sam,' said Sally, leaning forward. She held my free hand and stroked its knuckles with my thumb. 'This is what you are now,' she said. 'Either you find a job and we have to sort ourselves out, or you have to see this as your job and you've got to make it work.'

Another email from Nigel had confirmed again that I wasn't a desirable commodity at the moment. Also, and perhaps just as important, Sally and I had never been keen on both of us working full time, leaving the children to be looked after by someone else. Didn't appear I had much choice.

'You've got to work out where to find that pride,' Sally continued. 'You've got to keep looking at Peter and Daisy and realising how fantastic they are. Just imagine how you'll feel in twenty years time when they've left home as the confident, charming, decent people we hope them to be. You'll be terrifically proud of that, more so than running some FTSE company or whatever. Does that make sense?'

'It does,' I said. 'It's all very logical. I've just got to learn to feel it, I suppose, be more patient.'

'Exactly. And don't forget, it's incredibly tough when they're both pre-school. Everyone says that when they go to school, you get so much of your life back. And that's not far away. Perhaps you could do some consultancy or something a few years down the line.'

'Not a bad idea.'

'You don't sound enthused.'

'I know. Sorry.' I drained my wine. I think it was corked, but I couldn't be sure.

Monday 15 August

I bumped into Emily this morning who had her entire gang in tow, as did I. Nevertheless, the noisy abundance of our loinfruit did not stop her laying leaden hints regarding her availability.

'Jim's away next week,' she said, looking me straight in the eye.

She might as well have said, 'Would you like to have sex next week?'

'Perhaps if you're at a loose end you could join us for some dinner,' I said, knowing full well this wasn't exactly the invitation she was angling for.

'That would be nice,' she said.

'OK, I'll, um, get back to you with a day after I've checked with Sally.'

'Aren't you in charge of the social diary then?'

'Er, no.'

'I thought all housewives were in charge of such things,' she said playfully.

I was angrier than I'd been in a while.

'Listen, I have to run,' I finally said, desperately trying to think of a witty reply. 'I'm sure I'll see you soon.'

I left the shop, all but dragging Peter and Daisy with me.

Emily's comment has rattled me. Will I just turn into this hausfrau, who does little more than run around after the children and work out who's coming for dinner and when? If women can't take me seriously, then men certainly won't. And, the thing is, if nobody else will take me seriously then *I* most certainly won't.

There's no doubt that I'm at an all-time low. But if I can't be self-pitying in my diary, then where else can I be?

Thursday 18 August

I'm on autopilot at the moment. Drifting from hour to hour, performing the tasks of fatherhood perfunctorily. Peter and Daisy are being processed, not brought up. I think they sense my lack of joy and, as a result, they're being uppity. Peter has been whinging all day, and demanding TV, biscuits, his teddy, this and that. Daisy has been whining all day, and if she could speak no doubt would have regaled me with an equally long list of unsuitable demands.

I rang Nigel this afternoon, not to talk about anything in particular, but simply because I was feeling lonely. He said he was too busy and he would call me back a little later. He didn't.

Friday 19 August

It was watching one of those real-life-emergency-999-disaster-oh-my-God-we're-all-going-to-die programmes that gave me the idea. This episode of gratuitous near-death near-pornography was about a family who were trapped on the fourteenth floor of a blazing tower-block that was due to explode at any moment because there was lots of gas or something. As I was marvelling at the firemen climbing up God knows how many feet, and entering the smoke-filled building, I suddenly turned to Sally, and without thinking, said, 'I could do that'.

At first, she ignored me. She was flicking through some magazine, and simply sort of grunted.

'Listen,' I said, 'why don't I become a fireman?'

'A fireman?'

I had never seen Sally's gob so smacked.

'But how will you have time?'

'I wouldn't do it full time. I'd be some sort of retained fireman, you know, like a special police constable or something. Just do it in my own time. Voluntary work.'

'You're not being serious?'

'I'm being perfectly serious.'

Indeed I was. And the more I thought about it, the more I realised it was the perfect solution to my househusband woes. Suddenly, I would feel like a man again, a proper bloke. I might not be as rich as my friends, or sail the high seas of corporate finance, but here was a chance to hold my head up high the next time we went out for a Chinese. When they asked me what I was doing, their glazed expressions would perk up when I told them how I had just rescued a family from a towering inferno.

'I can't see you in the uniform,' said Sally.

I raised my eyebrows suggestively, provocatively.

'Sorry, firemen don't do it for me.'

'How about a policeman, then?'

'Even worse!'

'Doctor?'

'Getting warm.'

'Well, there's something I didn't know.'

'Enough of this,' said Sally, slightly abashed. 'We were talking of you becoming a fireman, not dressing up as a doctor. If you want my opinion, and if you're really being serious, I think it's a ridiculous idea.'

'But why? It would be the perfect way to make me feel that all my alpha male genes are being responded to.'

Sally harrumphed.

'I am being serious,' I said. 'Can't you tell?'

Sally looked back down at her magazine.

'One question,' she said. 'When would you do it? After all, you can't just run out of the house if you're looking after the children, and I assume the local fire station doesn't have a crèche. And I don't think it pays particularly well, so you'd be paying for childcare as well. '

'I could ask to be on call just at nights and at the weekends.'

'Would they allow that?'

'I'm sure they would.'

'Great,' said Sally. 'I can just see it. We're settling down to a nice Sunday lunch with some friends, and suddenly your bleep goes. Or, we're having a romantic night in, and beep beep, off you go. It would wreak havoc with the little time we've got.'

I didn't say anything at first.

'You've got a point,' I said, 'but don't you think it would help to, you know, cure all those things I was talking about the other day? Give me a purpose, that sort of thing.'

'I thought we said that Peter and Daisy are your purpose.'

'We've been through this,' I said.

I suddenly felt angry. This was a good idea, I knew it, and here was Sally once again pissing on my parade.

'I wish you weren't so negative the whole time,' I said.

'I'm not!'

'You are. Every time I have an idea you shoot it down.'

'That's not fair. I'm sorry if I'm not taking you particularly seriously, but a few minutes ago you were sitting here watching some dross on the TV and drinking your umpteenth glass of rosé, and now you've suddenly decided you're going to be a fireman. Fine, if that's what you want to do, then fine. But don't blame me when you find all our evenings and weekends are buggered because you've got to dash off to rescue a cat up a tree.'

'I'm going to give it a go,' I said, and stood up and left the room and came up to write this.

I've just looked at our local fire brigade's website. It looks like they're desperate for firemen during the evenings and weekends – perfect. This is serendipity, I'm sure of it.

The training looks a bit scary though.

Sunday 21 August

Have spent much of the weekend attempting to convince Sally that my becoming a part-time fireman is a great idea. I don't know why I feel I need to ask her permission, but ever since the Clarendon Incident (sounds like a Robert Ludlum novel), I'm treading on eggshells rather. Eventually, while we were washing up after lunch, she said, 'Oh all right then, get it out of your system. Anyway, I doubt you'll pass the training – you're far too much of a malco.'

'Me? A malco?'

'You were never exactly Mr Sporty, were you?'

'You were never Miss Sporty.'

'I know.'

'Just because I'm not sporty, doesn't mean I'm incapable of climbing up a ladder.'

'I didn't think you liked heights.'

'I'm fine with heights.'

'No, you're not. When we went to that church in France, you would barely look over the edge of the tower. Total vertigo.'

Sally had a point – she always does – but I wasn't going to admit any shortcoming. Instead, I went into pedant mode.

'It's not vertigo.'

'It looked like it.'

'It's acrophobia, actually.'

'Tomayto, tomahto.'

'Vertigo is dizziness, acrophobia is a fear of heights.'

'All right, smart Alec, you just tell that to your firemen friends.'

Lydia called again this evening. I told Sally what we owed her, and that I couldn't dishonour a debt. Lots of eye-rolling and tutting, but Sally acknowledged I was right. I'll send a cheque off tomorrow morning.

Monday 22 August

This morning, as soon as it turned nine o'clock, I phoned our local fire brigade. The chap on the line sounded like a good bloke, and although he was a little circumspect about my age – Christ! I'm not that old! – I said I was fit and everything was in good order. He then asked me what I did for a living and I said 'househusband'.

'Housewhat?'

'Househusband. You know, I look after the children.'

Silence. Awkward silence.

'Must be tough,' he said, 'doing that all by yourself.'

'My wife is around at the weekends.'

'So you've got a wife?'

'Yes.'

'Oh, I'm so sorry, I assumed that because you were at home, she had, um, passed on.'

'No, no,' I sighed, 'nothing like that. Just makes financial sense for her to work and not me.'

'I see, I see. So, um, why do you want to become a retained firefighter?'

I realised that saying 'excitement' or 'to prove I'm still a man' would not sound so great. So instead, I went for the vacuous job-interview coached reply.

'I want to put something back into the community.'

'Really?'

'Yes.'

'And not just because you want to do something exciting after a day spent with the kids?'

'Well, if I'm to be honest . . .'

'Good! Good! Don't give me all the community stuff. I want people who find it exciting. They're the keen ones. After all, you can give something back to the community by hosting bingo nights at the Bellevue Home for the Bewildered.'

I laughed obediently.

'You're right,' I said. 'So what happens next?'

'Well, we've got an assessment on Saturday morning. Have a look at the website to see what that's about.'

'I've already looked.'

'Good. It's at nine a.m. sharp. You can make it?'

'I can, yes.'

'Good, good. See you then, Mr Holden.'

'Great.'

'One thing.'

'I hope you don't get vertigo.'

'Of course not,' I lied.

It was not the time to be a pedant. Besides, I don't suffer from vertigo. Just a little acrophobia. There's a difference.

Thursday 25 August

I haven't felt like this since the run-up to Christmas when I was a child. Come tomorrow, I will be well on my way to being a fireman. I feel confident and fit – I even went for a run this evening when Sally got back and didn't feel as crap as I thought I would. Sally thinks I'm nuts, that much is obvious, but I think she likes the idea that I've got a spring in my step. Peter and Daisy have been affected by the change in my mood as well and are behaving a lot better.

This afternoon, in order to get the measure of how I'll perform with heights, I took them to Jungle Jim's Adventure Land, and once again, I vowed never to return. As usual, the place reeked of urine and chip fat, a smell intensified by the fact it was hot outside, thereby baking the greenhouse-like industrial unit Jungle Jim calls home.

I decided, when none of the people who pass for employees weren't looking, to enter the vast maze of rubber ramps and slides and ropes. Peter thought this hysterical, largely because I almost got stuck in one of the tunnels. A couple of other children looked at me strangely as I passed them up to the top of the long slide that forms the central feature of Jungle Jim's. When I got there, I looked down, and I found myself ever so slightly starting to shake. It did look a long way down, a very long way.

Peter came up next to me.

'What are you doing, Daddy?'

'I'm about to go down the slide, but I was, er, waiting for you.'

Peter didn't reply, but instead launched himself head first, and went whizzing to the bottom to crash land in a pit of small rubber balls. At first, I thought he must have hurt himself, but he extricated himself to reveal a huge grin.

It was now my turn. I paused. I was being an utter wimp, I knew it.

'Come on, Daddy!'

Taking a deep breath and, shutting my eyes, I launched myself down the slide. I must have been going at least 0.5

mph until I came to a stop halfway down. This was ludicrous. The slide was so shallow and my weight was such that the friction of my clothes against the surface had brought me to a halt.

'Come on, Daddy!'

I pushed myself forward again. This time I made it to the bottom and smashed at around 2 mph into the balls, which smelt even more rancid than I could have feared.

'Oi!' came a voice. 'What you doin' in there?'

I looked round to see a fearsome-looking fat woman of indeterminate age glaring at me from the other side of the net.

'You're not allowed in there!'

'I'm terribly sorry,' I said, 'I was just seeing if my son was all right.'

She eyed me suspiciously.

'Anyway, is that your daugh'er in the ball pit?'

'Yes.'

'She's been sick.'

She had been as well, all over the balls. I offered to pay for some new ones, but the woman told me it happened all the time.

'We wash 'em every week,' she revealed.

That's all right then.

When we got back home, I plonked the children in the bath and scrubbed every little molecule of Jungle Jim's off them. I then had a shower and did the same. I swear the water ran yellow off me. Yuk.

Saturday 27 August

Humiliation is a funny thing. Over the past few months, I've been humiliated in countless ways, and yet never learned humility. Self-pity, yes, but humility, no. But today I learned humility, and it feels extraordinary.

It all happened during my assessment to become a fireman.

I turned up keenly early, at about 8.30, and found nobody else was around. I sat in the car and listened to the radio, hoping yet another piece about Bob Dylan on the *Today* programme would calm my nerves. It didn't, but what did was an old cigarette I found in the glove compartment. It tasted foul, but the nicotine did the trick. I flicked the cigarette end in a bin and went into the fire station.

I was greeted by a tall friendly-looking man, who was wearing a fire brigade T-shirt and jeans. He had an enormous moustache, the type you see Para NCOs sporting.

'I assume you must be Mr Holden,' he said.

'Sam,' I replied, shaking his hand.

His grip almost fractured my knuckles. I did my best not to wince, and gripped his hand tightly back, but it was like holding a rock.

'I'm Geoff Brundage, the chief here at the station.'

I looked around the station, admiring the two gleaming orange fire engines.

'I always thought fire engines were red,' I said.

'Only Dinky toys are red,' he said. 'Ah! Here comes our lovely nurse!'

I turned to see a petite blonde woman in her early thirties walk in.

'Well hello, Sister Savage,' said Brundage flirtatiously.

Sister Savage fluttered her eyelashes a little.

'Hello, Mr Fireman,' she replied, even more flirtatiously.

Jesus, I thought, this was like a *Carry On* film.

'How many have you got for me today?'

'Half a dozen, and he's the first,' Brundage replied, looking at me.

'Shall I do you now?' she asked.

'Erm, yes,' I replied, not exactly knowing what she was referring to.

'Follow me,' she said, and led me into a small office with a teleprinter. She unpacked a black briefcase, and brought out all manner of medical kit and sheets of paper.

'Can you fill this in while I get ready?'

'Sure.'

It was a medical questionnaire. I usually find these fun to fill in, because I've always enjoyed good health. It's very satisfying ticking all the 'no' boxes, which I proceeded to do with gusto. I handed it back to her.

She checked my blood pressure and pulse.

'Hmm,' she said. 'Your blood pressure is a little high, but I expect it's the nerves.'

'White-coat syndrome?'

'Falling-off-ladder syndrome.'

'Come again?'

'You do know what you're in for, don't you?'

'I looked at the website.'

'You know you've got to hang off a ladder by one leg?'

I didn't, because I hadn't read the website properly.

'Um, how high is this ladder?'

'It goes up to about forty-five feet, but you hang off at about thirty feet.'

'By one leg?'

'That's right.'

'And what happens if I fall?'

'You won't fall. Nobody ever does.'

'What happens if I don't do it?'

'Then it's go back home time.'

Fuck, all I could think was, fuck. The fire station started to fill up with other applicants, all of whom looked about twelve. I wanted to run away, but I didn't want to lose face, at least not quite so quickly.

'Shall I take your blood pressure again?' Sister Savage asked with a wry smile.

'Best not,' I said, my heart beating as though it were trying to escape from my ribcage.

The first load of tests were straightforward, and gave me a false sense of confidence. We had to lift 50 kg weights, which were only marginally lighter than Sally, who I can lift easily. In fact, I carried her across the threshold into our first flat, and didn't even knock her head on the door frame. I was gratified to see I was able to lift the weights more capably than some of the pubescents. We then had to lift a 30 kg weight up to the top of a ladder, which once again I found simple enough. Just as I was completing it, a shout rang out.

'Fire!'

At first, us assessees thought it was part of the training, and we just stood around, smiling gormlessly.

'Fire!'

The shout was female, and it was coming from the other side of the fire station. We looked at Brundage, who ran off in the direction of the voice. We followed him, and came across Sister Savage.

'Quick! QUICK! The bin's on fire!'

I knew instantly whose fault it was. Mine. I felt weak. Shit, I thought, I would be the first aspirant fireman in the history of the world who burned down the fire station on day one. Within seconds, Brundage had grabbed a hose from one of the fire engines, and took it through the front doors to the bin. To watch him in action was an impressive sight, although not as impressive as the massive column of dirty smoke that was belching rancidly out of the bin.

The fire was soon out, replaced by a filthy cloud of steamy gunk. Brundage turned back towards us, a slightly menacing grin on his face.

'Well, fancy that,' he said. 'There's a turn-up for the books.'

'Any idea what may have caused it?' I asked.

'Cigarette, most likely,' said Brundage, 'that's what normally causes bin fires.'

Brundage looked at us, and I felt that his gaze lingered especially long on me. I knew he would not be able to prove my guilt, but my breath no doubt stank of the offending fag when I arrived.

'I do hope it wasn't one of you gentlemen who started it,' he said.

We all mumbled 'of course not', mine unnecessarily loud.

'Right, excitement over,' he said, and like schoolboys we scurried back to the yard. I felt an intense rush of relief when I realised I had not been busted.

Our next few tests were simple enough. Rolling out and rolling up hoses quickly, wearing breathing apparatus and negotiating a special course – mildly claustrophobic, but nothing too horrendous, not like potholing – as well as a fitness test that involved us running increasingly fast between a pair of markers several yards apart. It was absolutely exhausting, although I was determined not to be the first one to drop out. I really gave it my all, despite my hatred of running, and I was delighted to see a rather porky chap drop out just as the pace became really merciless. In the end, I was the third to drop out, and Brundage told me I had not disgraced myself considering how old I was. Grrr.

And then came the leg lock.

Brundage showed us how to do it, and naturally, after God knows how many decades as a fireman, he made it look simple. He scampered up the ladder as though he was an ape, and then, about two-thirds of the way up – so high that only his moustache was visible – he wrapped his left leg around a step, and engaged his foot on the outside of the left rail. Then, without pausing, he leaned his torso and his head all the way back, so he was looking directly at us.

'This, gents, is the leg lock,' he said, as though addressing people upside down and halfway to most flight paths was the most normal thing he could be doing on a Saturday morning. 'It's not just something we chuck in for show;

it's an essential skill. It means your hands are free to do whatever it is that needs doing, and you've got absolutely no danger of falling.'

Then, just for show, I thought, he wriggled his hands around, a huge upside-down smile bristling under his YMCA moustache.

'Right then,' he said, 'who wants to give it a go first?'

Us applicants looked around with nervous smiles. We all pointed at each other, with one of the guys saying, 'I think the oldest should go first,' and pointing at me.

'Good idea,' said another.

'Oh, no no no,' I said, 'you're only picking on me because you're too scared to do it first.'

'Bollocks!' went the accuser, a lad who must have been about nineteen with terrible acne, the poor bastard.

'All right,' I said. 'Why don't you and I toss a coin to see who goes first?'

'Done,' he said.

I extracted a coin from my pocket while Brundage made his way swiftly down the ladder.

'What a bunch of pansies!' he said.

'I know, I know,' I said.

I tossed the coin. My rival shouted 'tails' as it rotated in an arc to the ground. (I always like a man who chooses tails. Suggests something contrary in his nature which I appreciate.)

The coin landed on the ground and we looked down. It was heads.

'Right then,' I said. 'Up you go.'

'Fuck,' he said, staring up the ladder.

Once more, Brundage demonstrated the lock, but did

it at a lower level so we could see exactly how it worked. None of us looked convinced, least of all Acne Head.

'Um, one question,' I said.

'Yes?' said Brundage.

'What happens if I, I mean, if any of us fell?'

'You won't,' said Brundage. 'Not if you do it just as I've shown you.'

'But . . .'

'We'll be there to catch you, Mr Holden.'

I smiled weakly, and was glad to see I was not alone in looking queasy.

Acne Lad went up. I noticed his legs were shaking. Some bunch of firemen we were going to make, I thought.

'OK,' said Brundage, 'that's high enough!'

Acne stopped.

'Left leg as I showed you!'

With some nervousness, Acne did he was told.

'Now, let go and lean back!'

Acne's hands froze. We could all see he was terrified. I could feel my own legs starting to tremble. This would be me in a minute.

'Let go, lad!' shouted Brundage. 'If you don't, you'll never be a fireman!'

Acne let go with his left hand, and then, while everyone watched him in silence, he let go with his right. He wobbled. And then he leaned back a little, and wobbled some more. After three days, he eventually leaned all the way back.

'Excellent!' said Brundage, who then held up a playing card. 'What card am I holding up?'

'The Ace of . . . of Hearts!'

'Correct! All right, you can come down.'

Lots of back slapping for Acne when he returned to earth. I gulped. I didn't think people really gulped until then, but I certainly gulped. Like a frog.

'All right, Mr Holden, your turn!'

I briefly wondered why he kept calling me 'Mr Holden'. I could only assume he must have been in the army and I reminded him of one of his officers, one of his 'Ruperts'. As I climbed the ladder, I recalled how my friend Angus had once told me there were tons of gays and transvestites in the Paras – especially in one of the mortar platoons – and all this being macho stuff and joining the army was a way of compensating for a side of themselves they didn't like. Well, fair enough. In a way, it was similar to what I was trying to achieve by climbing that ladder, trying to unleash a part of Sam Holden that was being kept in check by a part of Sam Holden I didn't like – the househusband bit, the domestic bit.

'Stop there! That'll do!'

I looked around me. I was sodding miles up. I wasn't at thirty feet, I was at thirty thousand feet. Aeroplanes and clouds passed below, the space shuttle drew up alongside me, and I found it difficult to breathe. In fact, I was hyperventilating and damn near having what I suspected might quickly become a full-blown panic attack.

What was I trying to achieve? What was I doing up here in the middle of a fire station in the middle of a town in the middle of the country? Who was I doing this for? Me, or my family? Or maybe even the community? No, most certainly not!

'Come on, Mr Holden!'

The voice was very distant. I was entering into a limbo of consciousness – basically I was day-dreaming. I stood on the ladder, aware that I was there, but having some sort of Buddhist moment.

'Lock your leg!'

Henry Reed poem again. We call this locking the leg.

'Come on!'

Somewhere below me, my left leg went through the rungs and then tried to grip around the side. My legs were so gelatinous, they could have been made into fruit pastilles.

'That's it!'

Except it didn't feel like it. My left foot did not feel as though it could hold my left leg, let alone my entire weight.

'Now let go!'

We call this the letting go.

My hands were having none of it.

'Let go or it's straight back home!'

Home. What a nice place home is, I thought. Far nicer than being up a ladder, up here in the sky, where it feels wrong and terrifying.

I let go with my left hand, leaving my right hand clutching the rung ferociously hard in order to compensate. This felt so unnatural, and I felt such a malco.

'That's it!'

This was as far from the emergency-999 programme as it was possible to be. What the sod was I doing? I asked myself again. Sally was right. I was one of life's rosé drinkers, not a bloody action man. Who was I trying to kid?

Pride forced me onwards, narrowly beating fear in a

close-fought contest that left both sides punch drunk. A very pyrrhic victory for pride.

I let go with my other hand. For a few seconds, I got my balance, although not very well, and then I decided to go for it.

I leaned back. Slowly. My legs did the Shakin' Stevens.

'Keep going!'

I kept going, all the time thinking how much I hated doing this, and that even if I managed to read whatever sodding card it was that Brundage was holding up, I never wanted to do this again. I would be the type of fireman who only attended bungalow fires, or fires in fields. No ladders for Fireman Sam.

'They' always say that when something very bad happens, it happens in slow motion; I'd once heard this was because your brain, which is flooding with adrenalin in the expectation of some disaster happening to the body, is able to work at 200 per cent and receive and process so much more information than it does while at rest.

Well, that's all bollocks. With me, it didn't happen in slow motion, it happened very quickly. Extremely quickly. One yoctosecond I was sort of doing all right, and the next yoctosecond I was falling. Backwards. Head first. Plummeting towards the ground at terminal velocity. And as I fell, in the zeptosecond or two I had before I landed on the tarmac head first, snapping my spinal cord, and then entering into a world of death or quadriplegia, all I could think of were Sally, Peter and Daisy and how much I would miss them and how much they would miss me – their husband and father. I wasn't thinking about my fate per se, but about how my fate related to theirs. I felt an enormous sense of anger, even in that full attosecond in which this all happened, that I had been the most selfish husband and father ever.

You can't really brace yourself for falling head first from thirty feet, but what you can do is to flail your arms madly, and that is precisely what I did. And somehow, Christ knows how, a hand connected with a rung. I clutched that rung as though I were holding Peter or Daisy away from the jaws of a shark. I clutched it hard, and it stayed there. The rest of my body then sort of cartwheeled down the ladder, and I inverted and went a bit sideways, and ended up sort of the right way up, hanging by one arm just one foot above the ground.

I was alive.

Brundage rushed up towards me. He was saying something, but I couldn't make out what it was. All I can remember was the sound of my own breathing, and how much I wanted to get back home. I felt shame too, shame that I had wasted everybody's time in pursuing some gung-ho boyish fantasy that nearly got me killed.

A ringing.

It didn't register at first. Brundage was pointing at my pocket.

'. . . you going to answer that?'

'Answer what?'

'Your phone!'

I scrambled around in my trouser pockets and fished it out. It was Lydia. Fuck. I had forgotten to send her that cheque, and now she was going to give me a well-deserved rocket. I looked at the screen and debated whether to answer it, not that I could have done, because my hands were shaking so badly I could barely be sure of pressing the green button. I left it, coward that I am.

'You all right?' asked Brundage.

'I think so,' I replied.

'That was close,' he said, smiling broadly. 'Pretty spectacular stuff. You'd make quite the stuntman.'

'But not quite the fireman,' I said.

Brundage looked up the ladder.

'I'm willing to give you another shot,' he said.

I followed his gaze. My shaking subsided a little as I contemplated Brundage's offer. For some reason, I felt bizarrely confident. I had just cheated death, and so now I was invincible. Of course I can do it, I thought, you've just got to stop being a pussy and act like a man. Grrr. Tough talk.

But I didn't want to do it. I knew right then that I didn't want to be a fireman. I didn't want to climb up and down ladders and rescue people from tower blocks. The world didn't need me to do such heroics. There were others – like Acne – who could do all that. There was only one place for me.

'You know what?'

'What?' Brundage asked.

'I'm going to go back home,' I said.

Sunday 28 August

Sally can't believe my volte-face, and frankly, I don't blame her. Forty-eight hours ago, her husband wanted to be in line for a George Cross, and now he's emphatically stating that there's nothing else he'd rather do than bring up their two children.

'I just don't get it,' said Sally. 'I mean, I think it's great – you'll be a lot happier. But I just don't get it.'

We were walking along the river, Peter up ahead chasing imaginary baddies with a machine-gun stick, and Daisy kipping idyllically in the pram. In fact, everything was idyllic – the weather, the ducks on the water, the slightest of gentle breezes. A contented lunch sat in our stomachs, and both Sally and I had polished off a bottle of, yes, rosé. (Rosé is all anybody seems to drink during the summer these days. I think we've got through four cases so far. Disgraceful.)

'Look, I know it's not going to be easy, but there is not that much choice. And I'd rather do it a hundred per cent than wing it. I think I've realised that for the past several months I've got it all wrong. I used to care too much about what other people thought, and in the end, as cheesy as it sounds, the only people I should be caring about are you and the children.'

Sally held my hand.

'It's not cheesy,' she said.

'Come on,' I said, 'it's a bit *quattro formaggi*.'

'How about your friends?' Sally asked. I thought of other men I knew. I thought of Nigel and Paddy and Clive and Neil and all my other friends and former colleagues.

'What about them?'

'Won't you feel second class?'

'I've always prided myself at being adaptable,' I said finally. 'Well, I've got to adapt. It'll be fine. After all, if I wanted to have a life working in an office, then I should never have got married and had children. I don't want to sound too deep about all this, but what's the point of having children if you don't really want to see them?'

'I quite agree,' said Sally.

She let out a little sigh.

'I'm sorry,' I said. 'Insensitive of me. You must miss them enormously during the week.'

'I do,' she said, holding my hand harder. 'But I'm often so busy that I've barely got time to think of them. In a way, that's for the best. But then I feel awful when it occurs to me that I haven't thought about them.'

'I wouldn't beat yourself up about it.'

We stopped and looked into each other's eyes.

'Thank you for putting up with me,' I said.

Sally laughed.

'Not at all! Thank *you*. I know this is a big deal for you. And, anyway, it has been a fairly, um, interesting few months.'

'That's putting it mildly.'

We kissed and it felt good.

Daisy gurgled, as if she were saying 'stop it you two'.

Friday 2 September

Things are going well. In fact, they are going a lot better than I had secretly hoped, despite my outward Moonie-style conversion. Peter and Daisy have been a complete joy all week, and once again, I can't help but feel that their behaviour is unavoidably linked to my own mood. I don't want to think of them purely as offshoots of me, but there's no doubt that when I'm in a good mood, they are as well.

I've also been absolutely scrupulous about keeping busy. If you do sod all, then everybody gets grouchy, me most of all. So, we've been seeing some of Peter's playgroup friends and their mothers, buying shoes (bugger me, shoes are expensive), going to Drewfort Castle (twice), taking plenty of fresh air, and trying to enjoy what will undoubtedly be the last few days of summer. And even though it rained today, I made sure that there was no slumming it in front of the TV – we painted (most of the kitchen table) and even made some gingerbread men, many of which were either burned or dropped on the floor. No matter, they still tasted delicious.

Sunday 4 September

We had Nigel and Clare round for lunch today, and we spent the whole day in the garden drinking rosé and making sure the children didn't murder each other.

Had a long chat with Nigel about my future over a few of his Silk Cut Ultra Mild Incredibly Low Tar Sucking on Straw cigarettes. (I mean, what's the point? Alcohol, probably.) He asked me how it was going looking after the children.

'Very well,' I replied.

'Is it going to be permanent, then? I was under the impression that you'd had a bit of a wobble.'

I pretended not to be disconcerted. How did he know? I assume Sally must have told her sister, who in turn would have told Clare – and so on, in the endless vicious circle of gossip.

'Wobble? Well, a little, maybe. I can't deny that it's been hard to adjust.'

'But you're going to keep at it?'

'Yes,' I said. 'I like it, believe it or not. After the business at the fire station, it made me think about what's important. Sure, it feels a little strange when I'm with you and Neil or whoever that I'm out of the loop, but I'll just have to get used to that.'

'Don't worry,' Nigel said. 'It's not like you're boring. Anyway, your good friends will understand. I expect you'll weed out some of the dross.'

I took a drag on the cigarette, barely able to taste it, but doing so because the rosé was flowing through me.

'There's a lot of dross about,' I said.

We sat in matey blokey silence for a few seconds.

'Anyway,' I said, 'how's tricks with you?'

'Good, thanks. In fact, things are picking up. The market seems a lot more lively. In fact, and I've been debating whether to tell you this, there's a vacancy over at Ovett Filmer that I thought would be perfect for you.'

I sluttishly stubbed my cigarette out on the lawn. I felt a sudden frisson of excitement from what Nigel had said.

'Really? But I thought you said my day's past, blot on the book, etc.? No one would touch me with a barge pole?'

'Well, you never know. No harm in trying. It's exactly what you were doing before. New business. Good package, car and all that crap.'

'They'd never want me,' I said. 'I'm sure my name is mud.'

'Maybe. But you were good at your job and some will remember that too.'

Nigel was being the devil on my shoulder, dangling the carrot of work back in front of me, as if he were saying, 'Come on, be a real man again.' His tactic was working. He was flattering me, and there I was, thinking, 'Yes, I was good at my job.' And then all those feelings of pride returned. Pride that I was well paid and taken seriously. Pride that people in the industry knew who I was. Pride that I made the company money, and that I made things happen. I lit another cigarette and breathed out the barely tasteable cloud of carcinogens.

'You're a bad man,' I said. 'Just a few weeks ago you said there was no hope for me. I decide to stick it out as a househusband and now you're trying to schmooze me into a job.'

Nigel held up his hands in mock defence.

'What can I say? The position only just came up,' he said, rakishly holding a cigarette between his lips.

'Sure,' I replied. 'What's the commission on this one?'

'The usual trillions. Anyway, why not think about it?'

I looked at the children, who were naked and being chased by Sally with a hose.

'Maybe I will,' I said.

Tuesday 6 September

Nigel's words have been preying upon me. In fact, they've been keeping me awake. As much as I say I want to carry on looking after Peter and Daisy, it's tempting to go back to the world of work, take home two salaries and then feel rich. But at what cost? To leave Peter and Daisy to be brought up by someone else, a stranger with different values, different ideas? It doesn't appeal. I haven't dared discuss this with Sally, now the air has only just been cleared. Hell, I don't really want to think about it myself.

Thursday 8 September

Sincerity and willingness have come under sustained assault over the past forty-eight hours. Both Peter and Daisy have been afflicted by some mysterious bug, and I've cleared up more vomit and poo than I care to remember. It's when you're on your hands and knees, scrubbing vomit out of a living-room carpet, that management consulting and all its wankiness once again becomes appealing. By the end of the day, I was almost in tears, not least because I had literally not had a chance to take a crap.

Sometimes it's the small things in life that get you.

Friday 9 September

Took Peter and Daisy to the doctor, who said what I expected. 'Lot of it about, plenty of fluids, blah-blah, will go away soon, nothing to worry about, how are you feeling?' Until he said that, it hadn't occurred to me that I might catch the bug.

Saturday 10 September

The children are feeling better, in time for Sally and the weekend. This is just as well, as I've spent the past twenty-four hours either in bed, on the loo, in the shower, back on the loo again. I've almost considered putting an inflatable mattress in our bathroom and just kipping in there, but that seems too revolting.

Like all men, illness has put me in a foul mood. The slightest noise sends me into a rage, especially the noise of the children whinging about something downstairs.

God I feel wretched. Perhaps it's not a stomach bug. Perhaps it's cancer.

Sunday 11 September
2 p.m.

Feel miraculously better, and have even held down some toast. Perhaps it's not cancer. Sally has been a brilliant nurse, in that she has not been around. Yesterday afternoon, I asked if she and the children could disappear to her parents', and she was only too happy to do so. I much prefer being an invalid solo. The energy required for niceties is just too much, especially when one wants to sit in a peaceful living room watching war films all afternoon.

9.42 p.m.

Have just got off the phone and I want to get all of this down. I can't believe what I've just heard. The first phone call was from Clive, and, typically, he started with a load of small talk – the how are yous, and the how are the children, how is Sally, etc., etc. I then said he hadn't just called me to engage in social chitchat.

'No,' he said, 'you're quite right.'

'Well, go on – spit it out.'

'Remember Fiona?' he asked.

'Of course I remember her,' I said. 'She was my secretary. I'm not that forgetful. Anyway, what about her?'

'She's been sacked.'

'Fiona? Why?'

I was flabbergasted. Fiona's been with the company for years.

'I'm not sure. I'd heard it from Gary in IT, and he couldn't tell me a lot more. I thought maybe you'd heard something.'

'Not a sausage. When was this?'

'Last thing on Friday.'

'God, poor woman. I'll give her a call. I'll let you know as soon as I find anything out.'

I hung and up called Fiona. The phone rang and rang, and I assumed she was out, getting hammered at her local or something. (Not that that's the type of thing a woman like Fiona would do. Far too demure.)

Eventually: 'H . . . hello?'

'Fiona, it's Sam. I gather you've had some bad news.'

A long sigh down the line.

'I'm so sorry,' I said.

'It's not your fault.'

'What happened?'

'Fifteen years,' she said. 'Fifteen bloody years and then that's it. Summoned to David's office and he says, all smiles, that he's "going to have to let me go".'

I heard Fiona take a swig of something. Some ice clinked.

'Gin and tonic?'

'No,' she replied. 'White wine.'

'Turned into an alkie yet?'

'Nearly!'

'Did he say why?'

'Nope. Just "restructuring". He thanked me for all my "hard work" and then gave me the bit of paper and a cheque for fourteen months' salary, as per my contract.'

'So not sacked then?'

'No – just plain redundancy, but it feels just as bad.'

I didn't want to correct her. There is a vast difference between being sacked and redundo, but now was not the time to argue the toss. Another clink and swig.

'I'm so sorry,' I said again, helplessly, feebly.

'I'll be fine,' she said, her voice quavering.

'Would you like me to come round?'

(Like many single forty-three-year-old women, the only real companion in her life is a neutered Burmese called Alfred.)

'Don't worry,' she said. 'But it would be nice to see you during the week if you're around.'

'I'll have the children with me during the day, so it'll have to be the evening. I'm sure Sally won't mind.'

'Why not come during the day? I'd love to see them.'

'OK, when?'

'Tomorrow?' she suggested.

'OK, no problem.'

'And when you come, stand by to be surprised.'

'Oh yes?'

'I've got some very interesting pieces of paper here.'

'Yes?'

367

This sounded promising.

'Pieces of paper that seem to say that David and Chris are on the fiddle.'

My heart missed a beat.

'What pieces of paper?'

'Various records I've been hoarding over the past few months.'

'Jesus, Fiona! Are you sure about this?'

'No, but why don't you take a look?'

'I will. What time shall I see you?'

'In the afternoon? Threeish?'

'I'll see you then!'

This is enormous. Huge. If David and Chris really have been on the fiddle, it changes everything. And what's more, if we can prove it, I could even get my job back.

Except I don't want it, of course.

Monday 12 September

If David and Chris aren't on the fiddle, then they're pretty damn close. Thanks to what Fiona has shown me, there's no doubt in my mind what they're doing, and it's verging on the illegal. It's definitely immoral, and I'm determined to see they get what they deserve.

We turned up at Fiona's on the dot of three, and she answered the door before I had a chance to ring the bell. Her eyes looked red, but she was putting on a brave face, much of which was made out of make-up. For the first fifteen minutes, she spent a lot of time cooing over Peter and Daisy, which was enormously gratifying. (I knew she was saying all the right things, but I kind of believed she meant them.)

Typically, I had neglected to bring anything round. Luckily, Fiona keeps a load of toys for her niece, so we were able to fob Peter and Daisy off with those. Daisy seemed more interested in Alfred, who kept a low profile under a cupboard, which was probably sensible, as Alfred may have lost his tail or Daisy her eyesight.

As soon as the children were distracted, Fiona brought out a yellow box file and placed it gently on the kitchen table.

'This is it,' she said.

I opened it up as though I were Indiana Jones. I half expected a celestial angelic light to shine on my face as I surveyed the contents with awe and reverence.

Mind you, the contents were hardly the stuff of Hollywood. Far from being the Holy Grail, they consisted of sheet upon sheet of figures, emails, more figures, and all manner of graphs. In short, it was an accountant's wet dream, but a normal person's nightmare. Thank God, Fiona had helpfully circled the bits she thought were important.

'Where did you get all this from?' I asked.

She tapped the side of her nose.

'Let's just say I'm better at hacking into people's logons than you are,' she said with a smirk.

'I don't doubt it,' I said. 'I'd make the worst spy in the world.'

For the next ten minutes, Fiona talked me through what she had found. What was most bizarre about the papers was that they appeared to show the firm was making a loss. This had to be complete horse crap. As far as I was aware, it had been doing well.

And then Fiona pulled her rabbit out of her hat. Another document revealed the true performance of the firm, which was in fact good. However, the distribution of this information was just to David and Chris, rather than all the other senior management and members of the board.

'This is Italian,' I said.

'Italian?' asked Fiona.

'Italian firms keep at least three sets of accounts. One for the taxman. One for the shareholders. Another for the majority stakeholders, David and Chris in this case, which gives us the true picture.'

'But why would they do that?'

A crash from the living room interrupted us. I darted out the room to find that Peter had knocked over a coffee table, on which had perched a rather nice orchid, an orchid that was now looking most unhappy at being sprawled across the once-immaculate carpet.

'I'm so sorry,' I said.

'Don't worry about it,' said Fiona. 'It's my fault for not having a child-friendly house.'

'I wouldn't expect you to,' I said, and regretted it as soon as I did so. Fiona had been married once, but never talked about it. Tragic. She would have made a good mum. Or maybe she never wanted to remarry and have children and all that – I've never plucked up the courage to ask her.

We cleared up the orchid which looked more or less

salvageable, during which I issued Peter with a stern bollocking.

'But it's boring here!'

'Peter!' I snapped.

'I want to go home!'

Fiona laughed, but I thought it most unamusing.

'That's very rude!'

'Don't worry about it,' said Fiona as she righted the table. 'Anyway, back to where we were – they were making the firm look as though it was doing badly . . .'

'Because they want to buy it cheaply,' I said. 'That's it! It's one of the oldest games in the book. They run the company down, cook the books, and then get it for a bargain price.'

'But it would still cost millions.'

'They can borrow millions. It's not a problem. Anyway, as soon as they've bought the firm, they then run it brilliantly for two to three years, bring out the books which show how they've turned the business around, and then, this is the low-cunning part, they sell it to someone for a whole lot more than they paid for it.'

'But how much do you think they could make?'

'I'd say about five to ten million.'

'In total?'

'No, for each of them.'

'But surely it's criminal to do that?'

'Not necessarily. What *is* criminal is filing false accounts. If we can nail them on that, then it's Wormwood Scrubs time.'

'Prison?'

'Oh yes.'

I rubbed my hands in glee. Literally. Finally, I thought, I would have my revenge. Images of David and Chris being sent down ran through my mind. The judge wearing a black cap and sentencing them to death. Before my imagination got out of hand, the combined cries of a human girl child and an ageing feline filled the air.

Tuesday 13 September

Sally's not happy with my newfound obsession.

'I think you should just leave it,' she said over supper.

'But don't you see that I was right all along?'

'Maybe you were, maybe you weren't, but the point is, what do you hope to achieve? Get David and Chris banged up? Can't you see how unlikely that is, especially as the documents were illegally acquired?'

'I'm sure all that whistleblower legislation allows for this.'

'You think so? I think you'll be making things worse for yourself down the line. If this backfires and you ever want to consult again in a few years, freelance or whatever, then really no one will touch you.'

'No one would blame me for trying to clear my name. I just want some closure. I don't want people to think, "Oh, Sam Holden, wasn't he the one who snooped on his boss's emails and then got sacked and ended his days as a househusband?" No, I want them to think, "Sam Holden, he's the bloke who discovered that David and Chris were on the fiddle and saved the company and . . ."'

I paused.

'And what?' asked Sally.

I wanted to say '. . . and returned in glory to take his job back and ended up as head of the firm and became a millionaire and lived happily ever after.' But I couldn't say that, because Sally would have killed me with the carving knife I had minutes before used on the delicious piece of chicken we were eating.

'And . . . and that's it,' I said feebly.

'Hmm,' said Sally.

I stuck my tongue out. Sally had rumbled me. We both knew it, but I wasn't going to admit it.

'You smell of poo,' I said.

'You are a poo,' she replied, and we left it at that.

A long pause.

'Changing the subject,' said Sally, 'have you heard about Emily?'

'No. What?'

'My sister emailed me today to say she'd heard from a mutual friend that Emily and Jim are splitting up.'

'Really? How come?'

'Seems as though she fell for one too many fishermen when they were in Greece.'

'*What?* Explain.'

'Jim caught her with not one, but *two* fishermen in some sort of shed on the beach.'

'You're joking.'

'I'm not.'

'Wow. How racy.'

'Seems like this was the last straw for wife-swap Jim. Middle-class chaps, once in a while at wife-swap parties, fine. But seems like Emily went way over the limit.'

'That's putting it mildly. What's going to happen?'

'Emily is lying low with the children somewhere while Jim is up in London.'

'Think they'll stay in the village?'

Sally raised a perfect eyebrow.

'Darling,' she said, 'there are no fishermen in this village.'

Thursday 15 September

Have been having lots of chats with Fiona and Clive about what's going on. These conversations are often truncated by Peter and Daisy, who always seem to cause the most amount of destruction just when I'm on the phone. I'm sure it's attention-seeking, but how much attention do they bloody need? Do they really need to break things EVERY time I'm on the phone?

Anyway, Clive and I agreed that what Fiona had was not necessarily enough for us to take it to the board. What we needed was a definitive statement of intent from David or Chris, something that said they wanted to diddle the company in the way we suspected.

'But how are we going to get that?' Clive asked.

'God knows,' I said. 'The last time I snooped on their emails, I got sacked.'

'You can't get sacked again.'

'That's true.'

A pause. We were clearly both thinking the same thing.

'I'm just not techie enough to do it,' I said.

'To hack into the system?'

'Exactly. We need a nerd who can do it.'

'Do you know any nerds?' Clive asked.

'None,' I said. 'And besides, aren't all the computers behind firewalls and things like that?'

'But that's what nerds do,' said Clive. 'They get round things like firewalls.'

'Or,' I said, 'we just break into the office and try to guess their passwords.'

'That would be madness,' said Clive.

'It would,' I said. 'But can you think of a better way?'

'No, but breaking and entering is hardly our bag, Sam. We're middle class, remember?'

'Just because you're middle class doesn't mean you can't commit crimes, Clive.'

'It does in my book.'

'Look,' I said, 'I know you don't know the London office well, but do you know the fire-escape exit round the back?'

'No.'

I sighed.

'It's where everybody goes out to smoke. Nine times out of ten, that door is left unlocked. All we have to do is to nip in there in the middle of the night, sit at a computer, hack into one of their accounts, find what we're looking for, and we're away! Back in time for a fry-up.'

'This is nuts,' said Clive.

'Come on, it's got to be worth a try. Don't you want your revenge?'

Clive didn't reply.

'Let me think about it,' he said. 'I really don't want to go to prison.'

'We won't go to prison!'

'Why not?'

'Because a) we won't be caught and b) even if we are, all they can do us for is trespassing, which is not a criminal act.'

More silence.

'OK, I'll think about it. What about the security guard?'

'Terry? He just sits at his desk and reads the paper. There's no problem with him.'

'I'll think about it.'

I've found it hard to concentrate for the rest of the day. Sally has noticed that something is different about me, and has pleaded for me not to do anything about David and Chris. I sort of said I wouldn't, but not in a way that convinced her.

Friday 16 September

Clive called this morning. He said that he was on for it. I'm amazed, frankly.

'Are you sure?' I asked.

'No,' he said. 'But I want to get to the bottom of this. And besides . . .' His voice trailed off.

'Besides?'

'Besides,' he continued, 'I could do with some adventure. It's fucking boring sitting at home.'

I let that one go, and we agreed on a time. Tomorrow night, 11 p.m. We are both going to tell respective spouses that a last-minute piss-up in London has been arranged. They'll be hacked off, but it will all be worth it in the end.

I took the children into town today to buy some more clothes, and when we were at the shoe shop, I spotted a pair of black rubber-soled shoes. Normally, I wouldn't have given them a second look because they were so goppingly naff, but I decided they would be perfect for my newfound career as a cat burglar. I bought a pair. They'll go well with a pair of black jeans and my black polo neck.

Do I wear a balaclava? No – that would look ridiculous. Some tights over my head? Not a bad idea. A bit kinky, but would make identification hard if we're spotted on CCTV. I'll take a pair from Sally's knicker drawer.

Saturday 17 September
4 p.m.

Just about to leave for the station. Sally's really angry that I appear to have scuppered the weekend, but I told her I didn't have lads' nights very often, and I could really do with some male company. I said I'd make it up to her. I meant it, though. It's a bit rotten of me, but I really must do this. I feel incredibly nervous, but hopefully in a few hours' time, Clive and I will have enough evidence to get David and Chris utterly shafted. Wish me luck, diary.

That's a mad, gay thing to write. OK, best be off.

Sunday 18 September

What an absurd twenty-four hours. I'm back home, although I'm lucky not to be sitting in a police cell in the middle of London. My hands are shaking as I type this. Feel a huge sense of relief, excitement, failure, guilt, cheap thrill and adrenalin. Sally is furious with me, but that should blow over. The fact is, I'm back.

Everything started well. Clive and I met at 10 p.m. at the Two Chinamen at the bottom of the road from the office. Typically, Clive was completely and utterly wrongly dressed. He was wearing a pair of brown suede loafers, chinos, a pink button-down shirt, and a jersey tied round his neck. In short, he looked like a cheesy model out of one of those American mail-order catalogues called something like 'Hanthamanagasett', relaxing in the Hamptons during Labor Day weekend or whatever. Definitely no cat burglar was our Clive.

'Jesus, Clive,' I said as we waited at the bar, 'what are you wearing? This isn't bloody dress-down Friday.'

'What's wrong with it?'

'You're all pink and bright and visible and your shoes are leather-soled so they'll make a racket. You could at least put the jersey over your shirt.'

Clive did as he was told, but this only made things worse. I thought his jersey was blue, whereas it was in fact blue with the most revolting pattern of golfer-style Argyle diamonds down the front. I almost couldn't bear to stand next to him at the bar.

'Fuck, Clive, is Birmingham the town that taste forgot?'

'What's wrong with this?'

'It's something a middle-manager from the West Midlands would wear!'

'But I am a middle-manager from the West Midlands.'

'Good point well made.'

I ordered a couple of pints of lager and we drank them in conspiratorial silence. We both kept looking suspiciously around the room, as if we were now in Nazi Germany. I caught a glimpse of ourselves in a smokey, foxed mirror, and we looked like the least likely breakers-and-enterers imaginable. Clive may have looked a berk, but I looked like I was some crappy fringe-theatre director with my black polo neck, black jeans and dodgy black rubber-soled shoes. I nearly called the whole thing off, but another pint of lager gave me the requisite courage.

At 10.45, we were ready to go.

'OK?' I said.

Clive gave me a thumbs-up.

I was damned nervous. The last time I had done something like this was when I stole Mars bars from my headmaster's study was I was ten. The same chemicals flooded through me, causing the same nerves, the same sense of forbidden exhilaration. I looked at Clive's eyes. They mirrored the fear in mine.

'A quick sharpener before we go?' I suggested.

'Good idea,' said Clive.

I turned to the barmaid.

'Two double whiskies please.'

'Irish or Welsh?'

'Welsh? Don't you mean Scotch?'

'We don't have any Scotch. The landlord's Welsh and he can't stand the Scots.'

'All right,' I said circumspectly, 'two double *Welshes* please.'

So, five minutes later, fortified by two pints of strong continental lager and two large Welsh whiskies, Sam Holden and Clive Lofthouse found themselves walking down a dead-end alleyway that led to the back of the offices of Musker Walsh and Sloss (Consultants) Ltd. One or two Saturday night pissheads passed us by (a smell of urine in the air testified to the chief purpose of this alleyway at the weekends), but didn't give us a second glance. They should have done – we must have looked like a right couple of ponces.

The alleyway was reminiscent of the cover of *The Rise and Fall of Ziggy Stardust and the Spiders from Mars*. Cardboard boxes were stacked in nearly neat piles around doors, a dim yellow lamp shone above the back door of a defunct import/export company, and the night sky shone in that same electric-blue way. All that was missing was a blond bisexual wearing a turquoise jumpsuit unbuttoned to his navel that would have made it 1974mungus.

'Which one is the office door?' hissed Clive.

'That one,' I said, pointing to one at the end on the right. 'The office kind of straddles that corner.'

I could feel my heart thumping. This was it. We were about to overstep one very large middle-class mark.

'It's still not too late to duck out,' I said.

Clive looked back up the alleyway. Anybody who saw us would probably assume we were cruising.

'Perhaps we should,' said Clive.

His words were tempting, sorely so.

'But think of David and Chris,' I said. 'Those smug twats. Think of them in their manor houses or on board their yachts. Do you really want to let them have all that?'

I could see Clive's eyes glaring through his specs.

'No, I don't,' he said.

'Well, let's give it a go,' I said.

We shook hands.

'If anything happens,' I said, 'if anyone rumbles us, just run. Don't worry about sticking together. We can always phone each other. OK?'

'OK.'

I took a deep breath. For a brief moment, I thought of Sally, and how hog-whimperingly livid she would be if she knew what I was doing. I expunged her from my mind. Thank God for the booze, I thought, I really bloody needed it.

We approached the exit as quietly as possible. All around it were hundreds of fag ends, littering the ground like maggots. The door was nondescript – just a blank piece of wood that had been painted white, and bore the palm and handprints of hundreds of smokers. There was no handle on the door, but it was usually left ajar in a spirit of nicotinal fellowship. I was hoping that whoever was the last smoker on Friday night had done the decent thing.

He had. I restrained from letting out a whoop as I pulled the door open with the tips of my fingers.

'We're in!' said Clive. 'Great stuff!'

Ocean's Eleven this wasn't.

Silently, we crept up the stairs, or rather I crept and Clive clacked.

'Sssh!' I went, although it made no difference to preppy-boy behind me.

As we made our way up the stairs, their smell brought

back all sorts of memories. The recall was almost over-whelming – my first day here, my first big coup when I won the GFR business and, of course, my sacking.

Somewhere in the distance, a door creaked and slammed shut. Clive and I froze, our eyes meeting in the green glow of the fire-escape light. Clive's eyes were bulging, and I could see he was starting to sweat copiously. Clearly his ridiculous sweater was too hot.

We listened for more noises. None came. I assumed it would have been Terry, the same commissionaire who escorted me out of this building all those months ago. I remembered the humiliation of my bin bag splitting. David and Chris – those bastards. I was going to get them.

'This is the floor,' I said, and gingerly opened a wooden door with a circle of glass at head height. I almost expected the *Pink Panther* theme to start playing, except we were more Clouseau than jewel thief.

We stepped on to carpet, that same swirly brown-green-grey carpet that exists in offices to remind you that this is a place of work and not of pleasure. A school of computer terminals emerged out of the half light, their screen savers all playing an animated company logo in robotic unison. You were never allowed to have your own screen saver here, not ever.

'Which one?' asked Clive.

It didn't matter. Logic informed me it made sense to use the one closest to the door. I sat down on a brown executive chair, which was set so low I could only assume a dwarf must have joined the company.

I waggled the mouse and the familiar start-up screen

appeared. A sharp intake of breath from either me or Clive
or perhaps both. I then typed in Chris's logon: CHOLDEN.
Then came the password prompt.

LINSEY

The reply came back straight away.

ACCESS DENIED

'Fuck,' I whispered, although I knew it was unlikely he
would have left his password unchanged.

I then tried

BUYOUT

Once more, access was denied.

'What's his daughter's name?' I asked.

'Er, Amelia, I think. . . .'

AMELIA

A pause.

ACCESS DENIED

'How many goes do we get?' asked Clive.

'Dunno. Let's just keep trying.'

For the next five minutes, we tried every word that might
have had any relevance to Chris. I wanted to scream out
each time the words ACCESS DENIED appeared.

'What shall we do?'

'Keep guessing!' I hissed.

We sat in silence. I heard the distant sound of traffic,
and some singing. It was chucking-out time. Soon the
alleyway would be full of *les urinateurs*, which would provide
us with some useful cover.

We kept guessing and we kept guessing. Occasionally,
we thought we could hear a noise from down the main
stairs which caused us to pause. There was no doubt there

was a guard down there somewhere, but so far he had shown no interest in doing his job. What a strange twilight world these people must live in.

'How about "Dudley"?' asked Clive.

I grinned a Hollywood smile in the gloom. I tried to contain my excitement. Fool not to have thought of it before!

DUDLEY

A pause, an agonising pause.

And then: INITIALISING . . . PLEASE WAIT

'You fucking genius!'

Clive and I exchanged a very British sort of high-five, rather solid and formal and not really connecting properly.

'Yo brother,' went Clive.

Within a couple of minutes, the computer finally did its stuff and we had oh-so-not-allowed access to all Chris's files.

'Where do we start?'

'We've just got to go through them all,' I said.

'This will take hours!'

'Got anything else on?'

Clive shook his head.

Over the next twenty minutes, we silently searched through all Chris's files. Apart from confirming that his affair with Charlotte was still a runner, we found little of value. I punctuated our search with little expectorations of 'damn' and 'shit' and 'turd'.

'Now for his emails,' I said.

I opened his email program and did a search for 'Dudley'. Up came seventy-six emails between him and David.

'If it's going to be anywhere, it'll be in here.'

Methodically, I started going through them, noting some that I had seen before: the ones that had got me sacked.

Another noise from down the main stairs. This time, it sounded like footsteps. We froze. The footsteps were getting louder. I gestured to Clive that we should go back to the fire escape. I gently opened the door and we walked through. I then closed it and peeked through the porthole of glass.

'Fuck!' I whispered.

'What?'

'I've left the screen on! I should have activated the screen saver!'

'But won't it kick in after a minute or two?'

'It might.'

The footsteps were getting louder. Then, with almost a 'kerrang', came the noise of scores of tube lights switching on. The sudden brightness made me squint. Whoever was coming in was walking slowly. Maddeningly, the screen stayed resolutely on, displaying Chris's email program for all to see.

More footsteps. I craned my head, and over to the left, I could make out the figure of none other than Terry. Was he searching for us, or was he just doing his rounds? Still the screen didn't flinch.

'Save your screen, you fucker,' I mouthed.

Terry walked slowly around the room. He must have been doing his rounds, because he appeared not to be making for anywhere specific. At one point he yawned reassuringly. But the screen stayed put, and I couldn't rely on Terry's tiredness for him not to notice. Terry may have been a fat bearded sweaty sort of man, but he was no fool.

He walked near the screen. This was it, I thought, he was going to spot it. I held my breath and shut my eyes. I resolved that as soon as he saw it, Clive and I would dash down the stairs and out into the Ziggy Stardust night. I crossed my fingers as Terry neared.

And then, miracle of miracles, the company logo suddenly appeared on the terminal. Joy, such joy. I punched the air. I never thought I'd have been so happy to see a screen saver switch on. It was the type of thrill I imagine people in IT must feel when they get something right. A rare type of thrill, then.

As the screen bobbled and span and bounced its crappy logo, Terry walked past it, studying his fingernails. I held my breath, as well as an outstretched palm to bid Clive to keep absolutely still.

Terry stopped.

Get ready to run, I said to myself.

Terry then started undoing his trousers.

Oh my God, what was this? What foul thing did Terry do in the middle of the office in the middle of the night?

Terry then pulled down his trousers. He stood there in his capacious Y-fronts, looking sheepishly around.

Surely he wasn't going to . . . ?

Oh, yes he was.

He sat down at a desk – not the desk we were using – and began typing. Within seconds, the screen filled with the telltale lurid colours of the very foulest Internet pornography. From a distance it put anything Lydia looked at into a cocked hat.

I wanted to laugh, but the situation demanded silence.

Besides, within a few seconds there was very little to laugh at, because what I was beholding was the most revolting sight a man could witness. I slunk down from the window and turned to Clive, miming what Terry was up to with my hand. He put his hand over his eyes and mouthed 'yuk'. I pulled a face that expressed my sheer revulsion.

I looked at my watch. It was bang on twelve. Presumably this little episode was part of Terry's nightly routine – the midnight wank. For five agonising minutes, we waited. I then risked another peek.

Not good. Terry was still at it, and seemed to be watching some movie that featured very fat men dressed in nappies being beaten by very fat rubber-clad mistresses. How long was this going to go on for?

Five minutes later, I looked again. He was still doing it. I turned to Clive. He had a worried look on his face, and was pointing downstairs, suggesting we should scarper. I shook my head and pointed at my watch, indicating that Terry's time would soon come. As it were.

Once more, I edged up to the window and saw Terry was approaching a state of some rapture. There were at least twelve images on the screen, so he was presumably going for some sort of porn-mosaic effect.

Diddle-er-der, diddle-er-der-der.

My heart went crazy. It was my phone!

Diddle-er-der, diddle-er-der-der.

I saw Terry turning his head, and immediately ducked down.

Diddle-er-der, diddle-er-der-der.

Neither Clive nor I needed any encouragement to hotfoot it down the stairs.

Diddle-er-der, diddle-er-der-der.

We jumped down them as fast as we could, taking four or five steps at a time.

Diddle-er-der, diddle-er-der-der.

I cursed myself inwardly. This was the sort of error I expected Clive to make, not me.

Diddle-er-der, diddle-er-der-der.

And then Clive made *his* error. He slipped, his suede loafers proving themselves to be the least likely product to be endorsed by Cat Burglars Inc.

Diddle-er-der, diddle-er-der-der.

He thudded on to his right hip, and just from the way he landed with his full weight, I could tell it hurt.

'Fuck!' he yelled out.

'Who's there?' a voice shouted down the stairwell.

More 'fucks' from Clive, who was clearly in pain.

'Come back 'ere!' shouted Terry.

I helped Clive up. He winced in agony. I could hear Terry running down the stairs. In a few seconds he would be on top of us, an image rendered all too unpleasant after what I had just seen through that window.

Clive clutched his hip.

'Ow!' he went.

I started running, hoping Clive would follow me, but instead, he just sort of lamely hobbled. If this had been a war film, I would have shot Clive to save him from falling into the hands of an appalling enemy, but as it was, it was not a war film, and yet I still wanted to shoot him.

'Move!' I hissed.

I had enough presence of mind not to use my normal voice in case Terry recognised it.

'I can't!'

'Of course you can!'

I all but dragged Clive down the remaining two flights of stairs. He yelped with each one, as though he had been shot.

'It can't be that bad.'

'It bloody is!'

'Stop right there!' shouted Terry.

As if. Do burglars ever stop and go, 'OK, I'll wait here for you to catch me?' No, they do not, and neither did we. A few hobbled seconds later, we arrived at the door, the smell of urine almost welcoming.

'I can't run!' said Clive.

I put an arm round him and tried to get us moving, but it was useless.

'Leave me,' said Clive heroically. 'Save yourself. I'll be OK.'

With Terry's wheezing footsteps approaching rapidly, we were running out of options. As far as I could tell, I could:

1. Run off and leave Clive – tempting.
2. Stay with Clive and face music – honourable, but not tempting.
3. Try to drag Clive away. Impossible.
4. Deal with Terry in some way.

I decided on 4. There was no other viable option. But how was I going to deal with him? Talk him out of doing anything? Hit him?

I heard Terry's wheezing breath approach the door. In

a panic, I ran forward and decided to slam it shut. It was the only thing I could do. Perhaps I would be able to hold it for long enough to enable Clive to hobble away, and then I could sprint off. I should easily be able to outrun Terry and would just have to hope he didn't recognise me.

I slammed the door as hard as I could, forcing it shut with all my might. But before it met the frame, the door met something else. Something that felt heavy. Something that went 'gerdumf' as the air was expelled from it. Something that went 'crump' as it hit the floor. Something that was undoubtedly Terry.

I stopped. I could hear our breathing above the noise of the traffic. Somewhere, a drunk was singing a rugby song. But from the other side of the door, I could hear nothing.

'Shit,' I said.

A few seconds before, I had been praying for Terry to go away, to shut up, but now I was desperate to hear him speak.

I opened the door and peered through the gap, fearing above all else that I might have killed him. I looked into the gloom, and saw Terry's body – maybe corpse – lying across the floor. No noise emanated from him.

I bent down and listened, but I could hear nothing above the sounds of the city. I bent closer. Still nothing.

Shit shit shit.

I felt panicky. My legs almost buckled, and for the first time in my life – or at least since I was three – I almost wet myself. I had killed him, I had bloody killed him. My first instinct was to flee, to run to Dominica and live there as a gnarled fisherman.

'Is he OK?'

It was Clive, peering over me.

'I . . . I don't know!'

For about thirty seconds, we just stood there in a gorm-less middle-class way. I then bent down and checked if he was breathing.

He was, thank God.

'He's OK!' I whispered.

'What shall we do?'

'Leave him,' I suggested.

'But he may go into a coma.'

'Come off it,' I said.

'I'm serious,' said Clive, 'we should try to wake him up, just in case.'

'But if we wake him up, we'll get caught.'

We scratched our chins theatrically.

I gave Terry's leg a kick, but there was no reaction.

Another kick. Nothing.

'For fuck's sake, Terry!' I shouted. 'Wake up!'

Nothing.

'How about a glass of cold water?'

'I don't have a glass of cold water.'

We stood gormlessly again.

Diddle-er-der, diddle-er-der-der.

The Nokia ring tone. The most annoying noise known to man.

Diddle-er-der, diddle-er-der-der.

Terry's lips started smacking together.

'He's coming round!' I whooped.

Diddle-er-der, diddle-er-der-der.

I got my phone out my pocket and looked at the caller.

It was Lydia. Fuck, I had forgotten to pay her. But all my inefficiency was reaping serendipitous reward.

Diddle-er-der, diddle-er-der-der.

We stepped away quickly as Terry stirred.

Diddle-er-der, diddle-er-der-der.

Just as we reached the door, his eyes opened.

I shut the door and waited for a few seconds.

A grunt, the grunt of fat sweaty man who looks at revolting porn.

'Ouargh!' it went. 'Fuck me.'

I gave Clive a thumbs-up. He returned it.

We listened for a few more seconds and heard the sound of Terry trying to get up.

'Bugger me.'

It was at that point that we left.

I got back home late this morning. Clive and I stayed with an old university friend of his, who we elected not to tell. I haven't told Sally either, but she just knows something's up. She always does.

I do hope Terry is OK.

Tuesday 20 September

Turns out that he is, thank God. Fiona rang first thing this morning to tell me that she'd heard from one of the other secretaries that there had been a break-in at the office, and poor Terry had had his nose broken when he had a fight with one of the thieves. Apparently there had been four of them.

I couldn't help but smile, and used every ounce of my

unlegendary self-control not to tell Fiona the truth. Good old Terry, though, I admired him for talking up his heroism. No doubt David will give him a big pay rise for bravely trying to save the firm's resources. If David had known the truth – that Terry didn't check the doors, and that he spent half the night surfing the net for porn – then I expect he would be sacked. Instead, Terry will be lionised. I feel guilty about the nose, though, but I think it was already broken so it's not a total disaster. I shall make it up to him somehow. Perhaps send him some cash anonymously.

I asked Fiona if they knew who had broken in, but apparently it was a mystery.

'It wasn't you, was it?' she asked.

'God no!' I replied.

'It would be a mad thing to have done.'

'Nuts.'

We said our goodbyes, both knowing that the other knew. Good old Fiona, the soul of discretion.

All this farrago still doesn't get me any closer to the truth. Perhaps Sally is right. I should just leave it, and concentrate on Peter and Daisy.

Wednesday 21 September

Firmly back in the househusband routine. Peter to playgroup. Shopping. Cleaning. Playing with Daisy. It all feels rather flat after the excitement of the weekend.

Sally told me over supper that I had gone 'awfully quiet' about getting my revenge on David and Chris. It's true. I have. And it looks as guilty as hell. Coupled with this, I'm now annoyed that Clive and I failed in our mission. Initially I felt lucky not to have been caught – and not to have killed Terry – but now I'm angry. Those arseholes are going to get away with it, and there's nothing I can do to stop them.

Perhaps I should just go to Sir Roger Norris, the chairman, and show him what I've got. It won't be enough though.

Friday 23 September

Had a long discussion with Sally about my putative revenge.

'Why can't you just leave it?' she asked as I was doing the washing-up.

'It's a question of honour,' I said. 'You must be able to see that.'

'You make it sound so serious.'

'Well, it is. I'm sure they're up to no good, and I try to find out, and then the next thing I know is I'm sacked. It just feels unfair when they're the real crooks. I hate the idea of people like that beating me.'

'You're being so competitive, though.'

'I am a man. It's kind of programmed into us.'

'Women are competitive as well.'

'Yes – but not to the death.'

'I am.'

'I know you are, darling,' I said as I rinsed the sieve, 'and that's why you're so good at defending our country.'

'You're taking the piss.'

'Slightly.'

Sally passed me the ridged frying pan. How had it got so filthy when all I had done was grill a couple of tuna steaks on it? I started scrubbing with some wire wool.

'Don't use that,' said Sally, 'you'll scratch it.'

'What am I supposed to use?' I asked irritably.

'A normal brush and some elbow grease.'

'All right, all right.'

I scrubbed in silence while Sally tidied stuff away.

'How will you feel if you don't manage to get your revenge on David and Chris?' she asked.

'Angry,' I said. 'Thwarted. Frustrated. Thoroughly fucked off by the injustice. They'll be able to afford servants while I'm scrubbing grill pans.'

I paused. I knew that if I got rid of David and Chris, Sir Roger would offer me a very senior job, plus a fat pile of cash, and everlasting gratitude. In a few years, I'd be well on my way to earning hundreds of thousands a year. Or, I could look after Daisy and Peter.

Daisy and Peter getting sick	Fat pile of moolah
Washing Daisy and Peter's clothes	Massive company Mercedes
Clearing up Daisy and Peter's toys	Respect of my friends
Coffee mornings with the mothers of the friends of Peter and Daisy	A house in France
Cleaning the house	Guaranteed school fees paid
Supermarket shopping	All the latest gadgets

Making sure Peter and	Drinking Romanée-Conti
Daisy do their	for the rest of my life
homework	

Sunday 25 September

We've had another one of those idyllic family weekends. Blackberrying and pottering around the house and garden. Yesterday, Peter and I built a model Spitfire together. (I use the word 'together' loosely.) He got a little impatient at how the long the glue took to dry, and then even more impatient that the paint stayed wet for longer than thirty seconds, but by the end of the day, he and it were inseparable, and he even took it to bed.

Daisy is just about to walk independently. She can motor along with her trolley full of bricks, but lacks the confidence to go it alone. Shot lots of video of her scampering around the house, although I often have to extricate the trolley from a corner out of which she cannot negotiate.

All in all, a perfect weekend, right down to the session Sally and I had last night. We took a bottle of champagne to bed and pretended we were in a hotel. Nuff zed.

Why can't all weekends be like this?

It's my birthday on Wednesday. Sally says she's got the most superb present for me. I ask her if it's a new au pair, which earns me a vice-like grip on my nether regions. I then ask if she'll be willing to use the Lusty Girl Pleasurer (Plus Lusty Girl's Anal Love Bulb).

'If you're not careful, I'll use it on you,' she said.

Matron.

Tuesday 27 September

I'm stupidly, cretinously excited about what Sally is getting for my birthday. I'm so childish, I've asked Peter what I'm getting, and he said, 'A Lancaster bomber.' This is unlikely. I asked whether he knew I was getting anything else, and he said, 'Another Lancaster bomber.' He's a lot more discreet than I.

Spoke to Clive this morning. I asked him about his hip.

'I think it's fractured,' he said.

'It can't be.'

'It's got the most enormous bruise, you should see it.'

'No thanks.'

'I had a hell of a job explaining to Louise how I got it.'

'What did you tell her?'

'I told her I fell down some stairs when I was drunk.'

'Pretty honest of you.'

'Yes, well, I think the nearer the truth you are with your lie, the better.'

'I quite agree.'

'Anyway, what are we going to do now? I don't suppose there'll be any chance of getting into the office now.'

'I've no idea,' I said, which was true.

'Perhaps we can work with what we've got?'

'It's not enough.'

At that stage Daisy began to cry.

Wednesday 28 September

Boy-oh-boy-oh-boy was Sally right. She got me the best birthday present in the world. It's the type of present money could never buy, and I'll be for ever grateful to her. She gave it to me in bed. After I got it I repeatedly covered her in kisses until she had to brush me off as though I were a Labrador puppy. I know she must have hated doing it, probably found it a bit risky and demeaning, but boy did I love it. Total dream gift. What a woman.

It came in a large brown envelope.

'This feels like a load of paper,' I said.

Sally said nothing.

I unpeeled one end of the envelope slowly. I always like to spin out the excitement of my presents.

'What is it?' I asked rhetorically.

I slid out a thick handful of A4.

'A ream of paper, darling,' I said. 'Very useful for the printer. I was running low.'

'They're upside down you fool.'

'I know, I know. What is it? Some book you've been working on?'

I turned the pile the right way up and looked at the top page. After ten-seconds' perusal, my face erupted into a huge smile.

'You are a bloody genius,' I said.

I was being sincere as well.

'A bloody amazing fantastic gorgeous genius.'

Sally took a bow.

'A sexy brilliant intelligent thoughtful sexy woman.'

Another bow.

'I'm not going to ask you how you got it,' I said.

'Best not,' she said with a grin.

I looked through the pages.

'Is it just what you wanted? I thought I'd get you everything.'

'It's perfect,' I said, 'especially this bit.'

I cackled. I laughed. I think I may have even let out a few yelps. I certainly went 'ah-hah!' like a pirate several times.

Thursday 29 September

I walked into the office feeling like a conquering hero. My appointment was for ten o'clock, although I was ten minutes late. It didn't matter, because what I had in my briefcase was going to change everything. There, true to form at the reception desk, was Terry, a massive white plaster across his nose. Poor bloke, I thought. Still, it was all in a good cause, ultimately. If the firm collapsed, he would be one of the first to lose their jobs and, at his age, he would have little chance of getting re-employed. Guilt-inspired justification by me? Probably. But some truth to it.

'Jesus, Terry, what the hell happened to you?'

'A break-in,' he said.

'Where? At home?'

'No. Here. Six big fellas it was, trying to nick all the computers.'

'Bloody hell. What did they do? Hit you?'

'Not half,' he said. 'I'm lucky to be alive, I reckon. As it is, I've got away with just a broken nose.'

'Did you stop them?'

'Oh yes,' he said proudly.

'Good for you!'

I badly wanted to let on how much I knew, but I knew it would not have been wise for so many reasons.

'Anyway, Sam, it's good to see you again. Are you coming to work for us again?'

'I don't think so, no,' I said. 'In fact, I'm here to see Sir Roger. I've got a meeting at ten o'clock.'

Terry filled out a pass which he asked me to stick to my lapel. Normally I ignore such requests and stuff the bureaucratic piece of paper in my pocket, but I didn't want to hurt Terry's feelings. I'd hurt him enough as it was.

'Fourth floor, Sam.'

'Thanks, Terry.'

I went over to the lifts and pushed the up arrow. I felt exhilarated and a little nervous.

Ping.

The doors opened.

Our eyes met, bulged, and then narrowed.

'Sam Holden, what the fuck are you doing here?'

I smiled in as odious and as smug a way as possible.

'Hello, David,' I said. 'Just having a meeting with Sir Roger.'

'Sir Roger? What about?'

'A new business opportunity.'

'New business? I thought you spent your life wiping your children's arses.'

I didn't realise I could hate David any more than I already did. But that comment pricked me like nothing else. How dare he talk about my children like that? There was something so loathsome, so evil, so nasty about the way he said his last three words, that I was grateful for gun control. As it was, I had on me something better than any gun.

'You'll soon find out,' I said.

I stepped into the lift. David stayed in it while I pressed number four.

'Aren't you getting out?' I asked.

'Not until you tell me what you're doing here!'

'I've already told you.'

'No you haven't. Goddamn it! I'll get you thrown out unless you tell me!'

I held out my lapel badge.

'I have an appointment, David. As it is, I'm running late, so if you wouldn't mind . . . ?'

The lift doors shut and we started to ascend.

'I know what it is,' he said.

I nodded.

'It's about what you saw when you were snooping,' he said.

I said nothing.

'You think Chris and I are up to no good. Well you're wrong, Sam. Sir Roger knows exactly what we're doing. You're only going to look a fool.'

Ping.

'Am I?' I asked.

I walked down the corridor, David scampering after me. He could see I was carrying out my threat, and he was starting to crap himself. Who said revenge wasn't sweet?

'Are you really going to see him?' David asked with faux nonchalance.

'Yup.'

I reached an open door and looked through to an anteroom. There, behind a large oak desk was Sir Roger's secretary, Kirsty.

'Hi, Kirsty,' I said. 'Sorry I'm late. How are you?'

'Sam! How lovely to see you again! You look well!'

'So do you.'

She stood up and came round to give me a peck on the cheek. Frankly, I felt pretty damn cool. I was wearing my finest dark blue suit, a deep blue shirt, a subtle yellow tie, highly polished Oxfords, and had just had a haircut. After a lot of time in the garden, I was also tanned. I felt on top of the world. Jerry bloody Maguire. Not that I've seen the film, but I'm sure something like this happens. It always does in Tom Cruise films.

'Hello, David,' said Kirsty coldly.

'Kirsty, I need to be in on this.'

'I'm sorry, David, but Sir Roger told me this is to be a private meeting.'

Another smug Holden smile. Got you, you fucker.

A thick wooden door opened.

'Ah! Sam! How the devil are you?'

'Very well, thank you, Sir Roger.'

He then nodded at David with a brusque, 'David.'

'Sir Roger,' David started, 'I really think I should sit in on this.'

'No,' he said firmly.

That 'no' says all you need to know about Sir Roger. No 'Sorry, David', or 'I'm afraid not', just a plain, hard-arsed 'no'. I watched in triumph as David sloped off. As he walked into the corridor, he starting chewing his nails.

'Now then, Sam, in yer come, in yer come.'

Sir Roger speaks in a sort of Mayfair Cockney accent, what John Le Carré called 'the last vulgarity of the upper classes'. It's not 'Mockney' which is what Madonna's husband speaks, because it's still demonstrably upper class.

'Spain' is 'Spayne', 'Scotch' is 'Scatch' (not that the upper classes would ever use the word).

I noted the absence of an offer of coffee or tea, the type of thing Sir Roger thinks twee. And neither is he the type of man who keeps a drinks tray in his office, because that looks too American.

'So then,' he said, pointing directly at a small chair next to a low table, 'what is all this crap you've got for me?'

I perched and opened my briefcase. Sir Roger sat on a battered brown leather sofa, revealing a slight flash of old-man leg above his sock.

'It's proof, Sir Roger, that David Walsh and Chris Holden are filing false accounts in order to depress the value of the business before making a management buyout.'

Sir Roger showed no emotion. Instead, he put on his reading specs. He then clicked the fingers of his right hand.

'Show me.'

I showed him. Boy, did I show him. Whichever boffin it was in Sally's office who had hacked into the firm's servers, he had done a blinding job. Every document in Chris and David's logons, every email sent between them, every smear of their electronic existence was printed out on those sheets of paper. In order to help Sir Roger, I had marked out the most incriminating texts.

'How did you get hold of all this?'

'I'm afraid I can't tell you that, Sir Roger.'

He looked over his glasses. A man even lesser than me would have crumbled, but I was adamant.

'I believe under the whistleblower legislation I'm covered by the force of law.'

'You may well be right.'

He carried on looking through the sheets.

'Can I keep these?'

'Yes, they're copies. I have another set filed with my bank, and another with my solicitor.'

'Well done,' he said.

He stood up and stuck his specs behind a rather crumpled-looking handkerchief in his breast pocket. He then shook my hand.

'I'm very grateful to you, Sam.'

'Not at all, Sir Roger.'

'Has Kirsty got your number?'

'She has, yes.'

'Good. I'll give you a ring later.'

'Thank you, Sir Roger.'

And with that, I left the office, walked down the stairs, and left the building. I could have clicked my heels, but instead I tried to play it cool. Nothing was in the bag. I hailed a cab, and went straight back to the station. There, in order to calm myself down, I had a sly late-morning beer.

My mobile rang while I was on the train.

'Sam?'

'Yes.'

'Roger Norris. Listen, are you still in London?'

'Um, not really. But I can be.'

'I want you to come and see me.'

My heart palpitated. No kidding. It really did. I got off at the next stop and waited for the train back into London. What was he going to say? Was I walking into a trap? Perhaps a couple of policemen would be waiting for me, handcuffs at the ready.

It was a nerve-racking ninety minutes before I got back to the office just after one o'clock. Terry was still at his desk, eating a sandwich and reading the paper.

'You back again?'

''Fraid so!'

Terry filled out my second pass of the day.

'Something's going on, Sam,' he said, conspiratorially tapping the side of his nose, and then wincing.

'What?'

'I dunno. David and Chris stormed out of the building a few minutes ago. They looked livid, murder on their faces.'

I nodded. This was good news.

Ping.

This time the lift was empty. All I could think about was what waited for me on the fourth floor.

Ping.

Down the corridor.

'Hello, Kirsty.'

'This is becoming a habit!'

Another peck on the cheek.

'You'd better go straight in,' she said, her face suddenly turning serious.

Fuck.

I walked in. Sir Roger stood by the window surveying the rooftops. To be frank, it wasn't the best view in the world, but Sir Roger's stature made it look as though he were looking across half the world.

'They've gone,' he said.

'David and Chris?'

'Yes. Gone. They admitted it.'

I breathed out. Things had gone quicker and better than I could have hoped.

Sir Roger turned round.

'And I've told them to expect a call from the police.'

'Really?'

'Not really. I don't want the scandal. We've got a good name here, but I wanted to make those little bastards sweat.'

I smiled, and thought I could detect the trace of a grin on Sir Roger's face.

'I'll say it again. I'm very grateful to you, Sam.'

'Not at all, Sir Roger. I'm glad they've got their just deserts.'

Sir Roger looked at his watch.

'Look,' he said, 'I've got a lunch soon, so I'll be quick.'

I held my breath.

'You bloody well deserve your job back.'

I said nothing.

'Except I'm not going to give it to you.'

I nodded. It was fair enough. There was too much of a whiff of scandal about me. Cleanliness. I remembered Sir Roger was obsessed with cleanliness.

'I'm going to give you David's job. You deserve it, and you'd be bloody good at it. You're a bit young, but you've got what it takes. Besides, you'll have Derek to be your confidant down on the floor. I'm going to recommend you to the board on Monday morning.'

I gasped. Agog. Speechless.

A few days ago, I was breaking into this very building.

Just this morning, I had changed one of the very foulest of Daisy's nappies. While I was on the train home, I was thinking about what to cook the children for their supper. Fish fingers or sausages? And now I was being offered the job of CEO of one of the country's most successful management consultancy firms. It was a dream. People would have literally killed to be in my highly polished shoes.

I opened my mouth.

Then I closed it again.

Finally I spoke, slowly and hesitantly at first, then more confidently.

'That's a very kind offer, Sir Roger, but I'm afraid I'm going to have to refuse.'

Sir Roger looked incredulous.

'Who's got you?' he demanded.

I knew he wouldn't understand if I told him the truth. I had to give it to him in language he understood.

'It's a small start-up just outside London,' I said. 'But they've got some amazing growth potential. I've been kind of caretakering them for several months now, but I've decided to stay there permanently. I really feel I owe it to them.'

Sir Roger pursed his lips.

'Do you think they require some VC?'

Sir Roger was referring to venture capital.

'Well, you know start-ups, Sir Roger. Always hungry. But please don't feel . . .'

'Nonsense! We owe you. Just make sure they don't spend it all at once.'

And then he winked.

*

It's 6 p.m. Sally will be coming home soon. I can't wait to tell her.

Friday 30 September
Noon

This morning, so hungover was she, Sally pulled the first sickie of her life. Last night we drank four bottles of champagne and we both feel wrecked.

1 p.m.

I can't really face any more champagne, but I'm going to insist we force some down. A courier has just arrived from London with a small white envelope, inside of which was a small cheque for a very large amount. With it was a card from Sir Roger which simply read, 'Start-up VC', and then, 'Let us know if we can use you as a freelance one day. Best wishes, Sir Roger.'

This is the best of both worlds. I really don't deserve this. I can definitely afford to pay Lydia now.

Sunday 2 October

Daisy took her first proper steps yesterday. She cackled and gurgled as she did so, and looked so proud of herself. I'm so glad Sally was around to see them. A big day.

It will be my big day tomorrow – the start of my whole new life. No more looking back, just forward. In a way, I'll be taking my first steps as well.